'If Harry Potter smoked cigarettes and took a certain matter-

THE STRANGER'S WOES

MAX FREI

*Translated from the Russian by Polly Gannon
and Ast A. Moore*

Original text copyright © Max Frei 2003
English translation copyright © Polly Gannon and Ast A. Moore 2011
All rights reserved

The right of Max Frei to be identified as the author of this work, and
the right of Polly Gannon and Ast A. Moore to be identified as the
translators of this work, has been asserted by them in accordance with
the Copyright, Designs and Patents Act 1988.

First published in Great Britain in 2011 by
Gollancz
An imprint of the Orion Publishing Group
Orion House, 5 Upper St Martin's Lane, London WC2H 9EA
An Hachette UK Company

This edition published in Great Britain in 2012 by Gollancz

1 3 5 7 9 10 8 6 4 2

A CIP catalogue record for this book is available
from the British Library

ISBN 978 0 575 08980 8

Printed in Great Britain by
CPI Group (UK) Ltd, Croydon, CR0 4YY

The Orion Publishing Group's policy is to use papers
that are natural, renewable and recyclable products and
made from wood grown in sustainable forests. The logging
and manufacturing processes are expected to conform to the
environmental regulations of the country of origin.

www.orionbooks.co.uk

CONTENTS

Previously in THE LABYRINTHS OF ECHO ...

MAX FREI WAS ONCE A LOSER. HE'S A BIG SLEEPER (DURING THE DAY, that is; at night he can't sleep a wink). A hardened smoker, an uncomplicated glutton, and a loafer, one day he gets lucky. He discovers a parallel world where magic is commonplace, and where he fits right in. This is the city of Echo of the Unified Kingdom, a land where a social outcast like Max can be remade as "the unequaled Sir Max."

In this upside-down universe, Sir Max's deadpan humor and new-found talent for magic soon earn him a place in the secret police—night shift only, of course. As Nocturnal Representative of the Most Venerable Head of the Minor Secret Investigative Force of the City of Echo, Max's job is to investigate cases of illegal magic and battle trespassing monsters from other worlds. With this occupation comes an unusual band of colleagues—the omniscient Sir Juffin Hully, the buoyant Sir Melifaro, the death dealing Sir Shurf Lonli-Lokli, bon vivant and master of disguise Sir Kofa Yox, and the captivating sleuth Lady Melamori Blimm.

Plunging back into the threatening and absurd realm first portrayed in *The Stranger*, Book One of the Labyrinths of Echo series, *The Stranger's Woes* follows the new adventures and misadventures of Sir Max and his friends in this enchanted and enchanting world.

ONE

THE MAGAXON FOXES

"**C**ONGRATULATIONS, MAX. YOU AND MELIFARO GET A HOLIday. One day for both of you." Sir Juffin Hully was positively glowing with acerbity.

"Big deal. Have the Secret Investigators officially earned the right to keep a harem? Has there been a special Royal Decree?" I asked indifferently. To be honest, I had been out of sorts since morning.

"Even worse, boy. Much worse. It seems that the magnificent General Boboota Box is on the mend. Soon he'll be up and about."

"Well, it was bound to happen sooner or later, much to the chagrin of his subordinates. I've even missed him. It's so sweet to see him tremble in terror when I'm around."

"Is that so? Then you have reason to rejoice."

"Rejoice? Why?" I sensed a trap.

"To this day Boboota can't forget how you and Melifaro saved his precious backside from turning into pâté. The burden of his unexpressed gratitude has become too much for him. As a matter of fact, he sent you an official invitation. Tomorrow at sundown you are to cross the threshold of Boboota Box's residence. Happy?"

"Ouch, Juffin. What if I'm otherwise engaged tomorrow? I could deliver the head of some rebellious Grand Magician to you on a platter, or create a few new Universes. How about it? I'll do it in the wink of an eye, honest. But I regret to say I won't be able to make it to Sir Boboota's party. How unfortunate."

"Dream on. No, my boy, you've got to pay for your mistakes. Since you and Melifaro saw fit to save Boboota's life, you have to take the consequences. No need to pull such a long face, either. It will be fine. You just have to mention outhouses—Boboota's favorite subject. Then you come back to me and report the gist of your edifying chat. You're good at that. So you see, you'll both be happy—just not at the same time. I'm the only one who gets to be happy all the time."

"Does Melifaro already know about the pleasure that awaits him?"

"Of course, and he's delighted. He says that imagining you at Boboota's table sends shivers up and down his spine."

"Listen, Juffin, you've already done me in. You've knocked me flat on my back, wiped the wall with me, and rubbed my nose in the dirt. Now tell me, do I really have to go to Boboota's?"

"Well, I wouldn't say that you *have* to, but the poor fellow suffered a real blow from the pâté incident. He's been confined to his bed for days on end. And remember, he's turned over a new leaf. So he's counting on your visit. He's a very sensitive fellow deep down in his heart."

"Right, but your hands come up covered in blood after you dig down that far," I said. "All right, all right, I'll go. Otherwise, Melifaro will cry all day in the Chair of Despair. What would people think of us then?"

"Attaboy! But why are you so down in the dumps, Max? What's the matter?"

"Magicians only know," I said, shrugging. "On the surface everything seems to be just fine—but it's all wrong. Maybe it's a seasonal thing, like the mating dance of the Sysoo bird. You know I'm a simple guy. My mind is a very primitive mechanism."

"Sysoo birds don't do mating dances," Kurush said. "People entertain such strange notions about birds."

I stroked the buriwok's ruffled feathers. "I'm sorry, sweetheart. I'm an ignorant alien, and you're a wise Keeper of Knowledge. Forgive me."

"What's this I hear?" Juffin said, shaking his head in surprise. "By the way, I hope you aren't going to bed without the kerchief of the Grand Magician of—"

"Of the Order of the Secret Grass," I said. "I don't forget anything at all these days. I turn off the bathroom light and don't go outside in the nude. I do the famous Lonli-Lokli breathing exercises every morning and eat six times a day. Everything's just hunky-dory."

"No, Max. Not everything. What about your dreams?"

"That's just it: I don't have any at all," I said. "The trip to Kettari wiped out my ability to dream altogether. They're gone. Poof!"

"Hmm. Now we're getting somewhere. Don't exaggerate, though.

Nothing has been 'wiped out,' as you put it. It's a good thing you have that kind of defense mechanism."

"Oh, you mean a horror film series has been scheduled for my personal movie theater?" I asked, showing some signs of life.

"Be so good as to speak more clearly. Those metaphors of yours—"

"I just meant to suggest that all the nightmares of the World might be after my scalp."

"I didn't need you to tell me that," Juffin said testily. "But don't worry. They'll grow tired of you. It will pass. It's all for the best—you finally have some time to turn your attention to what happens when you're awake."

"Like a visit to Sir Boboota. You're right, Juffin. That's a nightmare right there," I quipped.

"That's better," the chief said, smiling. "Much better. Don't let any untoward wonders spoil your good nature."

"I have a good nature?"

"Absolutely. Especially after your fifth glass of Elixir of Kaxar. Well, wonder boy, it's time to get down to the task at hand."

"Did you send over to the *Glutton* for dinner?" I said.

"For pastries," Kurush corrected me.

Juffin pulled his hair in mock despair, and I burst out laughing. My own announcement that everything was "all wrong" did start to seem like an exaggeration. I really was fine after all. But a dozen days without a single dream—I wasn't used to that. I almost felt like a happy dead man who had managed to strike it lucky in the afterlife.

"I sense that we're in for a sea of pleasure today! Even more. Oceans of it. In a word, I'd like to be a pirate crossing those oceans of pleasure."

Melifaro was stretched out nonchalantly on his own desk, feet crossed, staring at the ceiling. I was sitting in his chair. I couldn't shake off the bizarre sensation that soon I would be sampling the festive delicacy that was laid out in front of me, elegantly wrapped in a bright turquoise looxi.

"Did you know there are lots of jokes making the rounds about Boboota Box and his men?" Melifaro said.

I shook my head no.

"What an innocent you are, Mr. Nightmare! Didn't your parents teach you anything? Shame on their bald and graying heads!"

Melifaro was already tired of lying on the desk. He jumped down to the floor, covered the distance from one corner to another in a few determined leaps, and arranged himself comfortably on the windowsill.

"Boboota and Foofloss are sitting in the outhouse in neighboring stalls, doing their respective business. Foofloss finishes, looks around, and sees there's no T.P. So he knocks on the wall to get Boboota's attention. 'Hey, boss. You have any T.P. over there?' And Boboota says, 'What's the matter, is your skaba too short?'"

I snickered, a bit surprised. Could it really be just a coincidence?

"Tell me another."

"Woo-hoo! I'm on a roll now! Go buy a ticket for the next show, first. Okay, okay, here's another one. Captain Foofloss comes up to Boboota and asks, 'What's the deductive method?'"

I started laughing, again taken by surprise.

Melifaro went on: "Boboota puffs out his cheeks and turns red in the face, he's thinking so hard. A half hour later he says, 'I'll make it plain and simple so even an idiot can understand. Did you eat yesterday? Yes, well then you've got a backside, too.' 'Goodness, boss. How did you guess?' 'I'll explain it one more time, this time for total cretins. If you ate yesterday, that means you visited the outhouse today. If you visited the outhouse today, that means you've got a backside. And *that's* the deductive method.' Foofloss, very pleased with himself, runs into Lieutenant Shixola walking down the corridor. You realize, naturally, that the joke was started long before Shixola was promoted to captain. Foofloss asks, 'Did you eat yesterday?' 'No, I didn't have time.' 'Well then you have no backside!'"

Amazing. I knew those jokes inside out. I had heard them many times as a kid in my own World. Sure, the characters had different names, but there was no mistaking it—the jokes were otherwise the same, word for word. Which just goes to show that peripatetic stories and jokes travel between Worlds far more easily than storytellers and jokers.

"Whoa!" Melifaro said. "A delegation has arrived. The cream of the crop, the pride and joy of the City Police Department and our White List. Lieutenant Kamshi and Captain Shixola, heroes of the popular imagination. Well, this was predictable. So, fellows, have you brought a petition? Here's your man, Sir Max himself. Grease his palm well, and he'll spit at your boss right across his own dinner table."

"Dream on," I mumbled. "I don't take bribes like some—"

"Like who?" Melifaro said.

"I don't know. I guess I'm the only one in the Universe who refuses them."

"No problem, mates," my daytime half said. "He'll wipe out your boss for free."

"You may think it's funny, gentlemen, but we're in a very difficult position," Kamshi said. Shixola made a mournful face.

"You're not kidding," Melifaro said in a jocular tone. "The Second Coming of General Boboota Box is nigh. If he's already sucking up to this freak of nature"—here he jerked his head irreverently in my direction—"he must be on his way to the House by the Bridge. Your happy days are over, boys. I feel for you."

"It was bound to happen sooner or later," Captain Shixola said. He looked like a prisoner waiting patiently on death row. "But it's such an inconvenient time."

"Ahem, and when would it be convenient?" Melifaro asked. "Anyway, guys, what gives? Something exciting?"

"Not exactly exciting. Let's just say some old traditions are being revived. Outlaws are coming out of the shadows in the Magaxon Forest again."

"Again?" Melifaro looked surprised. "It's only been thirty years since the World saw the last of Jiffa Savanxa and his henchmen. I guess a new batch of them is ready to roll. Their leader no doubt has a life-size portrait of Sir Jiffa in full outlaw regalia hanging above his bed. Charming. Well, is that all?"

"Almost, except that now our chances of cornering him are very slim," Kamshi said. "While Sir Boboota languishes at home in bed and his deputy Sir Foofloss goes pub-crawling, Shixola and I can act as we see fit. But what will become of our plans when General Box is back on duty? He'll start barking orders that we'll be forced to carry out. The gentlemen outlaws will be overjoyed, I'm sure."

"Hmm, I see." Melifaro nodded. "But what can we do to help? Cast a spell on Boboota that makes him allergic to giving orders? I'm afraid that's impossible."

"Of course. We were just thinking that hard work might undermine Boboota's already delicate condition," Kamshi said. "Perhaps you agree with us, gentlemen? And you could hint as much to Lady Box. Or, even better, you could inform General Boboota about your fears for his health."

"We're so worried we can't sleep at night," Melifaro said.

"I can tell Boboota that I spent all my free time learning the recipe for the pâté that poisoned him," I suggested. "And the experiment proved that the unhappy victims of that—what was that stuff called?

King Banjee, right—must under no circumstances overtax themselves. Otherwise they're doomed. But why didn't you try to bribe Abilat Paras? He's in charge of healing your boss. A warning like that from him would carry more weight."

"He is incorruptible, like Sir Max," said Lieutenant Kamshi, bowing to me ceremoniously. "I think the poor fellow is sick to death of being our boss's healer."

"Poor little Bobooty, nobody wuvs him," I said. "Should I adopt him? I can buy him candy and sit him down on the potty a hundred times a day. Wouldn't that be sweet?"

Melifaro turned aside and snickered quietly. That must have meant my friend was amused. The policemen looked at us almost in horror.

"Okay, boys, we'll do our best," Melifaro said. "Boboota will be white with fear by the time we're done with him. We'll take a great interest in the workings of his long-suffering intestines, and Sir Max will lecture him on the dangers of overexertion. With the Dark Magicians as my witness, we're on your side. Go forth, capture your brigands, and enjoy life."

The policemen left the office on wings of hope.

"You know this Lieutenant Kamshi isn't destined to stay too long with the City Police," Melifaro said after our guests had closed the heavy door behind them. "Sir Marunarx Antarop is already very old, and the post of Warden of the Prison of Xolomi is an onerous job."

"You think Kamshi will be the one to fill it?"

"Me? I don't think anything. But Sir Juffin once remarked that Kamshi was just the one to keep an eye on the walls of Xolomi. Juffin says he's made of the right stuff, heart and soul, and it's lucky if someone like that is born once in a century. Who do you think appoints someone to the post?"

"I don't doubt for a second that it's Juffin himself. And that's all for the best."

"And how! Well, are you ready to party?"

"No. And I'll never be ready for a party like this one. But if it's time to go, let's boogie."

❧

Boboota Box's mansion, the size of a stadium, loomed on the edge of the swanky Left Bank, where property started to get cheaper and neighbors were few and far between. The Left Bank was populated by those who didn't deign to take an interest in the price of land, or prices of any kind. People who wished to economize were rare in these parts. Only one or two houses, surrounded by greenery, were visible from Boboota's. This seemed to be where Echo ended.

"The old man sure lives in a grand style," Melifaro said. "This place looks like a fortress."

"Too grand for my tastes," I said. "Do you remember my apartment on the Street of Old Coins? For me that was already on the large side."

"Is this your inner real estate agent speaking?" Melifaro said. "To hear you talk, one would think you preferred living in a closet."

"You may find it hard to believe, but that's about what I was living in not so very long ago. How I managed to fit into it I can't imagine."

"You were probably just skinnier back then," Melifaro said, grinning. "And you slept standing up."

General Boboota Box met us at the door. He had grown so pale and thin during his illness that he actually resembled a human being. He no longer looked like a charging bull. He might even have been able to maneuver in a china shop without any upsets.

"Welcome, gentlemen," Boboota said in his most genteel manner.

His voice had become uncharacteristically mild. Melifaro and I exchanged wary glances. Was *this* gentle fellow the terror of his side of the House by the Bridge? What had happened to him, poor thing? Of course, as our host, he was obliged to be gracious and polite. Besides, we had saved his life, and he still feared me like he feared losing the spark, but this change in his demeanor was beyond comprehension.

After we had exchanged a few pleasantries, we went inside, where we were greeted by Boboota's wife. Strange as it may be, she was neither a harridan nor a doormat. As far as I've been able to judge, bullies like Boboota usually go for one extreme or the other when choosing a mate.

Lady Box was a very sweet, still pretty middle-aged redhead. She managed to be hospitable and unassuming at the same time.

"Thank you for saving my sweet dumpling, boys," she said with a bright smile. "It's hard to change your habits at my age, and I was already so used to falling asleep to the sound of his snores."

"Hush now, Ulima," Boboota murmured in embarrassment.

"Hold your tongue, worrywart! Have you forgotten our agreement? You invite the guests, and I amuse them, since the few times we tried to do it the other way around, it wasn't exactly a success. This way, please, gentlemen."

We were shown into the living room, where I was in for yet another surprise.

I was already familiar with the practice in Echo of cultivating luminous mushrooms in vessels that function as lampshades. These fungi are used to illuminate both streets and living spaces. When something irritates them, the mushrooms begin to glow. The light switch simply activates some bristles that gently but insistently tickle the caps of the mushrooms. General Boboota preferred this form of lighting, and it wouldn't have surprised me, but . . .

An enormous translucent vessel occupied the center of the living room. I suppose your average whale might have found it a bit cramped, but the whale still would have been able to fit inside it. The vessel contained a radiant mushroom of truly mammoth proportions. The ones I had seen before this were seldom larger than a three-year-old child. This enormous specimen not only cast a warm orange glow but also buzzed like an angry bumblebee. I was astonished. By the looks of it, Melifaro was as unsettled by the thing as I was.

"Are you impressed? This is my pride and joy." General Boboota was grinning from ear to ear. "I grew it myself. It's so smart, you can't imagine. You see, gentlemen, it began to glow as soon as we came in. And I didn't even have to go near the switch. It just knows when to light up."

"I'm afraid that mushroom simply hates my husband," Lady Box whispered to me. "When anyone else enters the room, glowing is the last thing on its mind. I always have to flick the switch."

"I believe my mushroom is the only one of its kind in the World," Boboota said, glowing himself.

"You, sir, are also the only one of your kind," Melifaro said with unfeigned enthusiasm.

"Thank you," Boboota said, making a deep bow. "And here, gentlemen, is another family heirloom."

He gestured toward a huge canvas that covered almost the entire wall. It depicted a battle scene. The foreground was dominated by General Boboota Box himself, decked out in some bizarre uniform and dripping with medals and bric-a-brac. His manly chest blocked from view a smallish elderly man with a bright expression and wind-tousled snow-white hair. Some claw-like fingers on a pair of emaciated dark hands were reaching out toward Boboota from the nether regions of the painting, while the General threatened them with his broadsword. In the background, a flock of wholesome, fresh-faced youths were cheerfully vanquishing some unattractive, unkempt gentlemen.

The painting struck me as horrible. It was pitiful to look at poor Melifaro, though—he was fighting a losing battle against his urge to guffaw.

Our host, in the meantime, launched into a lecture.

"This masterpiece is the work of Galza Illana himself. I was very lucky. Sir Illana was the Senior Master of Depiction at the court of His Majesty Gurig VII, may the Dark Magicians protect him. And who, if not he, could preserve the spirit of this outstanding and memorable event? It is an excellent rendering, is it not, gentlemen? Not like the work of our modern paint slingers. They may as well be smearing their backsides with their own crap."

The most striking thing was that good old General Boboota, our hospitable host, uttered this phrase in such a quiet and colorless voice that it sounded like an intelligent, even eloquent, critique.

"And what are those medals?" I said, my curiosity getting the better of me. "Amulets?"

"Right you are, Sir Max. Protective amulets made for us, the Royal Guard, by the Order of the Seven-Leaf Clover, the Single and Most Beneficent. In those days it would have been impossible to get along without them. We were up against the Orders of Magic! And a sharp sword and brave heart aren't going to get you very far against an enemy like that. If it weren't for those amulets, I wouldn't have had the joy of—"

"Joy of my heart," Lady Ulima interrupted him gently. "Don't you think it's time to feed the guests? That is why they're here, you know—to eat."

"Of course, my dear." Boboota turned to us, somewhat abashed. "Do you like the painting, gentlemen?"

Melifaro and I nodded silently. We were a hair's breadth away from desecrating the idyllic vision with a most irreverent explosion of laughter, but we managed to contain our glee.

For this we were rewarded with the call to dine. Dinner wasn't as unexpected as the prelude to the meal. Everything was *comme il faut*. The presentation of the dishes was lovely, Lady Ulima's society gossip was engaging, and the gallant Boboota deferred politely to her.

Weary of suffering in silence, I sent a call to Melifaro.

I wonder if he's always so proper when he's at home? Or could this be a lingering symptom of poisoning?

With such a sweet and affectionate wife around, it's possible he's always like this at home, Melifaro answered in Silent Speech. *The guy still can't figure out how he landed such a paragon of womanhood. For Lady Ulima, Boboota will refuse to speak above a whisper. He'll go down on his knees to put her dainty slippers on her little feet. At work, though, he cuts loose from the bottom of his soul, and it's no holds barred.*

Here I was forced to admit that the harebrained Melifaro understood people far better than I did.

❧

My body has its own notions of what constitutes good manners. For some reason that I can't fathom, it feels that when you are invited to dinner, halfway through the feast it's time to head for the john. Over the course of many years I struggled heroically against this urge, but I finally tossed in the towel. It was a losing battle.

The formal dinner at General Boboota's was no exception. In any case, I didn't have to worry too much. In this house, a little detour of that nature could only inspire indulgent approval on the part of my host. I left the dining room without troubling to invent all kinds of excuses.

Downstairs there was yet another surprise in store for me.

I had long before grown used to the fact that every house in Echo has at least three or four bathing pools. Usually there are many more. This could turn bathing into a complicated affair.

But a dozen *toilets* of various heights gurgling a discordant welcome to the visitor—well, this I was seeing for the first time. Even Sir Juffin Hully, the unsurpassed sybarite of all nations and epochs, gets along with just one, not to mention ordinary Echoers. I couldn't deny that Boboota Box was one of a kind.

I must have been looking somewhat bewildered when I finally returned to the dining room. My colleagues, especially the irreproachable Sir Lonli-Lokli, were always trying to persuade me to disguise my feelings, or at least not to wear them on my sleeve (right next to my heart). But my facial muscles gave me away every time.

Lady Ulima threw me a sharp glance, then burst out laughing.

"Take a look, dear! It seems that even gentlemen Secret Investigators can be caught by surprise."

"You're bringing shame on our organization, Sir Max," Melifaro said with a sniff. "Is this the first time it's ever happened to you? Didn't you know that all people do that sort of thing from time to time?"

"Very funny," I said. "Go have a look yourself." Here I switched to Silent Speech. *He's got a dozen toilets in there, I kid you not!*

Melifaro raised his eyebrows in disbelief and shut up. Just in case.

"No secrets, gentlemen," Lady Ulima said, smiling all the while.

"It's a perfectly appropriate subject for conversation—even at the dinner table, by way of exception. Tell them, dear."

Boboota began his story as if on cue. "When I was a young lad and had just entered the Royal Guard, about two hundred years ago, I lived in the barracks. They were glorious times, I'm not complaining. But something happened once—"

Lady Ulima chortled again. She clearly knew this saga by heart and was anticipating what was to come. General Boboota grew tongue-tied.

"You won't be shocked by hearing such an . . . unappetizing story during dinner, gentlemen? I can tell you the story later, over dessert, if you'd prefer."

Melifaro and I exchanged glances, then guffawed, unable to suppress our merriment any longer.

"You see? No need to mince words with these boys," Lady Box said, urging him on. "I'm not sure they'd be shocked even if you showed them. But do go on, please."

"Well, it wasn't even something you'd call an event," Boboota continued shyly. "I had a buddy in the service, one Shartzy Nolla, an excellent fellow. A real giant—a head taller than me, and with the physique to match. One day he and I received a Day of Freedom from Care and went to visit his aunt, Madam Catalla. Back then she was the proprietor of an excellent tavern, so our Shartzy was a lucky dog—and he was fed like a king. Since we were together that day, I lucked out, too. You might say we outdid ourselves, so much food did we consume. The next morning we returned to the barracks, and Shartzy made for the outhouse. He beat me to it, the old crapper!

"Back then we lived in barracks. There were four of us to a room, and we all shared one outhouse, if you can believe it. Well, I held it in, and held it in. Half an hour. An hour. The joker still wouldn't come out. He later claimed he was constipated, but I think he took his time on purpose. Anyway, holding it in any longer was beyond my control."

Melifaro made a terrifying spectacle. He was bright red from suppressed laughter. I even feared for his life, if not just for his sanity.

"Just let it out, Sir Melifaro," Lady Ulima said. "Why not? It's a funny story!"

"And that's when I decided," Boboota said in a solemn voice, "I decided that if I ever got rich, I'd have a dozen blasted toilets at my disposal at any given time."

Melifaro and I exploded into wild fits of laughter. We sounded like madmen. The General and his wife looked on benevolently. We were probably not the first guests who had laughed themselves silly after being regaled with this venerable tale.

❀

The dinner finally came to an end. Out of the folds of the Mantle of Death I ceremoniously drew a box of Cuban cigars. I had come by these rare delights when I was in Kettari. I had fished them out from the Chink between Worlds, where up until then I had found only cigarettes. Since that day I've never known what I would find when I reach my hand into that sinning Chink. In any case, I've learned that everything comes in handy sooner or later. Well, nearly everything.

To my shame, I had never liked cigars—or, rather, I had never really known how to smoke them. My coworkers had turned out to be even more clueless in this department than I was. Boboota was my last hope.

"What are these, Sir Max?" Boboota said.

"They're meant for smoking," I said. "I just received them from Kumon, the capital of the Kumon Caliphate. I've got kinfolk there, you see."

I was already in the habit of referring to the Kumon Caliphate whenever I had to explain the origin of the strange objects that turned up in my poor pockets more and more often. The Kumon Caliphate is so far away that the only person who might have caught me in the lie was Sir Manga Melifaro, author of the famous eight-volume *Encyclopedia of the World* (and of the infamous Ninth Volume, Melifaro Junior).

"You don't say! The Kumon Caliphate?" said Lady Ulima.

"Yes." I sighed. "Whenever I discover new relatives, it seems they always manage to migrate to the outer reaches of the World."

General Boboota, in the meantime, had lit up a cigar. "Sir Max!" The erstwhile victim of my cruel experiment gave a sigh of delight. "Even in my wildest dreams, I could never have imagined that such things exist. Are they really all for me?" His hands were trembling.

"They're all yours," I said, nodding. "I'll have my relatives send more if you like. They're too strong for me, but it's a matter of taste, of course. Glad you enjoy them."

"It's . . . it's . . ." He couldn't seem to find an uncensored word to describe his euphoria. Neither could I. The scoundrel with a big fat cigar between his teeth—that was a sight to behold. And Melifaro's restraint (he hadn't said a word through all of this) deserves a special word of praise. That was what you call a surprise.

❀

Just before we were about to leave, I recalled that the fellows from the Police Department had begged me to find something out for them.

"Sir Box," I began cautiously. "Have you fully recovered from your illness?"

"Yes, Sir Max. Thank you for asking after my health. I'm in tip-top shape now."

I sighed. Poor gentlemen police officers—though Boboota seemed to have become quite harmless. "So you plan to return to the House by the Bridge soon?"

"Yes, in a dozen days or so. Ulima, you see, thinks I should take it easy and not rush things."

I sighed again, this time in relief. Everything was sorting itself out without any help from me.

"You're quite right, Lady Ulima." I could have kissed the General's sweet wife then and there. "King Banjee is no joke. The slightest over-exertion, or, let's say, nervous strain, can lead to a relapse. I can vouch for it."

"Vouch for it?" Lady Ulima said, confused. "Did you eat some of that dreadful mess, too, Sir Max?"

"Praise be the Magicians, no. But I have spent a great deal of time investigating the consequences of others' misfortunes."

"Did you hear that, dumpling?" said this wonderful woman. "I don't think you should return to work until Midyear's Day, if not later."

Boboota nodded obediently.

Kamshi and Shixola's upcoming two-man antiterrorist campaign in the Magaxon Forest had been saved.

§

"Will you drop me off at home, Max?" Melifaro said, plunking down wearily in the back seat of the amobiler. "Juffin has no choice now but to free us from work for half a dozen days. I've never been so exhausted in my life."

"Really? What wore you out? Counting all Boboota's toilets? That's understandable—you don't have enough fingers to count them on."

"Are you making fun of me? That's not fair. I can't bear these for-mal dinners. They drive me to distraction. In my family, everyone eats when they please, including guests. So there's always someone at the table enjoying a meal or a snack, except at night, of course. That's what I was used to when I was growing up. But here, you sit in one spot for three hours with your mouth full, making polite conversation. I thought our hosts would be amusing, but they turned out to be such bores. Although Lady Ulima, of course, is charming. And the mushroom—that was something else!" Melifaro livened up a bit just thinking about it. "Yes, that mushroom is something to write home about."

"And the portrait?" I chuckled. "And the dozen toilets? And the family lore about how the youthful Boboota filled his pants? Holy crap!"

Melifaro brayed so violently that the amobiler jumped up and down.

Fifteen minutes later I deposited him in front of his door on the Street of Gloomy Clouds, in the center of the Old City. I watched him with envy as he went inside, then turned toward the House by the Bridge. I still had to go to work.

❀

The job that awaited me wasn't an easy one. It consisted of arranging my posterior more on the chair than off, placing my feet on Sir Juffin Hully's sacred desk, and imbibing an endless stream of kamra. The poor couriers would be running their feet flat, beating a path to the *Glutton* and back.

Relief came just in time. Kurush was pecking listlessly at his third pastry. His fondness for sweets seemed to be diminishing. At about the same time, I was beginning to fear that I might explode. Just then, in the doorway appeared the object of my long-standing envy: the splendid nose of Captain Shixola. He was on tenterhooks, awaiting my detailed report about our visit to the deathbed of General Boboota Box, Chief of Public Order.

I beamed at him. "Come in, come in. I can offer you a sea of kamra and some good news."

"You aren't busy, Sir Max?" the owner of the nose inquired tactfully.

"See for yourself," I said, grinning. "I'm swamped. The kamra is tepid, the mug heavy, and there's no end in sight to this hard manual labor. Don't you feel for me?"

Captain Shixola finally appeared in full. In spite of his unusual height and athletic build, he still seemed like an unnecessary afterthought to his own fathomless nose.

"But where is Sir Kamshi? Maybe he finally wore himself out with worry and headed for the Xuron to put a watery end to it. Too bad. Hope is supposed to die last."

"He's so tired after the last few days that he no longer cares. He just went home to sleep."

Shixola had the habit of responding to my wildest statements with a half-smile. It was universally applicable to all situations. If I was really joking—well, here's a smile for you. But if that Sir Max uttered something unbelievably stupid or outrageous—well, it wasn't a real smile after all.

"Okay," I said. "Let him sleep. Looks like you'll be the one to get all the good news. And all the kamra, too. I can't bear to look at it anymore, much less drink it."

"That's what Max always says," said Kurush. "Then he orders another jug of it. You people are extraordinarily contradictory creatures."

"You got that right, smarty," I said. Then I turned to Shixola again. "You owe me one, my friend."

"Do you mean that General Boboota—"

"You wouldn't even recognize him! He's the sweetest-tempered, most soft-spoken person on earth. He doesn't speak above a whisper. Is he always like that at home?"

"Quite the contrary. Lady Ulima is the only one who can tame him, and only half the time at that. But you know yourself how he treats us, Sir Max."

"Yes. What happened tonight was truly beyond belief. When the conversation turned to toilets, he inquired whether the subject was too shocking for us."

"That really is beyond belief," Shixola said, looking bewildered. "Is it possible he has changed that much?" He clearly couldn't believe his luck.

"Well, if I were you I wouldn't hold my breath. It might just be the consequences of the poisoning. And he has every chance of fully recovering. Be that as it may, for now the Dark Magicians are on your side. Boboota himself decided not to return to work for another dozen or so days. And after my little song and dance, Lady Ulima will keep him at home until Midyear's Day, I think."

"Sir Max, it's no wonder you're the stuff of legend around here. You—"

"What kinds of legends are they telling about me, Shixola?" I said, interrupting him.

"Oh my, hasn't Sir Kofa told you?" He was quite perplexed. "I can't repeat these silly things in front of Kurush."

"Don't worry. I'm asleep," the buriwok said dryly.

I laughed. Kurush may be the wisest of birds, but the things he comes out with sometimes! Too much exposure to people can't lead to any good, it seems.

"You see? Kurush is asleep. And I need to hear the bitter truth, so spit it out. Sir Kofa only wanted to spare my feelings."

"Well, they say you are Sir Juffin Hully's illegitimate son," Shixola said, after some hesitation. "But you must know that already without my telling you. And they say that you were imprisoned in Xolomi for five hundred years for the murder of the entire ancient royal dynasty that abdicated the throne in favor of the first of the Gurigs. That crime, by the way, is a historical fact, but the guilty parties were never found, no matter what people may think. They also say that you are the very first of the ancient Grand Magicians. You came back to life, dug your way out of the grave, stole one of Sir Juffin's numerous souls, and—"

"Wow, curiouser and curiouser!" The quote, which was known to me alone, sprang unbidden to my lips. "I see. What else?"

"More of the same. They say you are even more powerful than Loiso Pondoxo, but that you haven't yet come into your full powers since you first have to kill all the living Magicians—former Magicians, I mean. The ones that are left. That's why you entered the Secret Investigative Force, they say."

"Yikes! More powerful than Loiso Pondoxo? Oh, come on! I'm such a fine, upstanding guy. Sweet and inoffensive as a stuffed animal. Not without my little eccentricities, mind you, but even those are completely innocent. Come on, do people really believe all that nonsense?"

"Of course they do," Shixola said. "There's nothing they like better than being on intimate terms with a miracle, at least in their imaginations. Otherwise life is so monotonous, so dull."

"You're all right, Shixola. You have a clear and simple explanation for everything. I wish I did."

"Are you making fun of me, Sir Max?" Shixola said guardedly.

"Not in the least. But tell me about these outlaws of yours. Better yet, about their predecessors. Is it a tale of derring-do?"

"It's the stuff of romance and adventure, all right. Red Jiffa's men were known as the Magaxon Foxes. Those fellows were determined to become legends right from the start. Take Sir Jiffa Savanxa. He hailed from a very distinguished family—distant relatives of the king himself. It's not every day that gentlemen like him run off to become outlaws.

"His story began during the Troubled Times, but things were different at first. Back then, the Magaxon Foxes hunted down Mutinous Magicians who were fleeing to Echo from the Residences of the provincial

Orders of Magic. (These were the Junior Magicians, of course—the Senior Magicians were more than they could handle.) The Foxes were thus performing a service for the king, and for those who remained loyal to him.

"After the Code was introduced, Sir Jiffa refused to return to the Capital to collect his laurels. I think he had simply found his true calling. That happens, you know."

"You got that right, Shixola," I said grinning. "And what did these wholesome kids do next?"

"That's easy to guess. They kept on hunting. Only now they were more interested in ordinary people. Ordinary and rich. Merchants, for instance. At first the king tried to reason with Jiffa. Huntsmen from the Royal Court tried bringing him back into the fold for at least a dozen years. Finally the late king realized it was a lost cause. Jiffa and his brigands were declared outlaws, and the huntsmen had to try to chase them down out of other motives. Sir Jiffa was a master in the arts of secrecy and camouflage, and he taught his people all he knew. The Foxes knew how to make themselves invisible. Literally. Finally they were captured and their hideouts were discovered. You know, Sir Max, they hid underground, and Jiffa had his own palace down there. There was a whole system of passageways that led into the Magaxon Forest. The Foxes really did live like foxes, in lairs. It's no wonder that the huntsmen gave chase for five dozen years."

"What did they do with the stolen goods?" I said, naively recalling the legend of Robin Hood I had been so fond of as a child.

"They stuffed the corners of their lairs with the loot. What else can you do with treasure if you live in a forest? Actually, that slyboots Jiffa had the temerity to come sniffing around Echo. He managed to squander some of the fortune before they were hot on his trail. After that, Red Jiffa buried himself in his lair for good."

"Well, well," I said. There was no hint in the account of anything that smacked of robbing from the rich to give to the poor. And even in Robin Hood's case, I had my doubts.

"During the reign of the old king, things stayed pretty quiet," Shixola went on. "But when the present monarch, King Gurig VIII, took the throne, he decreed a Royal Hunt for the Magaxon Foxes. This time His Majesty enlisted the help of a bunch of former Magicians, though not Mutinous Magicians, of course. These fellows had their own issues with Red Jiffa. Back in the day he had cut down a number of their close friends. And so we add yet another detail to his portrait: he adored wielding cold steel. It made him dizzy with rapture."

"How vile," I said sincerely, recalling my own meager but unfortunate experience with dangerous sharp objects. "So tasteless."

"You must admit, though, Sir Max, that there's a certain fascination in it," Shixola said.

Touché! Live and learn, Max, I reminded myself. And don't forget for a minute that you are surrounded by intensely interesting people.

"So how did this tale of romance and adventure end?" I said.

"The only way it could end. The Magicians received special permission to resort to some unheard-of degree of magic. So the foxcubs crawled out of their lairs at a whistle, ready to be shot. You have to hand it to Jiffa—he wasn't an easy target. He and a few others held out till the end. Jiffa is a man of the old school, so he was able to counter every spell with one of his own. But there were many Magicians and only one of him. The fellows who held out with him were no great shakes. Capturing them was just a matter of time. In the end, they were able to lure Jiffa out of his den, too, but not before he killed four of the huntsmen. They did finally manage to quell his unruly soul, though."

"A happy ending for someone who wants to become a living legend, of course," I said. "As far as I'm concerned, though, it's better to live a long and happy life, completely devoid of romance and adventure."

"It's a matter of taste," Shixola said. "Aren't you being a tad disingenuous, Sir Max?"

"Certainly not. I'm a cautious and practical individual, very typical as far as they go. Haven't you noticed? Well, Captain, go forth and round up the Magaxon Foxes Fan Club. You won't be bothered by the good intentions of Boboota the Terrible any time soon. And be sure to fill me in on new installments of the legend, all right? You're quite a raconteur."

"Thank you, Sir Max. I'll keep you posted on developments if you're truly interested."

"I am interested in everything. Up to a point, that is. Good night, Captain. I see I've worn you out. You're so tired you can barely stand up. Go visit dreamland and put life on hold for a while."

Shixola, considerably more cheerful now than when he had arrived, drank the last of my kamra and went off to get some shuteye.

I looked at Kurush. "Did he tell the story right?"

"For the most part," the buriwok said. "Although he did leave out some important details."

"Details are the last thing I need right now," I said. "I'm fine without them."

I spent the rest of the night even more idly. I couldn't even get my hands on a fresh newspaper. For a dozen days I had been wondering which of the junior staff cleaned up the office. The fellow had a bad habit of chucking out the unread copies of the *Royal Voice* along with the trash. Of course, I kept forgetting to get to the bottom of it.

❀

Just before dawn, Kofa Yox put in an appearance. This time, he had chosen such an absurdly round, snub-nosed face for his pub peregrinations that I couldn't help laughing out loud.

"Give me a break," Kofa protested. "It's a perfectly ordinary physiognomy. We can't all look handsome and debonair." Then he passed his hands slowly over his face, and his own countenance returned to where it belonged. "Go home, Max. Feed your cats, milk them, clip their fur—or whatever it is you novice farmers do to your farm animals at sunrise. I'll be here until Juffin arrives, anyway."

"All right," I said. "Whatever you say. You have secrets to tell him?"

"No secrets. I'm just tired, that's all. There's a fury of a woman waiting for me at home. I've got to sleep sometime, somewhere, don't I?"

"A fury of a woman? At home?" I was surprised. I suddenly realized that I hadn't the slightest clue about my colleague's personal life. I knew about all the others, but up until then Sir Kofa Yox had been a blank spot in my personal gossip column.

"That's right. My cleaning lady. Yesterday I refused to marry her again. She claims my refusal was an anniversary—the sixtieth. Atili is a wonderful woman, of course, but I hate ceremonies. And some people are foolish enough to think they guarantee the longevity of feelings."

"Sir Kofa," I said. "I'm on your side, believe me."

"I guessed as much. Aversion to officially enshrined customs is written all over your face. In letters this big." Here he stretched out his arms to demonstrate. "Go home, Max. You're a perpetual party in my uneventful life, but, honestly, I'm so tired."

"I get the picture. I'm gone."

❀

And I flew headlong out the door. Let him rest, poor guy. I had to catch my luck by the tail. Who knew when I'd get another chance to tidy up my own apartment?

The need for a thorough spring cleaning was growing more urgent by the day. Armstrong and Ella, my cats, have a knack for turning everything upside down. Of course, I could have called in one of those unlucky people who have to earn a living by scraping the crap off other people's backsides, but the idea didn't sit well with me. Some mournful soul would traipse into my house, crawl around the living room on hands and knees, and slosh around a wet rag. I'd give instructions and then, feeling disgusted with myself, set out for the nearest tavern. After which the professional scrubber would breathe a sigh of relief, rummage through my desk and closets, throw away important papers, break a few things, and put everything else in places it didn't belong. No thanks.

Now the hour of reckoning had arrived, though. I'd have to pay for my convictions. You don't want to keep a servant, you don't have to, but keep your house in order, at least, I had told myself every morning since my return from Kettari. Then I would tell myself patiently, I'll clean it up later, when I have a bit more time.

In the meantime, the mess was entering a new phase. Chaos, plain and simple, reigned in my apartment. Life was becoming intolerable.

So it was now or never. With this in mind I drove home more slowly than usual—even more slowly than the local speed demons. Eventually I arrived home, though. Some things just can't be avoided.

I hadn't been able to get used to my new apartment on the Street of Yellow Stones. There was too little of me for six huge rooms. One of them became my living room, another one—on the second floor—my bedroom, and the other four constituted a testing range for all manner of experiments involving my cats. After a time, I concluded that two well-fed one-year-old cats can remain in a state of constant rapid and random motion for up to a dozen hours. Strange, when we lived in two rooms on the Street of Old Coins, Armstrong and Ella had been inveterate couch potatoes. Apparently, limitless expanses really do lead to an increase in uncivilized behavior in living species. I even caught myself in the secret wish to play tag, but I lacked suitable like-minded anthropomorphic playmates.

I took care of the empty rooms in record time. You get a real power surge when you're armed with a wet rag.

My bedroom looked fairly decent. That's where I spent most of my free time, after all, so the malignant mess hadn't been able to take hold there. I find that a small degree of disorder in my surroundings adds to the coziness. I just had to give the dusty windowsill a swipe and open the window to let in the fresh breeze . . . along with a million tiny particles of dust. It's a vicious circle.

I looked at the bed longingly, sighed, then told myself sternly, No you don't, buddy. There's still one more room in your palace. Have you forgotten?

Shocked by my own cruelty, I headed downstairs to the living room, which was the initial cause of all this madness. Along the way, it occurred to me that a small but amply packed tray of delicacies from the *Fat Turkey* would provide sustenance for a weary hero, and I sent a call to the tavern. Strictly speaking, the *Fat Turkey* was still closed at this hour. What people won't do for a regular patron, though, particularly if that patron had a habit of staggering down the street in the Mantle of Death.

Speaking of my Mantle, it finally dawned on me that it wasn't a bad idea to change my clothes if I was cleaning my house, so I had to go back upstairs. A thin everyday skaba decreased my discomfort considerably.

In the living room, I was greeted by the forlorn spectacle of the traveling bag I had taken to Kettari. It was planted in the middle of the room, just where I had left it when I returned home from the trip. Armstrong was merrily chasing after my magic pillow, without the least concern for the powerful spells of Maba Kalox. Ella was intent upon shredding the edges of the valuable Kettarian rug (which, to my shame, was still rolled up in a corner of the room). This, of course, did not exhaust the list of my domestic misfortunes.

The harsh working conditions at the Ministry had turned me into a real hero of labor. A few years ago I would have shuddered at the sight of this disorder and averted my eyes. Now I just swore under my breath a few times and got down to work. A half hour later, the table was as clean as a desert sky. This was a good start. Only minutes before, the surface had been evenly covered with a thick layer of debris. Since I lacked the courage simply to throw all the useless junk away, I had had to sort through it.

There was a knock at the door. It was my breakfast, accompanied by a terrified, sleepy delivery boy from the *Fat Turkey*. I had the presence of mind to thank him, so he carried out his delivery without completely falling apart. That was a good thing—I'm very lucky to have a *Fat Turkey* as my only neighbor.

After snacking a bit, I succumbed to another cruel onslaught of laziness. Then I gritted my teeth and started brandishing the rag again. I was waging the Battle for Cleanliness. Two hours later, when my work really was about done and I felt as though I had spent the past millennium voluntarily breaking rocks, there was another knock on the door.

"Come in! It's unlocked," I shouted. "I'm not your doorman."

Physical labor had never been known to improve my character. Besides, what's the use of being sweet and kind when the whole population of Echo takes you for an undead monster? The instructive chat with Captain Shixola had left an indelible impression on the tender surface of my soul. I heard the door slam, then the rapid clip of footsteps in the hall. In the doorway stood a strange creature. Even the heavy folds of an unseasonably warm looxi couldn't conceal its penguinesque rotundity. A rather pleasant face looked out from under a dark blue turban. I had seen that face somewhere before . . . Yes, of course! The stranger bore a striking resemblance to the poet Apollinaire, whom no one in this World had ever heard of. I wonder whether he's also a poet, I thought. Well, we'll soon find out. The last thing I need is a poet around the house.

"Are you in the service of Sir Max, young man?" my guest inquired amiably.

Sinning Magicians, he had a French accent to boot! And it was rather charming.

"How did you land it? Catch?"

"Land what?" I said, then launched into the penultimate cleaning ritual of the day: a quick dash around the almost pristine room with the wet rag.

"No catch? You don't understand?"

"Oh! I dig."

Now it was his turn to bat his lovely almond-shaped eyelids in consternation. This was tit for tat. Slang from two different Worlds, mutually unintelligible. I wanted to take my hat off to such a singular historical encounter, but, alas, I wasn't even wearing a turban.

"Who might you be, my dear chap?" I said, starting in on about the eighth windowsill. A hole in the heavens above this sinning palace of an apartment, and above Sir Juffin Hully who had found these "humble lodgings" for me!

"I am Sir Anday Pu, senior reporter for the *Royal Voice*," the stranger said. "Catch? Not from any old *Echo Hustle and Bustle*, but—"

"You're really a senior reporter?" I said, doubtfully. The last name wasn't familiar to me. Considering my passion for accumulating newsprint, this was rather strange. But I did have a bad memory for names.

"Well, one of the seniors. What's the diff?" my penguinesque friend said with a shrug. "Our editor, Sir Rogro Jiil, has asked me to do a story on Sir Max's cats, who will eventually become the parents of the first

Royal Felines. I decided I simply had to meet Sir Max in person. My colleagues, those cowardly plebs, whisper terrible tales about your master behind his back. By the way, could you stand me a mug of kamra, pal?"

When I paused in my chores and turned around, I discovered that he had already seated himself at my table and was distractedly rearranging my cups. Why did I even bother cleaning up?

"Look in the jug," I grumbled. "Maybe there's something left, I don't remember."

A soft gurgling sound ended my doubts. I sighed, then turned to face my final task. I started unfurling the weighty Kettarian carpet. If I had taken the trouble to lug the rug all the way from Kettari, I deserved the pleasure of seeing it unrolled, at least.

"Will Sir Max be home soon?" Anday said with his mouth full.

Drat, now he was scarfing down my breakfast.

"I don't know," I barked out. "He'll be back when he pleases. And I'm going upstairs to bed, so I'm afraid I'll have to interrupt your meal."

"Take it easy, man! I'll just wait for him in the living room. At the same time, I'll get acquainted with his cats. Where are they, by the way?"

"I guess they're sleeping on the bed in my room," I said. "Didn't it ever occur to you to just come back later?"

"You no catch," Anday blurted out. "I have to show my story to the editor no later than tomorrow. If Sir Max doesn't come home before evening, sound the alarm! And if I don't even manage to see the cats—well, the dinner's over."

His eyes were filled with such anguish that my stony heart started to crack ever so slightly. I shuffled the empty food bowls around on the floor invitingly, and in no time I heard the patter of their stubby kitty legs on the stairs. My furry beasties never turn down the opportunity for a little snack, no matter how often I feed them.

"Here they are," I said proudly, filling up their bowls. "Observe them, study their habits, but don't take it into your head to eat their food. They might turn violent. They'll go for the jugular, and it's curtains for you."

"It's what?"

"Curtains. Like, you're dead. Dig?"

"Ah, like somethin' *bad's* gonna happen. Where did you go to school, anyway? In college we used to say 'the dinner's over.' But I catch! By the way, is there anything to eat around here? I mean, Sir Max is a rich guy, and it's not going to make a dent in his pantry if I—"

"It's definitely not going to make a dent in his pantry," I said, laughing. "Only it's unlikely you'll find anything edible in this house. I've already eaten everything in sight."

Poor Anday looked so deflated it almost brought tears to my eyes.

"Oh, all right. I'll try to rustle up some food."

I thrust my hand under the table. This was a good excuse for me to try the trick with the Chink between Worlds, which still baffled me.

The rotund Anday Pu turned out to be a lucky guy. This time I pulled out not a broken umbrella or yet another bottle of mineral water (which happened all too often) but an enormous frying pan in which some eggs, covered with a generous portion of melted cheese, were already sizzling. This was more than I had expected.

"Be sure to clean up after your meal," I said sternly. "When Sir Max sees a mess on his table, he spits poison first, then looks for the culprit later. My advice to you is that it doesn't pay to wait. You were assigned to write a story about the cats? Well, here they are. Write to your heart's content, and make your editor happy. Got that? I'm going to bed." I didn't have the strength to send him packing. I was too tired for words.

"No catch! Where did this grub come from?" the flabbergasted visitor inquired of my weary back.

"From under the table."

"Well, knock me down with a feather," Anday exclaimed.

Ignoring his dumbstruck fascination, I went up to the bedroom and wrapped the powerful "rag"—the kerchief of the Grand Magician of the Order of the Secret Grass—around my neck with habitual ease. I had been strongly encouraged not to fall asleep without it these days.

Then it was lights out for me.

Praise be the Magicians, I finally had a dream. A very somber and meaningless one, but hey, I was willing to take any dream I could get. After that I awoke feeling absolutely refreshed. I was the happiest man in the Universe. Everything had fallen into place again.

I went downstairs in the most benevolent of moods. The absurd journalist, Anday Pu, was still sitting at the table. The mess I had banished just a while ago had been restored, despite my glowering threats. The coquettish Ella was purring tenderly in his lap. On the floor, Armstrong was tangling himself lazily in the hem of Anday Pu's looxi.

"Sir Max never came home," Anday said sadly. "I might as well give up. It's the absolute end of the dinner."

"You mean you're finished?" I grinned. "You don't know how lucky you are, buddy! He would have finished you off. What happened to the table?"

"Take it easy, kid! I don't know where to put all this stuff. That's your job, anyway. I'm sure you get paid a pretty penny for it. Come on, it won't kill you."

"I don't get paid a thing," I said cheerfully. "It keeps me alive, and that's enough. You see that door? That leads to the hallway, if you remember. There's a brazier in there, a big thing. Bring it here and dump everything you see on the table in it. It won't kill you, either, I hope."

"No, no, no problem," said the guest, formerly on the verge of rage but now nodding agreeably.

I nodded back, then went off to bathe. My good mood was unshakeable.

When I got back to the living room, my hapless visitor was piling up the dirty dishes on a large metal tray. His face wore an injured expression. At the rate he was going, he wouldn't be finished before midnight. I sighed, and in one bold motion swept the remains of the disorder into the brazier. Then I snapped the fingers of my right hand jauntily. I had learned this trick not long ago, and I couldn't pass up the opportunity to garner applause for it. The small mountain of junk rose up, turned a sickly shade of green, then disappeared altogether, to my indescribable relief.

"There," I said proudly.

"Was that Forbidden Magic? Whoa! Now you're really smokin', man. Everyone might as well give up," said the only witness of my modest wonder-working.

"No catch?" I sniffed. "There's nothing forbidden about it. Just ordinary manual dexterity."

There was a knock at the door.

"Excellent," I said. "That's either Sir Max, which I doubt, or my morning kamra, which I very much hope. Let's see."

My guest drew himself up, arranging the folds of his looxi.

These journalists have a thick skin. They aren't even afraid of a monster like me! I thought, going out to welcome my breakfast.

Naturally, I had to share my kamra and cookies with Anday Pu. I didn't actually mind. Ella seemed so fond of him already. But it began to look like he was planning to occupy my living room until kingdom come, and it was time for me to report for duty. Well, the poor sucker was just asking for a nervous breakdown.

After breakfast I went back upstairs, where, not without a touch of sardonic anticipation, I wrapped myself in the Mantle of Death. If they make a monster out of you, you've got to derive the maximum amount of pleasure from it. These were my thoughts as I was going downstairs again.

"Uh-oh, why didn't I catch right away?" Anday Pu burst out with fearful enthusiasm. "So *you* are Sir Max? I might as well give up. The dinner's over once and for all!"

I laughed. His pet phrase about the end of dinner was wonderfully apt. Moreover, the comical brazenness of the journalist was balm to my heart, fed up as it was with the timid glances and fearful silence of the citizens of Echo.

"*Now* do you catch?" I said, smiling. "Well, what was it you wanted to know about my cats? Hurry it up, though. I've got to go to work."

"The cats are to die for!" Anday said wistfully. "But I'll be on my way, if you're in a hurry. I've outstayed my welcome as it is. Forgive me, but I didn't catch. I hope I haven't caused you too much trouble." His boldness was quickly diminishing.

"Not too much," I lied. "You can send me a call if there are any questions."

"May I? Thank you, Sir Max. I'll definitely—"

Anday ducked into the hallway and shut the door softly behind him as he left, so I never had the pleasure of finding out what he "definitely." I shrugged and set out for the House by the Bridge. I still had time to run over to the *Glutton* and back with Juffin.

※

"You're looking great, Max," said Juffin. "Dining at Boboota's has really done you good. Maybe you ought to visit him more often."

"I knew you'd say that. Make light of the state of my health—it's all the same to me. Today I had a dream."

"A dream?" Juffin raised his eyebrows. "I wouldn't be so eager to rejoice about that if I were you."

"Oh, a hole in the heavens above it all," I said with a dismissive wave of the hand. "In the first place, it wasn't a nightmare. In the second place, yesterday even a nightmare would have been welcome. Have you already heard about Boboota's mushroom?"

"Just don't get it into your head to tell me about it." The boss's panic looked almost unfeigned. "I won't survive it for the eighteenth time."

"Melifaro told the story just five times, Juffin," Kurush interjected. "You sometimes have a tendency to exaggerate."

"No, joy of my heart, five times when you were here. He dogged my footsteps wherever I went, blathering on about that sinning mushroom."

"Melifaro beat me to it, the mangy dog," I said. "Too bad for you, Juffin. I could have told it better."

"I don't doubt it for a moment. But I've already had an earful of that story. Let's go to the *Glutton*. I have something interesting to report."

"What a treat!"

"No, not a treat. Just trivia. How you love your job!"

"I hate it," I said in a dignified tone. "It's just that I'm a shameless careerist and I'm trying to suck up, isn't that obvious?"

The upshot of the matter was that after a hearty breakfast, I received orders to deliver a certain character to the House by the Bridge. Sir Kofa had been observing his antics at the card tables of the local taverns for several days now. The fellow indulged everywhere in his penchant for Forbidden Magic of the sixth degree, which furthered his success considerably. Sir Juffin was of the opinion that my participation in the arrest proceedings would make a bigger impression. Terrible rumors were making the rounds in the city, so hard-boiled cardsharpers were turning into innocent lambs right and left. For the next dozen days it was better than nothing, of course. It's better to prevent petty crime than to catch someone at it.

So as not to seem out of character, I turned up my nose fastidiously at the task and lectured my boss on the futility of hammering in a nail with a microscope. Sir Juffin heard me out with amused equanimity, then nodded toward the door.

"I get the point," I said. "I'm on my way."

"Don't sulk, Max. You have to hammer the blasted nails in with something," Juffin said. "Good evening, Sir Microscope."

I wasn't sulking, of course. A pleasant meander through the taverns of Echo in the company of Sir Kofa was an enviable misfortune. It's just that my feeling of contentment is only complete when I am slightly indignant about something. And praise be the Magicians when there's a reason for it, even the most paltry one.

※

I returned to the House by the Bridge at around midnight. Not that arresting Toyo Baklin (he was the brazen card sharper) took so long. It's just that my presence improves Sir Kofa Yox's appetite, and the Master Eavesdropper wasn't in too big a hurry to get rid of me. I returned to the House by the Bridge in the best of spirits. If someone had happened to want to pull my strings, this would have been the time to do it.

I was about to turn the corner to our Secret Entrance when a painfully familiar penguinesque silhouette propping up a leafy tree by the visitor's entrance caught my attention. I whistled. Anday Pu in the flesh! This was getting interesting.

"Are you writing a crime story, pal?" I said. "What about my cats? Did you already finish that one?"

"Good night to you, Sir Max," Anday said in a gloomy voice. "I've been waiting here for three hours. I was beginning to think I might as well just give up."

"You're in luck," I said. "People usually have to wait much longer for me. We're even considering installing a bed for visitors right by the entrance. But why are you waiting outside, anyway? We have a comfortable waiting room. You can sit in an armchair, smoke, and . . . well, that's about all you can do there. But at least it beats waiting outside."

"I don't like your Ministry," Anday confided. "It's packed with rodents."

"Come again?"

"Rodents."

Finally it dawned on me. "Ah, coppers! Yes, there are quite a few running around in there. On the other hand, they've got to hang out somewhere. And if those fellows think they have something to do at the House by the Bridge, who am I to shatter their illusions? What's wrong? You scared?"

"I'm not scared. I just don't like them. I'm no chicken, but . . . you no catch, Sir Max."

"I dig," I said, laughing. "You may not believe it, but back in the day I couldn't stand them either. And I was scared of them, too. One didn't exclude the other. It wasn't so very long ago, either. Let's go, Fourth Estate."

"What did you call me?" The poor guy was almost beside himself with confusion.

"Forget it. Let's go to my office. We'll drink some kamra and eat cookies. Am I making myself clear?"

Anday cheered up considerably, and I went into the House by the Bridge. He followed close behind me, trying to hide from the stern gaze of Boboota's subordinates behind my Mantle of Death. Curiously, he didn't seem to be afraid of me at all.

"Well, what happened to you?" I asked, closing the office door behind me. "Or were you just bored? Go ahead and sit down. Grab an armchair. Truth doesn't hide in your backside—you won't be covering anything up. Come to think of it, I wonder where in the body truth does hide? You don't know by any chance, do you? You journalists are an informed bunch."

Anday sat down obediently, turning this way and that to see better. He glanced at Kurush, asleep on the back of a chair, and brushed my cigarettes off the table absentmindedly, not registering the slightest interest in what the stuff was or where it had come from. He didn't deign to notice the couriers either, but when the jug of kamra appeared on the table, he immediately dropped back down to earth and filled up his mug. Finally Anday allowed himself to spill his troubles.

"Sir Max," he began solemnly. "My editor, Sir Rogro Jiil, doesn't catch a thing. I think he's lost his mind. The dinner's over once and for all."

"Really?" I said. "What has he done? Did he kill and eat a dozen hopeful young journalists? Or something more original? In any case, no one at the House by the Bridge is going to help him. We could use a good doctor here ourselves. But that's a state secret, you understand."

"I catch, Sir Max," Anday said. "What a joker you are—sound the alarm!"

"It's nice to meet someone who appreciates me," I said, grinning. "All in all, today I'm full, contented, and happy, so I'm not in very good form. Anyway, back to your editor."

"He doesn't want to publish my article!"

I laughed, mainly from surprise. "The article about my cats? What an insult."

"No, no. The one about the cats he liked, and even offered to pay for it—tomorrow or a year from now, you never know with him. Sometimes he drags it out, sometimes he doesn't. No, no, it was another article he didn't like."

"You sure do write a lot," I said.

That was really no surprise. All the bureaucrats and writers of the Unified Kingdom have self-scribing tablets at their disposal. Your head has to be very empty indeed not to produce something under those circumstances.

"I wrote about you, Sir Max. It will be such a sensation that all those tabloid slaves might as well just give up."

"What kind of sensation is that? That I wash my own living rooms floors? For a lyrical outpouring like that, Sir Juffin Hully would bite your editor's head off, and yours, too, while he's at it."

"Oh, come on! As if I have nothing better to do than write about your floors."

Anday spoke with the intonations of a queen trying to insult a dozen stable boys. He pursed his lips, glanced haughtily at me, tossed his head, and turned his noble profile away from me. Then, just as suddenly as he had taken umbrage, he stared at me penitently.

"It won't kill you to take a look at it, will it?" he said, offering me two self-scribing tablets.

I peered closely at it. The story was called "A Tête-à-tête with Death." Simple and tasteful. The contents were completely in keeping with the title. The story implied that I had held the hapless journalist captive in my living room for a whole day. Enchanted giant cats guarded the prisoner, and I had to absent myself from the premises to perform my next murder. Anday didn't skimp on the details, describing my evil cunning, the bloodthirsty roars of Ella and Armstrong, and his own stouthearted courage.

"Take it away!" I threatened. "And destroy it. You're a swell guy, Anday, but if this is printed in a single newspaper I will personally spit on you. If you spread this blizzard of blather to your girlfriends, I wouldn't necessarily object, though."

"You no catch! I thought you'd like it," Anday said. "I thought you'd send a call to Rogro and he'd have to just give up."

"You thought I'd help you publish this garbage?" I said. "What do you take me for, friend? Do you think I can't read?"

"I thought you'd like it," Anday repeated, sighing. "But you no catch. Well, never mind. It happens. I'm sorry for bothering you, Max. Will you forgive me?"

He made a pitiful sight.

"Do you want some dinner?" I said, feeling generous.

Anday brightened up immediately. The tragic depths of his eyes melted, until he was literally beaming.

"Of course you do! What a fool I am to even ask." And I sent a call to the *Glutton*.

"Takeout from the *Glutton Bunba*?" Anday said with the air of a connoisseur, sniffing the contents of his portion. "Nice little place. How I used to live it up there back in the day. Sound the alarm! The crowns just spilled out of my pockets onto the floor, and I wouldn't even bend down to pick them up. I left that to the sweaty plebs."

"Really?" I was surprised. The fellow didn't look like a rich man, even a former one who was down on his luck.

"Ah, Sir Max, how little you know," Anday said, shaking his head. His face bore the mournful expression of a retired king. "Do you think

I've been writing these blasted newspaper articles all my life? Give it up! I wasn't even ninety when I became the Master of Refined Utterances at the Royal Court. I had just completed my studies, and I had real prospects. The werewolf lured me into a bout of drinking with that scoundrel from the *Echo Hustle and Bustle*. How we went to town that night. Sound the alarm! I just let my hair down and blabbed to him, friend to friend. I told him some Court gossip, and the next morning an article came out about it. The fellow didn't hesitate to stir up a sensation. He stood the whole town on its ear for a dozen days! The dinner was over once and for all. You catch, Max?"

"A sad story," I said. "That's how it goes. Don't worry, Anday. You have a good career now, too."

"It's not a career, it's a bunch of crap!" said the courtier-turned-reporter. "Writing for any old stinky pleb who can't even read without sounding out the words, if he can read at all. You think they pay me for that? You can forget about it. They just pay lousy rotten pennies, if they pay anything at all. I could be a real writer. Go to Tasher, and—"

"Why to Tasher?"

I knew about Tasher only from the account of my acquaintance Captain Giatta, who was forever in my debt for saving him from a most unpleasant and disgusting form of death. Sir Juffin had rather unceremoniously tried to liberate the poor guy from his valuable mother-of-pearl belt, a horrific bejeweled luxury item made by the mad Magician Xropper Moa. I stood by and, when it became necessary, was able to share the pain of the enchanted captain.

It was harrowing, but we both remained alive. Finally unbuckled, Captain Giatta settled down in Echo. He announced that he was duty-bound to repay my good deed with another. Until he repaid this debt of honor, he would live in the Capital of the Unified Kingdom so as always to be near at hand. I had tried thinking up a few trivial requests a few times, but the perspicacious Tasherian always responded sternly, "You don't really need me to do that." I had to admit, he saw right through me.

The clever captain lived quite comfortably in Echo. Guys like him always land on their feet in life. So maybe it was all for the best.

I never passed up an opportunity to collect information about this still unfamiliar World, so the Tasherian captain had to keep up with a barrage of questions when I was around. And his stories had not led me to believe that Tasher was a refuge for intellectuals—quite the contrary.

"You no catch, Max! It's warm there," Anday said with a dreamy look in his eye. "Fruit grows in your backyard. And I've heard that in Tasher anyone who knows how to read and write commands a great deal of respect. All the philistines bow down before even a semiliterate person. They worship the ground he walks on. You catch? Think of how they must treat a writer! Sound the alarm!"

"It stands to reason," I said, laughing.

"May I come in, Sir Max?" The impressive nose of Captain Shixola peeked in the door. "Oh, pardon me. Do you have visitors?"

"It's a friend. But we won't be long. Come back in a few minutes, all right?"

"Of course," said Shixola, withdrawing his nose from my office.

Anday's almond-shaped eyes turned sad again. Apparently he had hoped our entertaining discussion would continue. Maybe he even supposed that the free dinner would seamlessly turn into breakfast. "Wait for me in the reception room, friend. I have to discuss some matters with my colleague, and then we can keep on shooting the breeze."

It was a long time since I had been so agreeable. Had he put a spell on me by any chance?

"In the reception room?" Anday said gloomily. "Thank you, Sir Max, but I think I'll be going. You are no doubt busy, and I want to look in on Chemparkaroke. I could do with a hefty portion of Soup of Repose right now. All these sinning memories, you know . . . By the way, Max, how are you doing for cash these days? I mean, could you lend me a crown? I hope Sir Rogro won't forget to pay me for the story about your cats. Then I could pay you back tomorrow."

"I seem to have even more than one crown. How rich I am, unbelievable."

I fished out a few coins from the desk drawer. I'm not sure they were even mine. Juffin and I regularly emptied out the contents of our pockets in the drawer before we set out for another encounter with a lawbreaker. When loose change starts spilling out of the pockets of the looxi of a Secret Investigator at such crucial moments, it looks rather silly and undermines the criminal's sense of awe.

"Thank you, Sir Max. You sure do catch. Sound the alarm! Tomorrow I'll . . . or maybe the next day . . ."

"Don't bother to pay me back. Consider it the fee for your rejected masterpiece. By the way, I advise you not to show up with it around here anymore. I'm a nice guy. You don't even have to call me 'sir' if you don't want to. But for publishing filth like that I might just kill. Do you believe me?"

"Here, take my self-scribing tablets!" Anday thrust them at me. "Keep them in your office since you paid for the article. Don't throw them away, though."

"Wonderful," I said with relief. "That way everyone will be happy. Good night, Anday."

"Good night, Max."

My new friend abandoned the "sir" rapidly and easily, as one should always part with empty formalities. That approach to things always sits well with me. Anday Pu could hardly have guessed that he had found the shortest path to my heart.

❄

The penguinesque wonder disappeared temporarily from my life, and Captain Shixola materialized in his place.

"You really weren't busy, Sir Max?"

"Really and truly. What's going on?"

"Well, nothing worth taking you away from your work, but if you aren't working on a case . . . I came to fill you in on a few rumors since—"

"About me again?" I grinned. "You know, I think that's enough for the time being. I'm very impressionable, and right now I have to think about others. In the interests of the common good and state security."

"No, Sir Max. This isn't about you. It's about those outlaws who are giving us the runaround just now. I know it will sound a bit crazy, but I think you ought to know about even this kind of nonsense. I first wanted to discuss the matter with Sir Juffin Hully, but I didn't dare approach him with what are still just rumors. He's a busy man."

Right, I thought. A "busy man," Juffin is. Especially recently. First he yawns. Then he takes a sip of kamra. Then he has a little chat with Kurush. A very busy man, indeed. But my inner monologue didn't bear repeating out loud, so I kept quiet and nodded solemnly.

"I'm the one to bring your rumors to, you are quite right about that. Well, what are they?"

"Lately Kamshi and I have had the opportunity to interrogate many of the victims. I mean those who were relieved of some of the burden of their wealth—sizable sums—by the Magaxon Foxes. And those lucky ones who managed to get away and keep their belongings, as well. They have given us mountains of evidence, some of it useful and some of it garbage. And you know, a good fourth of these people claim that the outlaws are still in the service of none other than the late Sir Jiffa

Savanxa. Same red hair, same horrible scar running from the nostrils down the to the chest."

"A dead Sir Jiffa? Yes, that's been known to happen," I said, feigning wisdom.

"I think the explanation might be quite simple," Shixola said. "You see, all the victims noticed that the leader of the Fox gang bore a striking resemblance to Sir Jiffa, but he looked like a much older version of him. This is not unlikely. First, coincidences occur all the time. Second, it's likely that the new Magaxon leader wants to imitate the old one in any way possible. Then only one mystery remains: the scar. You know, in the Gugon Forest during the Epoch of Orders, Gaganova the Lemming led a band of outlaws. The fellow lost both of his ears in a single skirmish. Later he was killed, and his son, Gaganova the Cardsharp, became the leader. He hacked off his own ears to look more like his papa. This history of outlaw leaders cutting off their own ears continued for several centuries. There were several generations of Gaganovas, and they all hacked off their own ears until a sheriff of Gugon got wise and put a stop to these antics once and for all. Our gentlemen brigands are a romantic bunch, and for them Red Jiffa is like . . . like Loiso Pondoxo, for your clients."

"I see. A symbol. Do you think he dyed his hair red, sliced his face, and all the rest?"

"More than likely. Jiffa never fell into the hands of your department while he was alive. It's unlikely he would draw attention to himself when he was already dead. And yet . . ."

"What?"

"I guess it's better to tell all, even if it sounds utterly mad. All these guys who swear up and down that Jiffa is alive knew him well in their time. One of them Jiffa had robbed before. Others were wined and dined by him in the *Golden Rams*. The ones who say he only looks like Jiffa are just going on hearsay. I don't like these coincidences, Sir Max. We really ought to tell Sir Hully."

"Can do. I'll tell him in the morning. It's no problem for me to wag my tongue. But are you sure that's the only thing you want of him, Shixola? Be frank, now. It would ease your mind if one of us went with you, wouldn't it?"

Shixola shrugged. "Of course, but—"

"But you don't have the formal right to turn to us with an official request because when your boss is indisposed, only his deputy, Captain Foofloss, has that right. And you'd have to lure him out of the tavern and let him dry out a bit, which still solves only half the problem. Because then you have to explain to him a case that doesn't hold water, at least not yet. And this task is too big even for fellows as clever as you and Kamshi. Am I right?"

"You're a visionary, Sir Max," said Shixola, smiling broadly.

"Yes, sometimes I even surprise myself."

"Can you help us?"

"You know, Captain, if I had Booboota and Foofloss as my bosses, I would long ago have been slumbering in a hammock in a remote Refuge for the Mad. But not only do you not give up, you try to do some good. Shixola, I bow down before you. Oh, please don't take that amiss. I'm not mocking you. It's just a manner of expression. I mean it very sincerely. I'll leave no stone unturned for you if it's within my power. Sir Juffin, as far as I know, is already one of your biggest fans. So everything will be fine. When do you plan to start the spring cleaning of the Magaxon Forest?"

"Oh, we won't wait till spring."

"I was just asking when you were setting off to hunt down these Magaxon Foxcubs. Year, day, hour? It's all the same to me, but Juffin Hully will be curious since he may be parting with his comrade-in-arms."

"Thank you, Sir Max. You think he'll agree to it?"

"Don't you? Sir Juffin adores any flouting of official rigmarole and other acts of romantic daring."

"Kamshi and I planned to set out for the border of the Magaxon Forest tomorrow night, arriving there by next morning. The rest of the boys are already there. They left Echo one by one. Now they're passing the night in neighboring villages, collecting information, keeping an eye on things. If two dozen brawny fellows descended on a tiny hamlet in a big pack, it would look pretty suspicious, wouldn't it? But if there's just one lone guy snooping around each of the surrounding villages, it's not going to surprise anyone. Praise be the Magicians, they wouldn't even recognize your face, much less those of the city policemen, in the outlying regions. We'll all gather in force the day after tomorrow, early in the morning. Then we'll get down to work with a vengeance."

"You've planned everything so well. But why morning and not night? Can't your men see in the dark?"

Shixola bristled. "Are you joking again, Sir Max? All Ugulanders can see in the dark, even policemen. It's just that, as you know, these outlaws usually come out in the morning. They've only been seen once or twice at night." Shixola waved his hand dismissively.

I filled Captain Shixola's mug with kamra and stared at him expectantly.

"Well, what it comes down to is that Kamshi and I are leaving tomorrow night," he said after a long pause. "It's about a four-hour drive there. And if Sir Juffin agrees . . . You know, Sir Max, I feel awkward asking this, but Kamshi and I would feel more comfortable if you . . . well, if Sir Juffin would let you be the one to accompany us."

"Me? Why me? It seems to me that Sir Shurf Lonli-Lokli is the man you want. He'll make you feel like you're standing behind a brick wall."

"Of course, you're right. But with a person who once saved the life of Sir Shurf himself, one can feel even more secure. And it's very easy to get along with you, in spite of your—"

"Warped sense of humor?" I gave a snort. Then I said, "Where did you get the idea that I saved someone's life? More town gossip?"

"Sir Shurf and I are neighbors," Shixola said. "You know, maybe I shouldn't spread this around, but his wife is my little sister's best friend. By the way, I didn't mean to criticize the way you express yourself. I had something else in mind. Namely, that when a person wears the Mantle of Death, it's hard to expect him to act like a regular person. But dealing with you is pure pleasure."

"And that's why you're inviting me to the Magaxon Forest. For exemplary behavior." I was flattered. "I think Juffin will let me go. He adores collecting adventures, especially if I'm the one going through them. And if I find one on my own, he'll prepare us a basket with freshly baked pastries for the road, out of pure joy."

❊

Juffin was so happy to find out about my upcoming departure that I felt more like a mother-in-law than his loyal, beloved assistant.

"Splendid, Sir Max," the boss said with a dreamy smile. "Fresh air, the good men of the City Police looking timidly into your eyes. I'd like to be in your shoes."

"Fine, you're welcome to them. What's stopping you?"

"They didn't invite me," Juffin said. "Those mean policemen forgot to ask me to their picnic. And I'm proud by nature, so I refuse to beg."

"What are you so glad about?" I said. "Are you that sick of me? I thought I cheered you up."

"That you do," Juffin said. "It's always a barrel of laughs with you. I was afraid you were going to ask for a vacation, but after fun and games like this, your conscience will never permit it. And I'll have a good excuse for sending you to the werewolves when you come to me with all your summer plans."

"Ask for a vacation? Me? Magicians forbid." I screwed my face up in disgust. "No way! I can't survive more than three days without work. I start to suffer from imaginary aches and pains, and to bemoan my broken heart and wasted youth."

"All the better, then. I'm curious to know whether you'll be singing the same tune a few years from now."

"It will be the same tune you're singing. When did you last have a vacation? Five hundred years ago, when you were still young and foolish, I suppose?"

Juffin harrumphed. "Oh, no, five hundred years would be . . . but come to think of it . . . In any case, be careful in that forest. If you really do come face to face with some species of the living dead, though, I know you can take care of yourself. You seem to specialize in that lately."

"Thanks. It's okay as far as jobs go."

Juffin smiled his caustic smile. Then he looked at me earnestly and shook his head. "Well, if things start going wrong, you'll wriggle out of it, I'm sure. And if it's your everyday band of brigands, they'll just breathe fire, blow smoke out of their nostrils, and dive into the nearest trench. But I beg you, don't show off. Don't stand in the line of fire, and don't lead a regiment of overzealous policemen into battle. You don't know how to fire a Baboom anyway, and you're as good a target as any other human being. But I have to admit, this affair smells strongly of Forbidden Magic."

"Why is that? Did you have a presentiment?"

"None to speak of. But I'm familiar with Red Jiffa's story. There was a time when he offered his services to me. Of course, it was back when they called me the Kettarian Hunter and not Sir Venerable Head. Jiffa had a very romantic nature—but not a shred of talent. Not cut out for this kind of work at all. So I sent him packing."

"I wish I could have laid eyes on the Kettarian Hunter at least once," I said dreamily. "It's hard for me even to imagine."

"There haven't been any significant changes in me since that time, if you must know. Well, except that I look older. More distinguished. And I sleep more, of course. But it's the unlucky victims upon whom I usually make the biggest impression, so you don't stand much of a chance there, either."

"Okay, okay. I'll get over it. But I keep interrupting you. You should give me a cuff on the ear or something. You were talking about the 'talentless' Red Jiffa. What's the story?"

"I'll give you a cuff on the ear if it makes you happy. And as for Jiffa—you know, Max, people like him always come to a bad end. First he tried to do some conjuring, insofar as he was able. Then he realized he just didn't have what it takes, and he completely let himself go. In his bitterness, he killed some Junior Magicians. Then some former Magicians who had survived the new order tried long and hard to do him in. It's very likely there is an unfortunate coda at the end of his biography." The boss gently stroked the feathery crest of the dozing buriwok. "Kurush, my clever fellow, what do we know about the death of Sir Jiffa Savanxa? Come on, time to wake up."

"You people are so impatient," the wise bird said. "I want some pastry."

"All right, coming up," Juffin said. "Max, you want a couple of pastries, too, I assume?"

"A couple? I want three at least."

"They're on the way," Juffin told Kurush. "In the meantime, give me the low down, my sweet bird. I really only want to know one thing: the names of the ones in the punitive expedition who were connected with the Ancient Orders."

"Sir Pafoota Jongo, Junior Magician of the Order of the Holey Cup," Kurush began.

"Ah, a former colleague of our Lonli-Lokli," said Juffin. "I'll have to have a chat about him with Sir Shurf. Go on, my sweet bird."

"Sir Xonti Tufton and Sir Abaguda Channels, Junior Magicians of the Order of Time Backwards."

"Former young protégés of our friend Maba. Charming."

"Sir Pixpa Shoon, Junior Magician of the Order of the Barking Fish."

Juffin grimaced with displeasure but remained silent.

"Sir Bubuli Jola Giox, Junior Magician of the Order of the Secret Grass. Sir Atva Kuraisa, Junior Magician of the Order of Grilles and Mirrors. Sir Joffla Kumbaya, Junior Magician of the Order of the Sleeping Butterfly. Sir Altafa Nmal, Junior Magician of the Order of the Brass Needle. That's about all. Where's the pastry?"

"At the door, my dear."

The door opened as if on command. A sleepy courier placed a tray loaded with pastries and kamra on the table and disappeared into the darkness of the corridor again.

"Well?" I asked with my mouth full five minutes later.

"Well, what?" the boss said, starting in on his pastry again.

"Does it make more sense to you now?"

"It does and it doesn't. Go on your picnic, Max. If you have any questions, any matters to discuss with me, that's what Silent Speech is for. But first, you have to know whether there is anything to ask. Maybe there won't be. Maybe Shixola's imagination just ran away with him. It wouldn't be the first time."

"Okay. If you don't want me to know, fine. I'll remain ignorant. You're the one who has to put up with me. By the way, Kurush, what do you know about a gentleman by the name of Anday Pu? He's a journalist, one of the senior reporters at the *Royal Voice*, if I remember correctly."

"People often tell untruths," Kurush said. "I don't think he's a senior reporter since I don't know anything about him. And I keep bits of information about all the notable people of Echo. You need to go to the Main Archive, Max. I don't bother my head with trifles."

"What a self-important bunch you all are," I groaned. "The Main Archive sleeps sweetly till noon, so I'm not likely to find anything there. I'm abandoning you for my pillow."

"It's about time," Juffin said. "You have circles under your eyes and sunken cheeks, though you can still eat like there's no tomorrow. I'm tired of seeing your face, so scram."

"My sunken cheeks are the result of my spring cleaning. You won't believe it, but yesterday morning I actually did it with my own two hands." I waved my industrious extremities around under Juffin's nose.

"Why shouldn't I believe you? If you had told me you hired a cleaner like normal people, I might have doubted you. Sweet dreams, Max. Drop by this evening to say goodbye."

I did sleep sweetly, and I dreamed, too. This time, some exhilarating nonsense. So from the moment I awoke, my good mood soared to dangerous heights. I felt I might just explode.

When I went downstairs I discovered that the one and only Anday Pu was there. He sat timidly on the edge of a chair, wrapped up in a heavy old looxi, and stared at me forlornly with his warm, dark eyes.

Ella was purring relentlessly on his lap, and Armstrong sat at his feet. My little furries seemed not only to have fallen in love with the fellow but also to have teamed up to protect him from any untoward wrath on my part. I sighed.

"Hey guys, I hope I'm not disturbing you. Or is it already time for me to move out?" I asked the threesome. Ella mewed tenderly. Armstrong rushed up to me and rubbed against my leg, as if to say, "Don't move, Max! Yes, you are a nuisance, but we'll put up with you if you feed us right this very minute."

"I'm sorry, Sir Max. I catch that it's very rude to barge in uninvited like this, but I simply had no choice."

"Never mind," I said. "I'll bathe now, and then I'll turn nice again. You took a big risk, you know. In the morning I'm even more fearsome than people suspect. You're lucky this silly flirt is crazy about you." I nodded at Ella, who apparently considered Anday to be her new pillow, and wasn't in the least inclined to part with it.

While I was bathing I tried to recapture my good mood. It didn't work, though. I'm not the most companionable person in the Universe for the first hour and a half after I wake up, and the last thing I want to do is entertain guests.

Now he's going to say that he has nowhere to live, and since I have so many empty rooms, well . . . I thought gloomily. Then he's going to say he wants to eat, and after that he'll want to borrow my toothbrush. And no Mantle of Death is going to save me.

By the time I crawled into the fifth bathing pool, my irritation had begun to subside. By the sixth pool I had been rendered almost harmless. By the seventh I started thinking that it wouldn't hurt to have some good company for my morning kamra. And I didn't even get into the eighth since I was so weary of the whole bathing rigmarole. So I got dressed and went upstairs to the living room.

Now both cats were sitting on Anday's lap. How could he bear the weight, poor guy! Finally I melted altogether and sent a call to the tavern keeper of the *Fat Turkey*. I ordered a double portion of kamra and cookies. What else could I do?

"Well?" I said. "You had no choice. How is that possible? Let me guess, I no catch, right?"

"Righto!" Anday beamed. "Sir Max, I—"

"Yesterday we agreed that we could get along without any 'sirs.' And, just for the record, standing on ceremony is not the best way to improve my mood."

"Give me a break! That's not how aristocrats are supposed to behave. They no catch—"

"Who said I was an aristocrat? I'm way cooler," I said. "Anyway, what's the problem? Did your article get rejected again? By the way, you're no senior reporter for the *Royal Voice*. I checked up on you.

Don't worry, though. I'd boast, too, if I were in your place. That's the name of the game. Just keep in mind for the future that you don't have to lie to me. With everyone else—it's your call."

"I really do sometimes write for the *Royal Voice*. And believe me, those philistines at the paper, the staff writers, they knock themselves out trying to write like me. It's very clear that they badmouthed me to Sir Rogro, so now he won't offer me a long-term contract. So I thought, now the dinner's over once and for all! Then I found out they had been wanting to print a story about your cats for a long time, but no one was willing to risk showing up at your house to talk to you in person. And I thought, well, I have nothing to lose. Back in the day, my pen used to burn like a comet, let me tell you!" Anday shook his head and smiled meditatively, lost in recollection.

"Good." I stretched luxuriously till my joints cracked, which filled me with delicious pleasure, then poured myself another mug of kamra. "I understand all that. Come on, tell me your problem. I've got work to do, people to kill."

"Give me a break!" Anday said again.

I didn't get it. Either he really appreciated a good joke, or he approved of the hypothetical goal of my activities. Then he started arranging the dishes on my table with absentminded precision. A few minutes later a fairly intricate design of plates and leftover food had emerged on the tabletop.

I waited.

"Actually, I was just about to tell you that I wasn't . . . In short, now I really do have a chance to become senior reporter for the *Royal Voice*."

"You do?" Something seemed to dawn on me. "You told them that we were friends? Don't be afraid. Spit it out."

"It was my only chance," Anday mumbled. "If you only knew how these upstarts who've managed to scrawl their plebeian names on a full-time contract live. Especially the society columnists and crime reporters. They get a fat salary, and bonuses to boot. They get paid as much per letter as I get per line. So I went to Rogro Jiil and told him I get to see you every day now."

"What did you say? Every day?"

I was horrified.

"Well, I hinted so that he would catch. Of course, every day isn't absolutely necessary," Anday said. "But Sir Rogro didn't catch. He does-n't believe me. That jackass Jafla Dbaba, my former classmate at school, interfered again. In high school he used to sit in a corner and wait until someone sent him to a tavern for some Jubatic Juice. Now the guy shamelessly kisses Rogro Jiil's skinny backside. If it hadn't been for his gossip and scandalmongering, the contract would have been in my pocket more than a dozen years ago. Today he whispered to Rogro that I had made it all up, that I've never even seen you face to face, and that I found out about your cats from the neighbors."

"He forgot to consider that I don't have any neighbors."

This was the honest-to-Magicians truth. There were no houses near mine. The Street of Yellow Stones is one of the newest in Echo. Property here isn't cheap, and people are reluctant to part with it.

All of this rubbed me the wrong way. There are things I love and things I hate, and occasionally they switch places. But guys like Dbaba had always awakened in me a thirst for blood since in my time they had thrown plenty of crap in my general direction. I realized that this time Anday wouldn't be able to defend himself against evil tongues. Strange fellows like my new friend always attract plenty of ill-wishers, that's for sure.

"In short, Sir Rogro Jiil demanded evidence. I told him that he could send you a call and ask, but he wouldn't agree to it. I think he's afraid of you, too. Sound the alarm," Anday said sadly.

"You did the right thing," I said without any real enthusiasm. "Well, what do you want from me, *mon ami*? Do you want me to talk to him?"

"You catch!" Anday said, cheering up all at once. "Will you send him a call?"

"You want him to have a heart attack? Excellent idea. I'll do it right away."

"You catch everything, Max! A hundred percent!"

To be honest, I was very pleased with the compliment.

I drank down my kamra, put down the mug, and started concentrating to my utmost. I had seen Rogro Jiil only once before, for all of a moment. On the previous Last Day of the Year he had stopped by the Ministry of Perfect Public Order to attend the Royal Awards ceremony. Such a superficial acquaintance is really no basis for establishing contact through Silent Speech, but I tried my best and succeeded.

Good day, Sir Rogro. Max here, of the Minor Secret Investigative Force of Echo. I really have had several meetings with Mr. Anday Pu. It's possible that our meetings will continue. I hope this is evidence enough for you?

Of course, Sir Max. Please let me express my gratitude for the time and attention you've given to one of the senior reporters of my publication.

Sir Rogro Jiil was a tough nut to crack, but the understated courtesy of his manner gave me to understand that my protégé's fate had been decided in the most advantageous way. It also witnessed to Rogro Jiil's extensive experience in disseminating information.

Excellent, Sir Rogro. I very much regret that I was forced to disturb you. Perhaps it will surprise you, but I do hate injustice of any kind.

It is I who am guilty. I should be more trusting of people.

No, no, not at all. Let's just consider this a pleasant exception to the rule. Good evening, and I apologize again for the disturbance.

It is a great honor for me. Good evening to you, too.

We seemed to have ended our exchange almost as friends.

"That's that," I told Anday, who was fidgeting nervously. "Okay, time to quit gobbling. I'm a busy man, and now you are, too. Go sign your contract. And make sure your salary is twice as fat as everyone else's. I'm worth a lot, I hope. And don't even think about publishing your chefs-d'oeuvre without my knowledge. Another charming piece like 'A Tête-à-tête with Death' and I'll kill you personally. Got that?"

"All right, all right," Anday said, his enthusiasm plummeting. Then he brightened up. "But you burn like a comet, Max, you really do! You and me are going to give them all something to write home about!"

Anday Pu carefully deposited the yawning Armstrong and the dozing Ella onto the floor. The cats turned their unblinking blue gaze on me to make sure I wasn't going to offend or otherwise harm their new favorite human, then ambled over to their bowls.

I had to give him a lift. From my modest hovel to the New City, where the editorial office of the *Royal Voice* was located, was a two-hour walk. I didn't deny myself the pleasure of driving at maximum speed, so Anday paid me back royally for the trouble he had caused in the first half of the day. The fellow comported himself well. He didn't squeal but remained immobile and silent in the back seat. What was he doing? Praying? Unlikely —the inhabitants of this city are not in the least devout. Which is understandable, I guess. Why would they need gods when life is so good?

Finally I managed to part ways with my new friend. He set out to reap his rewards at the editorial offices, and I went to the House by the Bridge. All my roads lead to the House by the Bridge, whichever way they might turn.

※

"Good day, Max." Melamori was about to get up from her chair to greet me, but she reconsidered and plunked herself down again. "They say you're leaving town with the fellows from the Police Department."

"They say right," I said. "Who's they?"

"The policemen themselves are all talking about it. Do you really think you'll find something out there?"

"I don't think anything. Thinking isn't my line of work. You know that," I said. "We'll have to wait and see. Why don't you come with us? It will be a real picnic, I guarantee you. I supposed Juffin will let you go. If you can stand on the trace of the outlaws, you'll help the boys out, at least, since we've agreed to take charge of them."

Melamori looked so sad and perplexed that my heart ached for her. Time heals all wounds, of course, but so slowly. Too slowly.

"Sure, I'll let her go." The ubiquitous Sir Juffin suddenly materialized in the Hall of Common Labor. "A bit of practical experience isn't going to hurt you, my lady. And don't look at Max like that. He's offering you a case. Since we agreed to help them, we have to do a proper job of it. Otherwise, the terrible Sir Max and his trusty policemen are going to be playing hide-and-seek in the bushes out there for years before they find those foxcubs."

"You don't have to talk me into it. I'd be delighted."

Never in my life did I think a person could speak so sorrowfully with such a happy face. But Lady Melamori pulled it off beautifully.

"Go get some sleep, Melamori," I said. "We leave an hour before sunrise. Not the best time to hop out of bed to take a trip, but I didn't create this World. I can promise to treat all who take part in the expedition to some Elixir of Kaxar."

"Mine, naturally," Juffin put in. "You always leave yours at home out of sheer absentmindedness."

"That's been known to happen." I tried putting on a guilty expression.

"Kamshi said you were planning to leave two hours after midnight," Melamori said.

"Never mind what Kamshi said. He didn't take into account that I would be driving the amobiler. That means we'll get there at least four hours sooner."

"Right, and then the amobiler will shatter into smithereens. Poof!" Juffin said. "We've been through that once already, after our magnificent race car driver rushed home from Kettari."

"Come on, Juffin. I guess I may have been going three hundred an hour, but it was hardly top speed." I smiled a dreamy smile. "And it was only because I was hurrying to get Shurf back home before he got into another scrape. Well, I'm off to the Main Archive. I want to find out what kind of serpent I've taken to my bosom."

"That character you were asking Kurush about? What made you think of him?" Juffin said.

"That's just what I'm wondering. I'm going to look in on Lookfi Pence to try to find out. He's such an absurd fellow, that Anday Pu."

"Well, since he's absurd, go find out about him by all means," said Juffin. "Then come back and tell me all about it."

"I'll even show him to you, if you like. You'll get a sea of pleasure from it. See you tonight, Melamori. I'll pick you up."

"Good. Drop by a bit earlier, though, in case I oversleep. And don't forget the Elixir of Kaxar. It certainly can't hurt at that hour."

"I just happened to leave mine conveniently at home. But there's always a bottle to be found in the boss's desk drawer," I said, grinning.

Then I turned to Juffin and tapped the end of my nose with the forefinger of my right hand, once, and then again. This gesture is the essence of age-old Kettarian wisdom, meaning, "Two good people can always come to an understanding." Juffin's face melted into a smile, and he tapped twice on his own nose, too. Melamori was clearly baffled by this arcane little ritual.

Then we went our separate ways. I hurried to get to the Main Archive before the last rays of sun disappeared behind the horizon. I don't know what our buriwoks do after sunset, but I know they don't work.

"Sir Max, what a surprise! I haven't seen you in ages." Lookfi Pence came up to welcome me, his face beaming. On the way he overturned a chair. Actually, we had seen each other just two days before. Maybe our Lookfi has a different sense of time than other people do.

"Good evening, Lookfi. Good evening, clever ones," I said, bowing politely to the buriwoks. "I've come purely out of selfish motives, as always, I'm embarrassed to admit. But it can't be helped. Lookfi, will you ask your wise feathered friends whether they've heard of one Anday Pu? It seems that long ago he was a satellite at the Royal Court, but he was involved in some kind of scandal and fell from grace, if he's telling the truth. I just saddled Sir Rogro Jiil with him, and now I'm wondering what kind of mischief I've caused. Will Sir Rogro be hunting high and low for me all over Echo so he can punch my lights out?"

"Goodness gracious, Sir Max! Who would dare pick a fight with you? All the more since Sir Rogro hasn't fought with anyone for years.

He's very mellow these days," Lookfi said without a trace of irony. He went up to a buriwok. "Spush, tell Max about Anday Pu. You keep tabs on all the former courtiers, if I'm not mistaken."

"You're never mistaken," the buriwok said, bobbing his head up and down. "Dossier on Mr. Anday Pu. Born in Echo on the 222nd day of the 3162nd year of the Epoch of Orders."

I did some quick calculations. The Epoch of Orders ended in 3188, and now it was the year 116 of the Code Epoch. That means the fellow was just over a hundred forty years old, a little bit older than Melifaro, who was born on the first day of the Code Epoch. Funny, I was used to thinking of Melifaro as slightly younger than I was. But if you consider that natives of the World only outgrow their teenage blemishes at about ninety years of age, Melifaro really was slightly younger than me, however strange it may sound. And Anday Pu was about the same age as I was, though these calculations are enough to drive you mad. He was my age, and as much of a loser as I was at thirty years old in my own World. I shook my head, feeling somewhat chastened.

The buriwok continued. "His grandfather, Zoxma Pu, and his father, Chorko Pu, arrived in Echo in the year 2990 of the Epoch of Orders from some islands in the Ukumbi Sea. It is not possible to recover any information about their past, but since all adult Ukumbians are pirates, to some degree, it stands to reason that both Pu elders—"

"Were blackbeards!" I said.

"What are blackbeards?" Lookfi inquired.

"Well, there were some outlaws back in the Barren Lands, a whole clan of them, who went by that name. Spush, please proceed. I'm sorry I interrupted you."

"Not at all," the buriwok said. "You people always interrupt. First the gentlemen bought a house at 22 Street of Steep Roofs and lived on their savings. In 3114, Chorko Pu became the senior chef at the Residence of the Order of the Green Moons."

"Was that the Order of Grand Magician Mener Gusot?" I said. "The fellow who raised Phetans and was practically the archenemy of the Order of the Seven-Leaf Clover? The one who later killed himself, and after that they burned down the Residence, right? I lived just across from his house on the Street of Old Coins. That was some neighborhood, let me tell you"

"That is correct," the buriwok said. "Shall I continue, or have you already found out everything you wished to know?"

"Oh, no! Please go on, my fine fellow."

"Grand Magician Mener Gusot prized Ukumbi cuisine very highly, so the fortunes of Chorko Pu improved considerably. In 3117, Zoxma Pu began to assist his son as the Order's membership grew and more hands were needed. In the year 3148, Chorko Pu married Heza Rooma, a native of Echo. Her family—"

"Never mind her and her family, Spush. Let's talk about Anday Pu himself."

"Mr. Anday Pu was born on the 222nd day of the year 3162, as I have already told you. From the moment of his birth he lived with his maternal grandparents, since the presence of children at the Residence of any Order of Magic is prohibited. On the 233rd day of the year 3183, the Residence of the Order of the Green Moons was burned down by the combined forces of the king and the Order of the Seven-Leaf Clover. Zoxma and Chorko Pu, and Mrs. Heza Rooma, all died in the fire. Anday Pu continued to live in the home of his maternal grandparents.

"In the second year of the Code Epoch, the famous Royal Decree of His Majesty Gurig VII was issued. It decreed a special Royal Allowance for relatives of those who perished in the Troubled Times. This enabled Anday Pu to enter the Royal College in the same year. He was considered to be one of the best students, and he graduated with honors in the year 62."

I whistled under my breath. Incredible. Sixty years of schooling!

"Anday Pu's excellent academic record earned him a place at the Court. At the end of that year he received an invitation to assume the post of Master of Refined Utterances at the Royal Court of His Majesty King Gurig VIII."

Hmm, so it seems he wasn't telling tall tales after all, I thought. Well, I'll be.

"In the year 68, Mr. Anday Pu was accused of spreading petty secrets of the Court and excused from service to the king, without the right to be reinstated or the right to receive a pension. One Mr. Kuom Manio, a reporter for the *Echo Hustle and Bustle*, was also involved in the affair. He was not formally charged with anything, however, since he was fulfilling his professional duties, collecting information about current events. After his dismissal, Mr. Anday Pu moved to 22 Street of Steep Roofs, which he had inherited. Since his account at the Chancellory of Big Sums of Money was depleted, he was forced to rent out half of his house to the Pela family. He writes occasionally for the *Royal Voice*. He has been detained several times by the Echo City Police for rowdiness and unseemly behavior in public places. He has never

been detained for, or suspected of, more serious offenses. That's all."
The buriwok turned to Lookfi. "I'd like some nuts if you please."

"Thank you, Spush," I said, rising from my chair. "I have something
to add to your dossier. What day is it today?"

"The 113th, Sir Max," said Lookfi.

"Right. On the 113th day of the year 116, Anday Pu was appoint-
ed senior reporter at the *Royal Voice* by Sir Rogro Jiil, editor-in-chief.
It's the latest news. Moreover, it's the work of my very own hands.
Thank you again, gentlemen. Drop by for a mug of kamra on your way
home, Lookfi. I know you won't unless I invite you."

"Thank you," Sir Lookfi said, smiling broadly. "And you should
drop by to see Varisha and me sometime, too. Her *Fatman at the Bend*
really is one of the best taverns in Echo. I would never sing the praises
of my wife's establishment if that weren't the honest truth."

"Oh, what a nitwit I am! I should have done that long ago, especially since we're almost neighbors now. I also live in the New City. I'll visit
the *Fatman* as soon as I get back from the Magaxon Forest."

"You're going on vacation?" Lookfi said.

"Well, almost. Hunting, actually. In the company of Lady Melamori
and two dozen policemen. Sounds great, doesn't it?"

"You lead such a fascinating life, Sir Max."

On this note of optimism, we parted.

✺

Sir Juffin and I dined together, and for a few hours I regaled him
with the saga of Anday Pu. He clearly got a great deal of pleasure from
it, but I'm still not sure whether he was laughing at Anday Pu or at me.

After dinner Juffin set out for home, and I returned to the House by
the Bridge alone. In the Hall of Common Labor I ran into Sir Lonli-
Lokli. He was pacing back and forth from one corner of the room to
the other, his face absolutely deadpan and his hands, sheathed in their
enormous protective gloves, clasped behind his back. Dressed in a flow-
ing snow-white looxi, he was the picture of manly beauty. I nodded in
greeting.

"Where did you disappear to, Shurf? I haven't seen you in half a
dozen days."

"I didn't disappear," he said. "I've been right here the whole time,
sitting in my office and taking care of business. You're the one who's
been flitting about all over Echo. You even went to General Box's for
dinner. Are you off to the Magaxon Forest, Max?"

"You know the answer to that already."

"I do. What I don't know is what you're going to do if a dead Jiffa really does turn up there. Spit at him? Because you know your poison only works on the living. How do you plan to get around that one?"

"No idea whatsoever. From the start I insisted on you as the most likely candidate, but Shixola got it into his head that he'd feel more comfortable with me by his side. Imagine his disappointment if I screw up. And Juffin didn't object to the idea, either. Purely out of malice, I'm guessing."

"Sir Juffin knows you're still learning. He wants you to get the experience, and that's only logical, of course. But I've been feeling uneasy in my heart since this morning, so I decided to wait for you. Come into my office, Max. I have something to show you. Maybe you'll be able to pick it up without too much trouble. With you, anything is possible."

"Gladly. I love new tricks."

Shurf shook his head but kept silent.

Sir Shurf Lonli-Lokli's office was a remarkable place. An enormous empty hall, it was the most spacious room on our side of the Ministry of Perfect Public Order. In the far corner one could just make out a diminutive writing desk and a hard, uncomfortable-looking chair.

"Sit down, Max." Shurf pointed hospitably at the floor. "It's not going to damage your backside in the least."

"I should hope not," I said, arranging myself on the spot he had indicated.

Lonli-Lokli, in the meantime, drew from the folds of his looxi a very familiar holey cup. From his desk drawer he took out a minuscule ceramic bottle. He poured the contents into it, considered a bit, then extended the cup to me.

"Take it, Max. In Kettari you were able to drink from it, so you won't have any problem here, either."

I drank from it as he bid. The ancient wine tasted rather ordinary, and even slightly bitter. You'll never make a gourmet out of me.

"Am I going to start walking two feet above the ground like I did in Kettari?" I said.

"I hope not. I gave you only a very small portion. But get up and try out your legs yourself."

I got up and discovered with a mild sense of disappointment that my legs stood firmly rooted to the floor. No more defying gravity for me.

Meanwhile, Lonli-Lokli removed his outer protective gloves and then the death-dealing gloves inside. He went to his desk and hid them in a special box. Then he came back to me.

"Watch," he said, raising his left hand. His fingers were poised, motionless, as if to snap. And then he did.

Almost imperceptibly, but with a powerful thrust, a small white sphere of lightning exploded from his fingertips. I had no time even to notice how it rolled through the enormous hall, then dispersed in a fountain of sparks when it bounced against the far wall.

"Now you do it. Don't try thinking about how I did it. Just snap your fingers as you saw me do."

Apparently the sip of wine from the holey cup really had turned me into a wunderkind. The finger-snapping trick worked on my first try.

A tiny, glowing ball—not white, like Shurf's, but incandescent green—sped through the room and hit the wall with a loud crack. At that very moment it became huge and transparent, then disappeared.

"It's the first time I've ever witnessed such dexterity," Shurf said with something resembling surprise. "You've done very well. But your Lethal Sphere is somewhat off."

"You know things are always different for me than for other people," I said with a sigh. "I wonder if it can really kill? What was it, again—a 'Lethal Sphere'?"

"Yes, exactly. I'm afraid you'll have to test the effectiveness of your handiwork on your own, no later than tomorrow. In any case, Red Jiffa was never a Grand Magician, nor a respectable, run-of-the-mill sorcerer. So whether he's alive or dead, you'll be able to handle him. But it's a good thing to have another trick up your sleeve anyway. Don't forget to let me know how your green Sphere works when you find out yourself. A very curious natural phenomenon."

"Who, me?"

"I was referring to the color of your Sphere. But you, Max, are an even more curious natural phenomenon, that goes without saying."

"My, my, how ironic you've become, Shurf."

"It's your own fault for saving me from Kiba Attsax. Next time, think before you act." Shurf smiled with uncharacteristic warmth. "Anyway, Max, this is all well and good, almost too much so. Still, I can't shake the presentiment that there's trouble ahead for you. It's rather strange when you consider that your upcoming trip doesn't strike me as being terribly dangerous. Keep your head out of range of the slingshots, all right?"

"Yes, certainly." I have to admit, Shurf's words alarmed me. "Juffin has no such presentiments, it seems."

"If he had so much as the inkling of one, he'd never let you go,"

Lonli-Lokli assured me. "Perhaps the problem has nothing to do with this trip."

"Also possible," I said. "Maybe I'm just in for a stomach upset of colossal proportions, and this mishap is already registering on the radar of your sensitive soul. Which reminds me, I've got to remember to bring along some toilet paper."

"That wouldn't hurt," Shurf said. "Better stock up on it."

Sometimes it's impossible to know whether he's joking or being perfectly straightforward.

When I finally got to my office, I settled down comfortably in my chair, stretched out my legs, crossed them, and placed them on the shining surface of the desk. I didn't want to think about Shurf's presentiments and other unpleasant matters. I did want some kamra, though. I saw no reason to deprive myself of it.

By the time I was on my second cup, a courier's face appeared at the door, terrified, as always.

"Sir Max, there's some strange person here asking about you. He's standing outside at the entrance to the building, but he refuses to come in. What should I do?"

"A tubby fellow, wrapped up in a winter looxi?"

"Yes, sir."

"Tell him I'm in my office. If he doesn't want to come in, he doesn't have to, but I'm not moving from this spot any sooner than midnight. If he changes his mind, send him in. And may the Dark Magicians help me!" That last sentiment I addressed to the ceiling.

In less than a minute, the descendent of the Ukumbian pirates appeared on the threshold.

"I've come to thank you again, Max! Everything went off almost without a hitch," he said, settling himself uninvited in the chair opposite mine. "I thought, well, since you're just sitting there bored out of your mind, and I'm not knocking myself out right now either—look!" He pulled a dusty bottle out of the roomy pocket of his looxi. "This is no pig-swill firewater for the masses. It's left over from my grandfather's wine cellar."

"From how long ago? Is this leftover loot from a pillaged sailing vessel, or does it come from the wine cellars of the Order of the Green Moons? Thanks, either way."

"How do you know all that?"

"How? I'm not just any guy off the street. I'm a Secret Investigator, remember? Why didn't you want to come in at first, Sir Blackbeard the Younger?"

"It's full of rodents in here," Anday whispered darkly. "What did you just call me?"

"Blackbeard the Younger," I said. "It's one of those things that no one but me thinks is funny. Better get used to it. By the way, you've got to get a handle on your youthful fancies, or should I say complexes, about policemen. What does it matter what happened in the remote past? Everything changes. How do you think you're going to be a crime reporter if you're even afraid to poke your nose into the Ministry of Perfect Public Order?"

Anday said nothing and gave me a glum look instead. In the meantime, I wiped the dust off the ancient bottle and pushed a mug of kamra over to him. Then something dawned on me.

"Hey, have they given you an assignment yet, or are you still free as a bird?"

"I have to write an article about you or the Secret Investigative Force at least every dozen days. Easy as Chakatta Pie! Even once a day wouldn't kill me."

"Excellent. Listen, Anday. Tonight I'm driving to the Magaxon Forest with a sweet lady and a bunch of those—what do you call them?—rodents. Why don't you come with us? You'll be able to keep me company, and you'll make friends with the boys. And it will give you plenty to write about. You'll be able to report on our united victory over the Magaxon outlaws. If no one pops you with a Baboom slingshot, that is. Life is very unpredictable."

"Are you joking?" Anday said uncertainly. "The rodents will never agree to my coming with you."

"Who said anything about asking them?" I said. "Who do you think is in charge around here, anyway?"

"They take orders from you?" It finally started to make sense to him. Apparently, being detained several times for "unseemly behavior in public places" had made an indelible impression on Anday, and he had come to the conclusion that Boboota's underlings were the most powerful and fearsome fellows in the Unified Kingdom. I had the dubious honor of disabusing him of this notion.

"Right. I give the orders. So fear not. I don't advise you to throw your weight around, though. The main thing is not to get on my nerves. I hate squabbles and bickering. You'll all just have to be nice and make friends when I'm around. So you decide. Come along if you want to. If you don't, no problem."

"Okay, okay," Anday said. "You think a trip like this is more than I can handle?"

"If I thought that, I wouldn't have invited you. Now go home and get ready. Take a little nap. And come back here at around five hours after midnight. We'll crack open your bottle when we return. Tomorrow's going to be a hard day, and I have to drive the amobiler."

"Aw, come on, one glass won't kill us," Anday said.

"Oh, yes, it will. I want to be surrounded by sober people in good spirits. That's how I like it. Everything has to be the way I like it because—well, just because. Don't worry, Anday. Later there will be plenty of time for you and me to 'burn like comets,' as you put it."

"I catch," Anday said with a conspiratorial air. "I bet you really know how to party, Max, don't you?"

"Me? I don't know. It's been so long since I tried. Back in the day, though . . . Well, we'll see."

Then this latter-day son of pirates and chefs hightailed it out of my office. Amazing. He didn't even ask me to walk him through the rodent-ridden hallways to the entrance of Headquarters. Maybe he was already getting used to his status as friend of Sir Max the Terrible. I realized that my sudden notion to take him along wasn't half bad. He would keep everyone amused, me especially. What I was really happy about was that with this welcome rotund burden on my hands, I wouldn't be tempted to torment Melamori with my mournful gaze. Anday Pu was as necessary to me on this trip as a piece of chewing gum to someone who's trying to give up cigarettes. I just hoped he proved to be more useful than a pathetic piece of gum.

At around four hours after midnight, armed with a bottle of Elixir of Kaxar from Juffin's desk drawer, I knocked on Melamori's door. She opened right away, as though she had been standing there since the evening before.

"Are we off?" Melamori had already managed to get dressed and made up. Her face looked somewhat haggard, though, no doubt about it.

"I have to admit, I was really expecting to have to drag you out of bed by force at this hour. So we've got a whole hour to kill. We can go back to the House by the Bridge and have a bite to eat. I know the word 'breakfast' makes you queasy, but this should take care of that." I handed Melamori the bottle.

"Thanks. It turns out I don't have any Elixir of Kaxar in the house. Silly, isn't it? To be honest, I haven't even been to bed yet."

I smiled apologetically. Melamori took a large sip of the tonic and brightened up right away.

"Yes, let's go to Headquarters," she said. "Breakfast wouldn't be such a bad idea."

During the drive there, neither of us talked. Of course, the drive took all of three minutes. I flew through the night like a madman on wings, since at that hour the streets are as empty as the Barren Lands.

I had sent a call to the *Glutton* as we were leaving Melamori's house, so when we arrived at the Hall of Common Labor, breakfast was already laid out on the table. Melamori dug in with gusto.

"I arranged for some entertainment on our punitive expedition," I announced. "It should be here any minute now."

Then I told Melamori the story of the scion of our local corsairs. Judging by her hearty laughter, my narrative skills were in good working order.

"I'm afraid that I may have done a disservice to Sir Rogro. It was shameless of me, of course, but I couldn't resist the temptation to reverse the fortunes of the little guy who's been down on his luck for so long." This was the closing line in my predawn narrative performance.

"By the way, do you know anything about this fellow Rogro?" Melamori asked. "At one time he, too, 'burned like a comet,' as your new friend would say. Did you know he was a novice in the Order of the Seven-Leaf Clover? And a hero of the Troubled Times, too. This fellow threw himself into any turmoil or scuffle he could find, just for the fun of it, and he performed a number of unprecedented exploits out of pure foolishness. Then, right after the Code came into force, he landed in Xolomi for practicing Forbidden Magic of the sixtieth degree, I think, in a street fight. They kicked him out of the Order immediately, of course, although there was quite an outcry. He was universally loved and admired. At that time they were very strict. Even his battle scars couldn't save him. It was when he was serving time in Xolomi that Rogro came up with the idea of the newspaper and wrote a letter to the old king, who was delighted with the idea. So when Rogro was released from Xolomi, he was already a respectable man, editor-in-chief of the paper he himself had founded, the *Royal Voice*. That was the very first newspaper in Echo."

"Really? A World without newspapers . . . hard to imagine. A World without anything else seems plausible. But no newspapers? And Sir Rogro was the one who invented them. Boy, that guy must be a real genius!"

"You can say that again," Melamori said. "It's hard to believe nowadays, but back then the paper was free because none of the Echoers really knew what it was for. So the king footed the bill. Then people got so used to reading the paper that they couldn't break the habit even when Sir Rogro started charging for it. A dozen years later, the *Echo Hustle and Bustle* appeared. It's supposed to be published by different people, but Sir Rogro is behind that one, too. You can take my word for it. My father and he are good friends, so I know what I'm talking about. The *Hustle* is even more wildly successful. They write all kinds of nonsense, and people love it, you know."

"I know. Thanks for telling me, Melamori. Juffin advised me long ago to take a look at Sir Rogro's dossier. He said I'd get a kick out of it. That editor-in-chief is quite a guy."

"He certainly is." Melamori looked at me searchingly and said, "Max, what made you ask me to go along with you?"

"Well, I have a habit of doing stupid things, which I don't care to go into just now. Then I really might need your help. I have no desire to 'play hide-and-seek in the bushes,' as Juffin put it. If we're going hunting for these fellows, it wouldn't hurt to find them as quickly as possible. And the Magaxon Forest is big, if the map doesn't lie. And finally . . ." Suddenly I felt embarrassed and started fishing around in my pocket for my cigarettes.

"Finally?"

"You know, since Fate and Death and all the Dark Magicians are so concerned about our morals and all that, well, I thought it just wasn't meant to be. But maybe going out to catch Magaxon outlaws when we're locked in an embrace isn't such a bad alternative? I mean, there are many ways of getting pleasure from our common efforts, and we should try everything at least once, don't you think?"

"You're the most remarkable guy in the Universe, is what I think. Especially when your mouth's open and words come out. That's your normal state, I think. You probably even talk in your sleep."

"I swear up a storm when I'm asleep. Ask Lonli-Lokli. He'll recite one of my somnolent monologues to you."

"He already did."

By now, Melamori was in the best of moods, to my indescribable delight.

"Excuse me, Max. I'm not bothering you, am I?" Anday said. He stood in the doorway, looking Melamori up and down appraisingly, and casting significant glances at me. "I can wait out there, no problem."

"You don't have to wait for anything, Anday." I took a tiny sip of Elixir of Kaxar and stood up. "Here he is, Melamori."

"So I gathered." Melamori smiled.

"Anday, this is Lady Melamori Blimm, Master of Pursuit of the Fleeing and Hiding. If there's anything you need to be afraid of in this building, it's not the harmless policemen but her. And me just a tiny bit, of course, so I won't feel hurt. Let's go, kids. I'm sure Kamshi and Shixola have been pacing the floor in their office for hours already. When I told Shixola what time we were leaving, he nearly had a heart attack. They aren't aware of my talents as a race car driver."

"They're perfectly aware of them, Max," Melamori said. "But that won't stop them from worrying. Someone has to, before embarking on a grand operation like this one."

"Stands to reason. Okay, we're off. It's time."

Lieutenant Kamshi was already sitting in the official amobiler. His colleague was circling the vehicle—or, rather, making irregular ellipses around it, fiddling nervously with his pipe. They really did look like they were on pins and needles.

Then, to their visible relief, I got behind the levers of the amobiler.

"Gentlemen, this is Mr. Anday Pu." I nodded toward my protégé. "He's my personal scribe. I've become terribly conceited recently, and our healers can't do anything about it. So I ask you to love him, and not to hurt his feelings. He's your brother. Besides, he's very sensitive. I hope he'll get over that soon enough. Anday, remember—or, better yet, jot down—the names of your new friends: Sir Kamshi and Sir Shixola. They don't bite, whatever you might think. Melamori, you sit next to me. It will be a bit cramped there in the back. Our Sir Anday might not be a hulk, but he isn't the smallest kid on the block."

No one had time to say a word before I tore out of there as only I can. Shixola gasped in delight. "Well, it looks like we will get there on time," Lieutenant Kamshi said dryly.

"No way," I objected. "We'll get there earlier than we need to—by exactly one half hour. I always drive slowly and carefully in town. Beyond the city gates you'll find out what speed is."

Behind the levers of an amobiler I become completely unbearable.

What's true is true. As soon as we were out of the city, nothing could hold me back. I raced like I was trying to outsmart the devil at his own game. The fellows in the back seat clung to each other like orphans at a benefit dinner. It was all for the best, though. They say that suffering in company furthers mutual sympathy, and that the fellowship of misfortune becomes, in time, simply good fellowship.

"Would you get a load of this?" Anday whispered behind me. "Dinner is over once and for all!"

"Exactly," Kamshi said in a tight voice.

"Our race car drivers can go into retirement, every last one of them," Shixola said.

I puffed up with pride and sped up just a tad bit more.

Melamori was clinging to the seat, her knuckles white. I looked at her out of the corner of my eye. It had been a long time since I'd seen such a happy expression on that lovely face. Her eyes burned brightly, and a slight smile played on her lips. Her excitement seemed to have stopped her breath.

"I want to drive like that, too, Max!" she said. "Will you teach me?"

"There's nothing to teach. The speed of the amobiler reflects the driver's desire. When you get behind the levers, just remember this trip. You'll drive just as fast as me, you'll see."

"I'll overtake you," Melamori said. "It may take me a dozen years, but I will overtake you. Maybe I'll even manage sooner."

"Want to bet? I say it'll take you at least a dozen years," I said.

"Hmm, I don't know. Money is boring. You and I both have plenty, praise be Dondi Melixis and his Royal Treasury. Okay, let's just say that whoever wins gets to decide what the stakes are."

"Deal. But remember: I can drive still faster than I'm going now."

"Go ahead," Melamori urged warmly.

"I feel sorry for the boys back there. Maybe later."

"Okay. But I'll hold you to it!"

She went quiet and fixed her eyes on the darkness again. I was glad I had been able to make her happy. I never would have expected it.

"We're almost there, boys," I said forty minutes later. "Tell me where to go. I have no idea where our rendezvous point is."

Lieutenant Kamshi was able to get his bearings almost immediately, and following his directions we soon arrived at the meeting place half an hour early, as I had predicted. Melamori was the only one who had any regrets about this. The other victims of my inner speed demon crawled out of the amobiler more dead than alive, then sank down in the grass. I sighed and got out the Elixir of Kaxar.

"Have some," I said, holding out the vessel with the magic liquid. I'm convinced it can help in any possible situation. "Is it really as bad as all that? I wanted you to enjoy the ride."

"We did," Melamori said.

The lady was in excellent spirits. The others looked at her like she was mad.

"That was something else. Sound the alarm," Anday said weakly.

He lay back in the grass and stared up at the sky. Even a sip of Elixir of Kaxar couldn't restore his usual liveliness. The policemen were lying next to him, not saying a word. Melamori, meanwhile, was eagerly taking off her shoes. She couldn't wait to start the chase.

Here you see the difference between Secret Investigators and other people, I thought, looking at the happy Melamori. Shurf once told me that a completely normal person wouldn't be able to do our job. I'm pretty sure he's right. All you have to do is look at these normal guys and then at our lovely loony lady here.

"I'll go see what I can find," Melamori said. "I'll be very careful, and I won't venture farther than this grove. I promise."

"If you really mean to go no farther than that, be my guest," I said. "Only don't risk following someone's trail and getting lost in the wilderness, okay?"

"Please, Max! I'm not a kid," Melamori said.

I gave a skeptical sniff. Melamori was always a paragon of caution until it concerned her own work.

"No one has walked through this grove for a long time," Melamori said a few minutes later. "Max, I think it would make sense to—"

"To keep walking a bit farther, right? Fine, but only in good company." I turned to the policemen, who were still in a semi-catatonic state after the ride.

"Anyone alive there? There's a lady here who wants to walk through the dark forest."

The gallant Kamshi began peeling his behind off the damp grass.

"Max, I'll manage fine on my own," Melamori said.

"Of course you will. If someone can't manage, it will be me. My nerves won't hold out. I'll sit here imagining you falling into the paws of wild, uncouth outlaws. I'm just doing it out of self-interest."

"Well, in that case, let's be off, Sir Kamshi," Melamori said with a sigh. "The longer I work in this outfit, the more bosses I have. Doesn't that strike you as illogical?"

"I understand perfectly, Lady Melamori," Kamshi assured her, like the true gentleman he was. And he was no doubt speaking the truth, recalling his own superiors.

The two of them disappeared into the tangle of undergrowth. I could have gone with her myself, I thought.

The leaves rustled in back of me. Quick as lightning I spun around, determined to bargain for my life at a high price.

"It's all right, Sir Max. The boys are just getting ready," Shixola said.

"Yes, it's time. It's already getting light. How's it going down there, Blackbeard Junior? Alive and kicking again?"

"The dinner is totally over, Max," Anday called out weakly. This time he paid no attention to the pet name I had chosen for him. "I'm wiped out. Sound the alarm! I could do with another cup of Elixir of Kaxar."

"Sure." I handed him the bottle. "You, too, Shixola. You look rather drained. Heads up, guys. We're supposed to be having fun."

"Supposed to be," Shixola said with a sigh. "Thanks for the Elixir, Sir Max. It costs a pretty penny, I know. Half a dozen crowns a bottle is no joke."

"Yep. That's why I filch it from the boss's desk," I said.

Our small crew was gradually increasing in number. The policemen—handsome, hefty lads to a man—materialized out of the predawn mists as though gathering for a war council. The pupils of their eyes shone slightly phosphorescent. That's what the eyes of native Ugulanders, who can see perfectly in the dark, must look like, I thought. Their plain green looxis were damp with the dew. Their hair looked like it was tangled with tiny scraps of mist and the tender green shoots of the spring woods.

I stared at them, entranced. These can't be Boboota's boys. Surely they're elves of some sort!

At that moment, I seemed to realize once and for all that I was a stranger in this World. And it seemed so wondrous it took my breath away.

While I was gazing awestruck at my colleagues, I noticed their weaponry. It's strange, but until then I hadn't ever closely examined the most common firearm of my new homeland. The Baboom slingshot, which is used by all policemen (and scorned by Secret Investigators), is a fairly large metal slingshot that shoots tiny explosives. The deceptively small but powerful little pellets are stored in special leather pouches filled with a viscous, inedible fat. This serves as an indispensable precaution since the pellets can explode from the slightest agitation, never mind a real blow. Every slingshooter wears special gloves to extract the pellets from the pouch.

In spite of its seeming whimsicality, the Baboom slingshot is a rather dangerous weapon, which I have had the chance to observe on more than one occasion. Wounds caused by the exploding pellets are very, very serious. They take a long time to heal, and only then with the help of the local healers. A shot to the head means certain death, and a slingshooter with the slightest bit of real experience can't fail to hit his mark. Their accuracy is simply mind-boggling. In addition, all three ends of the slingshot are sharpened, so if you run out of ammunition you can switch to hand-to-hand combat. True masters of the art make this transition with admirable grace and facility.

Max, there's a very foul trace here! Melamori's panicky call struck me so suddenly that I shuddered. *I can easily stand on it, but I feel such loathing toward it.*

Don't do it on any account! I never suspected that I could scream so loudly in Silent Speech.

Wouldn't think of it. What should I do? Turn back?

Better wait for me. I'll be right there.

I tore off into the underbrush, sending a call to Shixola on the way. *Wait here. We'll be back soon. You'll hear from us if we need you.*

I flew blindly in what I thought was the right direction. How I managed not to get snared by a branch or plunge into a ditch, I don't know to this day. My flight probably lasted no more than a minute.

I'd never moved so fast in my life, and it was a personal record I'm not ever likely to break. At the end, I knocked poor Kamshi off his feet and finally screeched to a halt next to Melamori, who was sitting on her haunches nearby.

Melamori was shaking from head to toe, but the felling of the hapless lieutenant coaxed a weak smile from her.

"You can do that, too, Max? Why didn't you say so?"

"Do what? Throw big handsome men to the ground? Oh, Kamshi! Forgive me. I'm such a cretin. I was hurrying so fast to get here I overdid it. Are you okay?"

Kamshi was dusting off his looxi very meticulously. "I am all right, Sir Max. Don't mention it. I was lucky that you were on foot and not driving an amobiler."

I gave a sigh of relief and turned to Melamori. "Where's the trace? Was it really so much more loathsome than others?"

"Yes, rather. Try it yourself."

"How can I do that? Who's the Master of Pursuit around here?"

"Wait a minute. You mean to tell me you don't understand what happened just now?" Melamori said. "What do you think you've just been doing?"

"Me? I was afraid for you, so I rushed to you through the brush and bracken like a crazy moose. And barely made it here alive."

"Sir Kamshi, I don't think Shixola and the boys should be left alone," Melamori said, looking meaningfully at the lieutenant. "We'll come after you as soon as we get to the bottom of this sinning trace."

"Of course, my lady," Kamshi said, and his silhouette disappeared into the silvery mist. I admired the lieutenant's strength of character. I wish I could stay as calm as he when someone tells me to go to hell at such an exciting moment.

"Now tell me. How did you find us, Max?" Melamori stared at me relentlessly. "Do you have any clue yourself how you got here?"

"Nope. I haven't the foggiest," I admitted. "I sensed some kind of . . . You said something about a loathsome trace, I got pretty darn scared, and I raced over here. Intuition, I guess."

"Right. Intuition. You're not a human being; you're a perpetual surprise. I know what I'm talking about. You still don't get it? You stood on my trace without even taking off your shoes. That's not intuition; it's mastery of the highest degree. If there's anything that reassures me, it's your speed. You almost . . . Never do that again, Max, okay? I very much want to believe this has happened to me for the first and last time. I'm in a terrible state."

"I wonder how I managed?" I was really at a loss. "Lonli-Lokli told me I had special abilities, but I thought you still had to learn those things. And that Juffin just didn't want to teach me. And for some reason I didn't understand, he wouldn't let Shurf do it. It never entered my head that—"

"Don't you know why?" Melamori said sternly. "It's because when you step on someone's trace, it stops their heart. It only makes sense to do that if you want to kill someone. What you really need to learn is *not* to step on someone's trace. The sooner you get this under control, the better. Well, let's take a look at my quarry. Be careful, though, all right?"

"I'm so evil I even disgust myself," I said with a bitter sigh. "I'm sorry, Melamori. I ran over here to save you, and look what happened. What can I do?"

"It's simple. Before rushing headlong in pursuit of someone, ask her where she is, like any normal person would do. Then the way ahead will be clear." Finally Melamori smiled. "Why are you so upset? It's better to have a gift like that than not to have it at all. I wish I had it myself."

Then she stood up and walked over to an old stump at the side of the path. She stamped about softly, then turned to me.

"I don't want to pursue this sinning trace any longer. I've had enough for today. Try it yourself. You won't have any trouble!"

I circled the stump a few times, then looked at Melamori in perplexity. "Beats me! I don't sense a thing."

Melamori thought for a moment, then shrugged. "I can't really explain it. You really have to want to find it. And not doubt for a second that you will. But why should I tell you this? Just think about how you raced over here to find us. That's how it works."

I went around the stump a few more times, trying to remember what I felt when I came flying over to "save" Melamori. I didn't feel anything, really. I just desperately wanted to reach her.

I get it, I thought. Now all I have to do is want to get to the unknown source of this darn trace. Ugh, I'm afraid I lack the sincere conviction.

Still, I tried. I tried thinking about how dangerous this fellow must be, since Melamori was so unnerved by the trace. I decided I simply had to find the scoundrel who was sauntering through the forest leaving traces that spoiled the moods of perfectly decent people. All this smacked of a one-man play in an amateur theatrical hour.

Then I relaxed, and my mind was cleared of extraneous rubbish. I walked, attending to the sensation in the soles of my feet. Tracing circles around this absurd stump chased all the trivial thoughts from my head. Then I froze, as if struck by lightning. I couldn't budge from the spot. I stood there, immobile, slowly but surely turning into a statue. Now my breath was becoming more labored, and my tongue was numb and lolled around in my mouth. Still, I had time to summon help.

"Come on, get me out of this, on the double!"

I didn't have to ask twice, praise be the Magicians. A sharp blow at the back of my knees from Melamori's foot did the trick. I found myself on the ground, stunned. Since I managed to land on both my elbows and my knees, I hurt in four places at once.

"Thanks," I groaned. I noticed with relief that my tongue, and after that the rest of my body, was beginning to function again. "You level a mean blow, honey."

"I should hope so," Melamori said. "You see? You did do it, but the trace got the better of you. You succumbed, even worse than I did. I just felt queasy and frightened. Apparently our gift is a double-edged sword: the stronger you are, the harder you fall if something goes wrong. What kind of trace is it? Do you have any idea, Max?"

"Sure I do. It's the trace of a dead man," I blurted out, startling even myself. Right then and there I knew that I wasn't mistaken. What else could it have been?

"But that's impossible," Melamori said, looking at me fearfully. "Dead people leave no trace."

"Your information is out of date, my lady. Sometimes they do. It's the trace of Red Jiffa, I'm afraid. This is a sweet little case. The old geezer dug himself out of the grave. He was homesick for his old stomping grounds. I understand the poor guy. What I want to know is where he dug up the new Magaxon Foxcubs—from the neighboring villages or the neighboring graves? Too bad I can't step on his trace. I start dying myself—you saw it with your own eyes."

"Yes, you nearly scared the wits out of me," Melamori said. "Your face even started turning blue."

"I must have made a handsome sight," I said. "Well, what are we going to do?"

"Whatever you do, don't try that trick again. Besides, the blue of your face didn't match your clothes at all. It positively clashed. Send a call to the boys, Sir Max. There's no other way. I have to follow this sinning trace on my own."

"Won't the pleasure be too much for you?" I said. I didn't want to have to give the green light for this performance, but what choice did I have?

"There's no getting around it," Melamori said. "I'll have to grin and bear it. It won't be the first time. But let's really hustle, okay?"

"Like greased lightning," I promised.

"Good." Melamori smiled wistfully and buried her nose in my shoulder.

We stood like that until the first heroes of the impending battle burst forth out of the nearby thorn bushes.

Anday Pu brought up the rear. He looked so panic-stricken, and so eager at the same time, that Melamori and I couldn't help laughing.

"We'll follow behind Lady Melamori, the faster the better," I commanded my fiery but bumbling regiment. "I advise you to prepare for the worst. One of them is already dead, that's certain. I'm not sure about the others. Try not to lose your heads, whatever happens. Let's go!"

❦

Melamori stood on the trace, cringed, stooped, and put her arms around her body, as if she were cold. I really wanted to help her, but there was nothing I could do. She made a few uncertain steps, shook her head resolutely, and started running. We followed her.

I tried very hard to keep to the side of the invisible and dangerous trace. The last thing I needed was to collapse in the middle of a chase.

Luckily it was only a few minutes before Melamori was brought up short before the edge of a shallow ravine. She leaped down into it, dropped onto all fours, and started to howl. The unearthly sounds made my skin crawl.

"What are you doing?" I said, alarmed, jumping in after her.

"Nothing. The trace ends here. There's some kind of passageway— the trace leads right into it. I . . . I had to call him out, Max. Don't ask me why. I didn't want to, but somehow . . . the trace told me I had to," Melamori said. "Help me climb out of here, please!"

Her voice had returned to normal again. It was impossible to believe that this sweet lady had just been howling like an inconsolable werewolf. I helped her scramble out and followed close behind her.

"Max, he'll be here soon," Melamori said. "It will either be Jiffa by himself, or . . . much worse. Anyway, Jiffa's trace is the only one here."

"You got that, gentleman?" I said, turning to the policemen. "A bunch of living corpses are about to crawl out of that ravine. If you have a weak stomach, you'd better not look."

"Do you think you'll be able to handle them, Sir Max?" Captain Shixola said.

"How should I know? We'll soon find out—if we're still alive, that is. I told you Lonli-Lokli was the one to call on in a case like this, but you didn't believe me. That's what you get."

I stared into the bottom of the ravine. For some reason it seemed funny to me rather than terrifying, although I was not given to heroics and never had been. No, I had never tried to play the hero. I guess

I just couldn't believe in the reality of what was happening.

Finally I spied something truly suspicious. Something was moving around down there.

"The Magaxon Foxes lived in dens, didn't they, Shixola? Looks like these guys just moved into an empty apartment. That's good. It means they'll be crawling out of their foxhole one at a time. It's a den, after all. Melamori, you said you 'called him,' right?"

Melamori nodded. She looked none too cheerful.

"Do you know what's going to happen now? I mean, the one you called, is he going to be coming out of this foxhole and no other? For sure?"

"Yes, it will be from this one, but he may not emerge right away. He might put up resistance for a long time. Sooner or later he'll have to come out, though. Hey!"

"'Hey' is right," I said, raising my left hand and snapping my fingers. (Come one, come all, step right up and see my new trick, compliments of the one and only Lonli-Lokli.)

The tiny ball of lightning did not disappoint. It appeared right on cue, shimmering with a greenish light. Then it pierced the darkness of the ravine with a moist, smacking sound. I saw a youthful face, completely distorted with fear. My lightning hit the fellow right between the eyebrows. He gasped slightly.

The poor guy was still in one piece, apparently. My shot, which was supposed to be a mortal one, filled him with renewed vigor. He crawled toward me like a cockroach on the run. A second later the fellow grabbed a small thorn bush growing near my feet, pulled himself up, and . . .

The city policemen didn't waste any time. The first shot from the Baboom slingshot hampered his progress a bit. The explosion blew open his cheek and nose. I don't think you could have called this a trifling wound, but the bullheaded guy kept coming and climbed out of the shallow ravine at the same time I did. Without thinking, I spat at the horrifying face, disfigured by the shot from the Baboom. Even if the guy were alive, after our first encounter his time would have been up. My poison kills instantly, however stupid that might sound. But nothing of the sort happened. The spit left a gaping hole in his forehead, similar to the one on the carpet of my former bedroom on the Street of Old Coins. Of course, my "patient" was as dead as the nerve in a rotten tooth.

Then something incredible happened. This unsightly dead creature raised his dull eyes to me and shouted ecstatically, "I'm with you, Master!"

I jumped up and spat again at my "slave," from the sheer unexpectedness of it. This time I blasted a hole in his shoulder, but the fellow didn't pay the slightest bit of attention to it. The living corpse scrabbled along the edge of the ravine, his eyes fixed on me fawningly.

The policemen's collective nerves couldn't quite cope with this tender spectacle, so a volley of shots from their Babooms tore him to shreds. But even the shreds of his over-dead body kept crawling toward me.

"I'm with you, Master," the leftovers of his head cried out again and again.

I was pretty much beside myself at this point. Sometimes, though, when I'm pressed up hard against a wall, my mind works at the speed of light.

"Take it easy, boys," I said to the policemen. "It looks like I know how to get them to obey. And that's not bad, not bad at all. So don't rush to kill the others if there are any displays of tenderness toward me. We'll soon find out."

Down below something rustled again. I snapped the fingers of my left hand. There was another bright green flash of light, a disgusting *thwack*, and a weak, cracking voice that called out, "I'm with you, Master!"

I bristled but kept myself under control. The more people are with me, the better. Figuring out whether they're dead or alive is something I can do later, when this hullabaloo is over, I thought, provided it ever ends, of course.

So I said calmly, "Well, that's just fine and dandy, pal. Stand right where you are. Stand guard over me, and warn me the next time one of your comrades appears. That's an order! And tell me, how many of you are there down there?"

"We are many," my dead vassal said proudly. "Almost three dozen in number."

"Not too much to worry about," I said turning to the policemen. "Three dozen isn't three million, after all. We're in luck, boys. Only three dozen dead men, but at least we'll have something to brag about."

"We are alive, we will never die," the garrulous deceased man objected. Then he added proudly, "We've been together a long time."

"Ah, I see. Well, alive or dead, do you think you can tell the others to obey me?"

"They obey Jiffa. Jiffa ordered us to deal with you, though our time has not yet come. After a few hours we will become stronger, Master. There they are!"

"Many thanks." I made a comic bow to him and hurled some more green lightning into the ravine. As I had come to expect, another voice rose up out of the murky darkness, "I'm with you, Master!"

Just at that moment, a tiny but lethal piece of shrapnel from a Baboom flew at my head. "What a surprise," Lookfi would have said. My trusty slave executed a wild leap. The shrapnel was flying fairly high, but he managed to jump up several yards to intercept it, planting the lethal object in his own dead forehead. It blew off almost half of his head. I cursed everything under the sun, then snapped my fingers a few more times. The devil knew how many of these guys had come out. Bright green sparks melted into the chasm of darkness.

"I'm with you, Master!" A raucous chorus of voices convinced me of the wisdom of my action.

"Everyone stay put down there and guard us from the others!" I had learned to bark out orders remarkably fast. Turning to the policeman, I announced, "Now I'm going to retreat to the forest with my own hand-picked band of merry men. With brave lads like these, even the Dark Magicians are nothing to fear."

"Ask about their leader, Max!" Melamori's voice returned me to earth again. "These fellows don't carry a trace. They leave nothing at all. They don't count. I was following someone else. I don't think you'll have such an easy time with him. I called him, he should be coming out, but there's still no sign of him."

What a girl! She's brilliant to have reminded me, I thought. "Loyal slaves, tell Uncle Max—where is your Jiffa?"

"Underneath," the voices muttered. "Jiffa was called, but he won't come out. He sent us to take care of it."

In the meantime, the crowd in the ravine was growing steadily. I heard sounds of struggle. My "subjects" were trying faithfully to disarm their comrades. I would have to intervene. After snapping my fingers a few times, I became certain that now I had no fewer than two dozen corpses at my command. The fellows were crawling out of their lairs with such alacrity that there was no time for oaths of fealty.

"Max!" Melamori cried out. "Their leader is coming, I can feel it! It's something terribly powerful, much mightier than all the rest. Please take care."

"Yes, I will. I'm usually so careful I can't stand myself."

"Careful? You?" someone cackled nervously behind my back. It must have been Lieutenant Kamshi. He was still somewhat wild-eyed and shaken after my exploits at the levers of the amobiler this morning.

"Eagle scouts!" I said, calling my dead bodyguards to attention. "You must protect me from your Jiffa at any cost. Is that clear?"

"We are with you, Master!" the terrible troops assured me with languid enthusiasm.

I sighed. Some picnic this was turning out to be.

"More of our men are on the way, but Jiffa's not with them," a voice rang out from the ravine.

"Glad to hear it."

I snapped my fingers again. My regiment was growing by the minute. If only the poor blokes knew how sickened I was by their servile repetition.

※

A few more minutes passed. Finally I sensed the approach of something new. I was filled with a kind of dull relief. Here was something to break the monotony.

"Are you with me, Angels of Hell?" I said to the corpses.

"We are with you, Master!" they assured me.

"Your job is to capture Jiffa and bring him to me. Is that clear?"

"At your service, Master!"

They were as good as their word. I heard a melee, the sound of dull thuds, and hoarse, muffled curses. Then a remarkably striking face appeared at my feet. At one time the fellow must have been quite a beauty. Neither time, nor deep wrinkles, nor the unsightly scar stretching across his dirt-smeared face could mar such a lovely background. It was a face that asked to be photographed, not taken prisoner. His luxuriant bright-red crest lifted in the wind, and his blue eyes stared at me in cold fury. All three dozen of his former friends held him in a death-grip, but I wasn't so sure they'd hold it for long. I managed to snap the fingers of my left hand, and a green ball of lightning sped straight to Red Jiffa's left eyebrow, just at the point where the terrible scar began. The ball then scattered into a thousand tiny harmless flames that died out as if they had never been. Not wasting any time, I spat in his face. Nothing happened. Absolutely nothing—as though I wore the Mantle of Death just to pass the time of day.

If it weren't for my former exploits, I might have started doubting my professional expertise.

Red laughed spitefully. "You're a wretched wizard, stranger!" he said in an unexpectedly high voice that cracked like a boy's. "Maybe you're a bit better than I am, but my shield was made by a Grand Master!"

"He's telling the truth, Max," Melamori said. "This handsome lad doesn't have any special powers of his own, but someone forged an excellent shield for him. You can't harm him. You'll never break through it. Now I understand why it was so hard for me to step on his trace, and why you were completely helpless."

"And what does one do in such cases, O unforgettable one?" I said wearily. "Should I ask the boys to hold him tighter and then run after Juffin? Like, hold on a minute, I'll be right back? Or do you have any other suggestions?"

"Of course I do." Melamori burst out laughing. "Your loyal slaves can join forces with the trusty policemen and simply tie up their former leader. There isn't a single magic shield that can withstand a strong rope. In any case we have to transport him to Echo, where Sir Juffin can deal with him."

"Gentlemen." I turned solemnly to the policemen. "We need a strong rope, and fast. You see what a mean geezer we've got on our hands. Any suggestions?"

"Will belts work?" Captain Shixola began unbuckling the belt on which his weapons were fastened.

"Boys, take off your belts! We'll swaddle him up like a mummy."

"Do you need any help?" I asked the dead men.

"Yes, Master," they mumbled plaintively. "We need your help. We can hold him, but tell your men to tie him. He's too strong for us."

"Darn dead puppets!" Jiffa retorted in contempt. He looked at me with more sadness than wrath. "Never try to resurrect dead friends, stranger. It's bound to fail with such lousy wizards as you and me."

"I'm not such an idiot that I'd try to resurrect my dead friends. That's disgusting." I turned away from Jiffa hurriedly and addressed the policemen. "Well, gentlemen, don't just stand there. My lads need help—you heard them. Working beside them isn't terribly pleasant, I know, but if this mean gentleman breaks loose, it will be a whole lot worse. No need to wrinkle up your nose, Melamori. Your work is done, so my invitation doesn't concern you. Come on, boys, hop to it!"

"Thank you, Max," Melamori said with a slightly bitter grin. "How sweet of you. I think I'll take advantage of your offer. The sight of these beauty boys turns my stomach."

The policemen, judging from the expressions on their faces, concurred. They had no inclination whatsoever to go down into the ravine.

"Hey, what's wrong, did the whole bunch of you turn chicken? Feet stuck in the mud?" a voice from behind called out. Sinning Magicians, it was my own personal scribe! I had completely forgotten about him. Anday Pu, meanwhile, marched out in front and took the lead.

"Look sharp, people! Let me lend this moribund bunch a hand, Max. It's not going to kill me."

"Great, only make it snappy."

I had neither the strength nor the time to praise Anday Pu's efforts, but I hope my gratitude was written across my forehead.

The tubby fellow gathered the belts and slipped into the ravine with unexpected grace. Within a few seconds he had boldly assumed command of my dead assistants. Jiffa moaned, growled, gnashed his teeth, and cursed so eloquently that I was green with envy.

I turned to the policemen with selfless readiness. Lieutenant Kamshi took the remaining belts and followed behind. Shixola sighed and joined him. The other policemen shuffled their feet, glanced around furtively, and finally, one by one, crawled down into the ravine.

"Don't forget to gag his mouth," I called out after them. "You'll be the ones who have to listen to him."

Within the space of five minutes Red Jiffa was neatly gagged and bound in a leather cocoon. They had even remembered to fasten the buckles. Sinning Magicians, that shut him up!

Combining their efforts, they managed to pull Jiffa out of the ravine and place him like an offering at my feet. The three dozen dead men hovered nearby. Anday Pu, as grand as the statue of King Gurig VII, looked at them askance.

"You made your pirate granddad proud, old friend!" I said, and turned to the policemen, who were wiping their hands off fastidiously with clumps of grass.

"Well done, boys. Here are your Magaxon Foxes, the whole lot of them. Do with them what you will. I'm spent."

I slumped down in the moist grass and gazed with delight at the pale morning sky. There, above the trees, a solitary bird was circling. At that moment it seemed to me I loved that bird like life itself . . .

My musings were interrupted by a strange noise. I raised my head slightly, trying to look beyond the colored spots before my eyes. The policemen were standing in a circle around me and applauding, like passengers on an airplane when it touches the runway after a rough flight.

"Yeah," I whispered. "That's right. I'm a hero. I had a bottle of Elixir around here. Anyone know where it is?"

"It's in the pocket of your looxi, Max," Melamori said. "Do you feel like going beddy-bye or something?"

"Yep."

I rummaged around in my pocket. There was the bottle of Elixir, indeed. I took a sizable gulp, waited a bit, then realized it wasn't enough. I took another. The annoying spots retreated into the void. Little by little the world assumed its familiar outlines.

"Well, boys, time to go home," I said. "Or do you want to bring out the sandwiches for a picnic? No, I see that doesn't tempt you."

"Sir Max, what should we do with them?" Shixola said with an expression of horror.

"Nothing," I said. "I can't kill them—you saw that yourselves. I could keep spitting, but it would take until next year to get the job done. In any case, they'll come in handy. Let them carry their quarry Jiffa and follow behind me."

"On foot? But we have only one amobiler, and the boys all came on their own devices," Lieutenant Kamshi said, somewhat at a loss. "I guess we could find some transportation at the villages, but that will take until next year, too."

"Of course they'll go by foot. At a trot. If you sit at the levers, they'll easily keep up with us. What else can we do?" I turned to the corpses. "Are you coming with me to Echo, eagle scouts? Can you run fast?"

"We will follow you, Master!" said these ideal underlings in chorus.

"Excellent. Let's go, gentlemen. I'm wiped out."

"You do look terrible, Max," Melamori said. "Your lightning flashes must really drain you of energy."

"Most likely. But it's so easy to do."

"That's very common. For everything that comes easy you have to pay a high price in the end," Melamori said.

Then we went to the clearing where we had left the amobiler. My undead marched behind devotedly, toting the mummy-like load of their former leader. Anday Pu stayed right by my side, throwing supercilious glances at the dead men.

"We can stuff him in the amobiler," Lieutenant Kamshi said. "Then you and Lady Melamori can deliver him to Echo, and I'll go to the village with the rest of the boys."

"No, no," I said. "We'll return as we came, all together. Do as I say. Sit behind the levers, and go slowly so my little dead soldiers don't run out of breath. They'll manage. I think Jiffa will be happier in the company of his old friends, too."

"You are a cruel man, Sir Max," Sir Kamshi said quietly.

"You really think so?" I said, surprised. "That never occurred to me.

But cruel is as cruel does." And I laughed maliciously. "These fellows died long ago, by the way. And why are you so sure you know what's good and what's bad for them? Right now they're only interested in one thing—carrying out my orders. When these guys are trailing behind my amobiler trying to keep up, they'll be as happy as clams, believe me. As for Sir Jiffa, he hasn't been in the land of the living for a long time either, has he? What difference does it make what a dead body does if its master isn't there anymore?"

Kamshi shook his head and went to the amobiler. Captain Shixola threw him a puzzled glance and looked over at me. Then he shrugged and went to give his final instructions to his subordinates. They still faced a long trek to the Capital, making their way by their own means.

Melamori touched my shoulder gently. "Don't pay any attention to him, Max. Kamshi has always had his little eccentricities. And you were absolutely right."

"Right or not, what does it matter?" I smiled. "Thanks anyway. He did a good job of spoiling my mood, that's for sure. I don't even know why myself."

"You're just tired. Anything could spoil it. Try to get some sleep on the road if you can."

"I can," I said. "The trouble is, I could lie down and sleep right here. Get in touch with Juffin, okay? I don't have the strength to send him a call. Ask him if maybe I'm overdoing things here."

"Okay," said Melamori. She sat down on the grass and stared intently into space. A minute later she looked at me and winked. "Did you doubt it for a second, Max? Our chief is delighted with your idea. He says the Capital has never witnessed such a thing: a bunch of corpses marching in step through the whole of Echo behind an official amobiler of the Ministry of Perfect Public Order. And the noble Sir Kamshi can just eat the infamous giant mushroom of his boss!"

Kamshi was already sitting in the driver's seat. He looked at us and said coldly, "Are we going?"

"We are," I said. "Anday, old friend, you sit in front. You take up so much room! No offense."

"Yes, there's a lot of me," Anday said. "It's no matter. I'm never offended when someone is just stating the facts. Only uneducated philistines object to that."

"Ha! Get a load of that, Max." Melamori looked at me and laughed.

Captain Shixola hesitated a moment, then burst out laughing himself. Anday looked at them in supercilious surprise. Then I smiled, too, ever so slightly. I didn't even have the strength for that.

I rolled up in a ball on the back seat and laid my head in Lady Melamori's lap. My feet were propped up against poor Shixola's hips. I knew it was bad manners, but I wasn't capable of resisting the urge. I slept soundly in spite of the hefty portion of Elixir of Kaxar I had downed and the deliciously disturbing lap of Lady Melamori beneath my left ear.

It was the first time since my return from Kettari that I had fallen asleep without wrapping the notorious kerchief of the Grand Magician of the Order of the Secret Grass around my neck. Sir Juffin Hully adamantly discouraged such experiments, and I didn't have the least desire to risk finding out what the consequences of neglecting it might be. But now I didn't even think about my talisman. It had slipped my mind completely.

I had no idea what I dreamed about, but I woke up none too cheerful. This in itself was unusual, considering how much Elixir of Kaxar I had recently imbibed.

"We're almost in Echo, Max. Wake up," Melamori said, tugging at my nose playfully. "I don't think I can take a step. Your head weighs a dozen tons or more!"

"But of course. It's where I keep all my clever thoughts," I said, straightening my stiff back with difficulty. "How long did I sleep?"

"I guess about five hours. Kamshi didn't race. He crawled like an old man in his cups. He wanted to spare your loyal slaves, I suppose. Right, Sir Kamshi?"

"I just didn't want them to get left behind," the lieutenant said. "Sir Max, she pestered me the whole way. Tell her I can't go any faster."

"If you think I'm an expert on the optimal speed of living corpse-pedestrians, you are sadly mistaken. Do you think things like this happen to me every dozen days?" I mumbled sleepily, reaching into my pocket for the bottle of reviving liquid and looking aghast at the horrific procession straggling behind us. "Everyone here? I don't want to have to scour the country roads, rounding up the ones that got left behind.

"No one fell behind, Sir Max. I was watching to make sure the whole way," Shixola said.

"The whole way? You poor thing," I said with sincere sympathy.

"You could have looked away now and then. I'm forever in your debt, Shixola."

"Well, I must admit, I did turn around once or twice," the captain said.

"And it's good you did. How's it going, Blackbeard Junior?" I placed my hand on the plumply rounded shoulder of my heroic chronicler.

"The article is finished. Everyone can take it easy," Anday said cheerfully. "Want to read it? You'll catch, Max, I just know it."

"That's for sure," Melamori laughed. "After an article like that they'll put up statues of both of us, Max. Yours will be a bit taller than mine. But the biggest of all will be Sir Anday's, of course. Gurig's will just have to move over. Did I catch, Sir Anday?"

"Yes. Catch it she did," Anday said, a bit annoyed. He seemed to be talking not to us but to his favorite interlocutor: himself.

"Well?" I said to Melamori. "Should it come out in print?"

"Should it? It must—after Sir Rogro cuts a few strong passages about how reluctant the policemen were to enter the ravine, of course. And he will cut them, believe me. It is the truth, naturally, but you can understand the boys. And eventually they did go down into the ravine. That's something I never would have done. You have to be more magnanimous with people, Sir Anday. Have a heart. We are such fragile things, and our inner workings are so delicate."

Anday grumbled something under his breath. Lieutenant Kamshi looked at him in frank disapproval but kept silent.

"That's all right," I said. "Magnanimity is an acquired trait since it's a side effect of the good life and the offspring of prosperity. As for Anday Pu, all that is still ahead of him as far as I can tell." I patted him on the back. "Don't worry, hero. If Lady Melamori is satisfied, I won't even bother to read it now. I'll read it in the paper, that's more fun."

"Oh, come on. It won't kill you to read it now," he said, his grumpy petulance giving way to unbridled enthusiasm. "You were really smoking back there, Max! The heroes from the days of yore would have taken a back seat to you. You catch? It was really something!"

"I hear you. And they do, too." Grinning, I waved my hand in the direction of the window.

The streets of the Capital were swarming with astonished citizens. They stared in unfeigned horror at the gloomy procession of the undead from the Magaxon Forest.

"I never knew Echo was so full of do-nothings and gawkers."

"You can't blame them. A sight like this would make just about anyone drop everything and come out to look. I wouldn't want to miss a parade like this, either," Captain Shixola said.

"Can I get out here, Max?" Anday said. "It's a stone's throw to the editorial offices of the *Royal Voice*, and I may be able to get the story in for the evening edition."

"Sure you can. Why ask? You're a free man, praise be the Magicians."

Kamshi stopped the amobiler, and Anday jumped into the street with remarkable agility, shouting good day to us as he was already disappearing into the crowd.

"Well, what do you think of my find?" I asked Melamori.

"The dinner's over once and for all," she said. "The first half hour he really did write the article. After that he regaled me with stories of his student days and his adventures at the Court. He has such a sweet accent. I would have died of boredom if it hadn't been for Sir Anday. You were napping, Shixola didn't take his eyes off your moribund regiment, and Kamshi pretended he couldn't look away from the road— though at a pace like that, the amobiler could have gotten along without any driver at all."

Lieutenant Kamshi didn't say a word. He was sick and tired of the whole conversation, I think.

I don't know about my fellow picnickers, but I was darned glad to see the old walls of the House by the Bridge. It's so nice and quiet. Here Juffin Hully was in charge, and he would save me from this bunch of obedient corpses. For some reason it was extraordinarily unpleasant for me to look upon the fruits of my most recent exploits. I couldn't come up with any rational explanation for how I was feeling.

Sir Juffin came out to greet us. He gazed at the eccentric crew, snorted in amusement, cocked his head, and began barking out orders, to my great relief.

"Melamori, go home to rest. Scram! This monster in the Mantle of Death has run you ragged. If I need you, I'll call. Max, stop looking so mournful. If you don't smile right this second, I'm sending for the healers. And hurry up and hide this treasure in the small cell next to our office. I'm talking about Jiffa, not Lady Melamori. Then come back to your morbid flock, and help Shurf deal with them. You stay here for a few minutes, boys, and guard the quarry. By the way, which one of you decided to invite Sir Max on this picnic? Was it you, Kamshi? I'm curious."

"No. It was Shixola's idea. I insisted we should be acting on our own since the Magaxon Forest had never fallen under your jurisdiction. Besides, I had been planning the operation so long I really wanted to carry it out myself," Kamshi admitted.

"Really? Well, good going, Shixola. You're making progress. Intuition like that is very valuable. What are you waiting for, Sir Max? Come on, lead Sir Jiffa away and take a stone off my heart."

"You, and you," I said, gesturing toward the dead brigands who were holding the leather-bound mummy, the captive but not conquered Jiffa. "Come with me. All the rest of you, wait for me here. Understand? Forward, commandos!"

"Understood, Master!" they mumbled submissively.

"Wonderful!" Juffin said in triumph. "You're a born emperor, Max. Or, at the very least, a prince. And you said you didn't like giving orders."

"I hate it," I said bitterly.

"But you're good at it. You'll get used to it. You'll have to."

"I hope not. I prefer killing outright." I threw an acerbic glance at Kamshi, remembering the recent accusations of cruelty. What an idiot I was for getting upset. A reputation like that is very valuable in our profession. It should be guarded at all costs.

We deposited Jiffa in the small, narrow cage of a room, the secret door to which was located in the far corner of the office Juffin and I shared. The cell was just what was required: it was a miniature version of Xolomi. Leaving it, casting spells or practicing magic in it, and even using Silent Speech were all impossible. It was a sort of detention center for particularly hardened cases. I had never known it to be occupied, so Jiffa was a reminder of the glorious traditions of the beginning of the Code Epoch when this, the most reliable cell in the whole Ministry of Perfect Public Order, was never empty, even for a day.

"Put him down on the floor," I told my loyal subjects. "Like that, yes. Oh, I almost forgot. You can remove the gag from his mouth. Let him curse—it's every man's right. I'm for freedom of speech, even when it's objectionable. As long as I don't have to hear it myself."

Truth be told, they didn't give a rat's rear about my high-mindedness. They removed the gag, so Jiffa managed to wish us a pleasant journey, but a bit too eloquently for my taste.

The rest of the corpses continued their aimless shuffling in the corridor. Sir Juffin had already rushed off somewhere on other matters. And my comrades-in-arms, the brave police officers, their faces pale with rage, were listening to the harangue of their immediate superior, Captain Foofloss.

I started eavesdropping. Unbelievable. Foofloss was berating my heroic colleagues for not wearing their belts. I had always known that Foofloss was a bigger cretin than Boboota, but just how much bigger had escaped me till now.

"I think the best thing you could do would be simply to shut up and go to a tavern, Captain," I said amicably. "As for your subordinates' belts, at the present time they are adorning the wrists and ankles of a dangerous criminal, whom your gentlemen officers and I have just detained. I could go into detail, but as far as I know, you have a hard time understanding human speech. So please don't interfere when your men are doing their jobs."

Foofloss looked at me dumbfounded. I don't think he grasped a single word of my fiery speech, but he did understand one thing. He was being insulted, and he couldn't do a thing about it since the nasty rogue was Sir Max the Terrible himself. Nevertheless, the poor guy did try to defend his honor.

"Sir Max, it is inadmissible to speak in this manner to a superior in the presence of his subordinates. It undermines his authority."

"Authority?" I said. "Really? You are as much a superior as I am the Director of Cosmic Electroenemas. I repeat—get thee to a tavern, Foofloss! Do not incur the wrath of the Dark Magicians. Or me, while you're at it."

He looked at me flabbergasted. He hiccuped softly, not so much from fear as from intellectual strain. The skin on his lower forehead wrinkled up, revealing the inner workings of his mind. Finally, Foofloss turned around and fled without saying another word.

"Thank you, Sir Max." Kamshi was the first to recover. "Thank you for bringing this unfortunate situation to an end."

"Oh, I'm not finished with him yet. Not by a long shot. You all did such a fine job. So if this old douche bag raises his ugly head again, let me know. I'll have a little tête-à-tête with him. He'll be as sweet as pie afterward, seeing as I'm so cruel." I winked at Kamshi, and we both laughed with a sense of relief. The wall that had threatened to grow up between us crumbled.

"Sir Max, I didn't quite get your drift. What's a Cosmic Electroenema?" Shixola said. "And how can an enema, even a cosmic one, have a director?"

"Every Cosmic Electroenema must have a director," I said.

Further comments were unnecessary.

"I'm glad to see you, Max."

A towering snow-white figure appeared at the end of the corridor. Sir Shurf Lonli-Lokli in the flesh. I turned toward him joyfully.

"Look here," I said, somewhat shamefaced, pointing to the crowd of corpses. "I've brought you some visitors, my friend."

"May we leave?" Kamshi said.

"Of course, gentlemen. Thanks for the wonderful outing. I'll keep you informed about this matter if I can."

"You probably won't be able to," Kamshi said, nodding cannily. "This case smells like some ancient Order, if I understand correctly."

"We'll see," I said. "Besides, we never have a case without a lingering whiff of that piquant aroma."

The policemen left, and Shurf and I were alone. Not counting my corpses, that is.

"So, this is how my green lightning works. Are you happy? I'm not, actually." I looked at Lonli-Lokli uneasily. "Be a sport. Take care of these guys, will you?"

"Hmm, very interesting."

Lonli-Lokli examined the dead outlaws, who were staring at me in devotion. He even approached them more closely. Finally, he turned to me. "No, no, Max. Your Lethal Spheres are in good working order. They're as dangerous as mine. Only you know, they depend too strongly on your desires, and you don't know how to control them yet. You could destroy these corpses very easily, but you didn't want to."

"Didn't want to? You think I'm such a bleeding heart? All I could think about was saving my own skin."

"Of course, of course. But you see, Max, you still think that killing is bad. In any case, murder is for you the worst of all possible crimes. Deep inside you resisted killing them. You were hoping for something else—that they would be rendered harmless or, still better, useful. And that's what they became. It's quite admirable. You're a very pragmatic person, Max. Too much so, for my taste."

"Well, well. If you say so. And what should I do now? Go outside and kill a few dozen passersby just to get the hang of it?"

"You'll get used to it in time, whether you want to or not. No need to rush things. By the way, did it never occur to you that you didn't have to drag these dead beauties around with you?"

"Not drag them around with me? What was I supposed to do, leave them there to wander through the forest?"

"Don't you get it? They carry out all your orders, don't they?"

"Yes. So what?"

"You could have just ordered them to die there in the forest, instead of organizing this whole parade. The Echoers will remember the spectacle for a long time, of course, but I can't fathom why Sir Juffin approved of your decision. Well, a strange joke like this is quite up his alley."

"Wait a minute, Shurf," I said, dumbfounded. "You're saying that if I order them to die, they'll just lie down and do it?"

"Try it," Lonli-Lokli said. "It's not right for them to be shuffling around the corridors of the Ministry of Perfect Public Order. It's unaesthetic, to say the least."

"Unaesthetic?" I said. "That's a quaint way of putting it, friend."

"Come on, Max," Lonli-Lokli insisted. "Don't stall. All matters have to be taken to their conclusions, and unpleasant ones all the more."

"Fine." I turned to the dead men. "I order you all to lie down and die and crumble into dust. No reviving allowed."

I screwed up my face and played the fool, as I was for some reason sure that nothing would come of it. But my dead men lay down obediently on the floor. A few seconds later, they crumbled apart. The corridor became very dirty—dust and decay everywhere.

I felt an irresistible urge to grab Lonli-Lokli by the hand. To my delight, he was wearing his protective gloves. It occurred to me just then that grabbing Lonli-Lokli's hand could be considered a form of suicide. Leave it to me to come up with something so idiotic.

"They disappeared," I said, giggling nervously.

"Of course they did. You ordered them to. Did you ever doubt that they would?"

"Doubt it? I was sure that it wouldn't happen."

"Strange. When did I ever deceive you?"

"Never. But you know, Shurf, it just doesn't match up with my conceptions of my own abilities."

"Ah, I see. Well, no matter. No one has a real grasp of his own abilities. This holds for all people, and Magicians in particular, even good ones. Don't worry, you're capable of other misconceptions, too."

"Oh, speaking of lack of ability. This morning I unwittingly stepped on Melamori's trace. She was terribly put out. And I wasn't even trying."

"Let's go into the office, Max," Lonli-Lokli said. "Don't you think it will be easier to talk there than in the corridor? Besides, the cleaners are on their way."

"Okay," I said. "Yours or mine?"

"Mine. You see, Juffin considers your office to be his own. I wouldn't be surprised if that's where he is right now."

❊

After locking the door behind him, Lonli-Lokli sat down on his uncomfortable chair. I settled down on the floor and leaned up against his chair.

"You're tired, Max. How many Lethal Spheres did you launch this morning?"

"I guess about three dozen. I wasn't counting."

"Goodness! Even more than I thought. I don't know how you can still stand up."

I waved my hand wearily. "I'm sick to death of my own genius, Shurf. I'd like things to be simpler, honestly."

"That feeling is the result of overexertion. Tomorrow you'll feel fine. And you'll be dizzy with your own powers, believe me. The main thing is not to attach too much importance to either one state or the other. But tell me, how did you step on Lady Melamori's trace? Did it just come to you all of a sudden? Or did Juffin reconsider and decide to teach you how?"

"That's just it! He didn't teach me." And I gave Shurf a straightforward account of my morning exploit.

"This is getting serious, Max." Lonli-Lokli sounded concerned. "With such uncanny abilities, you've got to know how to control your actions. Otherwise it could be dangerous."

"Well, what should I do?" I asked for the umpteenth time that day.

"What should you do? My breathing exercises, for a start, but more often than you've been practicing them until now."

"That's all?"

"For now, yes. You only do them once every two or three days, don't you?"

"Sometimes more, sometimes less," I said with a guilty shrug.

"You'll have to be a bit more demanding of yourself," Shurf said. "There's nothing worse than real power in the absence of self-discipline. Forgive me, Max, but someone's got to be a nudnick, and I'm the only one around here who's willing to take on the role. If you don't get a grip on yourself—"

"You're absolutely right, Shurf," I said. "You have every right to remind me a dozen times a day. It seems that's the only way to deal with me."

"Are you sure it will help? I can remind you even more often if you like."

"I don't doubt it." I smiled at him. "But a dozen reminders a day should do the trick."

"Agreed," Lonli-Lokli said.

I sniffed. This was going to be a barrel of fun, I could tell.

"Let's go eat," said Shurf, standing up leisurely. "Sir Juffin is waiting for us in the *Glutton*. He just sent me a call and asked me to bring along 'all that was left of Sir Max.' Quote, unquote."

"I might have guessed," I muttered. "A message like that has Sir Juffin written all over it."

And off we went to the *Glutton Bunba*.

"Sinning Magicians, you're as gloomy as a hungry werewolf, Max!" Juffin said, tearing himself away from the contents of his pot of pâté. "Why do you always try to test your strength in the genre of high drama? It's not your forte, believe me."

"Max really did encounter some serious problems, sir," Lonli-Lokli said on my behalf.

"Problems? If only I had problems like his," Juffin said. "Everything is unfolding just as it should, even better. Since when did you become such a pessimist, Sir Shurf?"

"It was just a hunch," Shurf said.

"Really? I didn't have any such premonition. Strange, usually our premonitions are synchronized."

I looked at my colleagues in perplexity. I felt like a sick man consulting two outstanding specialists whose opinions strongly diverged.

"Everything is fine, Max. At least it will all turn out fine, I assure you." Juffin looked at me with uncharacteristic sympathy and warmth. "Do your breathing exercises. Someone in this World has to do them. And don't fret over things. It's always better when we remain calm. It's a law of nature— Sinning Magicians! What kind of idiot is practicing Forbidden Magic right under my very nose? Let's get out of here, boys. There's disaster afoot!"

And Sir Juffin rushed to the door of the *Bunba*. Lonli-Lokli was standing at the threshold in a flash, his white looxi billowing out like a sail in the summer breeze. I was at their side before I knew it.

Our Venerable Head looked around, puzzled.

"Either I'm completely incompetent, or . . . Lads, something's happening at the House by the Bridge! How curious."

We raced off to Headquarters.

"It's all over," Juffin announced as we flew. "That was really something—more than the hundredth degree, judging by how I was shaking."

"Can you feel it without a meter?" I said.

"I have to. You're not the only one who suffers under the burden of your own talents. You can't imagine how inconvenient it is. Especially at night."

We walked through the corridors of the Ministry of Perfect Public Order. Sir Juffin steered us into our office. In the doorway he momentarily froze, then let out a short, explosive curse: "Sinning crap!" After a moment, he stepped aside so Lonli-Lokli and I could see.

The secret door to our detention cell stood wide open. On the threshold lay Captain Shixola. His hands were clenched. On his face was an expression of dreamy serenity.

I rushed over to him and nudged him gently, though I already knew that it was no use. He was dead.

I turned to Juffin, distraught. "Was it Jiffa?"

"Not exactly." Juffin entered the empty cell and started to sniff something. "Someone helped him, that much is clear."

"Who?"

"The same one who helped him return from the World of the Dead to his beloved Magaxon Forest, that's who. Damnation!"

Juffin sat down next to the body of Captain Shixola and placed his hands carefully on his stomach. A moment later he sighed bitterly and got up to open the window.

"Well, things have gone terribly amiss. Poor Shixola was a very talented medium. How could I have overlooked him? The World knows only one like him in every dozen thousand. With those abilities, I should have stayed close by his side. I shouldn't have let him out of my sight."

Juffin sank into his armchair. Lonli-Lokli stood in the doorway nodding thoughtfully, then took a seat near the boss.

"Jiffa went down the Dark Path," he told Juffin coldly. "Granted, you can move a dead man only five or six miles, but that's enough."

"Yes," Juffin said. He thought a bit, then asked, "To the south?"

Lonli-Lokli shrugged and said, "You know I have no sense of direction."

Juffin frowned and sniffed the air. "Yes, southward. That's certain."

I stared at my colleagues in bewilderment. Their conversation seemed to me to be the most improbable event of this whole crazy day. After hovering around the doorway a bit, I stepped inside the empty cell.

"Don't go in there!" Juffin barked out. "If you step on Jiffa's trace, you'll find out the Dark Magicians are nothing to joke about."

I went back into the office and sat down on the windowsill. I wanted very much to cry, whether from anger, or helplessness, or simply because the death of the good Captain Shixola was incompatible with my notions of how events should unfold in my one and only life.

I didn't cry, of course, but just stared dully into space. Some kind of strange barrier had sprung up between me and the rest of the world—transparent but impenetrable. Even the boss's voice sounded like a radio coming from behind the wall.

"It was a real Master who revived Jiffa," Sir Juffin said. "He was the most vital of all dead men I can remember. And what a shield he had! I could easily have killed him—you too, Shurf—but no one else could have done it. But I couldn't dissuade him, couldn't reason with him. That's why I planned to take him to the Seven-Leaf Clover. There are a few old-timers there who might have been able to talk some sense into him.

"Melifaro, old chap, good you were able to make it so quickly. I need all the information I can get on Pafoota Jongo, Bubuli Jola Giox, Atva Kuraisa, and Joffla Kumbaya. Maybe that's enough for now. The others who took part in the Great Royal Hunt in the Magaxon Forest could hardly have anything to do with this, as far as I know."

"Pafoota couldn't either," Lonli-Lokli said. "I see him from time to time. Once every few years in the *Fat Skeleton*. It's a sort of tradition. I can witness to the fact that he's not capable of it anymore. The fellow squandered his power. He has a big family and doesn't practice anymore, obviously. He seems very happy."

"Really? All right then, Melifaro, you can wait on Pafoota Jongo. We'll get the other three. On the double, okay?"

"Of course."

I raised my eyes to greet Melifaro, but he had already disappeared. I just caught a glimpse of an aloe-colored looxi at the end of the corridor. I looked at Juffin.

"Pull yourself together, Max," he said. "We've got a lot of work ahead of us. If your grief could help Shixola, I would personally help you stay sad as long as possible. But it's absolutely pointless."

"Remember the breathing exercises, Max," Lonli-Lokli said. "It's the perfect time."

"Right. I'm sorry, fellows."

I tried to gather my wits about me. I have to admit, after doing Lonli-Lokli's famous breathing exercises for less than a minute, the invisible barrier that separated me from the World dissolved. A few minutes later, I was myself again. I was by no means lighthearted, but at least I could imagine the possibility.

"This resurrector of corpses, or whatever you call him, was he actually here in the House by the Bridge?" I said. "Then it should be no problem to find him. He's alive, and he leaves a trace."

"As if he'd be foolish enough to show his face here," Juffin said with mild contempt. "He doesn't need to go through the trouble. A good magician can use a sensitive medium as his instrument. Distance presents no obstacle to him. And in our Headquarters there was one outstanding medium, to my profound regret. Shixola had to open this sinning door and set Jiffa free. Naturally, no one but myself can open the secret door and remain alive. But that suited the one who gave orders to our Captain just fine."

"I see. Poor Melamori. She's not in for a good night's sleep now, is she?"

"Melamori?" Juffin frowned. "Yes, Max, she's probably the only one who can go after Jiffa. We can lighten her load, though. It will be far easier for her to trail Jiffa's Master than—"

"Maybe it's even simpler than that. Jiffa is very attached to his lair, isn't he? Maybe he just went back home again."

"Perhaps. Then again, perhaps not. Let's wait for Melifaro. I hope—"

"There's no use hoping," Melifaro said, storming back into the office like a green whirlwind. Who would have thought that fellow knew how to frown, too?

"Why is it no use?" Juffin seemed surprised. "Let's hear it."

"The buriwoks in the Main Archive claim that Bubuli Jola Giox, Atva Kuraisa, and Joffla Kumbaya are all dead. They died at different times, naturally, but all over the course of the past few years. Then I asked about Pafoota Jongo. Also dead, just a dozen days ago!"

"It's easy to check. Sir Shurf, send a call to your old mate," Juffin ordered.

"He truly is no longer among the living," Lonli-Lokli told us a few seconds later. "I'm sure of it. Shall I contact his wife? She might tell us something."

"Yes, go ahead." Juffin gripped the left armrest of his chair spasmodically. There was a resounding crunch when the thick piece of wood gave way. Juffin glared angrily at the fragments of the armrest and tossed them into a corner.

"At least I learned about the other members of the Great Royal Hunt in the Magaxon Forest," Melifaro said, looking timidly at Juffin, as if calculating how close he could approach without risk to life and limb.

"Dead?" Juffin asked indifferently.

"Yep, all of them. Isn't that what you expected?"

"Of course. Have the causes of death been established?"

"I don't know. Their deaths appear to have been natural. No one suspected otherwise, or they would have turned to us."

"Perhaps they turned to the police."

"Yikes! What a dunderhead I am." Melifaro clutched his head in mock despair. "Hold on." He disappeared into the corridor again.

"Have you managed to find out what happened to your former friend, Shurf?" Juffin asked, drumming his fingers on the table.

Lonli-Lokli raised the hand encased in the enormous glove, giving us to understand that his conversation in Silent Speech was not yet over. Juffin shrugged in annoyance, but a moment later his curiosity was satisfied.

"Pafoota's widow says it was an accident," Lonli-Lokli said. "He had had a bit too much to drink at a family celebration, went to the bathroom, fell down the stairs, and broke his back. A rather stupid way to die, I'd say."

"An accident, was it? This could be interesting," Juffin said, growing more animated. "Well, let's wait for Melifaro. He'll tell us something. But I'm already starting to figure it out, I think." He turned sharply to me. "What about you, Max? What do you think?"

"Many actual dead bodies, the former Junior Magicians of various Orders of Magic, comrades in the Great Royal Hunt in the Magaxon Forest—and among them, one imposter. He didn't die first, and he didn't die last. The causes of death didn't raise any suspicions. The family grieves. Everything is as tight as a drum. Is this what you mean?"

"Precisely," Juffin said. "What a mind you have—unbelievable! Hold your head high. It's your right. You've already improved my mood considerably. Now do something about your own. You'll need to soon enough. I want you to finish the job you began at the request of poor Shixola."

"I do, too."

I have to admit, I wasn't sure that I was up to the task. But I'm never sure of my own abilities. Right then, though, I wasn't in the least inclined to advertise my charming modesty and fish for compliments from Sir Juffin. Anyway, he always has plenty of them at hand at such moments. Hell, I myself was sure I had to close this case. Somehow.

"It's good to know that you want to yourself. But Sir Shurf has some objections of a metaphysical nature, doesn't he?"

"No," Lonli-Lokli said evenly. "If you both think everything will be all right, I have no objections."

"Go home, Max," Juffin said. "Wash up, pack only the most indispensable things, and dress in something comfortable and inconspicuous. Oh, and don't forget your talisman. There's no guarantee that you'll be sleeping at home tonight. Come back in two hours, no later. I'll call Melamori. I hope she had time to rest. In any case, the sooner you can start the better."

"Okay, I'll be back in no time."

I thought that someone sitting in the windowsill on the first floor of a building shouldn't have to wander through the corridors and passageways looking for doors. So I just turned around, stuck my legs through the open window, and jumped down onto the mosaic sidewalk of the Street of Copper Pots. It was only three or four feet to the ground, but for some reason the jump affected me like an electric shock. The unpleasant sensation stopped almost immediately, but I was discombobulated in the extreme. It was as though I were observing from the outside how my feet took one step after the other. Time passed unbearably slowly, as if it took an eternity for me to execute these few little steps.

"Max!"

I turned around. Juffin appeared in the window and beckoned to me. I had to go back.

"My congratulations, wonder boy!"

"Meaning?" I stared at him, uncomprehending.

"It's just that it's impossible to pass through this window. You can't enter through it, either. Did you really think there would be just an ordinary window in my office? Magicians only know what would crawl in! But you did it. So please accept my congratulations."

"Why did you tell me that? Just so I'd know, or because you wanted to congratulate me?"

"Both. But the main thing is that it's a good sign, Max. If you were able to jump onto the street through my window, I think you can be very confident that everything else will be just fine."

"I am confident. I have no more strength to worry. Sometimes I feel that nothing more is left of me, so there's nothing to worry with."

"That's a good state of mind to be in, lad," Juffin said, winking at me. "Just the one you'll need."

"Excellent."

I squeezed the semblance of smile out of myself and went to my amobiler. The boss was still following me with his eyes. The back of my head even started burning under his powerful gaze.

The first thing I did when I got home was to undress and head for a bathing pool. The cats stared at me cautiously from the far corner of the living room. I didn't seem to inspire them with much confidence. Oh boy!

In the fourth bathing pool, I suddenly relaxed. It was as if someone had flipped an invisible switch. I became myself again, with all the attendant consequences. I felt my nerves tighten, then slacken almost immediately. I was about to start bemoaning the death of the brave Captain Shixola. I was on the verge of tears, but then I thought about how I needed to search for the dead Jiffa in the company of Lady Melamori, and I cheered up. Then I thought about the same thing a bit longer and grew sad again. In short, I was the same as I always was.

Congratulating myself on my return, I crawled out of the bathing pool and went up to the living room. Armstrong and Ella padded up to me and rubbed against my ankles, purring loudly. I scooped them up in my arms, buried my nose in their soft fur, and gave in to a sense of relief. A tear rolled down my cheek. I shook my head indignantly, pulled myself together, and headed for the bedroom to get ready. By the time I was on the stairs I felt an unpleasant wetness on my left cheek.

Stop it, this minute! I commanded myself. *Or else.*

Or else what? The inner voice sounded terribly sarcastic.

I'll punch you in the nose! I was pitiless.

Go ahead! It'll be all the worse for you. It's your nose!

I couldn't keep up this idiocy any longer, and I burst out laughing. Long live the split personality—the shortest path to spiritual equilibrium!

Half an hour later, I tossed my half-empty traveling bag into the back seat of the amobiler. It held a change of clothes and a pack of cigarettes. A valuable bottle of Elixir of Kaxar rested in the pocket of my looxi. The kerchief of the Grand Magician of the Order of the Secret Grass I wrapped around my neck, just in case. There was a good chance I would forget to put it on before I went to sleep after a day like this. Everything else I planned to look for in the Chink between Worlds, if need be. I had to keep in shape.

In fifteen minutes I was already at the House by the Bridge. I approached the open window of Juffin's office. For a moment I just stood there, trying to figure out what I was feeling. I had no wish to repeat my recent exploit, so I went around to the side of the Ministry of Perfect Public Order and entered like all ordinary employees: through the Secret Entrance.

To my surprise, Sir Juffin Hully was sitting in his office in absolute solitude.

"Has everyone taken early retirement?" I said. "They decided their health was more important to them?"

"Finally you sound like the old Max," Juffin said, visibly relieved. "How did you manage, if it's no secret?"

"I took a bath, cried, and threatened to punch myself in the nose. A great method. You should try it."

"The third step would have been enough," Juffin said caustically. "You have an amazing capacity for going overboard. Okay, let's get down to business. Melifaro investigated the matter of the premature deaths of the Junior Magicians with the police. All well and good, but—"

"But they were simple accidents? All the former Magaxon Forest huntsmen died of natural causes? There's nothing to grab onto?"

"You guessed it. But there still may be something 'to grab onto,' as you put it. In two cases, the faces were terribly battered: Sir Atva Kuraisa from the Order of Grilles and Mirrors and Sir Joffla Kumbaya from the Order of the Sleeping Butterfly. The corpse of Atva Kuraisa was identified by his sister Tanna. No relatives were found for Joffla Kumbaya. He was a recluse, so a courier from the *Merry Little Skeletons* who delivered food to him had to identify him. Both Magicians had equal chances of being our clients. The Order of Grilles and Mirrors and the Order of the Sleeping Butterfly were very strong organizations in their time, so their Junior Magicians could easily have had some horrific secrets in their possession."

"Did someone send them a call? That's the simplest way of finding out whether a person is alive or dead. Or am I wrong?"

"No, you're not wrong, but a good Magician is capable of opting out of Silent Speech. He can create a sturdy shield, a perfect imitation of death, so that rule doesn't hold here. In short, you and Melamori will have to find Jiffa. I think they are together. If you're lucky, you'll find the trace of the Master next to Jiffa's. Then you'll be able to pick it up since you've already learned how. Give the bastard what he's got coming to him!"

"Yes. He deserves it, and it's for a good cause. By the way, why didn't you ever teach me how, Juffin?"

"Because I don't have to teach you," Juffin said. "To be honest, I just wanted to spare your nervous system. You learn too fast as it is."

"I agree with you a hundred percent," I said with a weary sigh. "Everything happens too fast. Maybe it's because where I come from we don't live very long. And I took such a running start at the very outset that I can't slow down now."

"Maybe yes, maybe no," Juffin said. "What difference does it make what the reason is?"

"I don't know. It's just that when I manage to find some watertight explanation for something, it improves my appetite."

"Like you have no appetite at all otherwise," Juffin said with a sniff. "You don't sit down to a meal more than eight times a day, poor boy."

⚘

"Where do we start, Sir Juffin?" Melamori burst through the door of the office. "As far as I understand, he didn't leave a trace behind. He went down the Dark Path, didn't he?"

"Yes. So this sinning trace, which doesn't actually exist, is where you have to begin. Not too promising, is it? Undoubtedly, the least promising task you've faced since you began working here. Do you think you can follow him down the Dark Path? You should be able to handle it, I think."

Melamori frowned, then nodded. "I think I'll manage. Following an ordinary trace down the Dark Path might be too much for me. But this one—it's pulling me along! Unpleasant, but that's just how it is."

Melamori's voice sounded calm and unhurried, as though the boss had just offered her a mug of kamra.

"You and I will go together," Juffin said suddenly. "You follow the trace, and I'll follow you. You never know what kinds of surprises we'll find there. You stay here, Max. I'll send you a call and let you know where we end up. Then you come to meet us, as quick as you can. Okay?"

"You don't have to ask. I'll be there before the words are out of your mouth."

"Good. Let's go, Melamori."

Melamori took her shoes off, went to stand on the threshold, and turned back to us in surprise.

"Did he walk right out of the cell?"

"Of course. When the door is open the cell becomes an ordinary room, just like any other, and you can cast as many spells there as you would in a regular kitchen."

"That's right. Okay, let's get on with it." She waved at me, and smiled. "Don't worry, Max. With Sir Juffin beside me, there's nothing to fear."

"You have to learn to conquer a woman's heart, lad." Juffin laughed. "With me she'll go to the ends of the earth."

"Will you teach me?"

"I'll teach you. If you behave."

Juffin touched the tip of his nose lightly with his forefinger. I felt like a true Kettarian when I answered him in kind.

Melamori swept into the cell, stopped abruptly, stood up on tiptoe, sighed, and . . . disappeared.

"Not too shabby!" Juffin said, letting out a low whistle. A second later, he, too, had disappeared. I looked at Kurush in bewilderment.

"Everyone's abandoned me!" I said plaintively.

"That's how people are," the bird said.

Max, can you imagine? Melamori and I ended near the Old Thorn, *just across the road.* Juffin had given me no time to feel sorry for myself. *Why don't you drop by? We're having fun over here.*

Fun? I replied, getting up from my chair. *Did you decide to mosey over to the* Thorn *for a cup of soup? What a pair of slackers.*

Don't curse, Max. Your expressions are sometimes too naughty. You're already in the amobiler, I hope?

No, I'm still in the office.

You're so sluggish today. All right, I won't keep you. Over and out.

A few minutes later I was already by the *Old Thorn.* I looked around and didn't see anyone, so I sent a call to Juffin.

Where are you?

Max, you mean to say you're already here? I planned to come out to meet you, but I didn't expect you so soon. We're in the little yellow house across from the Thorn, on the first floor. There are so many fresh traces here that Melamori is giddy with delight . . .

I crawled out of the amobiler and threw open the door of the yellow house. My colleagues were lounging about in a spacious, empty room.

". . . that she won't have to go following the trace of that dead bore Jiffa." Juffin concluded his thought out loud.

"That's music to my ears," Melamori murmured.

"So now it's my turn? You wanted me to 'wipe out the bastard,' right?" Much to my surprise, I felt the thrill of the hunt. My facial muscles tightened, and I smiled a predatory smile.

"Max, you have the makings of a real Master of Pursuit," Juffin said, grinning. Then he turned to Melamori. "Look at him! Whenever you're straining at the leash to pursue another victim, it's not a pretty sight, either."

"Really? That's what I look like? Impossible," Melamori said.

"Okay, you go ahead and amuse yourselves," I said. "I'm going to get down to business. Melamori, show me where the sinning trace is. Maybe I'll be able to follow it like I did before."

"Which trace are you after? There are two besides Jiffa's."

"Two?" I said. "Okay, show me both of them."

"Come over here. And why are you wearing boots? Oh, right. You were able to trace me without taking them off."

I went over to stand by Melamori. I stamped around a bit, trying to pick up some sensation in the soles of my feet. Nothing.

"You're fooling me, aren't you?" I said in an injured tone.

Melamori shook her head earnestly. Then I realized I had found the trace—and not just one but both of them at once. My left foot stood on one, and my right one on the other. It was like experiencing a true split personality. I was very much inclined to follow the left trace. The right one was far less attractive to me. My heart told me that it wasn't wise to follow it, and my heart was rarely wrong.

"Here they are! Both of them. The one on the right of me seems very dangerous, and the left one quite ordinary. We probably want the right one, don't we?"

"To me they seem equally dangerous," Melamori said, looking quizzical. "They even resemble each other, though it's hard to say how."

Sir Juffin came up and poked me lightly in the side. I moved away. He stood next to me for a moment or two, nodding thoughtfully.

"You're both right. The traces are very similar. And the right one is much more dangerous. It's good there are two of you. Max will follow the left trace, and you, my lady, the right one, since you're wary of it already. The suspects fled from here in an amobiler, I'm assuming. They aren't so lacking in brains that they'd try to get away on foot. It won't pose a problem for you to track them down, will it?"

"You know it won't be a problem. And for Max even less so, since he's able to find a trace with his shoes on," Melamori said enviously.

"Good. Go after them, and may the Dark Magicians help you."

"Let's go, Max. We've wasted enough time as it is. I can't imagine why," Melamori said dryly.

"I can tell you why. First, I wanted you to be able to rest a bit more," Juffin explained. "Second, who do they think they are anyway, making us rush after them hither and thither?"

"Brilliant," Melamori said. "Now I really do have a sense of my own significance. Thank you, sir."

Meanwhile, I had started moving along the trace. I crossed the threshold, went outside, and took a few steps down the sidewalk. My amobiler was parked a small distance away, but I felt a strong urge to get into it just where I stood. The urge was so strong that I had no power to resist it.

"Juffin, would it trouble you to drive my buggy over here?" I said politely. "I think I'm going nuts. I just can't force myself to go over there, Magician's word."

"Hmm, that must mean that this is where their amobiler was parked," Juffin said. "Now I'm sure you won't have any trouble tracing them. You've got it down pat. Here, Max? Is this where you want it?"

I turned around to look. My amobiler stood close by. Sir Juffin was sitting proudly at the levers.

"Just a bit closer," I said. "A tad."

"Here's your tad," Juffin said. The amobiler inched up even closer.

"Excellent."

By then I was already itching to get behind the levers. It was like an overwhelming hunger. I shot over to the driver's seat like a projectile, hardly giving Juffin time to vacate it.

"My whole life I've wanted a child like you to sit on my lap," he said bitingly. "You're just burning to get in this buggy and drive off, aren't you?"

"It's not so much about this buggy. You know, Juffin, it seems the guy whose trace I stepped on also sat behind the levers. I mean, he was the one driving their amobiler, not the other guy. Something is making me . . . Oh, I can't explain it," I said, feeling crushed.

"It's all right. I understand what's going through your brain," Juffin said.

He jumped out onto the paving stones. In the meantime, Melamori had settled down in the back seat. I turned to her in surprise, wondering why she didn't want to sit next to me. Then I understood: the one whose trace Melamori had stepped on had been sitting behind the driver. She intercepted my glance and nodded.

"If these guys really headed for the Magaxon Forest, you're going to need a guide," Juffin said. "I sent a call to the forester there, Sir Chvaxta Chiyam. A fine fellow. He knows the forest like the back of his hand, and Jiffa's lair, too. That's essential. After the Royal Hunt put an end to the Magaxon Foxes, he wandered through the lairs and passageways for several years, exploring them. I'm willing to bet Chvaxta collected some very useful household utensils during that time, but I have no objections to that. He'll be around if you need him."

"Do you really think they're such fools, sir?" Melamori said. "If I were them I'd flee somewhere beyond Uguland, or even leave the Unified Kingdom altogether."

"Jiffa can't survive very far from the vicinity of Uguland. The spells lose some of their power there," Juffin said. "Everything depends on how much his life is worth to his followers. All right now, get along with you. Keep in touch, hear?"

"You bet we will," I said. "Want to come with us?"

"I'd love to. Magicians as my witnesses, I'd love to accompany you. But a case has to be closed by the one who started it. With no involvement from outside."

"That's true. Absolutely crazy, senseless, and illogical, but true. I understand."

"Of course you understand," Juffin said with a sigh, more sad than mocking.

This time I drove even faster than usual, but I found no pleasure in it. I was overwhelmed by a single, anguished, uncontrollable desire: to catch up with the person whose trace I had stood on. Nothing else mattered to me—not the insane speed, or the intoxicating aroma of the flowering trees all around us, or Lady Melamori in the back seat, still and silent, in the grip of the same desire.

After about half an hour, I suddenly felt a sense of immense relief. I braked in astonishment and stared at the absolutely empty road.

"What's wrong, Max?" Melamori said anxiously.

"I don't know. I just have the feeling that I've arrived. Only where could they be?"

"I see. Your man has died." She sighed. "It's no surprise. How was he able to withstand even this much, poor thing?"

"He's dead?"

"Yes. I wasn't joking when I said that when you stand on someone's trace his heart stops beating. It was no mere metaphor, believe me. Okay, let's trade places. Your man may have died, but mine is still alive and kicking."

"As you wish. I'm not much good for anything right now," I said, climbing into the back seat.

Melamori got behind the levers. She had every chance of winning our recent wager. She took off at fifty miles an hour right off the bat—twice as fast as the average Echoer. It was quite an achievement for a beginner.

"I seem to be getting the hang of it, don't I?" she said. "I'm going a lot faster than usual, don't you think, Max?"

"You certainly are. You're doing great, Melamori. The rest is just a matter of time. In the beginning I didn't drive any faster than you're driving now, remember?"

"Speed is even better than reaching the end of a trace!" Melamori was ecstatic. "It's indescribable!"

Then she fell silent and concentrated on the road. I made myself comfortable, lit up a cigarette, and stared out the window. I thought for a moment, then sent a call to Juffin.

My man kicked the bucket, it seems. Now Melamori is our only hope.

Jeepers! Not bad. When you reach the spot where they got out of the amobiler, try to stand on the other trace. Maybe you'll bury the second one, too. Then Jiffa will be a sitting duck. You'll be able to catch him with your bare hands.

Okay, I'll try.

Good, good. Chvaxta Chiyam is already waiting for you at the edge of the Magaxon Forest. The trace is leading in that direction, isn't it?

"Melamori, are we still driving toward the Magaxon Forest?" I said.

"What? Yes, that's where we're headed," she said absently.

Correct, I told Juffin.

Fine. Everything is unfolding just as it should. Well, is it over and out yet? Any more questions?

I suppose not. Oh, wait! I wanted to ask you before—whose house was that?

Good question, Max. Our Main Archive produced some completely useless information. The house belongs to the Xitta family. A year ago it was rented out to one Lady Brisse Xlonn. Her papers are fine—like it's such an important document to forge, a rent contract. The neighbors claim that they almost never see her there. Who is this Lady Brisse Xlonn, anyway? There's no one in Echo with a name like that. I sent Melifaro to sniff out whatever he could. I'll let you know if I find out something. Over and out already?

Over and out.

I sighed, and then fell to thinking. Lady Brisse Xlonn. For some reason the name struck me as very unpleasant. But what could she have to do with anything?

An hour later, a tall figure in a dark-red looxi loomed up at the side of the road.

"Sir Chvaxta Chiyam, I presume." I touched Melamori's shoulder. "Stop here for a second, will you?"

"You're killing me, Max," she grumbled. "Okay, I'll try." And our amobiler came to a screeching halt next to the stranger.

"Get in, quick!"

I didn't have to ask the fellow twice. In a moment he was sitting in the front seat, staring back at me with round, owlish eyes of a nondescript color.

"Sir Chvaxta Chiyam?" I said.

How embarrassing if he were just a random fellow on his way to pick berries in the forest. Though a man with a vacant stare like that (what was he—a vagrant? a killer?) would hardly be out on a berry-picking expedition.

The man nodded and continued to study my face intently. Perhaps he just didn't know how to blink.

"You weren't sure who he was?" Melamori snickered. "Come on, Max! You should have found out before inviting him into the amobiler."

"I have my own methods."

"Oh, it's a *method*."

Hearing Melamori's voice, our new passenger turned to face her. It seemed to have just dawned on him that there was someone else in the amobiler besides him and me. Now it was Melamori's turn to have the strange eyes bore into her.

"Are you familiar with our case?" I tried to start a casual conversation about workaday matters.

The fellow turned to me again and shook his head. "I know that I'm supposed to show you the forest and the underground system of the Magaxon Foxes, if necessary. I'll show you," he said blandly.

He fell silent again and began contemplating a spot at about the level of my chest. Sir Chvaxta Chiyam was clearly not burdened with the knowledge of rules of social behavior. Either that, or he simply wasn't in the habit of following them. I truly envied his nonchalance.

Melamori turned down a narrow, overgrown pathway. Then we had to squeeze our way through some thorny underbrush. As a finale, we crashed unceremoniously into an empty amobiler, which had probably belonged to our victims. The flimsy, lightweight construction fell over on its side, but, praise be the Magicians, we were unhurt. There were a few scratches on the front of the amobiler and on one of my cheeks. I hadn't lost the opportunity to raze my face on the edge of the open window.

"I'm sorry, Max," Melamori said, confused and flustered. "I should have braked in time, but—"

"But it's not always possible," I said, and managed to smile. "Don't worry. Such is life."

The forester crawled out of the amobiler and began walking through the clearing.

"No lairs here," he said, and sat down on the grass.

"If they're not here, they're sure to be somewhere else," Melamori said.

She shifted her weight from one foot to the other, anxious to press on with the pursuit.

"Juffin suggested I try to stand on the second trace," I said. "Maybe I'll send the second guy to meet his maker, too."

"Who's Hizmaker?" Melamori said. "Is that a name?"

I smiled. "It's one of the Dark Magicians. The most powerful one."

"And you're personally acquainted with him?" she asked, awed.

"Sort of. But never mind that. Better help me step on the right trace, so I don't stumble upon Jiffa's by accident."

"Jiffa Savanxa?" the forester said, livening up suddenly. "Are you looking for him? I was sure he had died."

"Of course he died. That's the problem," I said.

Sir Chvaxta nodded solemnly, as though everything had now become clear to him. I looked at Melamori.

"So, where is it?"

"Right under my feet. Are you sure you want to try this, Max? You didn't like this trace at all."

"Yes, but that's beside the point when Juffin asked me to do it."

"What would you do if he asked you to jump off the roof of Rulx Castle?" Melamori said.

"I'd probably try," I said. "Though I am scared of heights."

"Me too," Melamori said. "What a pair of Secret Investigators, Terrors of the Universe, we are! We should be ashamed of ourselves."

"Would you happen to know where that corpse over there came from?" the forester broke in matter-of-factly.

"What corpse? Where?" Melamori and I jumped up in a mad frenzy.

"That one there." Chvaxta pointed casually to the overturned amobiler.

"Of course, Max," Melamori said with relief. "It's your client. Congratulations!"

"Thanks," I said. I went closer and found myself staring at the regular facial features of a middle-aged man. "Do you recognize him?"

"No. Ask Sir Juffin. Send him a call. Although what does it matter?"

"What do you mean, 'What does it matter'? Maybe Juffin knows what Order he's from and will tell us what to expect from the other one."

"No one knows what to expect of anyone in critical situations," Melamori said. "Go ahead and send him a call, though."

I sent a call to Sir Juffin Hully and described the corpse.

Ah, yes. Of course! He has light hair, doesn't he? And a large mole on his left eyelid?

I checked and confirmed this.

You have rid the World of Atva Kuraisa, retired Junior Magician of the Order of Grilles and Mirrors. By the way, Melifaro still hasn't dug up anything about the yellow house. So you beat him.

I never thought it would possible to beat Melifaro at anything. Well, what do you advise?

Try to deal likewise with the second guy.

Do you have any idea who he might be?

Not a clue. Who knows whom Atva might have taken on as his accomplice? Echo is a big city with lots of tourists. First find him, then we'll know. By the way, did you run into Chvaxta?

Yes. He's some character.

Yes, that he is. Well, I won't keep you. Over and out.

It seems that little expression was my lasting contribution to the parlance of the Secret Investigative Force of the Capital of the Unified Kingdom.

＄

"Come here, Max!" Melamori called. "Here's the sinning trace. Enjoy!"

I went to stand on the spot she indicated.

"Well?" she said.

"Nothing so far. But I'm a slow learner."

I tried to focus on my own sensations. This time, as before, everything happened very abruptly. I wasn't feeling anything at all when all of a sudden my legs were carrying me deep into the forest, where the evening gloom was already gathering. My heart was heavy with uneasy forebodings, but I was determined to stifle them, for the time being, at least. I flew like the wind, and Melamori and the forester stayed right at my heels.

Soon, everything seemed to come to a standstill. I didn't know how to proceed. I took an uncertain step forward and froze in place, unable to budge or even to breathe. Melamori was clever enough to realize what was happening to me, and again she kicked me behind the knees, as she had done that morning. My heels tore away from the ground, and I collapsed in the grass, heaving a sigh of relief. I was alive.

"I should have seen that coming," Melamori said. "It was completely predictable."

"Predictable? What was?"

"Jiffa just picked up and carried the one whose trace you were following. The fellow must have been in pretty bad shape. And that's when you stumbled right onto Jiffa's trace. But they forgot one thing: I *can* follow Jiffa's trace. And if that wasn't enough, I'm starting to get mad."

"Really? Way to go," I said and got up off the grass, rubbing the backs of my knees. It was already the second time that day they had suffered a blow like that.

"It gets dark early in the forest at this time of year," the forester said with studied indifference, the way people remark about the weather in polite society. "Night will be falling soon. If that's important to you, you should hurry."

"It's not important, but we still have to hurry," Melamori said. "But where is that sinning trace?"

She stared sullenly at the path, stepped on it, then pressed forward at a quick pace. The forester and I followed right behind. I could hardly believe my eyes. Only this morning it had been painful to see how Melamori suffered from standing on the dead Jiffa's trace. Now, not only did she stoically endure it, she seemed to glow with an inner radiance that stemmed from both anger and joy.

"Are you already able to cope with him so easily?" I said.

"I don't know. But when I'm good and mad, it always seems to help. I think perhaps he's just grown weaker, Max. Much weaker. Send Juffin a call, all right? He should know."

"Is there anything he shouldn't know?"

I sent a call to our boss and told him the news.

Good job!

Sir Juffin loves praising his flock.

I think I can guess why it has become so easy for Melamori to follow Jiffa's trace, Juffin continued. *Do you know when he was killed?*

About thirty years ago?

No, I mean the time of day. He was killed about an hour after sundown—just the time it is now. Try to capture him as soon as possible. Toward morning his powers will increase again.

Ah, I see. Now it all made sense. *But is time always so significant for them?*

Yes, it is. Every living corpse grows weaker at the hour of his death, then gradually gathers strength until the sun travels half the sky. I wouldn't want you to have to catch him at dawn, as you tried to do this morning. So hurry it up.

If only it really depended on me.

Who else could it depend on? It depends on you alone.

"We're almost there." Melamori clutched at my looxi. "Here's the lair. But I can't call him like I did this morning. I don't know why, but it's not working."

We're here, I told Juffin. *I mean, we're at the lair but not inside.*

Don't worry, you won't get lost with Chvaxta. Keep an eye on him, though. He's a very reliable fellow, though not much of a warrior.

As if I am. Okay, over and out.

Over. Have a nice trip.

I shook my head. A nice trip, is it now? Some of Juffin's quotes should be recorded in a notebook for posterity.

"Well, what did he say?" Melamori said anxiously. She crouched down next to an enormous boulder overgrown with moss. Sir Chvaxta Chiyam peered into a crevice behind the rock with an expert eye.

"He says we're lucky. Jiffa's weak as a baby now, so this is the moment to go after him. He'll perk up again toward morning."

"Let's hurry." Melamori turned to the forester. "Do you know this entrance?"

"Of course. I know them all."

"Come on," I said. "Melamori, you go first, and I'll follow. And you, Sir Chvaxta, follow right behind me so that I don't get lost."

"How could you possibly get lost?" Melamori said.

"Well, I'm not at all sure I can find my way in the dark. So I'm not the best companion at a moment like this."

"Give me a break!"

And Melamori crawled down into the passage leading to the lair, with me close on her heels. The noisy breathing of our silent guide behind me assured me that he hadn't given way to a sudden urge to go home and drink a mug of kamra.

Crawling on all fours through an underground passageway stimulates the imagination. I felt as if Melamori and I were entering the Underworld. In search of a dead person, no less. "Abandon all hope, ye who enter here!" My sentiments exactly.

I couldn't help turning around and stealing a glance at our guide. His round eyes glittered in the darkness like two red flashlights. His face looked far older and more formidable than it did by daylight. I even shuddered: this man didn't resemble Virgil at all.

"You're Charon, Sir Chvaxta. The spitting image!" I said.

It's stupid, of course, to introduce references from a distant culture at a moment like this, but I was agitated. The words flew out of my mouth before I was aware of it.

"Why did you call me that, Sir Max?" the forester said politely.

"Because you're leading us to the Underworld." What else could I tell him?

"Oh, I understand," the remarkable man said without skipping a beat.

I smiled. He understands, huh? Well, I'll be.

The passage, in the meantime, had opened up and become high enough to stand up in.

"Soon it will get even larger," Sir Chvaxta said.

"I hope so," I said, trying to wipe off my hands, soiled from crawling through the passageway down to Hades.

Strange, it didn't pose any problem for me to follow Melamori, although it was pitch-black. Can I really see in the dark? I wondered. It was a curious thing. It was as dark as a dungeon, yet I had no trouble seeing what I really needed to see.

Meanwhile, Melamori was tapping and stamping lightly, feeling her way forward with her feet. I felt uneasy. Our clients were no doubt planning an evening of entertainment and unpleasant surprises to help us while away the time.

"Are they close by, Melamori?"

"Not yet. But I can sense that they're sticking to one spot. They're getting ready, I suppose. Maybe Jiffa is getting weaker and now feels as rotten as I felt this morning. I only wish."

"Be careful, okay? Like you always are, but more so. I don't like this 'second client' one bit."

"He's probably some bona fide Mutinous Magician," Melamori said dreamily. "But never mind, you'll just spit at him, and everything will be fine, right? Your poison kills anyone who isn't already dead, doesn't it?"

"I hope so. The main thing is for them to attack first."

"They already did attack first," Melamori said. "Anyway, you haven't seen me fight yet!"

"I can imagine," I said, grinning and rubbing my elbow, which had been sore since the morning.

We turned to the left. Then the path twisted sharply to the right. Now we were making loops in what had become a true labyrinth, and I could no longer keep track of where we were. I looked hopefully at our guide.

"Will you be able to find the way back?"

"The way back? Do you already need to return?"

"No, no. Afterward, I mean."

"We'll get out of here somehow, don't worry," Chvaxta Chiyam said, with a dismissive wave of the hand.

❧

We padded along, zigzagging through the underground realm. My companions were silent. By this time, I had no idea where we were or how we had come, but I trudged on behind Melamori, as though it were the whole point of our journey, and of my own existence besides.

"They're around here. Very close by," Melamori said. "Max, please help me stop. I really don't have much self-restraint, and it's not a place to rush into so eagerly. They are well prepared . . . She is, I mean."

"She?" My surprise didn't prevent me from grabbing Melamori in a rough embrace. This was a crude but reliable way to stop her in her tracks. She shrugged me off in annoyance.

"Thanks. You're so ardent and efficient. Yes, it's a she. Why are you so surprised, Max? Your man, the second client, is a *woman*. I know that for a fact at this point. Very bad for us."

"Why bad?"

Melamori sighed. "A woman presents a problem. A woman, even your average Echo city girl, can wreak havoc that you men can't even dream of when she's afraid."

"Excellent. We'll have a contest—who can wreak the greatest havoc from fear, she or I." I laughed nervously. "Is she pretty? I've got to get a life somehow!"

"Very funny," Melamori said. "As for her looks, you're about to find out for yourself."

She tried to hurry her pace in spite of my efforts to hold her back. She even jabbed me lightly in the stomach with her elbow.

"Take it easy, my darling. You're the one who asked me to hold you," I said.

"I'm not yours, and I'm not a darling!" Melamori said, flaring up.

"Fine. You are someone else's, and you're a shrew," I said.

At that, Melamori burst out laughing and slackened her pace. "I'm sorry," she said. "I got carried away. Now you know just what I was talking about!"

"Well, let's just say I can imagine it," I said. "Say, isn't it time for you to take shelter behind my big strong shoulders? I'm planning to spit poison and all that."

"We'll walk side by side," Melamori insisted. "You never know who should go first when Lonli-Lokli's not around."

"Yes, his presence solves a lot of problems. It's too bad he's not here with us."

"We'll manage," Melamori said with a toss of her head.

Then she took me by the hand, and we advanced toward the other couple, no less strange than we were. There was another twist in the passage, then one more . . .

I didn't realize what was happening: a mild but unexpected blow to the throat, an unpleasant grinding sound, a burning sensation as though a flaming scarf had encircled my neck. My breath stopped for a moment. I plunged through the darkness gasping for breath, but couldn't reach the bottom, and in panic I grappled to reach the surface. Finally I burst through and was able to take my first gulp of air.

Everything ended as suddenly as it had begun. I was trembling violently—the usual reaction of someone who has been frightened to death. My throat and neck were still burning, but I could afford to ignore it since I knew the cause.

Melamori, screaming in a strange, guttural voice, let go of my hand and ran to take shelter behind the next bend in the passage. I tore after her.

There a new kind of darkness awaited us. In contrast to the former, almost tame gloom defined by the low ceilings of the passageway, here the nearly infinite blackness of open space reigned. As before, however, despite the cover of darkness, I could see everything I needed to see. I saw Melamori's bare foot planted in the stomach of a fair-haired woman whose outstretched arms shone with a livid glow. This malign luster was wrapping itself around Melamori's head like a hazy cloud.

I froze in horror. Something dreadful was happening. I couldn't have explained what it was, but I knew it was appalling.

A moment later the woman was lying on the ground. Melamori was a consummate fighter! But the blow that had felled the predator changed nothing. The pale haze that circled Melamori's head grew more and more viscous. I shouted in a frantic voice and almost mechanically snapped the fingers of my left hand, aiming my Lethal Sphere at the woman. Now I knew exactly what I wanted from her: I needed her to save Melamori by sticking her own head into the sinning mist. For some reason I never doubted that this was the only way.

The green sphere of lightning struck the forehead of the woman with a sickening *thwack*. She raised her eyes and looked at me with serene, unadulterated hatred. To be honest, it was a marvelous sight. But almost immediately her fiery gaze was extinguished. Her eyes grew dull and remote. The malevolent beauty stretched out her arm in front of her. The hazy cloud began to tremble and then disperse.

"Don't destroy it. Take it back!" I roared, getting ready to snap my deadly fingers again just in case.

The woman shuddered. Her hands fluttered up around her temples, the pale haze thickened around her own head, and she went limp.

"That's better," I said. "It's so satisfying to bring an experiment to its logical conclusion and watch what happens."

"What is happening, Max? Are you alive?" Melamori was sitting on the ground, looking around in bewilderment, but she seemed to have come through the ordeal unscathed.

Praise be the Magicians, it's over, I thought. I had no strength to utter a single word out loud. I looked at Melamori and smiled from ear to ear with relief.

A powerful jolt knocked me off my feet. What a fool I was to assume it was all over! An explosive din, the terrified scream of Melamori, and my own howls of indignation and outrage all combined to produce a short but heart-rending avant-garde piece for two voices and firearm.

There was no pain, though theoretically I should have been writhing in agony just about now. But no, my body had not yet had time to register it. This didn't prevent me from sitting on the floor and staring with dull interest at a rent in my looxi, at the blood and splinters of glass covering my clothing. Sinning Magicians, what blood? My fingers were drenched in priceless Elixir of Kaxar. There was some blood, but just a little. A few shards of the bottle had grazed my skin, nothing more.

"Aaiiie! You deceased filth, you!" Melamori threw herself at Jiffa, whom I had somehow forgotten about completely, and fastened onto him with a deadly grip. "Max, he shot you with the Baboom, can you believe it? I might have expected anything but this! This is going too far."

"I'll say. But we're dealing with a beast, after all."

"Yes, a beauty and a beast. What did you do to her, by the way?"

"I'm still not sure. Let me edge over here a bit closer. Now then, take that!"

I snapped the fingers of my left hand, and a green ball of lightning sped straight toward Jiffa's forehead. I was determined not to kill the red-haired robber before he could answer my questions. He didn't die. He went limp, just as I had hoped.

"I am with you, Master," Jiffa said.

Melamori sighed with relief and left the brigand in peace.

"I guess your shields didn't work, Jiffa," I said. "Talk about bragging! Well, sit here quietly, you abomination." And I turned to the woman. "Well, how are we feeling now? Not too well, I hope."

"Max, whatever did you do to her?" Melamori bent over our exquisite victim. There was a slightly hysterical note in her voice.

"I'm telling you, I don't know. Oh, sinning Magicians!" I gasped.

I was finally able to get a good look at my handiwork. A beautiful female body was lying on the ground, sheathed in a black looxi, but its head was that of a bird. It was a dead bird's head, with a pitiful, half-open predator's beak.

"I've never seen anything like it!" Melamori whispered. "How did you do it?"

"I didn't do anything. She did it herself!" I said. "I just convinced her that she needed to try her experiment on herself first, not another person. I think it's only fair. Look at my neck, by the way! It hurts like the devil."

"It's a burn," Melamori said, shaking her head in sympathy. "It's unpleasant but nothing serious if you consider that otherwise your head might have been around the corner, some distance away from your body."

"What do you mean?"

"Don't you understand what happened? However did you stay alive at all?"

"But what was it?" Suddenly I was gripped with fear, though it was already too late for this. In fact it was time to rejoice that it was all behind me.

"It was . . . Oh, Max, they launched the Thin Death at you! Haven't you ever heard of it?"

I shook my head. "What kind of odious thing is it?"

"It's a steel plate, much thinner than a human hair, almost invisible. It homes in on the victim by itself, so it doesn't even require any special skill from the one who launches it. It always slices off the head; it has absolutely no interest in other parts of the body. During the Epoch of Orders it was the most renowned weapon, though still very rare. Only a few of the Orders had preserved the tradition of using it. It's a terrible thing! When I saw the rainbow-colored sheen around your neck, I almost lost my mind. Oh, Max, I'm so glad you're all right!" Then Melamori sniffed loudly and wiped her nose.

"Well, we're on the same page there," I said with absolute sincerity, stroking my burning neck absently. Then it dawned on me. "You know, I'm the luckiest person in the Universe!" My voice cracked and a slight sob escaped. My imagination is too obliging, so the vision of my own head a few feet away from my body hovered before my mind's eye. I must admit, it was a sad sight.

"Did you just realize that?"

"No, but do you know what I did before I left home?"

"What?"

"I donned my talisman—the kerchief of the Grand Magician of the

Order of the Secret Grass. It's something Juffin entrusted to me, and after my return from Kettari he told me never to fall asleep without wearing it. In short, I thought our little hike might turn out to be a protracted affair and I would want to take a snooze at some point. And since I'm so scatterbrained, I put it on right away, just in case. Now the old rag is gone. I guess it burned up along with the Thin Death, or whatever it's called."

"The kerchief of Grand Magician Xonna?" Melamori frowned. "Yes, Max, you are incredibly lucky. Xonna's kerchief is probably the only thing that could protect you from the Thin Death."

"Ah, so that's his name. It's the first time I've ever heard it."

"That's because hardly anyone knows it. And whoever knows it has no desire to speak the name aloud. You see, the Order of the Secret Grass was renowned for its methods of defense. The members were very peace-loving people, compared to those in other Orders. They never attacked first, but they knew thousands of defense tactics against any danger or threat—including the Thin Death, luckily for you. As for the name of the Grand Magician, you can utter it out loud only if you are well disposed toward him. Otherwise you'll die on the spot, and no wisewoman or healer can save you. It's one of his little eccentricities."

"And yet you risk it?" I asked, alarmed.

"Oh, it's no risk for me. Grand Magician Xonna was one of my childhood heroes. And since his kerchief saved your life, I'd even throw myself at his feet if he showed up here!"

"Thank you, Melamori." Her confession just about left me speechless. "But where is he now, this Man with the Terrible Name? What is he doing?"

"No one knows. He went off to wander somewhere. In the very heat of the battle for the Code, he lost interest in the whole business. He announced that practicing magic in Uguland, the very Heart of the World, was without merit. A true wizard must acquire his powers in the back of beyond. In short, he abandoned everything and left his men to deal with the mess of war by themselves. But why am I telling you all this? Ask Melifaro—all his relatives were in thick with the Order of the Secret Grass. If it weren't for the Code, our Melifaro would be one of the Junior Magicians there."

"I'll ask him about it," I said. "Hey, where's our guide, the marvelous Sir Chvaxta?"

"I have no idea," Melamori said, looking around uneasily. "Could he have run off without us?"

"Juffin told me to keep an eye on him because he wasn't much of a warrior. As if we had time for keeping an eye on him! I'll bet he's already home by now."

Melamori gave a hearty laugh. I reflected for a moment, then chimed in. We sat on the ground at the feet of the surrealistic corpse with the bird's head and howled with laughter. It was impossible to stop ourselves, but after the adventures we had just had, it was no wonder.

"Chvaxta is very lucky that you didn't kill Jiffa. If you had, there would have been only one way to get out of here: standing on the trace of that deserter. Maybe we should punish the coward anyway?"

"No, we must spare Chvaxta. He's a funny fellow."

"Funny, yes." Melamori smiled uncertainly.

"Well, shall we go get a bit of fresh air?" I said.

"I'd love to! Call your trusty slave."

"Here Jiffa," I ordered.

The sad, red-haired dead man who had caused us so much trouble approached obediently.

"Take us up to the surface. By the shortest route. Understand?"

"Yes, Master."

I helped Melamori off the ground, and Jiffa led the way into the depths of the spacious underground chamber.

Melamori was still contemplating the deceased dame with the bird's head. "She wanted to turn me into that, didn't she, Max?"

"Who else was there but you? She thought I was already a goner. But don't dwell on it. It didn't happen."

"How did you deal with her?"

"Exactly how I dealt with the other undead. Lonli-Lokli says the Lethal Sphere obeys my inner desires. And in the depths of my soul, according to his theory, I don't want to kill people so much as to subjugate their wills like any run-of-the-mill tyrant or despot. Luckily, Shurf is an excellent theoretician."

"That's for sure. And you, praise be the Magicians, are good at putting theory into practice. I wonder who she is? I feel that I know her from somewhere."

"Who is this woman, Jiffa?" I asked my vassal.

"Lady Tanna Kuraisa, Master."

"Yes, of course! It's Magician Atva's sister," Melamori said. "He dragged her into this mess. What a wretch!"

"Did he lure her into it, or did she lure him, Jiffa?" I said. "Tell us how it was."

"Lady Tanna was in love with me," Jiffa said impassively. "I spent a few nights with her, but I attached no significance to it. When the retired Magicians deprived me of my band of men, Tanna forced her brother to find a way to return my life to me. Tanna was quite a witch herself: she had been brought up by the women of the Order of Grilles and Mirrors. But she had no knowledge of how to revive the dead. The women of the Orders are rarely taught how to do such trivial things. Atva feared her very much. At first his sister threatened to kill him for taking part in the hunt, but she spared him when he agreed to help her. As you can see, Atva restored my life to me, but he did a poor job of it. It would have been better if he had left well enough alone . . . At first I was just a moribund puppet like the rest of the undead. I wasn't the real Jiffa Savanxa. So I don't know how I lived in those first years. I simply don't remember. But Tanna didn't waste any time. She was a fast learner. Little by little, drop by drop, she returned my real life to me until at last I had become the person I was before they killed me. That happened early one morning in autumn, almost six years ago. I remember the day well. A cold wind was blowing, so strong the branches broke off the trees and fell to the ground, and a strange bird was screeching in the yard." Jiffa went silent, then murmured, "Now Tanna is dead, and almost nothing remains of me. It must be that some spells die with their conjurors."

"Well, you're in a fine mess," I said with real sympathy. "That's what you call 'love unto the grave.' And beyond, too. What all-conquering passion! All right, Jiffa. I think I understand your story, but who revived the others?"

"I did," Jiffa said blandly. "Magician Atva helped me a little. It wasn't very hard. But I couldn't make them as they were before, and Tanna didn't want me to. She didn't like the whole affair."

"Didn't like it?" I said in surprise. "She started the whole thing herself!"

"Tanna only wanted me. She thought if she restored my life to me I would stay with her forever, grateful and submissive. But I wanted to go back to the Magaxon Forest. I missed my former way of life. There was always a sense of something lacking, something that would make me feel completely alive again if I could only find it, and I thought—"

"You thought that if you went back to the forest and gathered your band of men around you, everything would be just as it used to be?"

"Yes," Jiffa said. "But nothing came of it. I found stupid puppets in place of my former merry men, and an emptiness in my chest in place of my former joyous heart. That's the worst thing—knowing something could be much better than it really is. Tell me, are you going to kill me now?"

"Probably. What else can I do with you?"

"That's good," he nodded, pleased.

Meanwhile, the earthen vaults were pressing down on us. Soon we had to begin crawling on our hands and knees. Then we emerged outside again and found ourselves in the same ravine where we had had our little picnic earlier that morning. Or in another one that looked just like it.

It was dark, damp, and very dank. While we had been wandering through the lairs of the Magaxon brigands, here, on the surface of the earth, it had been raining. I started shivering from the cold, and Melamori's teeth chattered. Only Jiffa remained unaffected by the climatic inconsistencies.

"Where is our amobiler? That's what I'd like to know." Melamori looked around angrily. "Grrr, just wait till I get my hands on that so-called guide."

"I've got a bag there with warm things," I said, and turned to face Jiffa. "Show us the entrance to the lair that you and Lady Tanna used earlier today."

"As you wish."

He turned around and marched into a thicket with a determined stride. We followed after him. Wet branches lashed at our faces, and mud squelched under our feet.

"I sent a call to Sir Juffin, Max," Melamori said. "I told him everything was fine. I described what happened—without all the details, of course. We'll get around to those later. I wanted to know whether we should deliver Jiffa to the House by the Bridge."

"And?"

"He said no," Melamori said.

"That's good. Why should he go back to Echo, a place he never really loved? Let him die here in his own forest, where he already died once before."

Jiffa, meanwhile, had stopped by the enormous boulder that marked the entrance to the lair.

"Here we are," he said. "Is that all? Will you kill me now?"

"Hold on a minute. Take us to the amobiler. Do you remember where you dumped it?"

"Yes." Jiffa set out hurriedly along a little footpath.

"Have you really found out everything you needed to know from him?" Melamori asked.

"I sure haven't! Thanks for reminding me. Where did you hide the treasures you robbed, Jiffa? In the lair?"

"No. We gave it to Atva, and he took it all away. I never even asked him where. Maybe he squandered it all—I don't know. It didn't matter to us. We didn't need it. We just robbed because we were used to that way of life."

"And who killed those who took part in the Royal Hunt? I mean all those Junior Magicians who killed you and your men back in the day?"

"No one killed them. Tanna cast a spell on them when she knew for certain that they had done her a disservice. She realized I would never be the way I used to be, and wouldn't stay with her, either. The women of the Order of Grilles and Mirrors know how to conjure, that they do. Tanna staged her brother's death just to deflect suspicions. Someone might have wondered why, of all the hunters chasing down the Magaxon Foxes, only Atva remained alive. Besides, she was afraid they would catch me and there would be dire consequences for her and her brother. Tanna was very angry with Atva and me when we revived the others and took up robbing again. Strange, isn't it? She must really have loved me—even the person I became only through her efforts. She stopped short of nothing. Atva died soon after you stepped on his trace. He always was a weakling. But Tanna—it didn't affect her in the least. It only made her furious. Well, here we are. There are the amobilers. I'm very tired. I feel that I'm fading away altogether. Soon there won't be anything left of me at all, only an inane walking and talking body, as stupid as all the others. I'm frightened! Better kill me while I'm still here."

"All right."

I felt no pity for Jiffa, but I was on his side in this story. I hate coercion, and what they had done to him seemed to me to be the worst form of coercion imaginable. I looked at the face of the red-haired robber, still beautiful but carved with wrinkles and gash-like scars, and I chuckled grimly to myself. Yeah, it's dangerous to be a ladies' man.

That's when I made my decision.

"I order you to become the real Jiffa Savanxa," I said firmly, with no second thoughts but not really understanding what I was doing. "I order you to vacate this World, to discover the place where Jiffa Savanxa will be happy, and to become him there. Come on, mate, do it!"

Dead Jiffa's dull eyes flashed with evil, joyous fire. He stared at me with hatred and admiration at the same time. Then he collapsed in the grass, bellowing not so much in pain as in ecstasy, and disappeared.

I slumped down on the ground, wiping the cold sweat from my forehead. I felt sicker than I had ever felt before.

"Max, what's all this about?" Melamori said in horror. "What have you done?"

"I don't really know," I said. "I think I may have restored justice. I think I acted right, but then why do I feel so wretched? And the bottle of Elixir of Kaxar shattered. Thanks to our dead redhead, by the way."

"Is it that bad?"

"Well, not so bad. Fair to middling bad. I just don't have an ounce of strength left, that's all."

"Why do you need to be strong now? We're going home. I'll take the levers, and you can lie down in the back seat. Sleep a little bit if you wish. Everything is over, isn't it?"

"I hope so. Help me stand up. I'm so dizzy."

Melamori held out her hand to me. Easily, as though I weighed nothing, she lifted me up from the wet grass and helped me into the amobiler. She climbed into the driver's seat. I stretched out in the back. I had to stick my legs out the window, but this pose was very much to my liking. I closed my eyes and got ready to dive into sweet slumber.

§

"Max, it won't start!" Melamori yelped, jolting me out of my blissful paralysis.

"Why? What could be wrong?" I groaned.

"Probably something with the crystal. It could have shattered from the impact of our crash. Let me take a look."

I heard the door slam, the hood creak as it opened reluctantly, and a few mild curses, after which the lady returned to her spot in the driver's seat.

"Just as I thought. It's broken, the rotten stinker!" she fumed.

"This is bad." I drew myself up into a sitting position and paused to think. Actually, there was nothing to think about. The magic crystal is the heart of the amobiler. Without it the sinning buggy won't move an inch.

"I'll have to send a call to Juffin," I said wearily. "Someone will have to come after us. It's not the end of the world."

"All the same, it's frustrating." Suddenly Melamori almost jumped out of the seat. "Look, Max, someone's coming!"

I tried to brace myself, just in case. You never know who might come along.

"Is that you? Where did you both rush off to? I was looking everywhere for you underground," Chvaxta the forester said, sticking his head through the window. "Is everything okay? Do you want some nuts?" A handful of damp nuts rained down on the seat, and a few rolled onto the floor.

Melamori and I looked at each other in astonishment, then burst out laughing. This was too much!

"Do you have an amobiler, Sir Chvaxta?" Melamori asked.

"Yes, at home, of course. Why don't you want to go home in this one? You don't like it?"

"Like it?" Melamori giggled. "Sinning Magicians, our crystal shattered!"

"Really? That's strange," the forester said, shaking his head. "Well, let's go to my place."

"Is it far?" I said.

"No. Close. An hour and a half by foot, not more."

"No way! Thank you very much, but no. I'm just spent. I couldn't make it that far if my life depended on it. How about this: you go home, get the amobiler, and come back for us. Sound good?"

"Okay. I'll be back in two hours. But don't go anywhere without me. You might get lost."

❀

"Do you think he'll come back?" Melamori said when the forester had disappeared into the undergrowth. "Maybe it would be better to send Juffin a call. It would take them five hours or so to get here, but they are certainly more reliable."

"Let's just hope Chvaxta keeps his promises. The guy is completely nuts, but he came to us with Juffin's stamp of approval."

"I think it must have been one of our boss's more questionable jokes. Did you hear him ask us where we had rushed off to?"

"All the same, I think he'll return," I insisted. "Two hours isn't too long. And if I take a little nap, I may be able to drive. Another hour and we'll be home. Maybe even sooner if I'm on a roll."

"Of course, try to sleep," Melamori urged. "And I'll—"

"Sit down beside me, okay? What if I have a nightmare or something?"

"After the adventures we've just been through it wouldn't surprise me in the least."

"Aw, shucks. What are a few little adventures? All the same, I don't have my talismanic kerchief, and Sir Juffin said that . . ." My head fell back on the soft seat, and I dropped off to sleep in mid-sentence.

This time my dreams took me so far there was no farther to go. I dreamed that I was in a completely empty place. There was nothing there. It's impossible to describe or explain, but there was truly nothing: no space, no time, no light, no darkness, no height, no depth, no gravity, no weightlessness. There was no me. At least, being present there didn't mean the same thing as *being*. More like the contrary.

Somehow I already knew the rules of the game. A few of them, anyway. I could get anywhere I wanted to from here. Not just to any city but to any World, uninhabited or inhabited. And to my surprise there were multitudes of them. I felt not only that I could but that I *had* to plunge into one of these unknown realities. I knew it would be dangerous to hesitate. If I didn't take the initiative, one of the Worlds would take me by force.

The Doors between Worlds—Juffin and Maba Kalox had often mentioned them to me. I had been dying to learn what they were like, and now I had the answer to that question. There was nothing here at all except those sinning Doors between Worlds! And they had all been flung wide open, as if to welcome me inside.

I stood frozen in the emptiness, knowing that now one of the Worlds would take me and that I would never find my way back to Echo. This seemed to me to be a disaster. I wanted to go home. What did it matter where and when I was born? My place was in Echo, and I wanted to stay there, because . . . *it was right*.

I had to get out of here immediately. To go back to the Magaxon Forest, to the broken-down amobiler of the Ministry of Perfect Public Order, where Sir Max, that me I very much liked being, remained. But I didn't know which of the doors in this eternity led home.

I demanded of myself that I stay. Easier said than done! The unknown Worlds were determined to get hold of me. I sensed their hunger and their power, which were absolutely indifferent to my desires, hopes, and plans for the future. With what could I counter this power? I had only my inborn obstinacy, which had almost driven my parents to an early grave. That and an irrational fondness for the mosaic pavements of Echo, and the habit of starting my morning with a mug of kamra. Not to forget my love for my friends, a feeling that was clear and profound, and that I had hardly even suspected until now. And the gray eyes of Melamori that reflected our mutual disappointment, and the longing for that which could never be ours. But even these things were not enough. I felt that I was disappearing, slowly but surely sinking into the crevice of another reality, and a new, already delineated fate.

※

A resounding slap brought me back to reality. I jerked awake, stunned, discombobulated, and boundlessly happy. I didn't remember where I was or what had happened at first. I just felt that I had been snatched back in the nick of time from some terrible danger. But what kind of danger was it?

Melamori, pale and shaken, was looking deep into my eyes.

"What happened?" I asked. "Why are you slapping me? Did I try to make a pass at you or something? I know I do all kinds of things in my dreams, but I never thought I'd stoop to that."

"Sinning Magicians, as if that were all that had happened! That would have been nothing! I'm sorry for slapping you, Max, but I had to wake you. You began to *disappear*. I was afraid that in another moment you would disappear altogether."

"That's not good." I shook my head, trying to come to my senses. "Where could I have gone? That's ridiculous. And what did it look like?"

"It was terrifying. When you fell asleep I sent a call to Sir Juffin to fill him in on the details of our hunt for Jiffa. At the same time I asked him to send a call to that crazy forester, to make sure he didn't decide to just go to bed and leave us without an amobiler. Then we gossiped a bit, you know how I goes."

"I know." I smiled in spite of myself. "And what happened then?"

"Then he told me that I should keep an eye on you, that your heart wasn't in the right place because you were sleeping without your talisman. Just in time! When I looked at you, you had already become half-transparent and were growing more so with every passing second. It was happening so fast! I was scared to death. Then I realized that if some misfortune was underway in your sleep I ought to wake you up. And that everything might be all right then. Obviously, I was right."

"Yes, you were," I said rubbing my jowls, still sore where she had slapped me. "How smart you are! Something terrible was happening to me, but what was it? I can't seem to remember."

"Max, I think you have to force yourself to recall it. Please, you must!"

"I'll try. Make sure I don't start to disappear, though. And don't slap the living daylights out of me next time, okay?"

"Did it hurt a lot?" asked this fragile lady with the strength of ten men. Then, blushing violently, she said, "I'm sorry, Max. I didn't mean to hurt you."

"Never mind," I said with a smile. "I enjoyed it in a way. Sort of. I'll save this bruise as a memento of a wonderful evening together. There must be some way to keep it from fading."

"I think the only way is to repeat the procedure from time to time," Melamori said tenderly. "I'm prepared to do it every day if you like. But don't get distracted, Max. Think. Try to remember."

Don't get distracted. Easy to say at a moment like this.

I closed my eyes, tried to relax, and allowed myself to doze off. Not to fall asleep but to doze, to inhabit the delicate, intangible threshold between sleep and waking. This is my tried-and-true method for trying to remember what I have just dreamed. It worked this time, too.

I was nearly suffocated by the flood of memories that poured over me, so strong it almost pulled me back down into sleep. I opened my eyes just in time, however, and, overmastering myself, shook my head free of the sweet vestiges of slumber.

"Were you able to remember? Was it really that bad?" Melamori asked. "You look like you're in shock!"

"It seems pretty bad . . . or maybe not. It's hard to tell. I'll send Juffin a call—he should be able to explain what happened to me. It seems I could have just disappeared into oblivion. Can you imagine? May I take your hand? I'm scared."

Melamori nodded and grabbed my big paw between her icy palms. I calmed down a little, then sent a call to Sir Juffin Hully. I hastily told him my strange dream. Juffin didn't interrupt me a single time, which was already suspicious.

I must say I expected something like this, the boss replied when I had finished my incoherent story. *It's good the talisman saved your life, but I'm very worried that it perished. I don't have another one. In fact, it was the only one of its kind. The Grand Magician of the Order of the Secret Grass had only one kerchief, unfortunately. He didn't like superfluity, you see. Don't worry, Max. This just means that you'll have to learn a few things very quickly. You would have had to acquire the wis-*

dom of traveling between Worlds eventually, in any case. I just thought it could wait a few years. Well, it's common to assume that it's all for the best. Maybe it is. Now you just have to prevent yourself from falling asleep until you reach me. Can you manage?

I can manage. Juffin, will I really be okay? I don't want to leave Echo.

What if the new World is as wonderful as Kettari? he asked cunningly. *You still wouldn't want to go there?*

No. I need to be here, in Echo. I so much want to . . . I can't explain it.

No need to explain, Max. I'm glad to hear you say this since everything really does depend only on you. Everything will be fine as long as you don't doze off before you see me, I promise.

There's no way I'll fall asleep. But when I'm awake . . . they can't take me from here, can they?

No, as long as you're awake no one can spirit you away. Over and out.

Melamori noticed my attention was no longer so focused and threw a questioning glance my way.

"Juffin says that everything will be fine," I told her. "The main thing is not to fall asleep. And I won't. What do you think, Melamori, will Chvaxta get back soon? Has it been two hours yet?"

"Almost."

Melamori crawled into the back seat, sat close beside me, and put her arm around my shoulders.

"Don't disappear, Max, all right?" she said.

"I'm not planning on it. You won't get rid of me that easily."

"This is no time for joking. I don't want to get rid of you. You know, everything is so trivial in comparison with this. It just doesn't matter. You've scared me to death three times today already—first with the Thin Death, then the shot from the Baboom, and now this. But here you are sitting beside me, and I'm so glad, enormously glad!"

"The feeling is mutual."

I tried to laugh, but an embarrassing sniffle came out instead. And not for the first time that day. I was really letting myself go!

Melamori and I sat in a silent embrace. We tried with all our might not to burst into tears, both from a kind of deep sadness and inexpressible joy. It was such a perfect moment that I never wanted it to end.

The noise of an approaching amobiler jerked us out of our pleasant stupor and returned us to reality. The large round eyes of the forester stared at us from the window.

"Are you sad?" he said. "You shouldn't be so sad about an amobiler, especially an official one."

Melamori and I exchanged looks and burst out laughing. This possibility was just too absurd. Sir Chvaxta got out and came over to us while we were recovering from this latest bout of hilarity. Then he asked in a concerned voice, "Do you need me to accompany you back to Echo, or can you make it by yourselves?"

"Of course we'll make it on our own," I said. "Thank you for rescuing us, though." I moved behind the levers of the forester's new amobiler. "We'll send someone back tomorrow. He'll return your buggy to you and pick up this wreck"—I waved in the direction of our defunct means of transportation—"after he supplies it with a new crystal."

"You think of everything, Max," Melamori said with gentle irony. "But are you sure you haven't forgotten anything?"

"I don't think so."

"What about this?" She waved my traveling bag in front of my face triumphantly.

"Oh, that. Of course," I said and smiled sheepishly. "I've got a sieve for a head. Throw it in back there somewhere, and get in beside it. I'm going to take you for a ride. Good night, Sir Chvaxta. Thank you for your help."

"Did I really help you?" The forester seemed surprised. "Good night. What a strange bunch you are after all, you Secret Investigators."

�֍

I drove through the forest very cautiously, much more cautiously than usual. I didn't want to wreck yet another amobiler. But when we finally turned onto the highway, I gave myself free rein. We were flying so fast that it seemed the wheels hardly touched the ground. Melamori was elated.

"Could I do that, too, do you think?" she said timidly.

"You can do even more."

She smiled with pleasure. "Really?"

"Really."

We were silent for the rest of the way home. No language contains the words we wanted to speak, and the crazy flight through the darkness offered a perfect alternative. It was even better.

"Here we are," Melamori said faintly, when I turned onto the Street of Copper Pots and stopped at the Secret Entrance to the House by the Bridge.

"Yep, it's the end of the line," I said. "You know, where I come from that expression has another meaning, too. Like 'Now we've done it,' or 'We're sunk,' or, as Anday Pu would say, 'The dinner's over once and for all!'"

"How true!" Melamori said laughing, and together we went into Headquarters.

❄

Sir Juffin Hully was sitting in his armchair just staring into space. I was always a bit afraid of his vacant stare, which seemed as heavy as an anvil. But when he saw us he broke into a smile and even stood up to greet us.

"Well, you certainly sorted out Jiffa and his ladylove," he said. "The boys next door in the Police Department will be glad to know that you're so keen on justice, and that you even know how to restore it when you're lucky. You were marvelous, too, Melamori, especially the restraint you showed. Please accept my congratulations! Well, I guess that's about it, then."

"The highest form of praise would be some Elixir of Kaxar," I grumbled. "I'm about to collapse from exhaustion. Did you hear about the sad fate of my own precious bottle?"

"I heard, I heard. And to think it's the first time you managed to take your own bottle with you and not mine!"

"Fate gives wise counsel," I said pedantically. "From now on I shall just filch your supplies."

"Iron logic," Juffin said, reaching into his desk drawer. "Okay, take it, you sponger. We need to petition Sir Dondi Melixis to open a new category of expenditures to cover your little penchant."

I took two enormous gulps of Elixir of Kaxar. The delightful vitality and cheer of a person refreshed from good night's sleep—how I loved the sensation! I felt light as a breeze again. Life seemed simple and wondrous. I closed my eyes in ecstasy.

"Delicious." I turned to Melamori. "I highly recommend it."

"I think I'd rather just go home and sleep for two dozen hours," she said. "And you really won't be needing me for now." Then she looked at the boss. "Sir Juffin, Max won't disappear anymore, will he? Are you sure of that?"

"I'm sure. And if he disappears, I'll snatch him back from wherever he ends up. I give you my word of honor. Are you satisfied?"

"Yes." Melamori put on the sad semblance of a smile, then came up to me and kissed me on the cheek, quite unexpectedly. "I hope I'm allowed to do that, at least," she said with a slightly bitter grin. "No objections from that bitch Destiny, the Order of Dark Magicians, and other Jackasses of Fate. Good night, gentlemen. I'm asleep on my feet already."

"Morning. It's already morning, Melamori. So good morning," Juffin called after her as she was leaving.

I just stood there with my mouth agape, like a fish on dry land. Juffin looked at me with sympathetic curiosity and shrugged helplessly. There was nothing else to say.

"Well, what are we going to do now?" I said.

"We are going to eat. Have breakfast. In short, we're going to stuff ourselves. We'll wait for the lads, we'll shift all the worries of this Refuge for the Mad onto their able shoulders, and we'll go to my house. You will go off to the Land of Nod. I'll sing you a lullaby. Maba has promised to hum along, so there's absolutely nothing to fear. After our musical accompaniment, you'll wake up just where you're supposed to, I guarantee it."

"I don't doubt that," I said smiling. "But what then? Will you and Maba sit next to me and hold my hand every time I go to sleep? You're going to get tired of that pretty quick, I'm sure."

"No, no, no. A problem like this has to be resolved once and for all. If this place has its eye on you, it's not going to let you go just like that. There's only one way out of the dilemma: you have to go there with an experienced guide. You'll pass through this fantastic labyrinth, look behind all the Doors, see the Worlds that they conceal, and learn to distinguish them by light and smell. What I mean to say is that you will have a map at your disposal. If the Corridor between Worlds beckons you again, you won't be an unhappy victim but a cheerful voyager, and you yourself will choose where to go. You will decide yourself when you wish to return. I think it will be a grand adventure. You really are very lucky, Max. I know quite a few powerful people who for centuries tried to go there, but it didn't want to receive them. But you it welcomes with open arms. Many Grand Magicians of old would be very jealous, if they only knew."

"The idea does have its appeal. But what then?" I asked again. "Am I doomed to go to that place again every time I fall asleep? To the Corridor between Worlds? And what about my other dreams? Maybe they're paltry ones in comparison with the infinity of new Worlds, but I still don't want to lose them. I don't want to lose anything, Juffin."

"If you don't want to, you won't," the boss said. "You still don't understand, Max. You won't be the *prisoner* of this strange place. You'll become its *master*. Do you still not fathom what that means?"

"Do *you*?" I said with a sinking heart.

"Yes. I know my way around there quite well. So I know what I'm talking about. Eat, Sir Max. Life is wonderful!"

I bent my head over my plate obediently. I had definitely worked up an appetite. What's true is true.

❀

Half an hour later, a weary Sir Kofa joined us.

"Well, did the Magaxon Foxes suffer a total rout, my boy?" he said heartily. "It seems you played your hand very skillfully."

"You think so?" I was flattered. In contrast to Juffin, Sir Kofa was very sparing with his compliments.

"That's what I say. What I really think is my own business, right?" said the Master Eavesdropper, grinning. Then he grew more serious. "The whole city talks of nothing else. And will talk of nothing else for who knows how long. It's a cause célèbre. Is it true that you lugged a bag with the head of Red Jiffa to the Ministry? The Echo dwellers are sure that you plan to hang it on display outside your house. They think it's your custom back there in the Barren Lands."

"Good morning, gentlemen." Lonli-Lokli appeared at the door and looked at me attentively, then shook his head. "So my premonitions didn't deceive me?" he asked. "You look pretty disheveled."

"At least I'm alive."

"I should hope so." Shurf sat down next to me and filled his mug with kamra.

"Have you been scarfing for a long time, or are you just starting?" Melifaro said, sticking his head into the office. "Anyway, I want some, too. I'm as tired as all get-out. Max, did you really schlep the head of that poor guy back with you? Do you really think that's funny? Personally, I think you've gone too far"

I sighed, and Juffin and Kofa laughed with sardonic glee.

"But do you know where the plunder of the Magaxon Foxes was?" Melifaro said proudly. "Mr. Nightmare, you're going to eat your skaba!"

"I can guess." It suddenly dawned on me. "In their amobiler, right?

They planned to hightail it out of Echo forever. Of course Sir Atva packed up his loot for the escape. What a nitwit I am! It never even occurred to me to search their sinning buggy. How did you find out? Did you already have time to drive to the Magaxon Forest and back? Pardon me for not believing you."

"Like I don't have better things to do than traipse back and forth to the Magaxon Forest. It was the forester who found it—that character Sir Chvaxta. I figure he filled his own pockets with the loot and sent me a call afterward. That's just what I'd expect from him. But never mind, he's got a reward coming to him for his good deed, in any case."

Melifaro fell silent, plunked down in the armchair, and began chomping loudly on some crisp pastries. I carried on with my self-reproach.

"Don't beat yourself up over it, Max. You can't hold it against a person who was nearly killed twice over," Juffin said. "You probably didn't even remember about the plunder, did you?"

"I remembered once, and I even asked Jiffa where it was, but I forgot about it almost immediately."

"Well, don't worry. You've got to trip up sometime. Otherwise, you'll become so insufferably perfect that no one will want to have anything to do with you." Juffin got out of his chair and stood up decisively. "Let's go, Max."

"Okay." I stood up and stretched luxuriously. "Good morning, guys." I went to the door but turned around just before I reached it. "Thanks for being who you are. Without you my life would just be one big blunder."

I felt a lump rising to my throat, so I rushed out into the corridor. Juffin caught up with me by the entrance to the building.

"Way to go, Max. You've got to say some things out loud from time to time."

❀

Sir Juffin Hully's amobiler was already waiting for us outside. Old Kimpa was sitting at the levers. I could relax. They wouldn't let me sit behind these levers at any price.

On the drive home we didn't say a word. Juffin seemed to be having a conversation in Silent Speech with some distant interlocutor. I wanted to get the impending improbable adventure over with. If I couldn't wriggle out of it, well then, the sooner the better.

"Welcome, Sir Max." Juffin made a comic bow, throwing the door to the bedroom wide open. I froze for a moment in the doorway and marched into the room. What would be, would be.

With that I quickly undressed and settled down comfortably under the fur blanket. I closed my eyes and tried to relax. The fair amount of Elixir of Kaxar I had downed didn't seem to make a bit of difference. I was dead tired. After a few minutes of pleasant hovering between sleep and wakefulness, I conked out.

I still can't make sense of what I dreamed about to this day. I remember a number of disconnected episodes, but I can't make them cohere into a single picture. Not anymore, at least.

I glimpsed a multitude of Worlds, some real and some that disappeared long ago. And some that exist only in the imaginations of particular beings, living or dead. Worlds that looked like familiar realities, like vestiges of dreams when I first wake up, like delirious visions, and sometimes like nothing I had ever seen before. In one of the dream places I met Red Jiffa. I think I sought him out myself because I was very eager to find out whether he was all right. I don't remember the details of our encounter, but Jiffa looked like a person who was absolutely happy with his lot.

I took a look around the World where I was born, too. I discovered that it wasn't any better, nor was it any worse, than any other. It just was what it was. I didn't attach any special significance to my short visit home. I didn't attach much significance to anything while I was there. I was in a wonderful state of mind: I didn't really feel like a human being but like a light, cool, disembodied breeze that penetrated the cracks of the flimsy Doors between Worlds.

At last I felt I had had my fill of solitude and new impressions. I had grown tired of the endless wandering, and I wanted to go home to Echo. I discovered that I already knew how to find the necessary door. I opened it, and woke up.

For a while I just lay still without opening my eyes. Lively little spots of sunlight seemed to be dancing a jig on my eyelids. I considered what I should do—pull the blanket up over my head or wake up to the world once and for all? I decided on the latter as the more promising option.

I opened my eyes and blinked, trying to get used to the daylight. Then I looked around me. The room didn't look like Juffin's bedroom, where I had recently fallen asleep. It was too small and had only one window, but it was very, very familiar. Finally I realized where I was. It was my own bed in my old bedroom. My first apartment on the Street of Old Coins, which I had since moved out of for purely sentimental reasons. Great, but the new owners might be rather distressed by this!

I shook my head in bewilderment and heard a rustle in back of me. I turned around to see a smiling Maba Kalox.

"Look how attached you are to this little room!" he said merrily. "What did you find here—can you tell me?"

"No, I can't. You know me, Sir Maba. I'm completely nuts."

"No false modesty, please. You're one of the most ordinary bores I have the pleasure of knowing. You're just a little eccentric, that's all. And it's for the best."

"What's for the best? The first or the second?"

"Everything. Everything is for the best. All right, now it seems I can safely leave to go about my business. You don't look like someone who is in urgent need of help. Besides, Juffin's on his way, beaming like a freshly polished star. He's bringing you your things, too. You don't have anything here, do you?"

"No. I'd have to cut a looxi out of the blanket and make my way home through back alleys under cover of darkness. Thank you, Sir Maba. Everything is fine with me now, isn't it?"

"With you? I don't know—you know best. Turn away for a second and let me disappear."

"Oh, sure. But do I really have to? Turn away, I mean."

"Of course not. But when no one's looking at you, it's a lot easier to disappear, and I'm very lazy."

I turned away, and Sir Maba was gone. The stairs creaked under the weight of Juffin's soft boots. The boss decided not to show off and came in through the door like normal people do.

"Well, voyager?" he said breezily. "Are you happy after your little jaunt?"

"I'm not sure yet. I guess so. But why did I wake up here and not at home?"

"It was you who wanted to. Otherwise you wouldn't be here," Juffin said matter-of-factly. "Maba and I were surprised, too. You are apparently very fond of this tenement. But you were right when you decided to move out of this apartment. Now you will always enter the Corridor between Worlds from here. And return here afterward. This is the place where your Door between Worlds opens. Very convenient, I'd say. Your practicality simply astounds me. Here, take your duds and go to the bathing pools to wash up. We've got work to do. Breakfast, for example."

Juffin tossed me a black skaba. I dressed with alacrity. As far as I'm concerned, a naked man looks far too vulnerable and defenseless.

Then I went downstairs to make myself presentable and to come to my senses. While I was bathing my thoughts also seemed to sort themselves out, without any help from me. As soon as I returned to the living room, where Juffin was pacing up and down impatiently, I asked, "What were you saying about how I would always leave from here and come back here? Do you mean to say that I can enter the Corridor between Worlds only from this bedroom? And in other places I'll only be able to sleep just like everyone else?"

"Exactly. At least for a while. This is just how you wanted it, and the Corridor between Worlds granted your wish, strangely enough. You've got it wrapped around your little finger! As far as I know, it's the first time some mere boy has been able to make demands of this queer and unaccommodating place. You're very good at having things your way, I must admit." Juffin looked me up and down appraisingly and smiled. "Come on, put on your Mantle of Death and let's go to the *Glutton*. They've missed you there."

"Missed me, right. You and I were there just yesterday." I looked at Juffin. "Or wasn't it yesterday? Wait a minute, did I sleep longer than two dozen hours?"

"A bit longer," the boss said, nodding.

I didn't like the crafty look on his face at all. "How much longer?"

"Well, to be honest, you spent more than a year there."

"What!"

"You heard me. Why are you so surprised?"

"Why do you even ask? Do you think something like that happens to me every day?"

"Not every day. But from now on it will happen from time to time. So you'd better get used to it. Time itself decides how to flow for someone who has entered the Corridor between Worlds. Only a very experienced traveler can perceive its actual flow. And you're not experienced. Although you're very capable, of course."

"But what about the guys?" I asked in dismay. "How did you manage all this time without me? And . . ."

For some reason I felt very hurt, like when you're a kid and you go home for lunch, and you're gone just an hour, but when you come back you find out that your friends have gotten along fine without you and even started a new game, the rules of which are a complete mystery to you.

"I told the crew that you had withdrawn to the Residence of the Order of the Seven-Leaf Clover, where you were carrying out a secret mission, which it was unadvisable not only to talk about but even to think about. They accepted it without a murmur. They said it was just like you, can you imagine?" Juffin chuckled. "Don't sulk, Max. Without you we were all at loose ends, wailing and gnashing our teeth and beating our heads against the walls at Headquarters. Believe me, it's no exaggeration. Not much, anyway. And every dozen days I stashed your pay in the desk drawer. Now the bottom's about to fall out of it! You've woken up a very rich man, son! Now are you happy?"

"Yes," I nodded pompously, watching my own reflection in the mirror. It didn't look bad, I must say. "Love me, pay me, and I'll be fine."

"Enough parading in front of the mirror. Let's go to the *Glutton*," Juffin said. "The lads are chewing their napkins already, I'll bet."

The *Glutton Bunba* was nearly empty. Only our favorite table between the bar and the window onto the little courtyard was occupied, by the Secret Investigators. They threw themselves at me in raucous joy when they saw me. Lady Melamori showed her mettle as a true fighter by reaching me first, so Melifaro got the rare opportunity to hug us both at the same time. Lookfi knocked over the tray of kamra in his excitement. Sir Kofa, a wise man, approached me from behind so he didn't have to throw himself into the fray for the privilege of touching me. Lonli-Lokli stood sensibly off to the side, contemplating the spectacle approvingly. This was fine: it's best to embrace such an impressive fellow on an individual basis.

I sat down at the table and began looking around. It turned out that a lot can change in a year. Melifaro, for example, had acquired a small triangular scar above his left eyebrow. I have to say it suited him.

"The easiest way to come by a hero's scar is to get it right in the kisser. That's the main thing, right?" he said. "What kind of hero was I before? A self-proclaimed one! Hey, you still don't know what our Lokki-Lolni managed to pull off. Show him, Sir Shurf! He'll get a kick out of it."

"Melifaro, you are simply begging for another scar," Lonli-Lokli said. "You can't persist in mocking my name with impunity much longer. I happen to like it."

"What did you manage to pull off, Shurf?"

"Have a look." Lonli-Lokli carefully drew off the protective glove from his left hand and showed me the palm of the death-dealing glove underneath. A sharp blue eye glared angrily from the center of it.

I gasped. "Whose is it?"

"It belongs to some fellow you don't know. It happened while you were gone. Beautiful, isn't it?"

"What does it do? Does it have any unusual powers?

Everyone guffawed at once. Only Shurf maintained his habitual composure.

"It winks, Max," Melifaro said, choking with laughter. "That's all it does—it winks!"

"I thought you'd like it," Lonli-Lokli said. "Now whenever I put my left hand into action I always pause, just for a moment. That gives my palm time to wink at the victim. You know, sometimes I think it's your joke. You whispered it to me once in a dream, I'm sure of it."

I smiled, flattered.

"It's definitely my style, but I'm not up to that yet. I've still got a long way to go. Thanks all the same."

After a long and wonderful breakfast I got behind the levers of Juffin's amobiler and drove home to the Street of Yellow Stones. I was very anxious about how my cats had fared. Darn it, I had abandoned them for a whole year! Some responsible pet owner I was.

"Come back by sundown, Max. You've got mountains of work to do," Sir Juffin called out after me. His words were like balm to my spirit.

Almost faint with worry, I rushed into the spacious hall of my apartment. There I was greeted by an idyllic picture: an incredible, indescribable, inhuman mess, in the center of which reigned Anday Pu, wrapped up in a house looxi. A slightly fatter Ella was curled at his feet, and Armstrong sat on his chest, purring. I shook my head in dismay, unsure of what to do: thank the guy, kill him on the spot, or simply cuss him out for all I was worth.

"Good day, Max! I catch, I shouldn't have stayed here without your permission, but your cats missed you terribly," said the amateur zoologist in his charming French accent. "And my house is full of tenants. Their lease doesn't run out for twenty years. Those plebeians have four kids who shout and bawl constantly, and I need to write. The dinner was over once and for all!"

I sank down on the floor and almost died laughing. My head was spinning round and round. But that's what my head is supposed to do, it seems: just keep spinning.

"You catch?" Anday said timidly, smiling a crooked smile with the left side of his loquacious mouth.

THE SHIP FROM ARVAROX
AND OTHER WOES

"MAX, THE LIVES OF ALL THE POLICEMEN OF ECHO ARE in your hands."

Smiling, Melifaro made himself comfortable atop my desk, knocking the self-scribing tablets on the floor and an empty cup in my lap. Melifaro didn't even blink. Instead, he hung over me, wringing his hands theatrically and demanding attention.

"Ever since Boboota ran out of those funny smoking sticks you gave him, his temper is even worse than it used to be."

"Impossible," I said in a calm voice. "It can't get any worse than it was. Nature's resources are not limitless. The boys simply forgot what their boss used to be like before he stuffed himself on King Banjee. Now he's completely recovered, that's all."

"So, you don't have any more of those smoking sticks?" said Melifaro. "Poor Apurra."

"No, I don't have any at the moment, but I can fetch some more. No problem. Who's Apurra?"

"Right, you haven't met him yet. Lieutenant Apurra Blookey. He's been with the police since Shixola died. As smart as the late Shixola, and almost as nice. You'll like him. Oh, and there's a new dame in the City Police, Lady Kekki Tuotli. Not only is she smart—I'd rather she worked for us, to be honest with you—she moves in the highest social circles. She's very prim and haughty. Boboota almost never uses foul language in her presence, can you believe it?"

"I can," I said. "If you'll remember, we once had a chance to observe him at home in his natural habitat."

"Right. As for the guy who replaced Kamshi, I don't want you to meet him. You're going to want to kill him right away," said Melifaro, smiling a malicious smile.

"Why? Is he a jerk?"

"Not really a jerk. Mostly, he's just an idiot. Lieutenant Chekta Jax has no sense of humor unless he's laughing at his own jokes—which are terrible but, fortunately, few. A serious fellow, mind you, and very muscle-bound. A true hero. I suspect you're not too keen on his kind."

"Oh, I can stand just about anyone as long as I don't have to stand them for too long," I said. "To think of how much has happened in just a year!"

"A year and forty-eight days," said Melifaro. "We've been keeping track during your absence. We made notches on a table in the Hall of Common Labor."

"You did? Unbelievable."

"But of course. Those were the happiest days in our lives. A man has the right to know exactly how long he's been happy."

"I see. Okay, you can be happy for another couple of hours. By the way, it's noon, and my shift doesn't start until midnight. So I'm off."

"You're off to where?" said Melifaro. "I'll bet you're going to get stuffed again. Didn't they feed you at the Seven-Leaf Clover?"

"You know how stingy they are there. Believe it or not, I haven't eaten once since I was gone."

This was true. I don't remember seeing any diners in the Corridor between Worlds. I even got visibly skinny during my magic slumber. Truth be told, I was looking forward to fattening myself up again.

"If you're headed to the *Glutton*—"

"If I *were* headed to the *Glutton*, I'd say so. I need to stop by my place. Do you know what's going on there? While I was away, one young man made himself right at home under my roof."

"Oh, that tubby journalist? He's a nice guy. Funny, too." In Melifaro's parlance, a recommendation like that weighed in as a real compliment.

"My cats think he's nice, too," I said. "The three were perfectly happy without me. You can't imagine what the place looks like now. I'm a minimalist, as you know, but this is beyond belief. They've turned the place upside down. The whole house needs an overhaul. My humble

Forbidden Magic skills are insufficient, so to fix the place up I followed the advice of Sir Shurf and hired professionals. Some pretty shady fellows, let me tell you. Possibly former Grand Magicians. Their leader says it'll take them no less than two dozen days to fix it up, and deep in my heart, I tend to agree with him. In any case, that's much too long for me to wait. I'm going over there to inspire them to hurry it up with my menacing countenance. Long story short, I'll be back in an hour. Then we'll go to the *Glutton* or some other place—you decide. Boy, I'm so agreeable today, I disgust myself."

"Yes, you're losing your touch," said Melifaro, smiling from ear to ear. "Get along with you now. But come back soon."

"You're letting me go? Really? Thank you, O magnanimous master."

I made a deep bow in the spirit of Melifaro himself and rushed out of Headquarters. I think I had the last word in that exchange, though when it comes to determining the winner of a contest of wits, even the Dark Magicians would be hard-pressed to choose between Melifaro and myself.

❀

At home, everything was fine, except that Armstrong and Ella were irked because I had locked them in the bedroom. I didn't think it was such a great idea for them to saunter around among sullen workers, building materials, and other unwholesome clutter.

"It's your own fault," I said, scratching the napes of my little furries' necks. "I should have locked your honey pie Anday in with you. I'm not done with him yet. Let this be a lesson to you: next time you'll think twice before demolishing everything in sight."

I knew very well that they wouldn't, though, if given another chance.

Two hours later, Melifaro and I were sitting at the *Glutton Bunba*. I was really going to make up for lost time.

"So, where are you going to live now?" said my diurnal half. "At Headquarters?"

"Uh-huh. Consider the Minor Secret Investigative Force to be temporarily disbanded. You guys are too much of a nuisance: you're noisy, and you're always munching on something. Seriously though, I still have my old apartment on the Street of Old Coins, remember?"

"That shed? Take it easy on the food, then, or you're not going to fit inside it. The reason I'm asking is because my nutty family is begging me to bring you out for a stay. I tried telling my folks that they'd live to regret it, but they're a bit slow, like all farmers." Melifaro's wit spared no one, not even his own parents.

"Is this an invitation?"

"No, it's the final warning. Don't you dare come poking your nose around my family estate! Well, unless it's under my direct supervision. I'm going there tonight to see my older brother."

"The big guy?"

"Who? Oh, you mean Baxba? No, I'm talking about Anchifa. The pride of the family, as it were. He's a real pirate. What else would my brother do in the wet, salty, boundless sea? The way I see it, pillaging merchant *fafunas* is the only worthy pastime under the circumstances. Anchifa got home just a few days ago, and it's been a nonstop celebration ever since. In other words, it's boring as hell there. Please don't let me die of boredom!"

"I'd love to save you, Melifaro, but you know Juffin. He'll gladly send me straight into a den of berserk werewolves, but on a pleasant trip to the country—I don't think so."

"Oh, but he will," said Melifaro. "I already talked to him. Juffin was pretty happy about it. I gather you're getting on his nerves big time."

"Really?" I said. "Good golly, I thought he'd tie me to the chair so that nothing would distract me from my work."

"That would be fantastic!" Melifaro said. "I should suggest it to him."

"Munching away, are you, boys?" said Sir Kofa Yox, who had materialized suddenly behind my back. "Good, good. I have some news for you, Max. You're going to love it."

"Is this a new joke?" I said.

I had already heard dozens of them. While I was gone, the locals missed me so much that they had come up with jokes (most of them quite obscene) featuring yours truly. I had no choice but to put up with them. After all, even Sir Juffin Hully hadn't escaped that dubious honor.

"Ha! Dream on," said Kofa. "You think they're going to come up with new ones every day now? Sorry, but no. You are an important person here, no doubt, but not *that* important."

"Praise be the Magicians! So, what's the news?" I said.

"Nothing special, except that I arrested a countryman of yours less than half an hour ago. In the *Sated Skeleton*."

"My countryman?" I felt like I was about to hyperventilate. A compatriot of mine had already appeared in Echo once before. He turned out to be a serial killer who had accidentally stumbled across my first Door between Worlds. The poor fellow used that metaphysical journey for the only purpose he could think of: sating his appetite and committing murders at double his usual rate. In the end, I had to put him out of his misery, and I didn't like it a single bit.

"But of course. Why are you so surprised?" said Sir Kofa with a sly wink. "True, the County Vook is quite remote from the Capital, but some people are very fond of traveling."

It was impossible to conceal my relief. The fellow in question was simply an inhabitant of the County Vook and the Barren Lands. According to the story of my origins that Juffin had concocted for me, those backwoods were my homeland. I'm pretty sure that none of my colleagues believed in that nonsense, but they were tactful enough not to voice their doubts. They were quite happy with me the way I was—what with the mysterious air and all.

"So, what did he do, this countryman of mine?" To be honest, I couldn't care less about the criminal adventures of some inhabitant of the Barren Lands. I had to stay in character, though, so I forced myself to feign real curiosity.

"Nothing special," said Sir Kofa. "The fellow fell victim to his own ignorance."

"What, he didn't know how to add two and two?" said Melifaro, guffawing. "I didn't know that was against the law."

Sir Kofa laughed, too, snatched a pastry from my plate, took a bite, and continued: "The guy had a signet ring that allowed him to read the thoughts of others. Nothing to brag about, really. During the Epoch of Orders almost every Echoer had toys like that. At the beginning of the Code Epoch, however, they were confiscated by special decree of Gurig VII. In the first place, it was White Magic of the twenty-fourth degree. And, second, it was a glaring breach of Article 48 of the Code of Krember, which stated that every citizen of the Unified Kingdom had the right to his or her own personal secrets. Your fellow countryman, naturally, didn't give a fig about 'personal secrets.' He got the signet ring from a 'good friend' of his some ninety years ago. I suspect that the 'friend' was one of the fugitive Junior Magicians. Back then they roamed the outskirts of the Unified Kingdom in swarms."

"What's going to happen to him now?" I said.

"Nothing special. In a few days, the innocent victim will have to part with his precious stone, accept monetary compensation for the confiscated talisman, and return home. Xolomi is overpopulated as it is. No need to detain him any further."

"Perhaps I should pay him a visit," I said. "After all, he's my countryman." I was curious to see a real inhabitant of the Barren Lands. I had the right to know what I was supposed to look like in the eyes of the Capital dwellers.

"Have you been missing the smell of manure?" Melifaro said. "You think you can find a piece and get a whiff if you search the fellow's pockets? I know what you're up to."

"You know, you may very well have to get involved in this case," Sir Kofa agreed. "The fellow didn't come to Echo alone. There's a whole caravan with him. Our compassionate citizens have already informed the terrified nomads that a countryman of theirs is a big shot in the Secret Investigative Force. I think they're already on their way to the House by the Bridge. Do you have any idea what you might be in for?"

"This is going to be fun." At first, I was exhilarated, but then I started thinking about the consequences. The whole business could easily blow my cover. I frowned. "I think I'm going to drop in on Juffin."

"I think you'd better, my boy," said Sir Kofa. "He also thinks you should drop in on him. Or he'll be thinking that soon. Anyway, I'm sorry I interrupted your lunch."

"That's quite all right, Sir Kofa. I'm ready to put up with a lot more than that from you." I stuffed the last pastry into my mouth and rose from the table.

"Wow, get a load of Mr. Busybody!" said Melifaro. "Don't even think of abandoning me now. We're leaving tonight."

"Don't worry. Have I ever passed up an opportunity to fill my belly at your expense? I love your parents' cooking."

"Such commitment," said Melifaro. "Such profound ambition in the name of a single idea. Such selfless service to one's own stomach."

"Yup, that's me," I said with pride. "Lonli-Lokli once taught me a series of excellent breathing exercises. They help me focus on the main goal and not waste my concentration on trifling matters. The result is standing before you now."

I found Sir Juffin Hully in his office. When I went in, he was trying to assume a serious expression. It didn't work very well, though. Instead, his refractory face betrayed a cunning smile.

"Ready to meet your fellow countrymen?" he asked.

"You know very well that I'm not. You can't be ready for something like that. By the way, it was your idea that I was supposed to hail from the Barren Lands. You've got to help me out now!"

"Don't panic. We'll patch up your biography in no time. No big deal. It goes like this: You're an orphan—you don't remember your parents. You were brought up by some old fugitive Magician by the name of . . . No, he kept his name secret from everyone, even from you. That is just what you might expect of a fugitive Magician. You lived in a small house on the boundless plains. The old man taught you magic, little by little. Then he died, and you set off for the Capital to find an old friend of your guardian's—me, that is. That should be enough. What do you think?"

"Sounds great," I said. "So vague, yet so watertight. I'm sure my accent is nowhere close to that of the real nomads—not to mention the rest of my quirks—but this hypothetical refugee Magician would easily account for all of that. I mean, who knows what he may have taught me?"

"Right. What you need, though, is a regular name. 'Max' is way beyond the pale. It doesn't resemble their names even remotely. Not to mention ours. A man has to know his own name, doesn't he? No one's going to believe that your guardian Magician wasn't powerful enough to learn your true name. That's just not how it works."

"Okay, let's make up a name for me," I said, somewhat flippantly.

"No, it has to be a real name. Can you remember one off the top of your head? You've read the third volume of the *Encyclopedia* to shreds."

"But that was so long ago," I said. "I can run back home and fetch it real quick, though. You know I'm as fast as lightning . . . No, wait, I think I remember one name. Fanghaxra. Yes, that's it, Fanghaxra from the Lands of Fanghaxra."

"Fanghaxra." said Juffin pensively. "Well, it does sound like one of their names. I think you remembered it correctly. If not . . . Oh, Magicians take those nomads. Why should we worry our heads over them?"

"That's right," I said. "What's the point? They're nomads. Let them wander where they will. For all I care, they can go to where it's hot."

"Well, that's just what it's like where they come from," said Juffin with a smile. "We must show love and concern for them, my boy. It's politics, you see. Our guests dwell on disputed territory—the very border of the County Vook and the Barren Lands. The Barren Lands, if you'll remember, do not belong to the Unified Kingdom, or any other country for that matter. I'd be happy to get rid of them in the quickest way possible, but His Majesty Gurig VIII is obsessed with the idea of hanging a new map of the Unified Kingdom in his dining hall. His Majesty envisions the Barren Lands as part of the Unified Kingdom. Naturally, the Royal Cartographers will simply draw a new map—no one really wants to wage war for the sake of some backwater. Seen in this light, the arrest of your 'countryman,' if you'll pardon the expression, is an event of national importance. We'll just keep him here for a little while, then let him go. We'll also prepare all the necessary papers, and in our reports the poor fellow will be referred to as a citizen of the Unified Kingdom. Do you follow?"

"It may come as a surprise, but I do follow you. This is called 'creating a precedent,' right?"

"Goodness gracious," said Juffin. "You're a smart boy. Perhaps you should think of a career at the Royal Court of His Majesty."

"As if! I know their salaries are no match for ours."

"What a greedy young man you are," said Juffin, smiling. "Okay, let's have a word with your countrymen, shall we? They've been crowding the reception room for a while now. Then you can go with Melifaro, and may you have a safe and quick journey."

"Can't wait to get rid of me, can you?"

"Me? Not at all. Can you guess why I let you go so easily?"

"Frankly, no. I haven't a clue. You spent so much time and effort explaining why I needed to keep a round-the-clock vigil in the House by the Bridge for days on end, because I've become so very indispensable, and then—all of a sudden—this. "

"I want you to spend the night in his grandfather's room," Juffin explained. "When you come back, you'll be as good as new. You deserve a good rest."

"Oh, yes, the room! Gosh, I almost forgot about it. That was quite an organization, that Order of the Secret Grass. I'd have joined it myself if they'd have let me, which I doubt. But thank you anyway, Juffin!"

"Don't mention it. I'm doing it for my own sake. Incidentally, back then they would have accepted you into any Order. Simply out of respect for your life story. Your *actual* life story, I mean. And now, run along to see your countrymen. Then come back and tell me about it. I'm burning with curiosity."

"All right," I said, standing up from the chair. "So, I'm Fanghaxra from the Lands of Fanghaxra. Boy, what a name."

"I suspect the others are even worse," said Juffin as I was leaving the office.

I went into the reception room.

I'm a strange bird. Up until the last minute I had been sure that the dwellers of the Barren Lands would be narrow-eyed, high-cheekboned Paul Bunyans wearing Mongolian robes, cone-shaped fur hats, and archer's quivers on their belts. That's what nomads looked like in my imagination, at least. My imagination failed to take into account that this was happening in another World.

At first glance, it might have seemed that a couple dozen ordinary Echoers had crowded into the reception room. Very commonplace faces—some of them pleasant, some less so.

Their attire, however, was a whole different ball game, let me tell you. On their heads they wore babushkas. These headscarves were counterbalanced by shorts that went down to just below the knees. To top it off, the nomads wore huge rucksacks strapped over their shoulders.

Jeepers, I thought. Is this what I was supposed to look like when I was younger? What a reputation I must have in the Capital.

I shook my head in amazement and just then noticed another incongruous detail: it was absolutely quiet in the room. Not only did the nomads not speak, they virtually *created* the silence. It seemed that they even held their breath. My "countrymen" stared at me.

Okay, I thought. Looks like they're not going to prostrate themselves before me. Which is good.

Finally, one of the nomads, an old man, his hair completely gray (he looked like the oldest of the bunch), stepped up to me.

"If you're one of ours, you must help Jimax," he said in a hoarse voice. "That is what the Law says, and what do we have but the Law?"

"Nothing," I said mechanically. "I will help Jimax. After the sun has taken leave of the skies several times, Jimax will return to you. That I promise. He will be compensated for the inconvenience. I will see to it personally. Fare ye well."

Having spoken my piece, I turned to go, with a sense of relief. My job here is done, I thought.

"Let us know your name," said the old man. "We must know the praiseworthy name of the one who abides by the Law, even so far away from the homeland. I mean your clan name, not the name the local barbarians gave you."

"I am Fanghaxra, from the Lands of Fanghaxra. Now I must leave, I have— What are you doing, gentlemen? Stop this at once!"

Now they were prostrating themselves before me. They fell on the floor all at once, with the discipline and enthusiasm of well-drilled soldiers.

"You have come back to your people, Fanghaxra!" the old man said reverently. He looked up at me, his eyes watering with emotion. "The people of the Lands of Fanghaxra hail thee!"

"Still, you should get up," I said. "Okay, I have come back to my people. All right, all right. Big deal."

Then I realized with horror why I remembered the name Fanghaxra. This was the name of a legendary child-king of some absentminded nomads who had lost their sovereign on the boundless steppes. Then, if I remembered correctly, his subjects had cursed their own existence. This was my favorite story in the third volume of the *Encyclopedia of the World* by Sir Manga Melifaro. Darn it, why had I remembered the name of that king, out of all possible names! The last thing I needed was to become an impostor king of the nomads.

"Look," I said dryly, "let's make a deal. You get up off your knees, walk outside, and go back to doing whatever you were doing. Nice and simple. And I go back to doing what I was doing. In a few days, you get your precious Jimax back, safe and sound, and that's it. Okay? Farewell, then."

I flung open the front door for them and froze in disbelief. A herd of moose was grazing in front of the House by the Bridge. Well, not really moose, of course, but of all animals, the so-called horses of the Barren Lands most resembled the moose. They were large and stooping, and they had antlers. The antlers were decorated with little thingamajigs: ribbons, bells, tiny jugs, and other bric-a-brac. It was very touching.

"Look, guys," I said, trying be conciliatory. "I didn't mean to hurt your feelings, but I'm really, really busy. So please get up off your knees, and never, ever kneel again. Before anyone. Got it? Such a nice, proud people. It doesn't become you."

"Your word is Law!" said the old nomad, assuming a vertical stance. "You have given us back our hope."

"Hope is a darn-fool feeling," I said, quoting Mackie Ainti in spite of myself.

Later I would come to regret my feeble attempts at wit, but what was done was done.

"Everything is going to be all right. Go now, guys," I said, pointing at the door.

The nomads went out without saying a word, mounted their weird steeds, and soon disappeared around the corner. I shook my head, somewhat dazed, and went back to Juffin's office to surprise him.

❀

"Now I'm a king, too," I said, standing in the doorway. "It's my own fault, though. I should have remembered some other name." I briefed him on the story of my sudden coronation.

"No big deal," the boss said. "So you're a king. Nothing to worry about."

"You're not going to send me abroad to fulfill my regal duties, are you?"

"Don't be silly, Max. Of course I won't. If anything, you'll just run off on your own. Then again, if you do I'll hunt you down. When I catch you, I'll force you to go without lunch for a week. Got that?"

"You're way too cruel, Juffin. I haven't eaten in a year!"

"You have been sleeping for a year, though," said Juffin. "Now, Your Majesty, be a good sport. Don your traveling robes, and go seek out Sir Manga Melifaro. Isn't he the author of your misfortune? Go and wreak your revenge."

"That's just what I'll do," I said. "I'll devour everything within reach on the table. That'll show him."

"Excellent. You have two days and no more. I seem to remember Melifaro saying something about three days, but you can forget about it. Two days, and not an hour more. As if he knows anything about anything."

"Exactly. He doesn't know anything about anything. No one needs more than two days of rest," I said.

On this uplifting note, we parted company.

❀

In the hallway, I ran into Melamori. She smiled at me with a mixture of joy and sadness. I think my face underwent a similar transformation.

"Leaving?" she said.

"Just for two days. It's nothing compared to an eternity, right?"

"But I haven't yet showed you how I can drive the amobiler. I still have a long way to go to catch up with you, but I think I stand a good chance to win the bet. One day I'll beat you, Max. I swear to all the Magicians!"

"I never doubted it for a second, Melamori. Do you want to give me a ride?"

"Of course, I do," said Melamori with a vigorous nod. "It's so good to have you back, Max."

"You didn't think I'd be back?"

"Well . . . not all the time. Though Sir Juffin said you'd definitely come back. It's just that sometimes I thought he didn't believe it himself. But you came back after all. Here you are!"

"It's me all right. Remember I told you it would take more than that to get rid of me?"

"I do, and I said I didn't want to get rid of you in the first place. But you disappeared anyway. Praise be the Magicians, you didn't disappear forever, but a year is still a long time."

"If it were up to me, I would—"

"I know. And if it were up to me . . . Strange lives we have, Max. Do you think we're capable of making our own decisions at all? It isn't really up to us, is it."

"I guess not," I said. "I'm getting used to it, but there was a time I was really sorry about it. And I'm still kicking myself over it."

Melamori forced a smile and nodded. "You know, just a few days before our little jaunt in the Magaxon Forest I had been thinking that maybe we shouldn't make such a big deal about those ancient prejudices—the Quarter of Trysts, destiny, death, and all that. Maybe we should have listened to our hearts, and whatever happened, happened, you know? But as soon as I started thinking I could just ignore the ancient taboos, you almost got killed in the Magaxon Forest. It seemed like a sign, so ominous that I got scared all over again. And then I decided I should just leave well enough alone, that it was all for the best. A year is an awful long time, and I've learned to live without you, and without regrets. Well, *almost* learned."

I leaned against the wall and wiped the perspiration off of my forehead. Boy, what a little exchange this was turning out to be! Certainly the first of its kind in the hallowed hallways of the Ministry of Perfect Public Order.

"The truth is, Melamori, I don't consider the local notions and omens to be silly superstitions anymore," I said after a pause. "I am glad that we're both alive, though. That's already a great thing, isn't it?"

Melamori nodded, embarrassed, and I fell silent for a while. Then the dam broke, and I opened my mouth to speak.

"Time," I said. "Everything takes time. I have learned tons of amazing things in the past two years, Melamori. Someday I'll learn to fool fate. This is not one of those resolutions I can learn to keep a day before the Last Day of the Year, is it? But someday I will. I just hope it won't be too late."

"It's never too late for that," said Melamori. "Things like that always happen on time, or they don't happen at all. We'll see. I'm glad you told me, Max. I really am. But don't hold it against me if I act as though we've never had this conversation. I'm tired of living with a void in my chest. I've got to cheer myself up. I've got to try, at least."

"And you will," I said, nodding. "You'll see. And so will I. Or have I already? Oh, I don't even know anymore."

Melamori gave me a long, penetrating look, shook her disheveled hair, waved goodbye, and disappeared into the Hall of Common Labor. I stood in the hallway for a few moments, then unstuck myself from the wall and left the Headquarters.

Melifaro was waiting for me at an empty table in the *Glutton Bunba*, fidgety with impatience.

"Where in the name of Dark Magicians have you been, Nightmare? Are you back to your old habits? How many have you murdered? 'Fess up!"

"Hundreds. Thousands. I don't know," I said absentmindedly. "I'm sorry, buddy. Something came up. See, I was being crowned. Becoming a king is no trifling matter, believe me."

"What do you mean 'a king'?" said Melifaro, blinking. "Is this one of your lame jokes from the Barren Lands again?"

"No, I'm being absolutely serious. I'll tell you everything on the way. Let's go, or my subjects will swarm in here, begging us to take them along on the trip. I have no idea how I've survived this far without a retinue."

"Boy do you have a warped sense of humor today," said Melifaro. "Let's stop by my place first. I need to pack a few things."

"Okay. Then I need to stop by my place, too," I said. "By the way, my subjects are way more practical that you. They carry all of their possessions with them. In rucksacks *this* big."

I stretched my arms as wide as they would reach. There's no harm in exaggerating a little bit for the love of my people.

Melifaro's place on the Street of Gloomy Clouds was a spacious, well-furnished, yet fairly desolate abode. It felt like the owner was an infrequent visitor to his apartment and used it solely for hitting the sack. I also noticed that, like me, Melifaro didn't keep servants. That was something I approved of.

"If you want a drink, look in the bookcase. I think I saw something there a couple of days ago," said Melifaro uncertainly. He glanced around his living room in perplexity.

"No, thanks. I'm driving. By the way, until now I was positive I was the owner of the most gigantic mess on either bank of the Xuron. Now I see that I was basking in someone else's limelight."

"You don't even come close," said Melifaro proudly.

"I guess you have to have some kind of edge over me," I said snidely in the direction of his back as he ran upstairs.

Melifaro pretended he hadn't heard me. Maybe he just didn't have a comeback ready.

A minute later he came down, waving a half-empty traveling bag in his hand.

"Let's go, Max. Can't bear looking at this filthy pigsty another minute. But that's all right. In two days, this place is going to be crystal clean. I decided to follow your example and hire some mysterious cleaning service. They say my lair is not as hopeless as it appears."

"I'd like to believe that. Actually, though, I like your place as it is."

"Really? Well, I guess compared to the flimsy tents of your people this does look like a nice place. By the way, you said you'd tell me about your coronation. How did that happen?"

"It was a little misunderstanding. I told them my real name, and it turned out I was their king. Rather, I have the same name as a king of theirs who disappeared as a child. That's about it."

Melifaro's jaw dropped. "Are you pulling my leg? Then again, knowing you, I wouldn't be surprised to learn that you were a—"

"Oh, come on," I said. "I'm a poor orphan with no kith or kin, gone astray in the murky darkness of remote memories of the past. A king? Of all the nonsense!"

All the way over to my place, Melifaro was silent, which was completely at odds with his usual habits. I think he was processing the new information. Then again, the ride wasn't a very long one.

✤

Chaos reigned in my living room. Almost a dozen gloomy workers were loafing around, and their supervisor paced the large room, pretending to be busy. I shook my head in reproach.

"You know what, guys? I'd really appreciate it if you'd get down to work, like right now," I said. "I have to live here."

The workers backed up toward the exit, and their supervisor opened his mouth to make an excuse. I could really feel for the guy. I wouldn't want to be working for someone wrapped in the Mantle of Death, either.

"Don't say anything. And don't be scared," I said. "Let's make a deal. You fix the place up real quick—in two days—and I pay you three times the amount we agreed on. For a rush job."

"But that's impossible!" said the workers almost in unison.

"A man is rarely aware of the true extent of his abilities," I assured them. "Especially in an emergency. And this *is* an emergency, trust me. Yours, not mine."

Having issued this ultimatum, I went upstairs to pack.

You do have a kingly manner, my friend. Melifaro's Silent Speech reached me on the stairs.

We do, indeed, I replied.

Ella and Armstrong were sleeping in my bed. I melted at the sight for just a short moment, then opened the closet. I grabbed a thin skaba and the first looxi I could find, and stuffed them into my traveling bag. That would be plenty, I thought. Then I ran downstairs. The sure way to kill Melifaro is to make him wait for more than a minute.

Melifaro was very much alive, though. He was talking to the supervisor.

"Oh, he will kill you, no two ways about it," he said to the poor supervisor. "He'll kill you first and ask questions later, believe me. You'd better do what he says."

"I second that," I added. "Excellent advice, Sir Melifaro. I'll never cease to wonder at the depths of your wisdom. We'd better go now. If I stay here any longer, I'll have to kill myself. And that will be a sad end to this fascinating story."

"What story?" said Melifaro.

"The story of my life, silly."

I rushed outside and settled behind the levers of the amobiler. I found it absolutely pointless to linger any longer in the construction site my house had become. Melifaro followed suit, satisfied after his meaningful exchange with the local proles.

I should really take a ride with Melamori, I thought, as we pulled away. I'm sure she's getting better and better at it. Well, looks like I'm not a lost cause, after all. I can still do something useful and not just destructive.

"I think you drive even faster now," said Melifaro. He was talking nonstop. "Now I know what you've been up to all year. You were made the personal driver of Magician Nuflin. The old man was longing for a rush of adrenaline. Am I right?"

"Yes," I said nonchalantly. "But then he got motion sickness. That was the end of my career. Now my only option is to become king."

Melifaro came up with a number of scenarios for my possible future, most of them quite risqué. I listened to him absentmindedly, speeding up even though I was driving at a dizzying speed already. I was overcome by a strange sort of stupor that left no room for words or thoughts. I had a vague premonition of something inevitable, vague, but vertiginous. The state I was in was more pleasant than not, though I couldn't be sure of that, either.

"Where are we going, by the way?" Melifaro asked.

"What do you mean? To your family estate, unless you've changed your mind."

"No, I haven't. But we should have made a turn a dozen minutes ago if we really wanted to get there."

"A hole in the heavens above you, Ninth Volume!" I said, making a U-turn at full speed. "Why couldn't you say so sooner?"

"I wanted to see if you'd figure it out. You see, my inquisitive mind strives to comprehend the incomprehensible. You, for instance. But then I figured that you were quite capable of driving us all the way to Landaland, so I had to stop my experiment. Don't miss the turn *now*, or we'll be driving up and down this blasted road until it's time to go back to Echo."

I pictured the amobiler plowing back and forth endlessly on the country road and laughed. Right then, my stupor dissolved and I was fine. Or was I?

"You're not yourself today," said Melifaro, looking at me with concern. "What is it? Is the crown too small, or is the robe itchy?"

"Your concern doesn't suit you at all," I said. "I'm always myself. Who else would I be? Just tired, that's all. I've got so much work now. It feels like while I was gone, you guys weren't doing anything except making notches on the table. Every last one of you. But don't you worry, a couple of nights in your grandfather's bedroom and I'll be as good as new."

"You will," said Melifaro. "That's for sure. Tell me, don't you get a little sick of the air of mystery that surrounds you, Nightmare?"

"Yep," I said.

Melifaro was so satisfied with my confession that he even went quiet. For no less than a dozen seconds. Then we arrived, and he had to open his mouth again to greet his father.

Sir Manga Melifaro was waiting for us at the gate. He hadn't changed at all since the last time I saw him, except perhaps for his thick red braid, which had become even longer. Amazing, actually, how becoming this unusual hairstyle was to the renowned encyclopedist.

"Your brother has gone completely insane," he informed his son, and then turned to me. "Good evening, Sir Max. I don't believe my eyes. Have you really come to visit us?"

"I find it hard to believe myself, but it looks like I am here, indeed."

"I went down on my hands and knees before this monster," Melifaro said. "For three days in a row I groveled, begging him to honor our humble abode with his presence. I was doing it for you, Dad, so you're forever in my debt. Which brother has gone insane, by the way?"

"Take a guess," said Sir Manga, rolling his eyes like a martyr.

"Well, Anchifa stands the greatest chance of losing it. He's more talented, and his life is full of adventure. Am I right?"

"But of course," said the head of this unique family. "I came outside to greet you so we could discuss one matter in particular. I was going to send you a call, but I kept procrastinating. Then, when I saw your amobiler flying down the road a few inches above it, I realized that it was too late to send calls."

"Flying?" I said. "Are you joking, Sir Manga?"

"I beg your pardon, Sir Max, but I am certain that the wheels were not always touching the ground. My compliment is thus based on facts."

"So, what did my brother do this time?" said Melifaro.

"He brought a guest from Isamon, no less," said Sir Manga. "And what a guest he is! You'll soon see for yourself. He's quite a phenomenon."

"A guest? I don't see anything unusual about it. It runs in the family. I mean, you're no saint in that department, and look what I drag in," said Melifaro, waving his hand in my direction.

I shook my fist in front of his nose. The fist, I'm afraid, was not hefty enough to inspire anyone with fear.

"Ah, but in half an hour you will see what I mean," said Sir Manga. "We can't kick him out, because he showed hospitality to our kinfolk in his homeland. Oh, how I wish Anchifa had spent that night out on the street! Your mother and I have reached the limits of our patience. She's threatening to run away to her relatives in Uryuland right after she casts her eyes upon you for the last time. You know, wives have never left *me* before, and I'm too old to deal with this now. Son, I'm begging you, please take this honored guest with you to the Capital. Maybe he'll get lost there. Echo is a big city, after all."

"Is he that bad?" said Melifaro. "Good golly, who *is* this guy? I'm really curious now. At any rate, you don't have to worry. If need be, I'll take him away. It's an old routine for Anchifa and me: he makes stupid mistakes, and I patch things up for him. But what does he think about it himself?"

"What do you think? Your brother couldn't be happier. This fellow is worse than a dozen sea cadets, so Anchifa can let loose his foulest curses on him. The fellow himself seems absolutely indifferent to them. On top of everything else, he's deaf. But we should go in to the dining room. I beg your pardon, Sir Max. I got carried away, talking about our family matters. It wasn't very polite of me."

"Oh, but it was very intriguing," I said, smiling.

"Do not despair, Father. I brought a professional killer with me, so everything is going to be fine. We'll bury his body in the garden. It won't be the first time. Right, Max?" said Melifaro with an innocent look on his face.

"That may be one way out," said Sir Manga pensively. "But only as a last resort. If he refuses to go to the Capital."

"Sinning Magicians! He didn't even notice I was joking," Melifaro whispered in my ear in alarm.

"Were you?"

Now it was Melifaro's turn to shake a fist in front of my nose. I heaved a sigh of envy: his fist looked much more intimidating than mine.

❀

The dining room was empty. Sir Manga sat down at the dining table.

"We seem to be in luck. I suggest you help yourself to a little snack, boys. The night is short, so don't miss your chance."

"I always obey my elders," I said, sizing up the multitude of dishes on the table.

"Oh, look at Mr. Do-Right here," said Melifaro, and dug his teeth into a tempting pastry.

"You just got here and you're already gobbling away! Way to go, brother. No need to keep your stomach and backside unemployed."

A small, skinny man appeared in the doorway. I knew at first sight that he was one of those slight, sinewy men you don't want to mess with. He could knock any opponent to the ground, weight category notwithstanding. On his head he wore a beautiful multicolored shawl, its ends almost touching the floor. A loose black looxi barely reached his knees—too short even by the fashion standards of the Capital. His checkered skaba wasn't much longer and revealed a peculiar sight: the high tops of boots decorated with intricate designs.

Behind the man stomped the giant Baxba, the eldest of the brothers, whom I had had the pleasure of meeting during my previous stay. He greeted us very courteously, sat down comfortably in a large chair, and focused on food. I think Baxba was the only quiet, meek member of the family.

Melifaro gave a cry of delight and rushed up to hug Anchifa. It was some time before the brothers finished their greeting ritual and Melifaro decided to introduce me.

"Anchifa, this is Max. They hired Max so that I could sleep at night." Then he turned to me. "You no doubt guessed that I was just embracing the terror of all shallow puddles, not to mention high seas, the irremovable stain of shame on the family name, and the only remaining hope of our father: Sir Anchifa Melifaro."

"And I was about to think that this was the fruit of your secret visits to the Quarter of Trysts, Dad," said Anchifa, chortling. "So, you're not my newfound brother, then, sir? That's too bad."

"It's quite possible, quite possible," said Sir Manga. "My memory isn't what it used to be. What do you think, Max? Perhaps the boy is right."

"I'm afraid not. I'd love to join the ranks of your clan, but no more than twelve hours ago I learned that I'm a descendant of the King of the Lands of Fanghaxra."

"This calls for a celebration!" said Anchifa, opening an enormous bottle made of dark-blue glass. He had already heaved himself onto the table. His left foot, clad in the beautiful boot, rested in a plate of cookies. Melifaro was starting to seem like a paragon of innocence compared to this brother of his.

"Have you lost your mind? No, seriously, are you crazy?"

An extremely long-nosed, slightly balding man then entered the dining room. I almost choked on my food when I saw his attire. He was wearing shiny red tights like a ballet dancer's. The tights proudly and honestly exposed the chubby thighs of their owner, along with the curves of his very feminine bottom. The bizarre tights formed an effective contrast to his heavy boots and short leather jacket. I guffawed in the most disrespectful manner. To my surprise, Melifaro was completely calm.

"Haven't you seen an Isamonian before?" he said, surprised. "They all dress like that."

"That's even funnier," I said, gasping for breath.

"It even looks good on them," said Sir Manga, lowering his voice. "Present company excluded, naturally."

"But you're all completely out of your minds! Simply out of your minds!" said the stranger, sitting down at the table.

He pronounced his *l*'s in a peculiar way, his voice was a bit nasal, and his diction and accent didn't help matters. I couldn't stop giggling. The stranger looked at me, offended.

"I don't see anything funny here, sir. It's not in the least bit funny. You've all lost your wits! There are guests in the house, I haven't been introduced, and no one bothered to call me down for dinner. I've arrived, but the caravan left without me. This will not do! What kind of a place is this?"

"This is my place," said Sir Manga sternly.

"What? Speak up. I'm a bit hard of hearing. If this happened back home in Isamon, elders wearing hats this big would have come down from the mountains." He stretched his arms to show us the improbable dimensions of the hats in question. "Yes, they would have come down, and then there would be trouble. Trouble, I say!" He made several significant nods and then looked at me again. "I still don't see what's so funny. Pull yourself together, young man!"

"Where I come from, it's customary to greet a stranger with loud laughter," I said. "It demonstrates one's joy at meeting someone. I'm just being polite, that's all."

Now it was Melifaro's turn to laugh.

"All right," said the stranger peaceably. "All right, I get it. My name is Rulen Bagdasys. I come from a family of highborn aristocrats, you know."

"And this is Sir Max," said Sir Manga said to the Isamonian. "His, as we have just learned, is a well-known *royal* family, you know."

"Yes, so I've been told," said Rulen Bagdasys. Suddenly he grew very serious. "That's fine— Hey, you!" he said, giving Anchifa a stern look. "You're out of your mind! Who dares sit on top of a dining table in the presence of royalty?"

"I do," said Anchifa. "I was vouchsafed the right by a special decree of His Majesty Gurig VIII in recognition of my outstanding service. So it's cool. Don't soil your pants from too much deference."

"What? Speak up! You know I can't hear very well," said the Isamonian indignantly, and immediately lost interest in the subject. He turned to the youngest Melifaro and said, "I've been told you can show me the Capital. Is that true? It's high time I moved to Echo. I can't sit in this provincial backwater surrounded by country dirt and stench any longer."

"All right, I'll show you the Capital," said Melifaro.

Sir Manga's face took on an expression of profound gratitude.

We amused ourselves in this way for another two hours or so. I found Rulen Bagdasys to be charming and odd. His rudeness, combined with startling innocence and slight deafness, could very well have passed for originality. If he had been staying at my house, of course, I'd have probably hastened to change my mind.

Finally, Sir Manga left for his study, saying that he had work to do. To my surprise, I realized I was exhausted myself. It was close to midnight, after all, and I was dozing off. So much for being a night owl, I guess. Granted, I had long ago forgotten about insomnia, which had ruined the first thirty years of my life.

"I'm getting positively sick of you guys," I said to the brothers Melifaro in a sweet voice. "I'm sure you're even sicker of me, so I'm off to bed."

"You're going to bed? It's not even midnight!" My colleague looked almost frightened. "What on earth has gotten into you, Max?"

"You've been asking me that all day today, and I've been telling you that I'm fine. I swear. I'm just tired, that's all."

"Our Venerable Head is driving you to your grave," Melifaro said sympathetically. "Granted, you're a cunning killer, a werewolf on the loose, and an all-around creep, but such cruelty is breaking my fragile heart."

"Spare me your sympathy and show me to the bedroom, instead," I said. "I don't want to get lost in your family mansion, roam the dark hallways for years, and survive on a diet of servants and guests. You'll find me ten years later, emaciated and bitter at all mankind."

"Okay, let's go," said Melifaro, reluctantly getting up from the table.

"You could very well be our brother, mate," said Anchifa. "A piece of advice: ask your royal mom who she was having quality time with in the bushes."

"I will," I said. "As long as someone brings her back from the dead. Though I hear it's not that difficult. Good night, guys!"

❀

The enchanted bedroom, handiwork of Magician Filo Melifaro, represented the delightful distillation of many centuries of wisdom of the Order of the Secret Grass. It was a cozy, peaceful refuge that I had been missing for a long time. Sweet wonders from my childhood years resided here: ghostly actors from the nighttime shadow theater, inconsequential midnight fantasies, and delicious dreams. I studied the intricate designs of the dark beams on the ceiling, lost in admiration. Then I fell asleep. In honor of my sojourn in the bedroom, a special screening of the Collector's Classics of my favorite dreams had been scheduled for me. Unfortunately, I didn't dream about the city in the mountains with the cable cars and tiny street cafés. Well, that was to be expected. Once, I had given this dream as a gift to another World. And you can't have a gift back, even if you really want it, right?

When I woke up, it was past noon. I had carried out Sir Juffin Hully's order and taken the opportunity to get my fill of rest. Not only did I feel I could go on with my life, I knew I could take pleasure in doing so.

Happy and peaceful, I went down to the dining room. Sir Manga Melifaro and his lovely wife were already crunching on some cookies.

"The boys are still sleeping," said Sir Manga. "Unlike you, they only stopped carousing after dawn. Are you jealous?"

"Not at all. Last night was the best night in my life. Your father's bedroom is a marvel."

"It is, isn't it?" Sir Manga and his wife said in unison.

"Where is he now, your venerable ancestor?" I said.

I was sure that my question was not tactless. I knew that the artisan of this magic bedroom could not just die of old age like an ordinary man.

"He's looking for his Grand Magician, a hole in the heavens above him," said Sir Manga. "Or maybe he's already found him. In any case, I'm sure he's happy. The thirst for adventure is in our blood, I'm afraid."

Are you up already, Max? Juffin's Silent Speech resounded in my head. *I'm very sorry, but you and Melifaro will have to come back a little sooner. Frankly, I need to see you before dusk.*

I can wake him up for you right now, I answered, not without a hint of sadistic joy. *Should I?*

Is he still sleeping? Well, let him snooze for another hour and a half or so. But not more. How about yourself, Max? Have you rested?

That's putting it mildly. Why? Did something happen?

No, nothing's happened yet. It will at dusk, however. The ship from Arvarox will happen. It's going to be a whole lot of fun for all of us. Trust me.

What kind of fun?

You'll see. We'll have plenty of time to talk when you get back. Over and out.

Over and out, if you say so.

I looked at Melifaro's parents with a guilty expression.

"I'm afraid I'm going to have to do something unforgivably rude. I must deprive you of your youngest son a day earlier than planned."

"But this is wonderful!" said Mrs. Melifaro, visibly excited. "Magicians be with him! We'll have plenty of opportunities to see him. He promised to take away that deaf idiot from Isamon, didn't he, Manga?"

"Oh, yes, yes. He certainly did."

"Is he really that bad?" I said. "To be honest, I thought he was rather cute yesterday."

"He is cute for the first two or three days," said Sir Manga. "But by about day four, you realize that he may not be as cute as you had originally thought. Then the oldest servants in the house threaten to give you notice, and your eldest son tries to find a pretext for spending the night in a rickety hut at the far end of the pasture. About half a dozen days later, you realize you can't get the thoughts of brutal murder out of your head. You know what I think, Max? I think that all this hospitality and good manners will be the death of us. I don't mean my family in particular, I mean the whole of humankind."

"Well, consider your troubles over. Unless your guest changes his mind about going to the Capital and decides to hibernate here instead."

"Goodness gracious, Max," said Sir Manga. "Please don't joke like that in my presence. You'll give me a heart attack!"

"I'm sorry," I said. "If worst comes to worst, I'll take him with us, by force. I have a trick or two up my sleeve."

I was telling the truth. I could place anyone between the thumb and the index finger of my left hand and take him away to the ends of the Universe.

※

An hour later I knocked on Melifaro's bedroom door.

"Wake up, my friend. Time to go to work."

"Work?" his sleepy voice came from behind the door. "What are you talking about? Relax. Everything is all right, you're in my home, and we don't need to go to work until the day after tomorrow. What you need is a good doctor, mate."

"Not me—it's Juffin who needs one. He just sent me a call. He said, and I quote, 'The ship from Arvarox will happen.' Ring a bell?"

"Ugh. It does," said Melifaro. "Our little vacation is over, I'm afraid. I'd rather you went insane. It would've been more fun to watch. Okay, I'm coming down. Is there time for breakfast?"

"Yes. There's even time for lunch. You know how fast I can drive."

"Right. You can be useful sometimes," said Melifaro. "Now get lost. I need to get ready."

I left. Instead of getting lost, however, I simply went down to the dining room. A few minutes later, my colleague, his hair still messy and wet but his spirits up, came downstairs, as well.

"Why so much fuss about some ship from Arvarox?" I asked both Melifaros, since I didn't know which of the two was more competent in this matter. "Are we at war with them? Or is it the Great Empire of the Dark Magicians, and we should always expect trouble coming from that direction?"

"It's an empire, all right," said Sir Manga, "but I doubt it's an empire of Magicians. If anything, their magic skills are quite weak. Their Great Shaman would hardly qualify as an errand boy for any wise-woman in Echo."

The young Melifaro was also going to say something, but with his mouth full, his attempt failed miserably. Sir Manga went on.

"Arvarox is the continent most remote from Echo. In my view, it is also one of the most interesting places imaginable. They have strange manners, a strange religion, strange philosophy, and even stranger logic.

Their plants and animals are nothing like ours. They look like they come from your worst nightmare. There are no metals in Arvarox, yet its citizens have devised quite original ways of getting by, and they do get by just fine. You will see for yourself, however. I understand that in the next few days you will have some firsthand experience with Arvaroxians. And, no, we are not at war with Arvarox, which is all the better for them. They wouldn't stand a chance against the Unified Kingdom. But apart from us, no one can compete with them. Alas, Arvarox is the major headache of our politicians. If it weren't for the well-balanced diplomacy of His Majesty and the Order of the Seven-Leaf Clover, the government of Arvarox would most certainly try to subjugate the rest of the World, much as they once subjugated their own continent."

"But do they pose any danger to us?" I said. The last thing I wanted was to get involved in a World War. The dirt of the trenches, the rumble of Babooms, and not a single bathing pool with hot water for miles around would bore me to death.

"Of course not, Max. If anything, it's we who pose a danger to them. But, you understand, no one wants the sovereigns of Arvarox to lord it over the Kumon Caliphate or, say, Isamon. They don't stand a chance against Arvarox, so they would send their ambassadors to the Unified Kingdom and drench the king's robe with their tears. What would happen next is that a couple of dozen highly trained specialists from the Order of the Seven-Leaf Clover would be sent to the battlefield. They would give the aggressor an object lesson on what happens to a turkey on the Day of Foreign Gods. There would be a lot of Forbidden Magic, a lot of bloodshed, and a lot of insults hurled back and forth. For this reason, the foreign policy of the Unified Kingdom regarding Arvarox boils down to this: We indulge them, look tenderly into their brave eyes, and strive to grant these eternal teenagers' every wish. We also make it very clear that the game will last as long as their military crusades, forays, skirmishes, and other such nonsense stay within the bounds of their own continent. If I understand correctly, we also secretly finance their rebels, guerillas, and other overage hoodlums. The Arvaroxian way of life provides a perfect playground for innumerable 'people's heroes,' so their sovereigns are never idle. Arvarox has been in a state of a permanent civil war since time immemorial, and this situation has been to everyone's satisfaction ever since."

"Boy, do I hate politics," I said. "But does anyone ask my opinion?"

"You're right. No one does," said Sir Manga. "No one asks mine, either." He then turned to Melifaro. "Don't forget to take our guest with you, son."

"Where is he?" said Melifaro.

"He's in the guest room. Still sleeping, I believe, judging by how quiet it is in the house."

✿

Waking up Rulen Bagdasys and persuading him to leave immediately, and not in two years' time, was no ordinary feat. Melifaro returned to the dining room almost an hour later. He was literally dragging the Isamonian by the scruff of his neck.

"We cannot make a member of a royal family wait forever." Poor Melifaro wasn't so much speaking as he was hissing and pointing his finger in my direction. It took me a second or two to remember that it was I who was the "member of a royal family."

"What's going on? What the devil is wrong with you! You've lost the last remains of your brain, sir! In Isamon the aristocracy never gets up before dusk. And I can't travel on an empty stomach. Are you out of your mind?" The nasal voice of Rulen Bagdasys filled the room. "You've got some half-wit cooks running your kitchen, but I simply must have something to eat right now! Don't you know that undernourishment leads to baldness?" he shouted in helpless indignation.

Sir Manga sighed, got up from his chair, and walked out onto the veranda. His wife had sneaked out earlier, as soon as she heard the Isamonian's first nasal utterances coming from the hallway.

"Sir Manga," I whispered, following him. "I need a definite answer from you. What should we do with him? Should we bring him back to you and Anchifa safe and sound, or should we put him on a ship to Isamon, or—"

"Oh, I don't know! Do as you please. For all I care, you can eat him. You know, Max, I am under the impression that he does not want to go back to Isamon. I don't think anyone's waiting for him back there. Anchifa is also getting tired of this exotic plaything from overseas. A sad story, if you think about it."

"Maybe not as sad as it seems. It's up to Anchifa to decide, though," I said. "Thank you for your hospitality, Sir Manga. I am sorry I couldn't stay so you could get good and sick of me. I'd love to, but I've got work to do."

"That's a law of nature, Sir Max. One of its most disagreeable laws, in fact. There is a saying in Tulan that goes, 'A nice guest always leaves early.' It's a great place, Tulan. One of my favorite."

"What about Isamon?" I said.

"Oh, no, it's the backwoods," said Sir Manga. "One of the most boring places I've ever been to. The only moderately amusing pastime there is entertaining yourself by watching the multicolored thighs of its inhabitants."

"Indeed. Their clothing is most peculiar," I said with a grin, and went back to the dining room.

❀

"Now we really do have to leave," I said.

I was exaggerating. We had about five hours before dusk, and I could get us back to Headquarters in no more than twenty minutes if I tried. After having slept in the bedroom of Filo Melifaro, though, I was surprisingly energetic. I had to start working off some of this new energy right away, or I would explode.

"Did you hear that?" Melifaro asked the Isamonian, who was practically licking the empty plate in front of him. "Run up and start packing. If you're not ready in thirty minutes, you're traveling light."

"What?" shouted the Isamonian. "Speak up, I can't hear you."

I began to lose hope for a peaceful outcome to our humanitarian mission. I sighed loudly and filled my plate again just to keep myself busy.

About two hours later, Anchifa, still sleepy, came down into the dining room. "I was just planning to go for a stroll, and this silly boy is already running off!" he said.

"If you need company, take Baxba," said Melifaro, chuckling.

"Thank you kindly," grumbled Anchifa.

"Better yet, come visit me in Echo," said Melifaro.

"What am I going to do there? Run around the Quarter of Trysts shouting, 'Hey, have you seen my brother? A dozen days ago he left for work and hasn't come back yet'?"

"For your information, running around shouting is not the only form of entertainment in the Quarter of Trysts," said Melifaro. "But it's up to you. If you change your mind, you can always count on a mat by my front door."

"I may change my mind. I just woke up, and I can't decide. By the way, say hi from me to those goggle-eyed fellows from Arvarox. Ask them what they thought of our latest skirmish by the Joxi Islands. Come to think of it, don't ask them that. It may provoke a diplomatic crisis."

❀

Finally, Rulen Bagdasys appeared in the doorway. He was wearing a pair of snow-white dress tights. His boots and jacket had not undergone much of a change, but his head was now crowned with a huge fur hat. It was the middle of the summer, for crying out loud! The fellow looked very satisfied with himself. His huge nose pointed skyward, his eyes sparkled like a gladiator's, and his lower lip protruded, giving his face a capricious, imperious expression. Apparently, the fur hat was an indispensable feature of the national pride of any Isamonian.

"Aren't you a bit overdressed?" I said cautiously.

"It is imperative to wear a hat out of doors," said Rulen Bagdasys, "or your brains will blow away."

The brothers Melifaro brayed like donkeys. The Isamonian looked down his nose at them, but said nothing.

I sat behind the levers of the amobiler, and Melifaro sat in the seat next to mine. Now *he* was eager to get back to the House by the Bridge. Judging by his expression, the ship from Arvarox promised to be a lot of fun.

Rulen Bagdasys got into the back seat of the amobiler. When I began gradually to pick up speed, he became frantic, started yelling, and even tried to grab the controls.

"Sit still, pal," I said. "When people grab me I spit venom. Didn't anyone tell you that?"

"I know," he said. "I've been told. But what kind of morons taught you how to drive? Get a grip on yourself! Let me show you how to drive properly."

"Should I punch him in the nose?" Melifaro said somberly.

"Go ahead, what are you waiting for?" I said. "Because if he doesn't quit grabbing me, we're going to crash."

"I didn't know that was how you drove around here," Rulen Bagdasys was quick to say. "I thought you were supposed to hold the levers with your palms facing outward, and you, sir, are doing it the other way around."

I burst out laughing from the sheer unexpectedness of it. I thought Rulen Bagdasys was unnerved by our speed, but he was worried about some technical matters.

"You hold the levers the way it feels comfortable to you as a driver," I said in a conciliatory tone, and increased my speed a little more.

I'm sorry to admit it, but I really wanted to scare Mr. Know-it-all. He wasn't a bit scared, though. Maybe the guy just didn't know what the average speed of an amobiler was. A few marvelous minutes later, during which the World around me ceased to exist, we pulled over by Melifaro's place on the Street of Gloomy Clouds, in the very heart of Echo.

"You just outdid yourself, Max," said Melifaro wiping the perspiration off his forehead. "This is a new record. Can't believe we're still alive."

"It was pure luck," I said, grinning.

"I think so, too."

Melifaro sighed and turned to the Isamonian. "This is it, Rulen. We're at my place. Get your stuff out of the amobiler."

Rulen, as it turned out, had lots of baggage. Melifaro was kind enough to help him take his numerous bags into the house. I suspected that they were chock-full of tights of all colors, fur hats, and manuals on how to hold the amobiler controls properly.

"Make yourself at home," said Melifaro. "Or you can go walk around the block. Do as you wish. Let's go, Max."

And we sped off.

"It's nice to have a highly disciplined driver," said Melifaro. "Maybe I won't fire you just yet."

"I'm going to tell Lonli-Lokli that you're mean to me. He'll teach you how to talk to a member of a royal family."

"Lonli-Lokli? No, please don't. My father is used to the fact that he has three sons. He counts us from time to time. He would be heartbroken if he came up one short. Wait, don't miss the turn this time!"

"When have I ever missed a turn?" I said, whizzing right past the Street of Copper Pots just to make my diurnal half happy. The diurnal half was pleased.

"Not too shabby, boys," said Sir Juffin Hully. He met us in the Hall of Common Labor. "Not too shabby at all. When I told you that I wanted to see you two here before dusk, Max, I sincerely believed that you would show up at exactly one minute before sunset. I even wanted to send you a call and hurry you up, but then I made a bet with myself. I wagered a dozen crowns. I sat here trembling with excitement and recalled all the curse words I have learned during my long, long life."

"How many did you recall?" asked Melifaro.

"No more than a couple thousand, to my regret. Back to the business at hand, however. At sunset, the ship from Arvarox will drop anchor at the Admiral's Pier."

"Why the Admiral's Pier?" I said slurping cold kamra from my boss's favorite cup. This was quickly turning into a ritual.

"Because it is an honor," said Juffin. "Also, it's a military ship, so officially that would be the right thing to do. But the most important thing is that this will honor *them*. Say, Melifaro, have you been present at a Customs inspection of ships from Arvarox? I can't quite remember."

"Oh, yes," said Melifaro with a nod. "I was still a rookie here. I remember I almost fainted when the proud chieftain of those barbarians started listing all his titles, and I had to stand there listening to all that nonsense with a straight face. But I persevered."

"A noble performance it was, indeed," said Juffin. "And today you'll both have to repeat it. Are you ready?"

"Well, no," said Melifaro. "But that's not up to us to decide, is it? By they way, why us and not Lonli-Lokli? He's much more imposing, and he certainly won't start cracking up during the ceremony."

"Sir Shurf can't step aboard any vessel. If he does, it will immediately develop a hole and sink. These are the consequences of his successful career in the Order of the Holey Cup. All his former colleagues suffer from the same problem. Didn't you know?"

"Whoa! No, I didn't," said Melifaro.

"Juffin, what does this have to do with us?" I said. "We're Secret Investigators, not Customs officials. Or am I missing something here?"

"You are, Max. The ship from Arvarox is a special case. Sending the actual Customs officials to it would be a deadly insult. The Arvaroxians would immediately try to retaliate, not because they're wicked monsters but because their code of honor says they must. Fortunately, for several thousand years the Office of Worldly Affairs has kept a thick *Guide to Good Manners*, which one must consult when welcoming guests from Arvarox. This sacred book was endorsed by both parties, but unlike us, the citizens of Arvarox know its contents by heart. Don't fret, Max. All you need to do is show up on the ship and glance over the contents of its holds. The truth is, there's no chance they're going to smuggle any contraband. That book states very clearly that the subjects of the Conqueror of Arvarox swear never to bring any contraband merchandise into the territory of the Unified Kingdom. And trust me, these guys keep their word. If we don't sniff around the ship, though, they'll think we don't take them seriously, and that constitutes another deadly insult to them. So please, remember to pretend that you are very interested in the contents of the ship's holds. You can even go slightly overboard with your zeal. Then you'll give them an official permit to stay in Echo, and that's it. Tomorrow they're visiting the Palace, and after that the fun will begin. We'll follow those innocent young men around and make sure nobody and nothing hurts them. You have no idea, boys, how I loathe this nauseating fuss and bother, but Grand Magician Nuflin believes it's best for everyone. I can't disappoint the old man, now, can I?"

"You? You certainly can," said Melifaro.

"Yes, I can, but I won't, of course. Now, scram. If you spend an hour or so waiting for the honorable guests on the pier, you'll be displaying the strongest grasp of the art of diplomacy. Don't give me that look. I'm not saying you can't stay for a cup of kamra."

"With pastries," I said.

"Kurush has a bad influence on you," said Juffin with a smile. "You've adopted his mannerisms, and his tastes, too. Next thing you'll know, you're going to start growing feathers."

"That wouldn't be so bad. In my book, buriwoks are much more highly evolved creatures than humans."

"You may be right," said Juffin, "but can you imagine what it would look like?"

"What do mean?"

"Feathers. In combination with your face."

Melifaro laughed. This, however, did not prevent him from grabbing a pastry from the delivery boy, who had just walked in and was looking very perplexed at the whole scene.

※

A half hour before sunset, Melifaro and I were standing on the Admiral's Pier. We had arrived early, but not too early: the ship from Arvarox, enormous and splendid, was approaching us swiftly. Against the background of the darkening eastern horizon, it looked like a majestic yet sad apparition.

"Look at you, Nightmare," said Melifaro. "You should be a poet, not a king."

"I was a poet once," I said. "Wasn't all that appealing, let me tell you. Especially the wages."

"What? Were you really a poet? But when?"

"Isn't it obvious? While I was riding my trusty nag through the endless plains between the Barren Lands and the County Vook. I had to do something to keep my mind busy."

Melifaro shook his head skeptically. I think up till then he had had a different picture in his head about the mysteries of poetic creativity.

The splashes of the dark waters of the Xuron reminded us that the solemn moment was nigh. The ship from Arvarox was approaching.

"I need to think about something sad right this minute, or I'll start laughing," said Melifaro. "How about my first love?"

"It won't help in my case," I said. "My first love was the most delightful moment of my life. I was less than a year old, and my chosen one was a few hundred years older. She was a friend of my grandmother's, and she took me in her arms from time to time. That, my friend, was true love."

❦

The black side of the ship's hull rubbed lightly against the pier, and a rope ladder landed at our feet. This took me by surprise: I had never had the chance to climb a rope ladder before. But I'd go to any lengths for the triumph of the foreign policy of the Unified Kingdom. Fear gave me the agility and dexterity I needed to climb the ladder. Seconds later, my beautiful boots, sporting dragon heads on their toes, landed on the deck of the ship with a soft thud. I have to confess, though, my knees were trembling.

In another moment, Melifaro joined me. We could relax and look around.

Frankly speaking, there wasn't much to see, apart from the ties and ropes of the ship's rigging above. The deck was empty. Whoever had thrown the ladder down for us had already hidden himself somewhere in the mysterious semidarkness of the ship's interior.

"That's all right," said Melifaro, nudging me lightly with his elbow. "The ceremonial exit of some Big Chieftain will start any second now. So start thinking about something sad. Maybe about your second love, since your first one was such a delight."

I wanted to come up with some witty retort about my second love but was distracted by a noise. It wasn't the thumping of heavy boots or a clattering of metal. It was a much more delicate noise: a soft knocking, rustling, and creaking. The author of this modernist piece of music was a human being of such striking beauty that it took my breath away.

A true giant, no less than seven feet tall, was coming our way. His snow-white hair was pulled into a knot on the top of his head. Even so, the ends fell down long enough to reach to his waist. His amber eyes seemed almost completely round. He had a very high forehead and a perfectly shaped face—too soft for a warrior's, but just right for a favorite with the ladies. The most striking, yet odd, feature was the combination of a predatory nose and a small, almost childlike mouth. His attire deserved special mention. His shirt and his pants, both of a very simple cut, shone with every color of the rainbow. They didn't seem to restrain his movements, but I noticed that the folds of the shirt, even though it was very wide, did not flap in the wind. The folds swayed slightly, making a very soft knocking sound when they touched. Later I learned that when one wore a shirt made out of the wool of Arvaroxian sheep, one had to use a considerable amount of muscle power just to bend one's arm, let alone do something else. His boots, on the contrary, seemed almost weightless: I could see the stranger's long, flexible toes through the thin skin of his footwear. To my surprise, he had not five but six toes. I looked at his hands, but the hands were all right: they looked like ordinary human hands with five digits on each.

On one of the stranger's shoulders, a large, furry, spider-like creature perched comfortably. Its numerous paws were shorter and much thicker than those of a spider, though. The creature was staring at me with eight pairs of tiny yellow eyes, the color of which matched those of its master. I returned the favor and gazed back with my own eyes, whose color had long been a mystery even to myself.

While I was playing stare-down with the wonder-spider, its owner slowly unfastened from his belt a weapon that looked like a machete. He threw it to our feet, and I noticed that the sound it made when it fell was quiet and dull. That's right, I thought. Sir Manga said that there were no metals in Arvarox. I wonder what these white-haired giants use for their weaponry instead.

An extraordinary article that looked like a gigantic flyswatter followed the "machete," landing on the deck just beside it.

Having disarmed himself, the giant approached us and stood an arm's length away. He looked at us for some time. There was no insolence, curiosity, or even tension in his gaze (which would be only natural under the circumstances). The stranger seemed to look at us with the expression of a bird, guarded and indifferent, simply because we happened to be standing in his line of vision. Finally, he spoke.

"I am Aloxto Allirox of the clan of Ironsided Hoob, ruler of Aliur and Chixo, Sternlooking Master of two times fifty Sharptooths, powerful and loyal warrior of Toila Liomurik the Silver Bigwig, Conqueror of Arvarox, who rules it all the way to the Ends of the World, immortalized in song by Xarlox the Pastry, the greatest storyteller among the living—"

Holy cow!

Melifaro's Silent Speech could have provoked an international conflict, but I managed not to laugh. I didn't even smile. I had to muster all my strength to maintain a diffident expression on my face. I still have no idea how I was able to pull it off.

Finally, Aloxto Allirox finished. I was sure that by then his ranks and titles were known to every single resident of Echo. The giant had a voice that could entertain an entire stadium without using any amplification system. Too bad his talent was completely wasted.

Now it was my colleague's turn to announce his title to the stranger.

"I am Sir Melifaro, Diurnal Representative of the Venerable Head of the Minor Secret Investigative Force of the Capital of the Unified Kingdom."

Melifaro gave an elegant bow, which, I assumed, was the appropriate gesture of hospitality for welcoming guests of honor from Arvarox, according to the *Guide to Good Manners* that Juffin had mentioned.

I thought that Melifaro's introduction was wanting in many respects, compared to that of the visitor from Arvarox. It was okay, but severely lacking in grandiloquence. I wanted to use a lot more window dressing for myself. I wanted the guy to wake up in cold sweat in the middle of the night and remember my name with envy. I took a deep breath and opened my chatterbox of a mouth.

"I am Sir Max, the last of the clan of Fanghaxra, Ruler of the Lands of Fanghaxra, Nocturnal Representative of the Venerable Head of the Minor Secret Investigative Force of the Capital of the Unified Kingdom, Death in His Majesty's Service, who generously kisses the condemned and spares the lucky, Leader of the Dead, and Terror of Madcaps biding their time in pubs."

Fortunately, Sir Aloxto was too impressed by the beginning of my speech to notice the irony of its finale. Later, however, I learned that the very notion of irony was completely inaccessible to the citizens of Arvarox. Their ways of looking at the world simply lacked the notion of irony altogether.

This was probably for the best, because my last phrase was intended solely for Melifaro's ears. I was getting back at him: now it was his turn to try not to laugh. The poor fellow turned bright red, to my utter delight.

You . . . you . . . Couldn't you find a better time for your jokes? I'm going to kill you sooner or later, and this World will lose another crazy poet. It even makes me a little sad.

Praise be the Magicians, at that moment Melifaro could only take revenge by resorting to Silent Speech.

While Melifaro was trying to maintain a serious expression, our Arvarox guest lowered his head in a sharp movement and began contemplating the boards under his feet. Apparently, this was the equivalent of a bow in Arvarox. In any case, I decided to go ahead and assume that he was bowing.

"I will make sure to convey my special thanks to your king for this honor," said Aloxto Allirox in a thunderous voice. "The presence of both of you on my ship is a sign. You are the face of the day, granting rest, and the face of the night, bestowing death. I could not have dreamed of the honor of such an encounter. My heart did not deceive me in sending me on this journey. Welcome to the deck of *The Surf Thorn*, under the bright cloak of the Conqueror of Arvarox. My Water Tamer will show you anything you find worthy of your interest. You are free to do whatever you like here."

The fair-haired giant turned away from us and shouted so loudly that my ears started ringing, "Kleva! Come here, Kleva!"

Another giant, this one red-haired, appeared before us. He was only a little shorter than Aloxto, but more broad-shouldered. Flung over his shoulders was a long dark cloak. I noticed chain mail underneath the cloak, glittering in the twilight.

Remembering that Arvarox knew no metals, I thought that his mail must be imported. Later I learned that an Arvaroxian warrior would never buy arms or armor from outlanders. They made their mail from the hard shells of the Eube bug. Arvarox was full of these insects, which provided enough material to supply everyone with armor.

"Take the keys, Kleva." Aloxto handed his subordinate several bundles of keys. I had no idea that there could be so many locks on the ship.

"Show these gentlemen everything they wish to see."

The rest was easy. Led by the silent Kleva, we took a short trip around the holds of the ship. Here and there we saw huge, handsome men wearing dark cloaks. They looked at us indifferently while we listened to the jangling of the keys in the hands of the captain and pretended that we were looking for contraband goods. Boy, was it ridiculous.

An hour later, Melifaro and I decided to call it quits. Melifaro produced a standard self-scribing tablet of the Customs Service from the pocket of his looxi, then pulled out a thick sheet of bluish paper from the chancellory office of Gurig VIII. It was an official permit for staying in Echo for the crew of the foreign warship. With the precious documents in our hands, we went to look for the leader of this gang of Mr. Universes.

We found him exactly where we had left him an hour before. He was sitting, his legs crossed, contemplating his weapons, which were still lying on the deck.

"Thank you for the hospitality, Sir Allirox," said Melifaro, bowing. "I have your papers. I have almost finished filling them out. There is just one other matter we must discuss. I must inquire of you the purpose of your visit to the Capital of the Unified Kingdom."

"We have come to find out whether the filthy Mudlax, last of the vile kings of the edge of the earth, who fled in disgrace from the victorious army of the Conqueror of Arvarox, is hiding here," said Aloxto.

"All right, I'll just note it down as 'justice and revenge,' then," said Melifaro, nodding matter-of-factly. "Here are your papers. His Majesty King Gurig VIII will be happy to welcome you tomorrow to his Summer Residence, the Anmokari Castle. His messengers will arrive at the ship at noon to accompany you. Good night, Sir Allirox."

"Good night, Sir Sternlooking Master of two times fifty Sharptooths," I added.

"Good night to you, too. I will be honored to see you again, gentlemen," said Aloxto, lowering his head ever so slightly again in a bow.

We departed from under the hospitable "bright cloak of the Conqueror of Arvarox"—disembarked *The Surf Thorn*, that is—and stepped down onto solid ground.

"I feel tiny and ugly," said Melifaro. "Why did the makers of the Universe expend most of their generosity creating the citizens of Arvarox? I just fail to see any logic in that. Do you see any logic in it, Max?"

"They are too handsome for me to be indignant about it, or to envy them," I said. "I can't compare myself to them. We're too different. It wouldn't be comparing people to people. It would be like comparing people to something else. Does what I'm saying make sense?"

"It does. But I still feel bad."

It was no wonder that when we returned to the House by the Bridge we still felt crestfallen after witnessing the otherworldly beauty and grandeur of the subjects of the Conqueror of Arvarox.

"Say, boys, are you sorry that your mothers didn't marry some handsome boys from Arvarox in their time?" asked Juffin, who could read our faces like an open book. "Don't envy them too much, though. Their lives aren't all song and dance. Besides, they rarely live to see their hundredth birthday. Can you really hold it against them that at least something about them is perfect?"

"Why don't they live longer?" I said. "Too many wars?"

"That, too. And they don't consider life to be worth all that much. Neither theirs, nor anyone else's. Life is a cheap commodity in their eyes. One could say that they don't live long because they want to die. That would be, perhaps, the most accurate explanation. You see, many Arvaroxians die young, but not necessarily on the battlefield. Sometimes a handsome young giant will sit down in a corner to think, and an hour later, when they call him for dinner, he is already stiff and cold."

I shook my head in disbelief. "How is that possible?"

"It just is, Max. There are old people in Arvarox, but they are few and far between. A gray-haired old man in Arvarox is considered to be a great wonder: a senseless one that nevertheless clearly witnesses to the great might of the powers they worship. Anyway, boys, go get some rest. I'm truly sorry I had to take you from Sir Manga so soon, and on such short notice."

"That's all right," said Melifaro. "Someday it will be tit for tat. And thank you, sir, for the information about Arvaroxian customs. I don't envy them anymore. It's strange that Father never told me about them."

"It's not strange at all. If Sir Manga hadn't been bound by numerous vows of secrecy, his *Encyclopedia of the World* would have comprised not just eight, but eight dozen volumes. Didn't you know?"

"Vaguely," said Melifaro. "To be honest, I never thought much about it. Let's go, Max."

I looked at Sir Juffin Hully in bewilderment. "Don't I need to stay at work?"

"No, not today. I'll need you tomorrow at noon. Try to look your best. You will meet one of the most avid admirers of your exploits."

"And who might that be?"

"Where is your intuition now, Sir Max? Why, His Majesty King Gurig VIII, of course."

"Oh, no!" I said putting my head between my hands. "Please, Juffin, have mercy! Look at me. What impression will I make at the Court? Plus, I feel shy. And nervous."

"Don't, Max. He's very pleasant and quite harmless, believe me. I have to deliver a report about our work at Court tomorrow, and the king begged me to bring 'that mysterious Sir Max' with me. It's only fair: one must meet in person the man whose cats will give birth to the first Royal Felines. Who knows what kinds of tricks you might teach them?"

"Aw, look at him," said Melifaro. "He wasn't shy or nervous in Jafax, but he's scared to see His Majesty. Trust me, Max, you wouldn't want to miss it. There will be plenty of amusing people there. And His Majesty himself is a quite a cool guy."

"See?" said Juffin. "If Sir Melifaro himself approves of it, you're going to like it. That I can guarantee you. Now, go ahead and have some fun, you poor victims of long-standing diplomatic ties."

❀

And away we went. That day, our way of having fun was one of the simplest varieties. We went back to Melifaro's place to pick up the man from Isamon, who was patiently waiting for us in Melifaro's living room with a proprietary air. The three of us then went to the *Fatman at the Bend* in the New City. The tavern belonged to the wife of our colleague Lookfi Pence. I had promised Lookfi I would visit their tavern, and this was an excellent opportunity.

Lookfi was waiting for us at the door.

"Sir Max, Sir Melifaro! Goodness, what a pleasant surprise! Do come in." He took a step back to make way for us, knocking over a heavy wooden chair. A female customer shrieked in fright, and Lookfi was very embarrassed. "I'm so sorry, so sorry. I'm such a klutz. Varisha! Come and see who's here!"

"Are you all right, hon?" said a beautiful red-haired woman rushing down from her post behind the bar. Her violet eyes were filled with such tenderness that Melifaro and I both sighed with jealousy.

"No, no. I'm quite all right. I'm used to knocking over this chair. I do think it stands too close to the entrance," said Lookfi.

This reassured the beautiful Varisha. She gave us a kind smile and told us that her chef had been instructed to charm us with his culinary skills. She returned to her post behind the bar, and Sir Lookfi invited us to sit at a cozy table by the far wall of the dining hall. It took us only a few minutes to persuade him to keep us company. A moment later the chef brought in a tray with food. As far as I could tell, the food here was on par with the food at the *Glutton Bunba*.

Rulen Bagdasys, who had been left to his own devices for a time, blustered and swaggered and then grew shy by turns. He gobbled down the contents of the plates in front of him, but the expression on his face was that of a person who was being poisoned. He was quiet for about thirty minutes, but after that he could no longer contain himself.

"You call this turkey? Are you out of your freaking minds? Who's the moron who—"

Melifaro leaped up in shock and covered Rulen's mouth with his hand. Rulen had to choke back the rest of his utterance.

"Is this man with you, gentlemen?" asked Lookfi.

"Unfortunately, yes," I said. "Sir Anchifa Melifaro just returned from a world cruise and brought back a present for his younger brother. How do you like him?"

"A present?" said Lookfi. "But it is prohibited to own slaves in the Unified Kingdom. Only servants."

"To my profound regret, he's neither slave, nor servant," said Melifaro. "He's a petty household disaster."

"Oh, I thought the gentleman just happened to be sitting at our table. I am sorry, sir, that I have been neglecting you all along."

Rulen Bagdasys opened his mouth. He saw Melifaro's clenched fist hovering dangerously close to his large nose, and nodded without saying a word. Then he sat quietly for a while, and the tension in the air dissolved. Melifaro and Lookfi picked apart the two new policemen who were at the top on our White List: Lieutenant Apurra Blookey and Lady Kekki Tuotli. They also didn't fail to mention Lieutenant Chekta Jax, whose mental abilities left him no hope of ever making it to our top dozen—though combining his brawn with someone else's wit, according to my colleagues, could be very fruitful. I listened to this with half an ear and grieved over the fact that I hadn't had the chance to meet the new heroes of the City Police Department personally.

"It's not that you have been too busy," said Melifaro. "They could have stopped by your office and introduced themselves. That's the way it's usually done. But you see, they are a little shy. Probably scared of you, too. You know, Nightmare, that's the best shortcut to fame: stir things up big time, and then disappear for a year. By the time you return, you're already a living legend. Say, was that why you disappeared?"

"But of course," I said. "Why else would I disappear? I've always wanted to become a legend. Since I was a kid. And, mind you, a *living* legend. By the way, where's the precious token of your brother's esteem and affection? Where did your family treasure go?"

Rulen Bagdasys no longer graced our table. Maybe he had grown bored with our chatting about work and left to find adventure.

"Huh? Beats me," said Melifaro, looking around. "Well, it's all for the best, anyway. If he gets lost, I'll inherit a hundred dozen pairs of red tights from his luggage. He left his stuff at my place. I just hope he won't remember where I live. On second thought, I think the poor fellow is still here. Is someone taking a pounding in that part of the hall, or what?"

"A pounding?" said Lookfi. "No one takes a pounding in my tavern. The *Fatman* is a respectable establishment."

"It *was* a respectable establishment," said Melifaro. "Until tonight. You shouldn't have been so persuasive with your invitation, Lookfi. Now, we've ruined your tavern's reputation. Oh, look! It *is* a fight!"

"Baan!" Lookfi shouted in distress. "Varisha, where's Baan? There's a fight going on there."

"I know, hon," his better half answered from behind the bar. "Baan is already dealing with it. Some customers had a little quarrel with that funny man that arrived with your friends. Did you just notice? They've been going at it for quite a while now."

"Is this man really with you, or is he lying to me?" A short but sturdy man was looking askance at my Mantle of Death. He dragged the Isamonian by his ear over to our table. Rulen had been fairly roughed up, and his left eye was turning, slowly but surely, black and blue.

"Unfortunately, he's not lying," said Melifaro. "What happened to him?"

The short man looked at Lookfi uncertainly.

"Don't be afraid, Baan," said Lookfi. "You did the right thing. Now, tell us what happened."

"Well, two ladies caught this gentleman's fancy, and he decided to introduce himself to them. The ladies were surprised and told him that they'd come here to eat, not to seek a partner. He insisted on joining them and sat down at their table. The ladies began to protest, and that attracted the attention of some other customers. They tried to explain to your guest that his behavior was unacceptable, but he wouldn't listen. Then he started grabbing the ladies. Lady Varisha called me, and I had to use force. If you only knew what kind of language he used in front of the ladies, sir. I grew up by the port, and you know what kind of people you run into there, but I swear I'd never heard anything like that before in my life."

"What kinds of things was he saying?" asked Lookfi.

I was dying to know myself, and Melifaro was already groaning and laughing in anticipation.

"I'm sorry, boss, but I can't repeat such foul obscenities. Let him tell you himself."

"That's quite all right, my friend. You may go now," said Lookfi. Then he turned back to us. "I think there must have been some misunderstanding."

"That son-of-a-gun hit me!" said Rulen Bagdasys.

"Figures," said Melifaro. "You're lucky I wasn't there. Lookfi, I think we'd better leave now. Next time we drop by, we'll come without this skirt-chaser, I promise you."

"If you feel lonely, you should go to the Quarter of Trysts," Lookfi said to Rulen.

"The Quarter of Trysts? What is it? What is it? Tell me!" said Rulen Bagdasys.

I pictured this funny, fat-bottomed man becoming someone's "destiny," if only for a night. This should have been amusing, but my good mood had been completely ruined. Sometimes I take other people's troubles too close to heart.

Half an hour later we took leave of Lookfi (who was falling asleep) and his wonderful wife. Rulen Bagdasys demanded that we take him to the Quarter of Trysts right that very minute.

"You can't go there with a black eye," Melifaro lied. "So you're going to have to wait it out."

The Isamonian became visibly upset. A few minutes later I pulled up by Melifaro's house on the Street of Gloomy Clouds.

"Want to stay at my place?" said Melifaro. "Yours probably looks like a Mutinous Magician's playground right now."

"It probably does," I said. "Thank you, pal, but since I'm back in Echo, I'd better go say hi to my kittens."

"Oh, that's right. You're a family man now," said Melifaro. "Well, up to you, then. Say hello to His Majesty Gurig VIII for me."

"Good golly, I almost forgot about that! Why, oh why did you have to remind me?"

As I drove off I heard Rulen Bagdasys shouting. He was trying to find out from Melifaro who "that son-of-a-gun Gurig" was.

To my surprise, my place was spotless and tidy. The workers had gone, leaving on the table a bill for an astronomical sum. I thought they deserved the money, though. Ella and Armstrong, shocked by the changes, were sitting by their bowls. I lay down on the Kettarian carpet and combed my little furries' long silky hair. They purred so happily that the walls trembled. Life was perfect. Almost perfect, anyway.

I showed up at Headquarters at noon, as I had promised. Sir Juffin Hully hadn't really dressed up for the occasion, but his expression was quite stern and sedate. I was astounded.

"Whoa!" I said. "Sir, are you sure the king is some guy named Gurig, and not you?"

"Have I gone a little overboard with the stateliness? Should I tone it down a bit?" said Juffin.

"No, no. Don't change a thing," I said. "It's a direct hit."

"I certainly don't need to hit anyone."

Juffin hurried out into the hallway to look in the large mirror. He returned quite pleased with himself.

"You have a talent for overstatement, Max. I look perfectly fine," he said, and turned to the buriwok. "Are you ready, my friend?"

"I am always ready," said Kurush calmly.

"You're absolutely right," said Juffin. He stroked the bird affectionately and placed it on his shoulder. "Shall we, Max?"

"We shall. I'm prepared to march to the ends of the earth in such company."

❀

Well, "the ends of the earth" *was* an overstatement. The Headquarters of the Ministry of Perfect Public Order is called the House by the Bridge for a reason. It stands on the very bank of the Xuron by the Royal Bridge, which connects the Left and the Right banks of the river with Isle Rulx. On the island stands the tall Rulx Castle, the main Royal Residence. As we crossed the bridge, I admired the old castle walls. They breathed the aura of ancient and forgotten mysteries.

Then we crossed Louxi Bridge and stopped at the main gate of the Summer Residence of Gurig VIII. If anything, the Anmokari Castle looked like an oversized but neat country villa.

"How underimpressive," I said with hauteur. "Call that a palace? Now, the Rulx Castle is one heck of a palace."

"Don't be such a snob," said Juffin. "I, for one, prefer the Summer Residence. It doesn't have that alarming, creepy-crawly feeling of old sins and ancient curses that the Rulx Castle has. Did you feel that?"

I nodded and said, "To be honest, that's just what attracted me to it."

"Really? That's wonderful! You're back in shape, then. A single night in the bedroom of old Filo was more than enough for you. Who would have thought? If I remember correctly, just two days ago you were sick and tired of mysteries, your own in particular."

I looked at my boss, surprised. I didn't remember saying anything like that to him. I generally try not to complain. It's just not my style.

A few moments later I remembered part of a conversation with Melifaro. "Don't you get a little sick of the air of mystery that surrounds you?" he had said. "Yes," I had replied. Just some worldly chitchat, nothing more.

"Juffin, do you really eavesdrop on every word that flies out of my mouth? And you still haven't gone mad?"

"Eavesdrop? Oh, spare me, Max. Your mindless chatter isn't the least bit interesting to me. It's just that I always know what's going on with you. It's a quirk I have, a character trait."

"No, no, it's okay. I'm flattered," I said and smiled. "Besides, it's very useful, too, because I don't always know what's going on with me. You should tell me."

"I just did."

❦

We got out of the amobiler and entered the Anmokari Castle. Juffin walked slowly and carefully so as not to disturb Kurush, who was dozing on his shoulder.

We stood before a cool, empty hallway that seemed to go on forever. When I made my first step in it, my knees trembled: the floor, walls, and ceiling had mirror-like surfaces. They were made from dull, smoky glass that multiplied our reflections infinitely and rendered them into sad, beautiful ghosts. The misty multitudes of creatures timidly copied our every motion. It sent my head into a tailspin.

"I know. You can really lose your equilibrium if you're not used to it," said Juffin with a nod. "A strange place this is, but the king likes it."

We managed to cross that mysterious infinitude and finally ended up in front of an open door leading to a relatively small and cozy hall.

"You should be happy that this is a business visit and not an official one," said Juffin, winking at me. "Remember what happened at Sir Makluk's?"

"Do I! Compared to that high-life reception, all the rest of the events in your neighbor's house were a joke."

"Indeed. Well, an official reception here would have been even more entertaining."

"I can only imagine."

"No, you can't, Max. I swear by the Magicians you can't. We are, however, going to take a small ride. Get ready."

"Well, if it's just a small ride, I don't mind."

We were surrounded by a few dozen young courtiers in embroidered looxis. They bowed so low that their heads almost touched the floor. They gave us looks of poorly concealed curiosity. Not without pleasure I noticed that my Mantle of Death inspired respect rather than superstitious horror. Maybe the courtiers were nice, well-educated young people, unburdened by superstitions.

Finally, the palanquin bearers arrived. I had acquired social graces by now, so I immediately flopped onto one of them. Sir Juffin graciously settled himself onto another. The bearers took us to a large hall that was modestly called the Minor Royal Study. It was as empty as most living quarters in the Capital. In Echo people don't like to crowd rooms with too much furniture, and I, for one, welcomed this custom wholeheartedly.

The palanquin bearers disappeared, leaving Juffin and me alone. The king was nowhere to be seen, though.

"This is all part of the etiquette," said Juffin. "His Majesty has been burning with curiosity since morning, but good manners require that he make us wait at least a minute. He rarely keeps his visitors waiting longer." Juffin tickled the soft feathers on Kurush's back. "Wake up, my friend. Time to get to work."

Kurush, displeased, puffed up his feathers. He always hated waking up. I understood him very well.

❀

His Majesty King Gurig VIII didn't wait even the customary full minute. A little door at the far end of the room opened, and a handsome, youthful man who looked like a young Johnny Depp appeared before us. He was wearing an elegant, hand-embroidered purple looxi. Instead of a turban, the favorite headgear of all local dandies of the past few centuries, he wore a simple hat. Later I learned that the shape of the royal headgear had been canonized many millennia ago. This was the kind of hat favored by Mynin, the most illustrious monarch of the Unified Kingdom, who had reigned centuries before.

"I see you as in a waking dream!" said the king, covering his eyes with his hands and turning to me.

I smiled. I hadn't had the opportunity to show off the official greeting that I learned on my first day in this World. I mostly met guys who didn't think much of all these highfalutin manners. But praise be the Magicians, I had practiced enough in my time to respond to His Majesty accordingly.

"You only visit me when you run out of excuses, Sir Hully," said the king reproachfully. "I was expecting you a hundred days ago. Not with a report, like today, but just for a friendly visit. You did get my invitation, didn't you?"

"I did," said Juffin. "But you know as well as I do what went on at the Ministry this spring, Your Majesty. We had to manage without Sir Max, just like in the old days. So instead of enjoying your company, seated at your table, I ran around Echo like an errand boy, chasing the mad Magician Bankori Yonli. He almost killed Melifaro, I should add. The boy now has quite a neat-looking scar on his face. I suspect he deliberately put too little healing ointment on it, so he looks like a true hero."

"What are you saying? The youngest son of Sir Manga nearly died? That would have been very bad. Very bad, indeed. And who is this Yonli? I do not recall," said the king, frowning.

"The Grand Magician of the Order of the Tinkling Hat—remember that odd sect of King Mynin worshipers? Yonli fled from Echo during the reign of your father, and returned this spring to take revenge on Grand Magician Nuflin. I couldn't imagine why he'd want to do such a thing. Our Sir Nuflin Moni Mak is such a gentle fellow. Never hurt as much as a fly in his entire life."

His Majesty was kind enough to burst out laughing. Even I couldn't hold back a smile, though I felt extremely shy. I always needed time to relax in the company of new people. Considering the fact that I had never had the pleasure of being in the company of a king before, the paroxysm of shyness was severe.

I could feel, though, that His Majesty Gurig VIII was also feeling uneasy. I realized that he and I were plagued by the same feelings. I'd never thought there might be shy kings, to tell the truth. Right away I felt a great bond with His Royal Majesty. It was so satisfying to learn that he, too, shared my insignificant human problems.

"Please be seated, gentlemen," said the king. He pointed at a set of high, soft armchairs by an open window. "The treat for Kurush was brought in beforehand. Help yourself, dear sir."

I liked the way Gurig addressed our wise bird with such dignity and called him "dear sir." I even felt a little envious that I hadn't thought of it first myself.

"Darned protocol," said the king. "My courtiers believe that the study should only be used for business affairs, and that I should have meals in the dining room. Is it not ridiculous? I prefer to combine these two pleasurable activities, just as you do, Sir Hully. What do you think, Sir Max?"

It struck me then that His Majesty was genuinely interested in my opinion on the matter.

"Your Majesty cannot be more correct in saying so. It would be impossible to survive at the House by the Bridge if one were otherwise disposed."

I had to muster all of my will to speak in a normal voice, and not to mumble under my breath, staring at the floor.

"Would it, indeed? It is comforting to know there are still contented people in this World," said the king solemnly. Then he brightened up and said, "But this morning I told my Master of Ceremonies that I would resign if he didn't at least serve us kamra here. The poor old man ground his teeth but had to submit in the end. Today I won't have to feel that I am the stingiest master of the house in the Universe. Sir Kurush, are you prepared to do some work for us?"

The bird stopped eating peanuts and began relating the great deeds of my colleagues to the king. I think I listened to him even more attentively than the king did. I finally had the opportunity to find out, in great detail, what the guys had been up to while I had been roaming the labyrinths of unexplored Worlds. Their lives seemed much more productive and full of events than my own otherworldly existence. It even made me a little upset: I had been missing out on all the fun for a whole year.

Kurush talked for almost four hours. While he was at it, though, he managed to empty a whole plate of peanuts and even ask for another helping.

We didn't have to starve, either. It turned out, though, that the kamra-making skills of the Royal Cooks couldn't compare with those of the cooks at the *Glutton Bunba*. It occurred to me that I would never consider getting involved in a plot to overthrow the king and appropriate his crown—his hat, that is. There was simply nothing to gain by it.

When Kurush finished, the king nodded his head in frank admiration. "You are the only citizens of the Unified Kingdom for whom the adventurous spirit of days of yore has not become just another page in the book of history. I must confess, I envy you, gentlemen."

"But Your Majesty, we are certainly not the only ones," said Juffin, smiling. "I'm sure the lives of our clients are much more adventurous."

"Yes, indeed, but they have to pay a very high price for it," said the king.

"Sometimes they do."

"I think retribution is always unavoidable, for they have to deal not just with anyone but with you. Well, I have truly enjoyed your company, gentlemen. May I ask you to stay for the official visit of the warriors from Arvarox?"

"When are you expecting them?" said Juffin.

"Quite soon," said His Majesty, looking out the window. "If the sun is not deceiving me, they should be in the Minor Reception Hall any minute now. I should very much like you to stay—primarily because those gentlemen may be in need of your assistance and, of course, your guardianship."

"Sir Max and I will be happy to fulfill any of your wishes, Your Majesty."

"Any of my wishes, you say?" said Gurig, laughing. "I will bet a hundred crowns that I have at least a dozen wishes whose fulfillment is unlikely to make you very happy."

Juffin mused over the thought for a moment and then said, "I would have to decline the bet, I'm afraid."

"I thought so," said the king, winking at Juffin.

I was steadily leaning toward becoming a monarchist. I was growing to like the head of the Unified Kingdom more every minute. It's too bad we're both so busy, I thought, and have such different occupations. Under different circumstances, I think I'd become friends with this fellow.

"I think this gentlemen has just fallen asleep," whispered the king, pointing to Kurush.

"That is his most natural state," said Juffin, smiling as he gently covered the bird with the flap of his looxi. "Would it offend Your Majesty if the bird slept through the entire reception?"

"Sir Kurush may do as he pleases in my palace." Gurig VIII looked at the buriwok with the genuine admiration of an amateur ornithologist.

The Minor Reception Hall was in reality so huge that I couldn't make out the faces of the courtiers standing by the wall opposite me. Beautiful Aloxto Allirox was standing immobile in the middle of the hall. This time he showed up without his spider-like pet. He probably had no idea that the king was such an avid lover of animal life.

By his feet lay his weapons, and behind him stood his entourage—about a hundred mighty warriors, clad in the same inflexible capes and soft boots, all light-haired, yellow-eyed, and handsome like Aloxto Allirox. The courtiers looked at them with well-meaning curiosity.

With a barely noticeable movement of the hand Sir Juffin Hully motioned me to come closer to him. We stood to the left of the Royal Throne, which was the rule. The area to the right of the throne was crowded with numerous noblemen. Next to them stood a single middle-aged gentleman. He was wearing a blue-and-white looxi, which meant that he belonged to the Order of the Seven-Leaf Clover, the Single and Most Beneficent. He bowed ever so slightly to Juffin and me. A more formal greeting was not allowed by the rules of etiquette.

Finally, the king entered the hall. Slowly he ascended the gem-encrusted stairs to his throne, the back of which seemed to tower over him. He bestowed a sympathetic smile on Juffin and me, then solemnly sat down on the throne. His expression was now one of unassailable, icy grandeur and boredom.

"I greet you, stranger." When the king spoke to Aloxto, his lips barely moved. "Tell us who you are and what matters have brought you to us."

Aloxto lowered his head in a respectful bow and began with the same old song that I had heard on the ship: "I am Aloxto Allirox of the clan of Ironsided Hoob, ruler of Aliur and Chixo, Sternlooking Master of two times fifty Sharptooths, powerful and loyal warrior of Toila Liomurik the Silver Bigwig, the Conqueror of Arvarox, who rules it all the way to the ends of the World, the Waterer of the Royal Tree of Spicy Flowers, the Keeper of Table Rugs, the Bearer of the Third Cup at the New Moon Feast after the Spouse and the Senior Cupbearer, the Eternal Helmsman of the Royal Boat on Lake Ulfati who has the right to wear bone boots on Zoggi needles, the Locker of the Royal Chamber and Master of Fifty Keys, the Chief of the Reprisal of Isisorins, the Speaker of the Ninth and Twelfth Words during the Royal Game of Launi, the Slayer of the Kulyox Bird with just two glances, one hit, and a bit of wit, the Bringer of Three Handfuls of Coins to the Tomb of Kwarga Ishmirmani, the Maker of Fire under the Royal Vatla Caldron, the Speaker of the Tongue of Morions, the Eater of the Mayushi Pork in two and a half gobbles, and he who made two times fifty songs about his own great feats."

Will you listen to him? Such an important guest. Juffin couldn't restrain himself any longer and sent me a call. *You and I will never live to see the day when we get half that many titles, my boy.*

Yeah, especially since yesterday there were half as many of them, I replied. *He must have stayed up all night coming up with new ones.*

I'm afraid I'm going to have to disappoint you, Max. No citizen of Arvarox is capable of "coming up" with anything of the sort. Yesterday, he simply thought that you and Melifaro were too low in rank to hear all the titles of such an important personage. Naturally, our king deserves the honor of hearing him deign to reveal a little more about himself. I think when this guy gets to the gala thrown by his mighty Dead God, or whatever they call their maker, he'll be talking about himself for twelve years in a row, nonstop. That would be the first chance in his life to say absolutely everything there is to say.

Juffin's silent broadcast was interrupted in a most unusual way. Kurush, who had been dozing under Juffin's looxi, finally woke up and wanted to get out.

"I want to look at those people," said the bird.

"Of course, my friend, of course, but please be quiet," whispered Juffin to the buriwok, and put him on his shoulder.

Then something incredible happened.

Aloxto Allirox, the "Master of two times fifty Sharptooths," whose back never bent low in a bow, fell silently to his knees. His forehead met the thick carpet with a soft thud. His entourage followed suit.

"O mighty buriwok!" moaned Aloxto, his voiced tight with constrained excitement. "O mighty buriwok!"

I thought our esteemed guest had lost some, if not all, of his marbles.

A wave of confusion swept through the Minor Reception Hall. Even Gurig's majestic expression had to give way to ordinary human surprise.

"Citizens of Arvarox tend to exaggerate our mightiness somewhat," said Kurush in a calm, quiet voice. "Although all humans are inclined to exaggerate."

"You're right, my friend," said Juffin, smiling. "But let's not try to persuade this nice man otherwise. Perhaps he should keep his delusions. They may come in quite handy. Don't you think, Your Majesty?"

"I completely agree with you," whispered the king. "It's such a pity that we didn't know this before."

Meanwhile, Aloxto had more or less come to his senses. He looked at Kurush with great reverence and admiration. "I am honored beyond words! How can I repay you for this honor, O mighty buriwok?"

"I am here because such is the will of His Majesty King Gurig VIII and the Venerable Sir Juffin Hully, by whom I am employed. If you wish to express your gratitude, you should express it to them, for it is they who have honored you. Now, get up from your knees, my children."

Juffin and I exchanged a couple of dumbfounded glances. Kurush had spoken so regally that if I had been the king, I'd have given up my throne to him right there and then.

"Never in my life have I dreamed of such an honor," murmured Aloxto nervously, his lips turning pale. "Toila Liomurik the Silver Bigwig, Conqueror of Arvarox, will never forget the honor that has been bestowed upon his messengers. He will order that no less than a thousand songs be written to commemorate this event, and I will write the first one myself."

The king, praise be the Magicians, had already gotten the hang of the situation. He smiled indulgently and said, "We have decided to bestow the honor upon you because of our friendly feelings toward Toila Liomurik, which have remained unchanged. In addition, we are still ready to assist you in your difficult ordeal. I should be very, *very* happy if you would be kind enough to accept our help."

The last sentence sounded more like a command, however politely phrased.

"I will do as you wish," said Aloxto.

"Your words please me," said the king, smiling ever so slightly. "Sir Juffin Hully, who is present with us now, will be waiting for you tomorrow in the House by the Bridge. I am certain that he and his colleagues can turn the World upside down to restore justice, the longing for which made you cross all the oceans of the World, chasing the brazen fugitive. Fare you well, gentlemen. I have been delighted with your company."

I knew that Gurig was being absolutely honest. We were all delighted, especially Kurush.

❦

We went back to Headquarters. On the way there, Kurush behaved like a newly crowned emperor.

Juffin locked the door of his office, and we both gave the puffed-up bird a long inquisitive stare. The buriwok was cleaning his feathers nonchalantly.

"Don't you think you ought to explain yourself, my dear fellow?" said Juffin. "What happened between you and the beauty boy back there?"

"Nothing much. The people of Arvarox worship us buriwoks like gods. Their idolatry is not completely unfounded. Where we are abundant, the World is the way we want it to be. Arvarox is the only place where buriwoks are abundant. We like beautiful people, so the people of Arvarox are beautiful. The color of their eyes matches that of ours, for we love this color. They are taciturn, for we are not interested in their conversations. They are active, for we derive pleasure from discussing their deeds. We live in isolation, but our elders go to die among the people of Arvarox, simply to enjoy the sight of them. After all, they are the result of our common efforts. People of Arvarox love to die, for they believe that they will be reborn as buriwok nestlings. This *is* just a superstition, but sometimes we think they are capable of it—though not everyone, of course. In other words, to the people of Arvarox we are, indeed, like gods." Kurush blinked and helped himself to a few peanuts.

"Yes, I know all that," said Juffin, nodding. "But are you saying that the people of Arvarox also know about your powers? I would never have believed it."

"They don't know it—they feel it. People of Arvarox don't know much, but their feelings rarely deceive them," said the buriwok.

"Hmm, this is news to me. Well, in any case, this *is* good news. Now we can wrap them around our little fingers."

"No, you can't," said Kurush. "They will, of course, do whatever I tell them to do, but if I tell them to do something that is contrary to their rules and laws, they will die. It is easier for them to die than to do wrong. People of Arvarox see death as the best solution to any difficult situation."

"Like samurais," I said.

"Like what?" said Juffin.

"Samurais. Believe it or not, in my World there were guys like this, too. But I see now that their lives were much more miserable—they didn't have buriwoks."

"That's unfortunate," said Juffin. "Life without buriwoks would be a crying shame. Am I right, my dear fellow?" Juffin scratched the fluffy back of the wise bird. "Can you imagine what would happen to that guy if we took him on an excursion to the Main Archive?"

"Will we?" I said, brightening up.

"Maybe we will. If he behaves. Or if he doesn't behave. Then we'll have to take some measures—although I have a strong feeling that the brave heart of Aloxto Allirox might not be strong enough to withstand the shock. So I think we should avoid such drastic experiments." Juffin got up and smiled a wicked smile. "I'm off to get some rest. You stay here and keep working. How cruel I am! Does that shock you, Max?"

"No, it doesn't. We've known each other for a while, and I'm used to anticipating the worst from you. I just hope the Elixir of Kaxar is still in the same drawer."

"Where else would it be? You're the only one drinking it."

"Then I'm going to drink half a bottle and start carousing, because I'm bored," I said with a dreamy smile on my face. "If I get the picture, I won't have much work to do tonight. The fun doesn't start until tomorrow, right?"

"That's right. By the way, I wouldn't mind if you took a leisurely little walk. Pretty soon, none of us will have any time for that, so grab your chance while you can, boy."

"I can try," I said.

And Juffin left.

After thirty minutes of complete boredom I sent a call to Melifaro: *How's the human souvenir from overseas been doing?*

Wonderful. He took a walk around the city during the day. Unfortunately, he didn't get lost. He did get another shiner, though. This time on his right eye. Looks great. By the way, don't you want to have him now? Maybe you're bored or something. You see, I'm beginning to get tired of him.

No, thanks. I'm doing just fine.

Are you? I thought as much. Okay, I have great plans for tonight. I'm thinking of taking this piece of work to the Quarter of Trysts. Maybe he'll ease up there, or get lost once and for all. Do you want to come along?

As a spectator? Gladly.

As a spectator, of course. What else? As the woman of his heart? You need to shave more often for that.

I shave often enough. But I'm also hungry, you know.

You're always hungry. Okay, come over to the Lucky Skeleton. *That's between my house and the Quarter of Trysts. At this time of day, the guys usually dump some of their leftovers. I think they'll let you root around in the pile.*

Oh, is that what you usually do for dinner? I didn't know that. I'll keep it in mind for future reference.

I was about to leave when I saw my own traveling bag. I couldn't be happier because I was finally able to change. My joy was complete.

"You may rule this world in solitude, O mighty buriwok," I said, bowing to Kurush.

"Don't forget to bring me a pastry," he reminded me.

This was a sacred tradition. Whenever I slipped away from work, Kurush got a pastry. Then again, even if I stayed in the office all night long, Kurush still got his pastry. Deep in my heart, I wholeheartedly shared the Arvaroxian views on buriwoks.

☙

When I arrived at the *Lucky Skeleton*, Melifaro wasn't there. That was strange, because according to my calculations, the strapping young lad should have already been sitting at the table finishing off his dessert. I looked around to make sure, but my colleague was nowhere to be seen. Surprised, I sat down at a table in a cozy booth and fixed my eyes on the door.

Melifaro arrived some thirty minutes later. Following behind him was Rulen Bagdasys, wearing orange tights and a new fur hat, the size of which extended beyond anything remotely imaginable. His shiners glowed dimly under a thick layer of powder. I was impressed and waved to them from my cozy corner.

"Impressive," I said to Melifaro. "I had no idea you were capable of running so late."

"I had help," he said. "Rulen was getting ready before his love affair. It took him so long to choose a pair of drawers, powder his black eyes, and comb the hat that I thought I'd go crazy. Have you already eaten your food?"

"That's all right. I'll order more."

I hadn't had anything since morning, but I tried to keep up my image of a glutton. If you want to be an idol of the masses, you'd better have a few harmless—and, preferably, amusing—flaws.

We buried our noses in the heavy menus. Rulen Bagdasys was prudently silent. I think he had been briefed on how to behave in respectable society before leaving the house. I even began to have my doubts about his second shiner—could it be courtesy of Sir Melifaro?

"Where did you get that one, poor thing?" I asked Rulen.

"Some half-wits," he muttered. "Dirty half-wits with their busty females. They should've been happy that I bothered to glance their way. In Isamon even some poor noodle cutter wouldn't marry them!"

"Quiet, you!" said Melifaro, and turned to me. "Same thing as yesterday. He was pestering some respectable gentlemen. He thought they'd be happy if he grabbed their wives' buttocks. Well, the gentlemen didn't appreciate the honor."

"What is wrong with you?" I said to Rulen. "Haven't you ever seen a woman before?"

"Are you out of your mind!" Rulen shouted. "I'm an old ladykiller. In Isamon females like those chase me day and night!"

"Well, in the Unified Kingdom, we don't call women 'females,'" I said dryly. "That's a sure way to get your face smashed. By me, for instance."

"Forget it," said Melifaro. "I'd love to see you as an enforcer of manners, but advice of this sort doesn't work on him. Trust me, I've tried. He remains completely deaf to it."

"What? Speak up, I can't hear you!" shouted the Isamonian, as if he wanted to prove the observation of my colleague. We laughed and began to eat.

I was so eager to tell Melifaro about our visit to the Court and Kurush's secret that I couldn't chew my food very well. Melifaro was laughing like a madman. Even Rulen Bagdasys temporarily forgot about his libido and listened to my story with his mouth wide open. His deafness seemed to have magically disappeared. His head was spinning from the words "King," "Court," and "courtiers." He was so excited that he had a bit too much Jubatic Juice. I thought we ought to postpone the visit to the Quarter of Trysts for another day. By the end of the dinner, the bleary-eyed Isamonian was falling asleep over his plate. When the waiter brought the bill, he suddenly woke up.

"Okay, take me to the females now!" Rulen Bagdasys shouted so loudly that some other customers began throwing our table curious looks.

Melifaro frowned with disgust. "I don't think you're in very good shape, buddy. You should probably catch a few Zs."

"Have you sucked out your own brains?" Rulen shrieked. "I can't think of sleeping. It's time to grab some fat butts! Right now!"

"Okay, then," said Melifaro, giving a short laugh. "It's your call. Let's go get you some 'fat butts.'"

I was a little worried about the tone of his voice. I looked at my colleague and asked, "What's going on?"

"You'll see. You're going to love it. Trust me."

Now I was intrigued.

It took us about ten minutes to walk to the Quarter of Trysts. All the way there Melifaro was whispering in Rulen's ear. I didn't dare interfere.

We stopped in front of the first house for Seekers. I thought it was logical: I just couldn't see Rulen Bagdasys as a Waiter.

"Go on," said Melifaro. "Remember how to behave there?"

"What? I never forget anything. All the busty females will be mine!" shouted the Isamonian. "What are we waiting for?"

"Alas, we have some business to take care of," said Melifaro. "We'd love to accompany you, but unfortunately, we're otherwise engaged."

"The wind blew away your brains a long time ago! Hello? Business? What business can you have at this hour?" shouted Rulen Bagdasys.

He didn't waste any time trying to persuade us. He set his fur hat straight with a proud gesture and headed toward his first erotic adventure in Echo.

"Let's hide around the corner," said Melifaro. "I think one of the biggest brawls in the history of the Unified Kingdom is about to begin."

"Figures," I said. "What did you tell him?"

"The truth. Well, almost. I said he should walk in, pay, and pull out a token. And then I made a few things up. A bit of wishful thinking, so to speak. I told him that the number on the token denoted the number of women that were required to go with him. Can you imagine what will happen if he pulls out a token with the number seventy-eight?"

"Oh boy." I couldn't resist a smile. "I just hope it won't be a blank."

"Even if this lover boy pulls a blank, he's going to start a brawl without any extra help."

"True that. But don't you think this is extremely cruel? He's a human being after all."

"Oh, look at you," said Melifaro. "Since when did you become such a humanitarian? What do you think a person who calls women 'females' and grabs their behinds deserves?"

"Sooner or later I'm going to have to arrest you for disturbing the peace," I said. Then I laughed, because the first shouts from the semi-closed doors of the Trysting House had reached our ears. I think it was something about brainless females that were out of their minds, unless I had misheard.

"The show has begun," said Melifaro in a loud whisper. "Sinning Magicians, the show has begun!"

"At least no one will have to spend the night with him," I said. "I wouldn't want to be in the shoes of that poor woman."

"Then again, she will miss the best show in her life," said Melifaro.

Meanwhile, the door of the Trysting House opened, and Rulen Bagdasys shot out of it like a cannonball. His orange hips flashed a few times as he sailed past the lights of the lampposts. The hat magically remained on his head throughout his entire flight. Had he glued it on?

"You half-wit! I'm coming back, you know, and then something terrible will happen!" The Isamonian was shouting nonstop. "I'll show you! I'll show you all! I have connections at the Royal Court!"

"By the way, his 'connections at the Royal Court' are you," Melifaro said, winking at me. "See, you're his final resort."

"If you don't calm down, I'm going to call the police." The voice belonged to the owner of the Trysting House. "And praise be the Dark Magicians that you are a foreigner. That is why I'm letting you leave without any serious consequences after what you've done."

"I can come back, you know," said Rulen brazenly as he stepped away from the door to a safe distance. "I'll come back and then there'll be trouble!"

"There will be trouble, indeed," promised the owner, shutting the door with a loud bang.

"Let's go, Nightmare," Melifaro whispered to me. "Quietly, though. I'm so sick of him. Can I sleep at your place tonight?"

"Sure. Is he that bad?"

"Oh, you wouldn't believe it," said Melifaro, hanging his head. "He wakes me up at night to tell me some stupid stories about his youth. He yells at people out of my windows and drops his fingernail clippings in my breakfast. I think I'm going to move out. Let him have it all."

"Too bad," I said. "I really liked your humble abode."

"Believe it or not, I was also quite fond of it. So, can I go to your place?"

"And probably take my amobiler, too? I'll bet you left yours at home."

"You're not a very good psychic, you know. I'm going to take one of the Ministry's. After all, if I have privileges, why shouldn't I use them? On principle."

When we got to the House by the Bridge, Melifaro fulfilled his threat. He jumped into the back seat of one of the official amobilers of the Ministry. The driver woke up, trying to look brisk and alert.

"Feed my cats," I said to Melifaro.

"I will. And I'll comb them, too. Don't worry, Max. I'm a country boy. A simple but very trustworthy country boy," said Melifaro, smiling.

✿

I stopped by the *Glutton* to grab some pastries for the "mighty buri-wok" and went back to the House by the Bridge. I was going to catch some sleep in the armchair.

To my surprise, the armchair was occupied. The Master Eaves-dropper was sleeping in it. This was an unusual event: normally at this hour, Sir Kofa was on duty in one of the numerous pubs of Echo.

"Well, I'll be," I said. "What's going on, Sir Kofa? The world has turned upside down: I'm running around town and you're sleeping at Headquarters."

"I dropped by to have a chat with our wise bird about the guys from Arvarox," said Kofa, yawning. "The city is full of rumors about them. I got curious. I suspect that it will be up to us to find that 'filthy Mudlax,' so it's best to be prepared."

"Would you like some Elixir of Kaxar? I've never seen you this tired before. And I thought that everything had been quiet recently."

"It has," said Kofa with a nod. "Don't pay any attention to it, boy. I'm worried about my own, let's just say personal, problems. Let's have a drop of your Elixir. It might be just the thing at this moment."

"Maybe I can help you," I said, fumbling in Juffin's drawer for the bottle of my favorite energy drink. Until now it had never occurred to me that someone else besides me could have "personal problems."

"You?" said Sir Kofa, giving a resonant laugh. "You definitely can't help me, boy. Don't bother your head about it."

"My head is quite big and empty. I'd love to fill it with something," I said. "Why did you mention finding that filthy what's-his-name?"

"Mudlax," said Sir Kofa. "Why? Because we're going to help those courageous yet simpleminded, handsome boys find him."

"But that's going to be super easy. People of Arvarox are so differ-ent from the rest of the people of the World. Even I noticed it."

"Of course. But have you ever stopped to think that if I can change my appearance, as well as the appearance of others, maybe other people in the World can do it, too? I think even that sinning Mudlax had enough brains to make sure no one will recognize him. He's as aware of the customs of his homeland as anyone is—the vendetta and all that. Besides, there are quite a few fugitives from Arvarox living in Echo."

"Really?" I said. "I've never seen them before."

"You probably have. It's just that none of them risks showing off his pretty face in public. There are plenty of people in Echo who can dis-guise their appearance. Trust me on that one."

"Whoa!" I said. "Looks like I've been a fool all this time."

"Ah, no big deal," said Kofa, smiling. The Elixir of Kaxar was evidently doing its job very well.

"Is there a method for testing whether a person's face is real or not?"

"Maybe, but no one knows of such a method. Fortunately, we don't need one. From talking with Kurush I learned that buriwoks can detect a native of Arvarox, no matter how well he disguises himself."

"That's great news."

I remembered about the pastries. I handed them to Kurush, who had almost fallen asleep. Better later than never.

"I thought you forgot," Kurush grumbled. "People tend to forget their promises."

"Hey, when did I ever forget my promises?"

"On the eighth day of the year one hundred sixteen. Granted, that was the only time."

Sir Kofa was getting a kick out of our little exchange. "Okay, boys," he said. "I think I'm going to take a night walk through Echo. You've revitalized me completely, Max. Make sure you stock up on your wonderful Elixir. There are some dark days ahead."

"You're all trying to scare me," I said. "First, Juffin told me to have some fun, hinting that it may be the last time. Now you. Is it that bad?"

"Not particularly bad, just messy. When I hear the word 'Arvarox,' my head is attracted to my pillow like a magnet. Whenever those white-haired, goggle-eyed, handsome boys appear in Echo, life becomes a particularly tiresome endeavor."

Kofa left, and I was so confused by his premonition that I fell asleep right there in my armchair. I didn't even change into the Mantle of Death, which I was actually supposed to do.

Juffin Hully woke me up in the morning. His freshness and vigor were revolting. I extended my arm mechanically to the table where the Elixir of Kaxar sat, but Juffin chuckled and moved my arm away.

"You'd better go home and finish your sleep there. Come back at noon. There's nothing for you to do here before then, anyway. The people of Arvarox get up late, you'll be glad to know."

"Really?" I said, still sleepy. "So very considerate of them."

Back at my place, I encountered Melifaro, as sleepy and gloomy as I was. But my poor colleague was in an even worse situation: unlike me, he had to go to work. Neither of us felt any inclination to wish each other good morning.

"This is the darkest hour," I said.

"What?" said Melifaro.

"The darkest hour," I said. "The time just before dawn when the night—that is, me—is expiring, and the morning—that is, you—hasn't yet arrived. Too gloomy for my tastes." And I headed up to the bedroom.

"Looks like you *were* a poet once after all," Melifaro called after me with a heavy sigh. "I'm so glad you quit that job. Such unwieldy metaphors at this early hour are more than I can handle. You, sir, are a nightmare, indeed."

"Yup," I said, slamming the door shut. I had three more precious hours, and I wasn't going to waste a second.

⁂

I woke up around noon and muttered to myself, "Now, that's better."

In my book, a person should sleep long and soundly and wake up as late as possible. I began to sympathize with the people of the distant land of Arvarox—finally, I had found someone who shared my point of view.

I got to the House by the Bridge at the same time as Aloxto. I managed to enter the Hall of Common Labor a few moments before him, however, because I used the Secret Entrance. The poor fellow had used the regular visitors' entrance. Our team had already assembled. Even Sir Lookfi Pence came down from the Main Archive. He was burning with curiosity.

"You're late because of some silly dream, I'm sure," said Sir Juffin. "I'll bet you didn't even have breakfast."

"Right you are, sir. I didn't. But the dream wasn't all that silly. In fact, it was a pretty good one, though I can't remember any of it."

The door opened. Aloxto Allirox stood in the doorway. On his shoulder, once again, sat the furry parody of a spider. Aloxto stared at Kurush in wonder, cried "O mighty buriwok," and fell to his knees.

Watching my colleagues was a special treat. Even Lonli-Lokli's famous imperturbability underwent a rigorous test. Melifaro, who knew from me about the events at the Royal Palace the day before, also looked puzzled. But maybe yesterday he thought that I was making the whole story up.

"Get up from your knees, son," said Kurush. "I hereby relieve you of the obligation to kneel every time you see me. You may simply greet me with polite words. That would suffice."

"I thank you for this honor, O mighty buriwok. I will annex this privilege to my title presently," said Aloxto, getting up.

Having come to his senses after this exchange with the buriwok, he studied us with a long look. When he saw Lady Melamori, his yellow eyes shone with a suspicious luster. I even thought he might drop onto his knees again. But no, Aloxto simply blinked, which I don't think he had done until then.

After that the dweller of the mysterious land of Arvarox gave us a brief but densely packed autobiography. In other words, he introduced himself. The guys returned the favor—everyone except Melifaro and me, because we had already done so earlier. Sir Juffin Hully also refrained. According to the customs of Arvarox, a man in such a high position is not obliged to tell anyone anything about himself.

"I invite you to partake of this noon feast with us, Sir Aloxto," said Juffin. "This is necessary, because we are about to pursue a common undertaking."

"I appreciate the honor bestowed upon me," said Aloxto Allirox, nodding his head slightly.

"It's great that I skipped breakfast at home," I said, laughing. "I economized. Life's full of pleasant little surprises."

"Ah, thank you for reminding me," said Juffin. "I'll deduct the cost of this feast from your salary. That will teach you not to show off."

I think we managed to dispel the tension in the air again. Lady Melamori snickered, and Melifaro lowered himself into his favorite chair, making a lot of noise and smacking his lips in anticipation. A minute later, jugs of kamra and plates with sweets began to appear on the table. The delivery boys from the *Glutton* cast terrified glances at our guest, like horses in a fire. He paid no attention to them, because he was busy showering looks of admiration on Kurush and Melamori, in that order.

"You're in great shape, Max," Lonli-Lokli whispered in my ear as he sat down beside me. "You have become light in spirit. This has never happened before."

"Oh, yes," I said with a nod. "My life has become very easy and carefree since I became a king."

"A king?" said Shurf. "Is this a joke? I am sorry, but I don't find it funny."

"You shouldn't, because it is not a joke." I turned to Juffin. "By the way, when are you going to release my loyal subject? My Majesty is beginning to get angry with you."

"Your subject? Oh, a hole in the heavens above me! I completely forgot," said Juffin. "He's free to go, of course. Any time."

"Okay, then, I won't declare war on the Unified Kingdom," I said magnanimously. "I have spoken."

"If you keep up this attitude, I'm going to make you the King of the Nomads for real," said Juffin.

"Got it. I'll shut up then." And I covered my mouth with my hands.

Sir Kofa Yox looked at me in disbelief. "Strange, but I've heard no rumors of that kind in the city."

"My people can keep a secret," I said proudly. "Especially the secret of their ruler."

"Indeed," said Juffin. "His compatriots are absolutely sure that he is their king. They complain that he doesn't want to reign because we pay him more."

Sir Shurf shook his head disapprovingly. "You're always getting yourself into some kind of scrape like this," he said, and turned back to his plate.

My colleagues burst out laughing all at the same time. Juffin laughed the hardest. He looked at me like a mad painter examining a work he had created under the influence of a heavy drug—unable to fathom how on earth he could have conceived it.

While we were having fun, Aloxto Allirox was busy chewing. I think that even if we had all taken off our clothes and danced on the table, he would have continued chewing as if nothing had happened. He was eating, and he was busy. The rest simply didn't exist. Later I learned that people of Arvarox were, indeed, capable of giving themselves over completely to whatever they did.

When Aloxto finished eating, he gathered the crumbs from the table and fed them to his furry spider. The little creature ate the treat and then . . . *purred* in the sweetest way. I jumped up in my chair when I heard its tiny voice.

"So, you want to help me catch Mudlax," Aloxto said to Juffin. "Your king said that I should be seeking your assistance, although I don't know why. We are capable of finding that filthy man ourselves."

"Of course you are, but you are not familiar with the city. In addition, you are not familiar with the tricks and habits of the citizens of Echo. If you act on your own, you will lose a great deal of time. Besides . . . tell me, Sir Allirox, can you recognize Mudlax if he changes his face?"

"I don't understand," said Aloxto dryly. "How can someone change his face? Everyone should be content with his own face. This is not a choice."

I must say that the phrase "everyone should be content with his own face" sounded somewhat disingenuous coming from him. It was easy for him to say.

"Show him, Kofa," said Juffin.

Sir Kofa Yox nodded and passed his hands over his own thoroughbred face. A moment later, a completely unfamiliar countenance was staring at us. This time, the Master Eavesdropper had turned into a lopeared, snub-nosed young man with large blue eyes and a wide frog-like mouth. I think he chose such an unappealing appearance precisely to make a point.

Aloxto was taken aback. He stared at Sir Kofa so intently that it seemed he was trying to make the apparition go away by the power of his will. A few moments later, Aloxto managed to come to his senses.

"You are a great shaman," he said to Sir Kofa with admiration. Then he added dismissively, "But Mudlax can't do that."

"Perhaps Mudlax can't, but . . . watch this."

Sir Kofa turned to Melamori, who was sitting beside him, and moved his hands down her face. Now, a wrinkly old lady with a disproportionally large nose and little beady eyes was sitting before us. Everybody laughed. Melamori produced a pocket mirror, looked at it, and shook a small but menacing fist at Sir Kofa. Aloxto Allirox looked like he might faint dead away.

"Now do you see why Mudlax doesn't have to know how to do this? All he needs to do is find someone who can. And trust me, there are plenty of people who can in Echo," said Sir Kofa, and took a sip of kamra from his mug.

"You are indeed a great shaman," muttered Aloxto. "Will you now give this woman back her face? It was beautiful, much more beautiful than the one you just gave her."

"You're mixed up," Melifaro intervened. "This mug *is* her real face. The lady simply borrowed the pretty face you were so fond of for the occasion. The poor thing is over eight hundred years old, so we've learned to be understanding of her whims."

"Is that so?" said Aloxto. He was visibly upset.

"He's lying," said Melamori. "Sir Kofa, give me back my face right now!"

"Here you go," said Kofa. With an air of nonchalance he restored it. "Say, were you scared, girl?"

"Scared? What nonsense. It's just that I find it more convenient to be young and beautiful than old and ugly." She turned to Aloxto. "Melifaro always lies. Don't listen to him."

Now Aloxto was completely confused. He was blinking nonstop.

"I wonder what they do with liars in Arvarox," I said. "I'm sure they kill them on the spot, don't they, Sir Aloxto?"

Suddenly, Kurush flew up from the back of Juffin's chair, where he had been sleeping all this time, and landed on the armrest of Aloxto's chair. "Here in Echo people often speak untruths," the buriwok said. "You will have to get used to it. Sometimes they speak untruths only to have a good laugh. They like it, so don't pay any attention to it. They meant no harm to you or the lady."

Kurush returned to his place on Juffin's chair, and Aloxto nodded. "I understand," he said. "Everyone has his own customs." But to be perfectly sure, he asked Melamori, "Are you sure you have not been offended or hurt, my lady?"

"Sinning Magicians, of course not! And if they did hurt me, I would've shown them. Trust me."

Aloxto looked at her in disbelief, but decided not to object.

"Tell me, Sir Allirox," said Juffin, "how long has it been since that filthy Mudlax left the land of Arvarox? I need to know when he might have turned up in Echo."

"Seventeen and a half years ago," said our guest. "One needs about half a year to cross all the oceans, so this man, whose name is not worthy of mention, came to your land around seventeen years ago. I am sorry that I cannot be more precise."

"You don't need to be any more precise than that," said Juffin.

"And you waited all these years before setting off to chase him?" said Melamori, surprised.

"That is correct," said Aloxto. "Why is this surprising? Throughout these years there has been not a single day that was auspicious for setting off on a long journey. That is why we had to stay home."

"And what about Mudlax? Did he manage to leave on an auspicious day?" I said.

"No. He was in such a hurry to take his miserable body away from Arvarox that he didn't confer with the shaman. Thus, I am sure we will find him with ease. Such an imprudent journey could not have reached a favorable outcome."

"I see," said Juffin. "I think it's time we got down to business. Correct me if I'm wrong, Sir Allirox, but as I understand it, your duty dictates that you take action even if the chances for success are negligible?"

"That is correct," said Aloxto. "It is true, I cannot sit and do nothing, and wait for a favorable result. It's easier to die."

"Well, I hope it won't come to that," said Juffin, shaking his head. "I want your men to guard all the city gates. Two fifties of them should do the job nicely. Tell them to keep an eye on everyone leaving the city. Mudlax has disguised himself, but your men can feel him, right?"

"If my Sharptooths see Mudlax, they will recognize him," said Aloxto with a nod. "They are warriors and this is their job—to sense the enemy."

"Very well, then. Now, since you don't know where the gates are, you'll need a guide. Kofa, can you disguise yourself as a man from Arvarox?"

"Of course."

"Excellent. Do it, then. It will look very natural if Sir Allirox walks in the company of one of his compatriots. And Sir Allirox, you can't find a better guide than Sir Kofa Yox. In the meantime, we'll stick to your plan."

"Take heed of the advice of your companion, my son," said Kurush, looking at Aloxto indulgently. "He is indeed a very wise man."

"Thank you, my friend," said Sir Kofa Yox, flattered. He stroked the buriwok gently, massaged his own face, and suddenly turned into a handsome young yellow-eyed man. Aloxto Allirox stared at him, his eyes and mouth wide open.

※

As soon as the two had left, Juffin began issuing orders.

"Melifaro, we'll need the help of the best policemen. Head straight to their half of the building and assemble them. You, Max, go with him. Your task is to talk Boboota into it. If he sees me, he'll start whining about an official warrant signed by the king, and then, being the stool pigeon that he is, he'll go spreading lies about me again in his reports. With you, on the other hand, he's as tame as a kitten."

"That's true," I said. "General Boboota and I are soul mates. But you're going to have to wait a bit. I'm sure he's expecting the promised present from me."

"Oh, the smoking logs?" said Melifaro.

"They're called cigars," I said with a sigh. "Hold on. Give me a minute or two. I'll try my best."

I stuck my arm under the table, trying to find the Chink between Worlds, an inexhaustible source of exotic treats and complete garbage. Almost immediately, my hand became numb. This was a good sign that I hadn't forgotten my best trick ever.

A few moments later, I threw a pink umbrella into a corner of the room. Somehow I ended up pinching umbrellas from the Chink between Worlds more often than anything else. My colleagues looked at me with silent veneration. Even Juffin's eyes showed genuine interest. I sighed and tried again.

This time I tried to focus. I thought about cigars and people smoking cigars: portly elderly gentlemen with gray sideburns, lounging in leather armchairs and looking down at the rest of world from the unreachable heights of their capital. Then I dumped that image and tried thinking about the members of the board of directors of a company I used to work at part time. Almost immediately I saw those clean-shaven fops, not much older than myself, wearing expensive jackets, smoking cigars at the end of a business lunch, when an imperturbable waiter brought them tiny cups of coffee and slightly warm cognac in fat, fogged-up glasses. At some point I thought I could spot the ever-so-slightly noticeable spots on one of their shiny, greasy cheeks, and was surprised at my own gloating delight over this discovery.

"Max, don't overdo it! Where do you think you're going?" Sir Juffin Hully was shaking my shoulder. He looked pleased but a little perplexed.

I looked around, slightly puzzled myself. Then I retrieved my numb arm from under the table. A wooden humidor fell on the floor.

"Ugh, Sumatran," I said with disgust after reading the label. "I knew those fops were too cheap to shell out some cash for a box of real Cubans." I turned to Juffin. "But I did it! I really wanted to get cigars, not a blasted umbrella, and I did it!"

"You're getting good at it. Sir Maba will be more than pleased. He was sure it would take you at least a dozen years to master this trick."

The others looked at me as if I were a new acquisition in the city zoo—with cautious curiosity, trying to figure out if I would bite their hand off if they tried to feed me.

"Where did these strange objects under our table come from?" asked Lookfi Pence all of a sudden. "Have they been lying there a long time? Our janitors have become far too lazy lately."

❧

Then Melifaro and I set out to visit our venerable police force. I slowed down by the office of Boboota Box. Some incomprehensible exclamations were coming from behind the closed door.

"Something about outhouses," I said tenderly. "Sinning Magicians, just like the good old days."

"Okay, you go ahead and talk to your soul mate, and I'm going to enjoy a conversation with some more intelligent people," said Melifaro. "To each his own."

"If you keep teasing me like that, I'm not going to give you a fur hat like the one Rulen Bagdasys has," I said menacingly.

Melifaro laughed and went to meet some "intelligent people." I threw open the door to Boboota's office. To my surprise, he was there alone. I had thought that the brave police general was reprimanding one of his subordinates, but I was wrong: he was talking to himself.

"Bull's tits! Who the hell is there?" Boboota roared. Then he looked up, saw me, and shut up with a guilty look on his face.

"That's all right, sir," I said. "One can't go against one's nature, right? I just stopped by to lift your spirits."

"You, Sir Max? Lift my spirits?" Boboota was stupefied.

"Uh-huh." I put the humidor down on the table in front of him. "Just got it in the mail this morning. It's from my relatives in the Kumon Caliphate. You did like these, didn't you?"

"I did like them very much!" Boboota smiled at me in ecstasy. He opened the humidor, grabbed a cigar, and began to fumble with it impatiently. He almost wept with emotion. "You saved my life again, Sir Max! How can I repay you?"

"Funny you should ask," I said with a smile, "because today is the day you can do it. I need the help of your best policemen, and right away. We'll be happy to do all the paperwork, but it'll take about two days. So, what do you think? Can you and I arrange it so that your boys start working for us now, and the paperwork—"

"Oh, forget about the paperwork. Flush it down the toilet!" said Boboota. "What paperwork can there be between friends, Sir Max! Take as many of my boys as you wish. Take them all."

"Well, we really don't need all of them. And we're not going to flush any paperwork down the toilet. We'll give it to you, instead, and you may deal with it however you deem appropriate, including flushing it down the toilet. How about tomorrow or the day after? Would you mind?"

"Mind! How can I say no to a man who brought me such a precious gift and . . . and . . ." Boboota stopped short and fell silent, confused.

And wears a Mantle of Death and spits venom whenever he sees fit, I thought. I thanked him and got up to leave.

"Sir Max, with your gift you have just patched a large hole in my life," said Boboota. He finally managed to find words that could express his feelings.

Now that's what I call a metaphor, I thought approvingly.

Melifaro hadn't returned to the office yet. Lookfi Pence had already left for the Main Archive, his place of duty. Lonli-Lokli was contemplating the runic ornaments on his protective gloves. Melamori and Juffin were whispering to each other.

"So, what did Boboota say? Did he try to object?" said Juffin.

"I don't think he'd object even if I took a dump right on his table," I said.

"Really? Of all the miracles you've been so quick to pick up, this is the most unfathomable. You've outdone me, Max. I tip my hat to you."

"You just don't have any common interests that would call for heart-to-heart talks," I said with a smile. "The poor guy is longing for a sophisticated interlocutor, an expert in outhouses."

Melamori smiled absentmindedly, staring off in the distance, then got up from her chair and left without saying a word. I couldn't quite figure out whether Juffin had just entrusted her with an important task, or whether she just wanted to go for a walk. That was very much like her.

Melifaro, his emerald-green looxi flashing, rushed into the Hall of Common Labor with a dozen policemen trailing behind him. I knew some of them, but others looked unfamiliar to me.

"Here he is, boys, the monster you've heard so much about," said Melifaro pointing his finger at me. "Sir Juffin, here's our entire White List for you. And Sir Chekta Jax to boot."

A short, brawny, gloomy-looking fellow frowned at Melifaro but didn't say a word.

"Don't pay any attention to him, Chekta. Unfortunately, this is not the first time we've had to deal with Sir Melifaro. It's time you got used to him," said a cold female voice.

I examined the voice's owner, a pretty, gray-eyed lady. She was tall—

almost as tall as me—with a body shaped according to the canons of beauty of Ancient Greece. She had an air of grace and refinement about her.

The owner of the ice-cold voice noticed me looking at her, covered her eyes with her hand, and said, "I see you as in a waking dream. I'm glad to speak my name: I am Lady Kekki Tuotli."

She seemed to have more of an air of high society about her than the king himself (who, I thought, was a very down-to-earth fellow). I immediately assumed a serious expression and greeted her according to custom, cleverly balancing smiles and the appropriate intonations. I had to atone for the sins of that dunce Melifaro.

Lady Kekki Tuotli listened to me patiently, gave me a dry nod, and turned away haughtily. What a shrew, I thought, taken aback. Then it dawned on me that the poor thing was simply very, very shy. That's how it is with some people: the shyer they are, the more arrogantly they behave to disguise it. It was amusing, so I sent her a silent call.

Don't worry, my lady. I'm also very shy among strangers. And take it easy on Melifaro. The world wouldn't be the same without him.

She looked at me in surprise and grinned slightly. I sighed with relief. I hate working in a strained environment.

"I'm also glad to speak my name: I am Lieutenant Apurra Blookey." A dapper middle-aged gentleman in a bright looxi looked at me with poorly concealed curiosity. "Lady Tuotli and I have been meaning to come by and meet you, but—"

"But you have a great deal of work to do," I helped him finish his thought.

"We do, indeed," said the lieutenant readily.

"Okay, boys, let's consider this the end of the official introductions and get down to business," said Juffin.

"How do you mean 'the end'?" said Melifaro. "What about synchronized bowing to the 'mighty buriwok'?"

"Later," said Juffin. "By the way, how come you're still here and not at the Customs?"

"At the Customs?" said Melifaro. "What am I supposed to be doing there?"

"You're not too quick today, I guess. That 'filthy Mudlax'—a hole in the heavens above his home—came to Echo seventeen years ago, right? I'm sure they would have remembered him passing through. One can hardly forget an event like that. Afterward, send a call to Melamori. Maybe she can pick up his trace there. Beats hanging out here doing nothing."

"Got it," said Melifaro. "I'll sniff out whatever I can and then call Melamori. I'll be back in no time."

"That's for sure," said Juffin and smiled. Then he turned to the policemen. "Now, while Sir Melifaro is drowning himself with Jubatic Juice in the company of Sir Nulli Karif and the ghost of old Tyoovin, we can *finally* get down to business."

❀

Thirty minutes later, after the briefing, the policemen went to the Main Archive. When they returned, each of them was carrying a buriwok. It seemed that the birds were puzzled: On the one hand, they were burning with curiosity. On the other hand, these feathery little beasts are not too keen on changing their habits all of a sudden. Most of them hadn't left the cozy vaults of the Main Archive for more than a hundred years.

"And don't forget, gentlemen: at dusk all the buriwoks must be back here along with their companions," said Lookfi Pence, "or they will refuse to work with you tomorrow."

"There's not a whole lot of time before dusk, so consider today's stroll to be a rehearsal," said Juffin. "But if someone meets a man from Arvarox in disguise, bring him here and I'll have a man-to-man talk with him."

"I can only imagine the kinds of rumors that are going to pop up all over the city," I said with a sigh, looking at the policemen and the birds as they left the House by the Bridge. "We're going to scare him off, that Mudlax. Or aren't we?"

"Of course we are," said Juffin. "But that's exactly what we're after. I want to scare him so that he panics, tries to flee the city, and lands right in the welcoming arms of his compatriots. That would be the easiest solution to the problem. Too easy, I should say. I don't quite believe that this plan is going to work, but then again, who knows."

"I see," I said. "What do you want me to do?"

"You? How about some highly intellectual work? Go get something to eat," said Juffin seriously.

"Oh, now that's an important and difficult task," I said. "I'm not even sure if I can manage on my own."

❀

Melifaro returned about four hours later, tired and vexed. By that time, Lonli-Lokli and I had managed to empty out half a dozen jugs of kamra, and discuss any and all philosophical problems that deserved an iota of attention. Sir Shurf apparently thought that was just as it should be, but I felt like a shirker and deserter.

"It's always nice to see true professionals," said Melifaro with venom in his voice. "The gentlemen killers are just biding their time, waiting for me to bring them their next victim. Such an idyllic scene."

"Yeah, we don't waste our time on trifles," I said.

Lonli-Lokli ignored Melifaro's grumbling altogether. He merely gazed out the window in deep concentration at the slowly darkening sky.

"I'm going to turn myself in to Juffin. Let him cut my head off," said Melifaro, sighing. "I don't know about the others, but I failed big time. Sure, the guys at Customs remember that fellow, but then what? He didn't tell them where he was going to stay. And Melamori didn't find so much as a hint of his trace there. No wonder, it's been seventeen years, and many a horde of mad barbarians has gone through Customs in both directions since then. Now she's feeling better, though. See, the lady's taking that goggle-eyed gold standard of male beauty and his furry beast for a walk around the city. They stare at each other like kids looking at an ice cream stand. That's all right, though. Someone's gotta be happy in this World."

The vehemence of Melifaro's anger surprised me. Sir Juffin poked his head out of his office.

"Don't be upset, son," he said. "Frankly, I didn't expect you to return with any good news. The policemen took long strolls with no results, either. The buriwoks didn't see any Arvaroxians. They're going to go through the whole rigmarole again tomorrow. By the way, does anyone have any idea where we should be looking?"

"Sir Kofa is usually full of ideas," I said. "At least he should know everyone who specializes in disguise. Maybe we should begin with them?"

"Yes, I thought so, too," said Juffin. "Kofa's already on it. Maybe he'll bring some good news. I sure hope he will. But it is strange, isn't it? You'd think that finding a man from Arvarox in Echo should be easy as Chakatta Pie."

Finally, everyone else went home to sleep, and Kurush and I stayed behind at Headquarters. I was fine with that because Melifaro was sleeping at my place again. He said he was in too foul a mood to enjoy the company of Rulen Bagdasys.

"I'm pretty sure I'd beat him up," Melifaro confessed. "You know, when things don't go well for me, I just don't find certain things funny."

✸

At midnight I went out for a walk. My whole body hurt from sitting in the chair. For some time I just followed my nose. The multicolored stones of the mosaic sidewalks shimmered under my feet. The few passersby looked mysterious and attractive: the orange light cast by the street lamps wrapped their ordinary faces in a veil of enigma. The cold wind from the Xuron also took a walk down the narrow lanes of the Old City. The wind and I seemed to be taking the same route the whole way, but I liked its company. That night I liked pretty much everything. Unlike poor Melifaro, I was in a good mood, which was enough to make me wary.

My nose led me to the Victory of Gurig VII Square. I looked around, bewildered—how did I end up here?—and was going to turn around to sneak back into some cozy dark alley when I saw the silhouette of a tall man sitting at a table in a street café on the square. I took a closer look. But of course. It was none other than Aloxto Allirox. As far as I knew, there was no other man in Echo who had such beautiful white hair. Surprised, I decided to approach him. After all, it was only yesterday that Juffin had said we should be protecting our guests—unobtrusively—from possible trouble. As soon as I had taken a few steps toward him, I realized that the fellow was already under the protection of one of the employees of the Minor Secret Investigative Force. Lady Melamori's tastes remained unchanged. I never understood why she liked this busy place so much.

I smiled and went back to the House by the Bridge. On my way there I desperately tried to get upset or, at least, surprised. No go. I had known from the beginning that it would end this way. As soon as I had seen Aloxto, I knew that my fair lady would soon "cheer up," to borrow her own expression. Until now I just hadn't thought of expressing this knowledge in words.

I smiled involuntarily at the thought that if I had been a girl, I would have . . . There was no need to deny it, that Aloxto was a true work of art! How far can this go? I wondered with a mixture of curiosity and indifference.

To be honest, I didn't recognize myself. I should have been furious, cursing everything and everyone. This was what I would usually do in such situations. But recently I had undergone changes that were even more improbable.

Long story short, by the time I got back to the House by the Bridge,

I was in a very good mood. Kurush got not one but three pastries. I think he was surprised at my generosity. Then again, you could never tell from his expression what was on the buriwok's mind.

Sir Juffin returned early in the morning and was kind enough to let me go home and catch some sleep.

※

I returned to the House by the Bridge not long before dusk. The only person in the Hall of Common Labor was Lonli-Lokli. There was still no work for us to do. There were plenty of killers out there—two times fifty Sharptooths were eager to cut the throat of Mudlax, who had turned out to be not just "filthy" but also impossible to catch.

"Lady Tuotli and the buriwok that is accompanying her did manage to find one native of Arvarox," said Shurf. "They are on their way here."

"Excellent," I said. "Finally, something in this case has budged. That Lady Tuotli has a ton of luck on top of her other virtues, huh?"

"Perhaps you are right," said Lonli-Lokli and nodded. "Do you not find her . . . strange?"

"Well, I don't know her very well. I just met her yesterday. At first I thought she had a terrible temperament, but then I realized she was just very shy. Funny, isn't it?"

"Shy? I never would have thought that. What made you so sure?"

"I don't know. I just sensed it. It seemed pretty clear to me."

"Was it? Well, then, it's not all that bad, if you are correct."

"What's not all that bad?" Now it was my turn to be surprised.

"I mean her 'terrible temperament,' as you said. That was a very good way of putting it."

"Was she rude to you?" I said. "Uh-oh, what a woman!"

"She . . . Well, perhaps she was. You know, nobody has been rude to me for a long, long time, so at first I was quite puzzled."

"You? Puzzled? I can't believe it. I simply cannot believe it."

"And yet I was."

※

"Is Sir Hully in?"

The gray-eyed Amazon walked into the Hall of Common Labor with great determination. Following her was a large old man. Only his height and athletic body gave away his Arvaroxian origin. His face was quite inconspicuous. Any tavern in Echo is full of such faces at any hour of the day. The man was absolutely calm, and it was pleasant to look at him.

"He is. He's expecting you," I said affably.

The stern lady raised the corners of her mouth in an attempt to smile. She looked like she'd forgotten how.

Juffin's Silent Speech put an end to our courtesies. *Max, it's great that you decided to show up after all. I was worried that you were going to fall asleep for another year. Come in with Kekki and her trophy. Just in case.*

I turned to Shurf, somewhat shamefaced, and made a helpless gesture to show him I wasn't leaving on my own accord. My silent apology was in vain. Shurf had already changed his expression to one of complete indifference and was buried in a thick book. I looked at the cover. Good golly! The magnum opus was called *The Pendulum of Immortality*. I shook my head in disbelief. Was the promising title a reflection of the author's unsophisticated poetic tastes, or did he really intend to unveil to the reader a trick or two about how to become immortal? One could expect either from the local literature, so I promised myself I'd browse through the book at my leisure.

After I finished musing about life, death, and literature, I followed Lady Tuotli and her prisoner to Juffin's office. Right before I went in, I heard the familiar "O mighty buriwok" and the dull sound that a head makes when it meets the carpet. This was getting old. Fortunately, by the time I was in Juffin's office, the Arvaroxian had already assumed the vertical position. Perhaps Kurush had taken care of it.

Lady Tuotli was already on her way out. I guess Juffin had decided her mission was over. The lady was desperately trying to demonstrate her complete lack of interest in further developments in the office. I really felt for her. How would you feel if you did your job and were dismissed immediately, never to learn what happened next?

"I am Naltix Ayemirik," said the old man. "And I have not done anything worthy of mention."

I shook my head in admiration. It was an art in its own right to speak of one's worthlessness with such aplomb.

"And what sort of business made you leave Arvarox?" asked Juffin.

"I would rather not talk about my past," said the old man calmly. "I give you my word of honor that I am not the one you are looking for.

No one is looking for me, for no one deems it honorable to defeat one who has been deprived of his powers."

"I'm sure that's the case here," said Juffin. "Okay, let's not talk about your past. What I want to know is whether you knew King Mudlax."

"I was his shaman many a year ago, until the powers left me."

"This does happen," said Kurush confidently. "Such mishaps happen as a matter of course, but the people of Arvarox believe them to be a great misfortune. A shaman whose powers have left him must go away to a distant land and take his curse with him, the farther the better. That is the law."

"A sad story," said Juffin, "but I'm interested in something else. Tell me, Naltix Ayemirik, have you met Mudlax here in Echo?"

"Yes, I have met him and his men. They came here seventeen years ago. At that time I was helping your people maintain the peace at Customs. The pay was decent, so I was not disgusted by the labor involved."

"Excellent." Juffin was pleased. "Say, would you happen to know where he may be now?"

"No, I wouldn't. Mudlax bought himself a new face, just as I did. He does not wish to be found. That is why he parted with me before he changed his countenance."

"I see. And do you know who helped Mudlax to change his countenance?"

"I do, but I gave my word of honor never to tell this secret. I am truly sorry, sir."

Juffin gave Kurush a desperate look. "Help me out here, friend."

"Is this important?" said Kurush.

"This is very important."

"All right." Kurush blinked his round yellow eyes and flew over to Naltix Ayemirik's shoulder. Naltix almost fainted from excitement.

"You must break your promise," said the bird. "This is an order."

"I will do as you say," said Naltix Ayemirik rapturously. "My duty is to obey the Almighty Bird." He turned to Juffin. "Hear me then. I took Mudlax and his men to the Street of Bubbles, to Varixa Ariama. He was the one who changed my countenance. He is very competent. Unlike others, who can only change your face temporarily, his magic is permanent. Mudlax and I parted on the porch of Ariama's house. I have never seen my king since then."

"You bet you haven't," said Juffin. "Sir Varixa Ariama, the former

Senior Magician of the Order of the Brass Needle—goodness me! What people won't do to make money these days. I'd never have thought that— Hey, what on earth are you doing?"

Juffin's cry startled me. I looked at our visitor and froze in horror: the old man was clenching his throat with his own hands. He was literally strangling himself. How was that even possible? And yet there was no doubt that he would finish what he had started.

"Don't try to stop him," said Kurush. "He must do it. If you stop him now, he will try to do it again at another time. A man of Arvarox who has broken his word of honor must die. Nothing can be done about it."

"A funny custom," said Juffin, turning away to the window. "Max, is this too shocking to you?"

"Not too shocking," I said, my lips numb. "Just shocking enough."

"My sentiments exactly . . . Is he dead now?"

"I think he is. Or will be in a minute."

"He is dead," said Kurush. "People of Arvarox can die quickly. Don't be upset. Such things happen frequently in Arvarox. Besides, this man died happy. He has seen me, fulfilled my command, and died as a true warrior of Arvarox. To him this was more important than living a long life."

"Right, right," said Juffin. "You might not believe me if I tell you that I've never seen anything like this before in my life. I had no idea I could still be knocked out of my saddle that easily. In any case, we have received some important information. Let's go back to the Hall of Common Labor, Max. I think we can stand to have a cup of kamra while they clean up here. I've already sent a call to Skalduar Van Dufunbux, our Master of Escorting the Dead. By the way, Kurush, what's the proper way of burying him? I mean so that we can please him."

"To the people of Arvarox it doesn't matter," said the buriwok. "Nothing matters after a man dies."

"That's a very healthy attitude," said Juffin.

❦

We went to the Hall of Common Labor. Skalduar Van Dufunbux, a good-natured, portly gentleman who carried out the responsibilities of a coroner, hurried into the office with a preoccupied air, nodding to Juffin on the way. Sir Shurf lifted his head from his book, sized up the situation, gave a sympathetic nod, then went on with his reading. I grabbed a mug of kamra and took a sip, but couldn't taste anything. Then I remembered a good method to improve my mood and come to my senses: chatting with my colleagues. Sure beats staring at the same spot in utter silence. Fortunately, I had a lot of questions.

"There's something I don't understand. If Arvaroxians are so indifferent to death, why is Mudlax hiding from his pursuers so diligently? And why did he flee to begin with? I mean, he could have chosen to die fighting or to strangle himself, like that other hero, and called it a day. As Sir Aloxto Allirox put it, 'It's easier to die,' right?"

I was counting on an answer from Juffin, but the boss was not forthcoming. Lonli-Lokli, on the other hand, put down *The Pendulum of Immortality* and said, "Oh, that's a very good question. Naturally, this isn't about saving one's life. No Arvaroxian would put so much effort into staying alive. This is clearly a matter of honor. It is one thing for a warrior on the side of the victors to accept death and die in battle. That is an honorable death. When a vanquished warrior dies, however, it means his complete and ultimate defeat. Robbing the victor of the opportunity to take your life is the last chance of the defeated to even the score, his last chance to gain a small but memorable victory."

"This is true," said Kurush. The buriwok was pleased to play his new role of chief expert on Arvaroxian psychology.

"I see you have soaked up some of their philosophy, Sir Shurf," said Juffin. "You're not planning to emigrate to the land of Toila Liomurik, Conqueror of Arvarox, are you? Don't get too carried away."

"I never get carried away. I am simply stating a few facts that I already knew," said Lonli-Lokli. "It's amazing the information contained in some books . . ."

"Gentlemen, something unbelievable has just happened!"

Lookfi Pence, tangled in the folds of his looxi and grabbing the railing, ran down the stairs.

"It's the first time this has happened as far back as I can remember." He was almost shouting. "I read that it was almost impossible!"

"What? What happened?" said Juffin.

"The buriwoks in the Main Archive had a nestling! It happened just now! Can you believe it? The strangest thing is that I hadn't even seen the egg. How did they manage to hide it from me all this time?"

"They didn't hide it. It is extremely rare for people to spot a buriwok egg. One moment there's nothing there, and the next thing you know there's a nestling and some broken pieces of eggshell. That's just the way it is," said Kurush. He paused for a moment and then added, "I told you that an Arvaroxian can sometimes fulfill his dream and become reborn as a buriwok nestling when he dies. I don't know how the people do it, but they do."

"Not a bad ending to the story, huh?" I said.

"Yes, Max, such things happen," said Kurush.

"Do you think I can take a look at it?"

"I think you can. But not for too long. Little creatures get tired of too much ogling."

With Kurush's blessing I went up to the Main Archive. Sir Lookfi Pence followed me up.

"This is amazing, simply amazing," he kept saying. "Buriwoks rarely lay eggs, and they need to be left alone for a long time to be able to do so. They almost never have offspring even in their natural habitat, not to mention when they live among people. No one would ever have thought that something like this could happen here in the House by the Bridge." He opened the door of the Main Archive and threw me a questioning glance. "Would you mind waiting here for a moment, Max? I'm going to walk in first and ask them if you can come, too."

"Of course," I said. "I'll do whatever they say. No offense taken."

A moment later Lookfi poked his head out. "They say they don't mind. They say that you can come in."

I smiled from ear to ear and went inside the Main Archive. I said hello to the buriwoks and hesitated, looking around.

"The nestling is in that corner," said Lookfi. "You can come up a little closer."

And come up a little closer I did. A tiny fluffy ball was crawling around on a soft mat. Unlike the adult buriwoks, the nestling was white and had touchingly cute little pink legs. Its large yellow eyes, however, were as wise and indifferent as those of the adult birds.

The nestling looked at me, blinked its eyes, and turned away. I could have sworn it looked at me as though it knew me. No particular emotions, though. It just recognized me, nodded, and turned away. That made sense: I hadn't been friends with Mr. Naltix Ayemirik, the late shaman of King Mudlax. We didn't even know each other very well. My frightened face was the last thing he saw before he died.

I gasped. Whew, it looked like I had just brushed against a mystery so incredible that my recent trip between Worlds seemed like nothing more than a walk in the country by comparison.

Lookfi tugged on the fold of my looxi. I nodded and tiptoed toward the exit.

※

"Well?" Juffin said with unconcealed impatience.

"It's him. I swear it's him."

I tried to describe my impressions of the newly hatched buriwok for Juffin. It turned out that words for describing it in human language were lacking, but Juffin understood me anyway. He nodded and stared at his empty mug for a long time while he processed the information.

"To die and be reborn. An unusual and strange endeavor," said Lonli-Lokli.

"Indeed. What hoops people are willing to go through to entertain themselves," I said.

We might have gone on talking about life and death for a long time, but a courier rushed into the Hall. "Sir Max, your . . . they say they are your subjects. They've come to see you," he said.

"My subjects?" I said. "Sinning Magicians! That's all I need." I turned to Juffin. "Have you already released that—what's his name? Not Mudlax but—"

"Jimax. Yes, yesterday already. I think they came to thank you. Let them in, then. The more the merrier."

"Whatever you say," I said. "Although I don't find them particularly merry."

※

The nomads came in—babushkas, brightly colored shorts, large rucksacks and all. This time they didn't kneel, praise be the Magicians. That's right, I thought. I had told them not to kneel before anyone anymore. The proud inhabitants of the Barren Lands simply made a deep bow. The gray-haired old man from before, the head of this small horde, pushed forward a tall, wide-shouldered middle-aged man. "Thank your king, Jimax," he said sternly.

The man opened his mouth, then shut it, bowed so that his head almost touched the floor, and finally mumbled, "You have saved a man of your people, Fanghaxra. From now on, my soul belongs to you, and my body belongs to you, and my horses belong to you, and my daughters—"

"Thank you, thank you, but I'll do fine without your soul, body, horses, and daughters," I said dryly. "Keep them and be happy."

"Did you hear that?" said Jimax, turning to his companions. "Fanghaxra told me to be happy!"

The nomads looked at him as though he were a saint. The indefatigable old man stepped up and said, "We've come to ask for your mercy, O Fanghaxra. Your people have been cursed ever since the day we lost you. Forgive us, Fanghaxra!"

"Okay, okay. You are forgiven," I said.

That was easy, I thought.

"And please return to us," the old man went on. "You must rule your people, O Fanghaxra. You are the law!"

I gave Juffin an imploring look. He was treacherously silent. I knew I had to deal with it on my own.

"I will not return to you," I said. "I have unfinished business here in Echo. I am the law, so submit."

"We will wait for you to finish your business," the old man assured me.

"I will never finish my business. My business is simply impossible to finish. You know, I am Death in the Royal Service. Have you ever heard of Death finishing his business? So go back home and live in peace."

I'm afraid my monologue left them cold. Perhaps the guys weren't too keen on listening to what I had to say and just enjoyed the sound of my voice. I gave Juffin another look of desperation. He was smiling from ear to ear, but he wasn't going to interfere. Lonli-Lokli had closed his book and was watching my sufferings very attentively.

"Your people cannot live without you, Fanghaxra," said the old man with the tone of an experienced blackmailer.

"Of course my people can," I said. "My people have been living without me all this time. Don't tell me you just dug yourselves up out of your graves."

It was clear that my "compatriots" had no sense of humor. They looked at each other and then stared back at me. Pleadingly.

"Goodbye, gentlemen," I said firmly. "Finish up your business and go home. Say hello to the boundless steppes of the County Vook, follow the command of His Majesty Gurig, and you'll be all right. M'kay?"

My "subjects" bowed and left in silence. To my horror, I noticed an expression of hope mixed with stubbornness on their faces.

"I fear this is only the beginning," I said gloomily after the heavy door had closed behind them. "Now they'll find out where I live and pitch their tents under my windows."

"Funny." Juffin looked as happy as a kid who had just seen the traveling circus. "I don't know why, but I liked all of this very, very much."

"That's because you're a very, very mean person," I said, "and it makes you happy to see other people suffer."

"Right you are," said Juffin. "Look, Max, could you do me a favor? Since you're their king, could you tell them to change their headgear? Those headscarves are truly a shame. Why can't they at least wear turbans or hats?"

"The lower the cultural level of a people, the stronger they cling to traditions," said Lonli-Lokli.

"Perhaps," said Juffin absently. "Well, this is all fine and dandy, but let's get back to work. You two go ahead and bring me that master of disguise, Varixa Ariama. I want him alive and kicking, but if you scare the pants off of him—all the better."

"Okay," said Lonli-Lokli. "Let's go, Max. Or do you prefer your royal name? After all, you chose it."

"Oh, look who's talking," I grumbled, getting up from the chair. "You know that I'm no Fanghaxra."

"That is irrelevant," said Shurf. "If those people consider you their king, you *are* their king to a certain degree, and you have to accept the consequences."

"To heck with the consequences," I said. "Let's go, already, philosopher."

When we were outside, I hailed one of the official amobilers of the Ministry. The driver sighed and got out. All our employees had gotten used to the fact that I always drove the amobiler.

Then I heard some loud singing, coming from far away:

> He came at dusk.
> *The Surf Thorn* foamed the ocean,
> To the city where
> Filthy and cunning Mudlax hid.
> Many a Sharptooth came with him,
> Thirsty for Mudlax's blood.

"What is it, Shurf?" I said.

"Oh, you haven't heard it before? That's our good friend Aloxto Allirox singing a new song about his feats to Lady Melamori Blimm on the Royal Bridge, if my sense of direction isn't deceiving me."

"What?" I was completely dumbfounded. "And she likes it?"

"I think she does. If she didn't, she'd ask him to shut up. You know how Lady Blimm is."

"I guess I do," I said. "He's a beautiful man, that 'Master of two times fifty Sharptooths,' but I couldn't stand to listen to his singing."

"To each his own," said Lonli-Lokli. "Let's go, Max. You say you don't like the song, and yet you are standing here listening to it with your mouth agape. Don't you think that's a little inconsistent?"

"I do," I said, laughing. "You're so wise you scare me, Shurf."

I grabbed the levers of the amobiler and we took off under the lyrical outpourings of Aloxto the scribbler:

> . . . he came and met a girl,
> But his sword is not rusting in its sheath.

"Un-be-*lievable*," I said. "This is an ordinary case of disturbing the peace."

"Is it upsetting you?" Shurf said cautiously.

"Oh, no. Not at all. This Aloxto is a great fellow. I'm happy that he and Melamori are not too bored with one another, and all that. But when I hear bad poetry I get furious."

"Really?" said Shurf. "Is it really that bad? Frankly, I like Arvaroxian poets. Their poetry is marked by a peculiar masculine innocence, which endows their creative verses with palpable, primeval authenticity."

I sighed. To each his own, indeed. It was useless to argue about taste with Sir Shurf Lonli-Lokli. He was equally versed in snuffing out "unnecessary lives" and unnecessary opinions. I had much to learn.

A few minutes later we stopped by a yellow two-story house on the Street of Bubbles. Lonli-Lokli carefully took off his protective gloves, revealing the death-dealing gloves underneath, gleaming in the twilight. The mad blue eye stared at me out of his left palm. I shivered—I still couldn't get used to this novelty.

"Come on, Max. I hope he's home. Lady Melamori won't be too happy if she has to come here and step on his trace."

"Right," I said. "She won't have the chance to listen to the end of the song."

We entered the house trying to make as much of a racket as we could. It is thought that representatives of law enforcement organizations must be rude and have poor coordination. Only when these two conditions are met people do people agree to fear and respect us.

We did our best. I was so eager to make noise, stomping around with my boots, that my heels began to hurt.

An elegant young man looked out of the farthest room on the second floor. When he saw Lonli-Lokli, his jaw dropped in horror. Then he saw me and caved in completely. Frankly speaking, one of us would have sufficed for arresting Varixa Ariama, the former Senior Magician of the Order of the Brass Needle—he wasn't such a big shot, after all—but the boss had the habit of going overboard from time to time.

"What is the matter, gentleman?" said the young man, his lips white.

"We must take you away from your business for a short while, Sir Ariama," Lonli-Lokli said politely. "The Venerable Head of the Minor Secret Investigative Force will be much obliged if you find some time to visit him for a short discussion."

"You must be looking for my father, Sir Varixa Ariama," the young man said timidly. "I don't know where he is now, but—"

"You should come with me, nevertheless." Shurf was implacable. "Maybe this gentleman is telling the truth, and maybe he's posing as his own son. This is often the case during an arrest," he explained to me. "Sir Juffin will sort it out."

"Then I'd better stay," I said, "and send a call to Melamori. If this gentlemen is not the one we're looking for, she'll have some work to do here."

"That would be wise," said Shurf. He turned to the young man. "After you, sir. If what you say is true, the discussion will not take much of your time."

And the poor fellow shuffled over to the door, followed by Sir Lonli-Lokli.

When I was alone, I took my time searching every room, making sure that there was no one else in the house. Then I came down to the living room and sent a call to Melamori.

I'm sorry to disturb you in the middle of a breathtaking performance. I'm at Number Fourteen, Street of Bubbles, and you and I may have some work to do here. Then again, we may not. Still, it would be better if you came down.

All right. By the way, Aloxto has finished singing already. I'll be right there. Over and out.

I put my feet on the table, found a crumpled cigarette in the pocket of my Mantle of Death, and lit up.

To my surprise, Melamori arrived very quickly.

"If you drove here all the way from the Royal Bridge, it's a record. Congratulations!" I said.

"No, just from the Victory of Gurig VII Square," she admitted.

I did some quick math in my head. "Well, it's impressive, so congratulations are still in order. Tell me, though, did you really like that horrible song?"

"Oh, I did like it, very much," said Melamori, laughing. "I've never heard anything funnier in my life. What's more, I also sang him a song about my exploits. I think it was quite a good parody. Aloxto took my parody very seriously, though. He was ecstatic."

"So you had a great time," I said.

"I'm trying, Max," said Melamori. "I'm trying my best. I like Aloxto. He's so beautiful and . . . different. Alien and strange. Exactly what I need right now."

Max, that boy that Shurf brought in, he really is the son of Varixa Ariama. Juffin's Silent Speech interrupted our attempts to come to an understanding. *Is Melamori there already?*

Yes. She just got here.

Excellent. Try to find Ariama Senior quickly. I don't think he's hiding from us. Most likely, he just left on some errand. The best way to start tracking him down is to start from the bedroom. Ariama Junior says that his father was taking a nap there after dinner and then left. The bedroom is on the second floor, left of the stairs. Over and out.

"Guess what? Let's check out the bedroom," I said to Melamori, and winked at her.

"What for?" She sounded surprised.

"What do you think?" I was going to go on with my stupid joke, but seeing Melamori's face turn white, I realized I was being a jerk. "We'll be looking for the trace of Sir Varixa Ariama. What else can one do in a bedroom?"

Melamori gave a hesitant laugh and took off her shoes, and we both went upstairs.

"Yep, here's his trace," she said as soon as she crossed the threshold. "Maybe this Sir Ariama was once a Senior Magician, but I don't think he was an especially ferocious wizard."

"No, not one of the Grand Magicians," I said. "Just some young talent."

"I wouldn't be so sure. During the Epoch of Orders it was often the case that some Grand Magician retired or took too much time pursuing magic of his own. Then the real power in the order was exercised by Senior Magicians. Junior Magicians, who were pretty numerous, were rarely taken seriously, even when there was every reason for it. But you know that yourself."

"Let's go, though." I nudged the garrulous lady softly toward the stairs. "Let's find this old geezer real quick, and then I'll treat you to a mug of kamra, for old time's sake. Okay?"

"No," said Melamori, smiling. "I'd rather have something stronger."

"As you say. Everything will be as you say. Absolutely everything."

"Indeed. Sooner or later, somehow or other."

I winced. I could clearly hear the tone of the Kettarian Sheriff Mackie Ainti in Melamori's voice. But she shook her bangs and laughed, and we went out into the street. There the wind from the Xuron quickly swept away the remains of my delusion.

We found Varixa Ariama in the *Irrashi Coat of Arms*. He was about to dig into some exotic dish. By the time we arrived, the poor fellow had lost his appetite and was suffering from heartburn. When Melamori steps on someone's trace, even worse things happen to people.

Our prey glanced warily at my Mantle of Death and took his arrest as the lesser evil. Granted, his heartburn disappeared as soon as Melamori stepped off of his trace. We took the former Senior Magician to the House by the Bridge and turned him in to Juffin.

"I promised to treat the lady to some poison," I said. "May I be excused?"

"Yes, you may," said Juffin. "Until tomorrow. And please try to get some sleep tonight. Tomorrow may turn out to be a tough day. Or it may not—but I want to see you in my office tomorrow before noon. Mind you, I want to see *you*, not just your body snoring under my table."

"You're being unfair. I never snore under your table. I have learned to make a decent bed from the chairs." I turned to Melamori. "Shall we go?"

"If we can decide where," she said with a nod.

✸

We went out onto the street by the House by the Bridge and hesitated at the intersection. Sometimes choice is a curse rather than a blessing. Then I heard Melifaro's voice in my head.

What's up, Max?

I'm standing on the Street of Copper Pots with Lady Melamori, trying to decide where to go for a drink.

Shirkers. Okay, tell our Lady Moonstruck that her goggle-eyed pretty boy is walking around the city with his hairy beast. He's so depressed, it pains me to look at him. No one except our Melamori will listen to his songs. By the way, I'm getting tired of following him around. Does Juffin really believe that someone may hurt this big hulk? Anyway, I was going to ask you to keep me company, but I see you're busy.

Not at all. Where are you?

In the New City, not too far from your place. Oh, our overgrown teenager just dropped into the Armstrong & Ella. Looks like a nice little tavern.

Say what? What is it called, again?

You heard right. It's the Armstrong & Ella. They named it after your cats. The place opened right after that tubby guy you adopted wrote about them in the Royal Voice. I thought you knew.

How could I have known? I was out of town for a year. Oh boy! This is something I've got to see. What's the address?

It's Number Sixteen on the Street of Forgotten Dreams. So, are you guys coming?

You bet!

I turned to Melamori. "Melifaro's waiting for us in the *Armstrong & Ella*. Can you believe it?"

"Oh, the one named after your cats?" she said, smiling. Then the smile disappeared. "Do you really want to go there? Because I don't. Sir Melifaro's acting very huffy toward me. He won't let us talk."

"But I'm not in a huff. Isn't that enough?" I said, and lightly flicked the end of her nose. "Besides, it wasn't his idea to go there. He's guarding your precious Arvaroxian treasure, who at this very moment is enjoying himself over there."

"Really?" said Melamori. "Then let's go. But may I drive, please?"

"You not only may, you must. You promised to give me a ride, and this is your chance."

✸

Melamori drove very fast. For someone who thought that thirty miles an hour was the maximum speed of the amobiler for the first hundred years of her life, she was doing great. All the way to the tavern we were silent—the contemplative, peaceful silence that grows between two old friends. I was beginning to understand that a strong friendship had its advantages over passion, as Juffin Hully once wisely observed.

The Street of Forgotten Dreams was easy to find. It crossed the Street of Yellow Stones just two blocks from my house. Strange that I had never walked here.

"There's Number Sixteen," said Melamori. "Hey, look! *Armstrong & Ella*. That's a real honor."

"True," I said. "You know, I'm honestly flattered."

❀

A tall, slender girl in a black looxi flew out of the tavern toward us. Her head was surrounded by a shock of thick silvery curls that looked like a halo. Her dark eyes stared at me. She seemed to find the spectacle so attractive that without a moment's hesitation she dashed up to me and draped herself over my shoulder. When she touched me, I felt as if I had been struck by a bolt of lightning: I was hot, and colorful spots danced before my eyes. I shook my head, trying to get a grip on myself.

"You are Sir Max."

It wasn't a question; it was a statement. I didn't want to disappoint her, so I nodded and began waiting for the situation to unfold.

"Amazing," said Melamori. "Women fall all over you."

"They do, don't they?" I said, looking intently at the woman who was gripping my shoulder. "Has something happened?"

"Come with me. There's a fight going on in there," she said, pointing at the tavern. "They're killing everyone!"

"What?"

I dashed for the doors, Melamori following close behind me. We burst into the tavern and stopped dead in our tracks. Sir Melifaro was standing on a table with the air of a conqueror. Aloxto Allirox, though covered in blood—his or someone else's—was alive and imperturbable. He was wiping off his "machete" with the fold of his cape. When he saw Melamori he smiled the lovesick smile of a Romeo, which even the mighty Arvaroxian genes weren't immune to, it seemed. About a dozen dead bodies lay on the floor. Their faces looked like those of ordinary Echo dwellers, but their bodies betrayed their Arvaroxian origin.

"What took you so long, Nightmare? We could have used some of your infamous poison around here. Still, we managed on our own, as you can plainly see," Melifaro said proudly. "You missed your chance to witness the greatest battle of the Code Epoch. But now you're here, and the caravan has already pulled away, as my Isamonian guest likes to put it."

"So, what happened here?" I said, heaving a sigh of relief and sitting down in an uncomfortable chair.

Melifaro hopped off the table and sat down beside me. The woman in the black looxi went behind the bar and started filling glasses. I finally realized that she was the proprietor of the tavern. She returned and placed the glasses before us on the table. I sniffed the unfamiliar beverage. It smelled of apples and honey but scorched the throat something awful.

"Thank you," said Melamori, the first to recover her good manners.

"Don't mention it. I'm just doing my job." The woman smiled and retreated behind the bar again. I could feel her dark eyes drilling into the back of my head.

Aloxto Allirox bowed to Melifaro. Unbelievable! Until now, this great warrior had barely deigned to nod, even when greeting the king.

"I am grateful to you," he said. "If it hadn't been for you, I would have had to die without finishing my business. What could be worse than that? You are a hero and a great shaman. Thank you."

"Don't mention it. I was just doing my job," said Melifaro.

The proprietor of the *Armstrong & Ella* laughed quietly on hearing Melifaro repeat her words.

"I'm still all ears," I said.

"Well, here's what happened. Sir Aloxto was sitting at that table over there, and I was sitting at the bar. I was just waiting for you and trying not to bother our guest too much. Then I heard the door open and thought it was you. When I looked around I saw these beauty boys shaking their battle slingshots. One of them fired at Aloxto with his Baboom, but Aloxto managed to duck just in time. To tell the truth, I lost my bearings for a moment, so the boys had time to fight for real. If you can call six against one 'for real.' How many did you kill, Aloxto?"

"I wasn't counting. I was fighting," said Aloxto.

"You were indeed. Anyway, after Aloxto laid one of them low with his flyswatter—you won't believe this, but it turned out to be a lethal weapon—I ordered this sweet lady to clear out and launched my Lethal Sphere at them."

"I didn't know you could do that," I said.

"I'm not completely a lost cause," said Melifaro. "Granted, I hate doing it. I always get a headache after exploits like that, and it puts me in a terrible mood. But that's okay. After a couple of glasses I'll be in tip-top shape. They serve Ossian Ash here, the best booze in the entire Unified Kingdom."

"Oh, yeah, I like it, too," I said. Then I turned to Aloxto. "Those were Mudlax's people, right?"

"Yes," he said. "The pitiful servants of that filthy man. I sensed their presence all day. I hoped that Mudlax would appear soon after them, but he did not. Only a man who has forgotten his honor sends his useless servants to fight in his stead."

"Melamori, take Sir Aloxto to Juffin," I said. "The boss will be happy to hear the news. And he'll patch him up in no time. Your right arm is wounded just above the wrist, isn't it, Sir Aloxto?

"You are correct."

"How did you know?" Melamori looked at me, her eyes wide as saucers. "He's covered in blood. How could you see a wound under all that mess?"

I was slightly embarrassed. "When I look at Aloxto, my own right arm begins to hurt just where his wound is. It's called 'compassion.' It happens to me."

"Whoa!" said Melifaro. "Say, does it come with the ability to heal, too?"

"I doubt it," I said, grinning. "Killing—that's my job. Making someone feel better—not my thing."

"You are speaking an untruth," said Aloxto suddenly. "You do not like to kill, and when you look at me, my pain subsides."

"Really? That's news to me. Then again, I can't keep looking at you forever, and Sir Juffin cures wounds much better than I do. You can take my word for it."

"Let's go, Aloxto," said Melamori. "Max is absolutely right, we'd better hurry. I'm also going to send the policemen over here to take away the bodies. Is that a good idea?"

"It's a brilliant idea," I said. "This summer, interior designers do not recommend decorating with dead bodies."

"Good night, then."

Melamori took the hand of the handsome Arvaroxian and they left.

"She could've thanked me for saving her boyfriend," said Melifaro, and then turned to the proprietor. "Sweetie, I'm getting drunk tonight, so bring your entire stock of wonderful booze over here."

"All of it? You're going to burst like a dam, hero," said the woman. "There are already more dead bodies here than living people."

"I'm not going to burst," said Melifaro. "I'm going to get drunk. I feel like crap."

"That's just the way it goes sometimes. But it always passes, or life would be unbearable," said the woman, putting a jug on the counter. "Have a seat, gentlemen. My face isn't much to brag about, but it sure beats that pile of dead bodies you've been staring at."

I loved her gutsy way of talking. She can be even ruder than me, I thought. How cool is that!

"Then I'll brag about it for you," I said. "If you don't let me, I'll get offended and go off to cry in a corner."

The dark-eyed lady looked at me as though she was trying to decide whether I believed my own words. My head started spinning again, but I didn't mind. If it felt like spinning, I had no objections this time. It could spin all it wanted, as far as I was concerned.

I moved to a tall barstool. Melifaro sighed and sat next to me. The woman gave us each a clean glass and sat down across from us. She hesitated a moment and then poured herself a drink.

"Actually, I was going to drink kamra and have something to eat," I said.

"I make the best kamra in town. You'll see." She put a jug on a tiny burner. "But as for something to eat—you know, I don't have a cook. It's so boring to feed people. My customers come here to have a mug or two, smoke a pipe, and hurry back to their errands."

"I'll be darned," I said, surprised. "Back in . . . where I used to live, they called places like this 'coffee shops.' But even in a coffee shop you could get a sandwich."

"A coffee shop, huh? Sounds funny. I'm sorry, but I don't even serve sandwiches."

"Then my time's about up," I said. "I'm not complaining, but the World won't be the same without me, don't you think?"

"You're right, it won't," she said, nodding seriously. "All right, this is against the rules, but I can give you half of my own dinner. I'll be right back." She jumped down from the stool and disappeared into the semidarkness behind a small door.

Melifaro gave me a gloomy look. "For your information, I'm hungry, too. Didn't it occur to you that the *Fat Turkey* is just a few steps from here? We can go there instead of depriving this poor lady of her last crumbs. She already looks anorexic."

"I'm not going anywhere," I said firmly. "And she's not anorexic. She's just thin and very elegant, Mr. Connoisseur of Fine Women."

"Fine," said Melifaro. "Then I'll have to get drunk on an empty stomach. You'll live to regret this."

"I'll let you have a bite," I said. "I promise."

"Two bites," said Melifaro. He seemed to be feeling better by the minute.

"Two bites it is, then. But please, no drunken brawls, okay?"

"Oh, there will be a drunken brawl for sure. You just wait," said Melifaro. "Sinning Magicians, I'm such a dimwit. I should have waited for those guys to mow down that goggle-eyed ladies' boy and *then* showed off with my Lethal Spheres. I'd have one less problem to deal with."

I looked searchingly at Melifaro. Deep down, I had thought that Melifaro's long and mostly fruitless attempts at courting Melamori were just one of the many things my colleague did for amusement. I guess I was a lousy psychologist.

"That bad?" I said.

"Worse. But let's not talk about it. I'm not too good at playing the part of a rejected lover. Just not in my line."

"Yeah, and you won't get any standing ovation, either," I said. "No fun in that."

"Absolutely."

"But you were darn good as an invincible hero today. I envy you so much that I think I'm going to poison you. I'll just spit in your glass and call it a day."

Melifaro looked flattered. He smiled and took a large sip of the not-yet-poisoned drink.

❀

The dark-eyed proprietor of the *Armstrong & Ella* came out carrying a sizable paper bag.

"Here," she said. "This is dinner *and* lunch. It turns out I forgot to eat lunch today, but I still don't feel hungry. And here's your kamra, Sir Max. If you say it's no good, I'll get insulted and take the food away."

"You won't have time," said Melifaro. He had become considerably more cheerful and was busy opening the bag.

"I am awfully sorry for my insolence," I told our lady-to-the-rescue, "but would it be too presumptuous of me to ask the name of the woman whose food I'm about to gobble up in the most shameless manner?"

"I'm Tekki Shekk. I thought you knew everything about everyone, Sir Max."

"Almost everything," I said. "Everything except addresses, names, and dates of birth. For those things we keep buriwoks. I'm glad you're not scared of my Mantle of Death like the others, Lady Tekki. I'm beginning to feel like a normal person again."

"But you shouldn't," said Melifaro. "Because you're not a person—you're a bloodthirsty monster. So don't even try to pretend."

"And you, mister, have already had your two bites," I said, taking the rest of the sandwich away from him.

"Why should I be scared of you?" said Tekki Shekk. "Since I opened this place, I've been hoping that you'd drop by out of curiosity. After all, the place is named after your cats." She produced a small pipe from the pocket of her black looxi and began to fill it. "As for your famous Mantle of Death and other scary stories for the general public . . . You know, I'm not afraid of death. I should thank my heredity for that."

"Has everyone in your family been a hero?" I said.

"Oh, no. Don't be silly," said Tekki, lighting up her pipe. "It's just that everyone in my family has already died and become a ghost. I'll also become a ghost when I die. Maybe 'ghost' isn't the best term, but I can't think of a better one. I see my late brothers from time to time, and trust me, they're having much more fun now that they're dead. Then again, I can't say they didn't have any fun when they were alive."

"That's fantastic," I said. "You're very lucky, Lady Tekki. No frightening unknown future for you, then—the curse of the rest of humanity."

"You can say that again," she said.

"I want to be a ghost when I die, too," said Melifaro.

I took a note of the fact that he had already killed approximately half of the jug.

"For that you should have been born my father's child," said Tekki. "That's the only surefire way I know of."

"Really?" said Melifaro. "Well, that might be a problem. And Sir Manga might take offense. I guess my only option is to stay alive. The longer the better."

"Not the worst option, either," said Tekki.

I looked at her with increased admiration. The lady sure knows how to joke, I thought. Or does she? Deep inside, I knew that she wasn't joking at all.

✺

Finally, a police patrol, headed by Lieutenant Chekta Jax, arrived at the tavern. The lieutenant greeted us politely and looked at Tekki with interest. She was probably not his type, though, because almost immediately he turned away, became somber, and started grumbling at his subordinates. They quickly removed the bodies of the elusive Mudlax's dead servants and left.

"Shixola was much more fun," said Melifaro. "Too bad he didn't become a ghost. He'd have made a good one."

"Yes, he would have," I said. "A stupid death, his was, huh?"

"Death is never stupid," said Tekki. "Death is always right."

"I beg to differ. Death is a fool. Trust me, I'm the biggest expert around on that subject."

"We're both right," she said. "When people talk about things like that, they're all right. In a way."

"Well, I'll be," said Melifaro. "Look at you two philosophers. By the way, my lady, how about another jug? This one's empty."

"Never knew you had such a talent for consuming spirits," I said.

"Believe it or not, I didn't know, either," said Melifaro. "But this Ossian Ash is something special." And he began helping himself to the second jug, never ceasing to grumble. "A hole in the heavens above Arvarox! What crazy demiurge created that cursed continent? I'm going to quit the Royal Service and ask Anchifa to take me away on his ship. Even as an ordinary sailor. If he's not lying, his guys teach those goggle-eyed beauty boys a lesson from time to time. I'd love to give them a hand."

"Look, sooner or later he's going to go back," I said.

"Yeah, *sooner or later*," said Melifaro, knocking his glass to the floor. It shattered into a thousand tiny fragments with a sad tinkling sound.

"You're good at breaking glasses," said Tekki, laughing. "I've never seen a glass break into so many pieces.

"Want me to teach you?" Melifaro offered. He grabbed my glass, still full, and put it in front of him.

I was watching my friend in amazement. Even now, life was full of surprises.

"Aren't you tired yet?" I asked. "I think it's time for you to go to bed."

"I am tired," said Melifaro bitterly. "This kind of thing happens to me sometimes: I want to have fun, and I fall asleep instead. I'm so ashamed of myself."

"Oh, no," I said. "You've got a long way to go before you have anything to be ashamed of. Come on, I'll take you to my place. Unless the company of Rulen Bagdasys is still so precious to you."

"No no no! Take me home please," said Melifaro stubbornly. "I live there. You live at your place. Isn't that obvious? And Rulen Bagdasys, for all I care, can go to the Quarter of Trysts and get himself a few more shiners. They make him look a whole lot better, don't they?"

"Fine. Your place it is, then," I said.

If Melifaro wanted to go back to his place to sleep, who was I to prevent him? I looked at Tekki. She was diligently filling her pipe. It seemed she was looking a little less happy than a tavern keeper normally would when someone removes a customer who had taken a drop too many.

"Are you going to call it a day?" I said.

"I don't know. Why?"

"Well, I really liked your kamra, and . . . In other words, I was going to put this hero to bed and then come back, if it's okay with you."

"Do you really want to come back?" she said, surprised.

"I do. What's so strange about that?"

"Everything," she said with a helpless smile. "Come back, Sir Max. I'll even send out for dinner."

"Brilliant!" I said. "To sit in one tavern and send out for dinner to another one. This is a first for me."

This time I had every reason to hurry. I outdid myself driving to the Street of Gloomy Clouds and arrived in a matter of minutes.

Melifaro was sleeping on the back seat of my amobiler. I tried shaking his shoulder, but to no avail. He was sound asleep, though he still tried to kick me a few times. I sighed—this wasn't going to work without resorting to magic. There was no way I was going to carry this guy on my back. Moving heavy objects had never been my favorite pastime. So without further ado, I did one of my all-time best tricks. The next thing I knew, a tiny Melifaro fit snugly between my thumb and my index finger.

"A beautiful girl is waiting for me, and I'm stuck here with you," I said to my left fist.

Naturally, if he had been conscious, Melifaro would have just told me where to stuff it.

When I walked into Melifaro's living room, I was in for another surprise. Three men besides Rulen Bagdasys were sitting there. Judging by their huge fur hats, they were also from Isamon. The table deserves special mention. It was the most disgusting mess I had ever been privileged to see—a late, late show featuring a special guest: garbage. Normally, achieving such spectacular results would require a lot of food, drink, smokes, lonely tipsy men, and a whole week. These gentlemen had managed in just two days.

"Enjoying ourselves?" I asked sternly.

The men looked at me indifferently. They weren't impressed by the Mantle of Death. But of course, I thought, I'm not wearing one of their fur hats.

"Have you sucked out your own brains?" Rulen Bagdasys hissed at his buddies. "This mister is from some aristocratic family. He's very close to the Royal Court!"

"I suggest that you try to clean up this sinning mess and get out of here," I said. I was trying to be scary, but it wasn't quite working. "The master of the house is asleep, but he could wake up any minute now. He's in a very foul mood, and he's the kind of fellow who is used to choosing his own guests, so—"

"Don't you understand who these people are?" Now Rulen Bagdasys was hissing at me. "This is Mr. Ciceric, Mr. Maklasufis, and Mr. Mikusiris! Don't you know them? Where did you leave your brains! These are titans! You're out of your mind!"

"I don't have time to deal with you now," I grumbled on my way to the stairs. "Mark my words, when Sir Melifaro wakes up, there's going to be trouble. Big trouble. I don't even think your fur hats will come out of it alive."

Exhausted from dealing with so many Isamonians, I went upstairs to Melifaro's bedroom. Bending over the bed, I gave my hand a vigorous shake. Melifaro, suddenly his regular size again, tumbled onto the sheets.

"Don't throw me on the floor," he said angrily without waking up.

"My, my, how fragile we are!" I said. "Okay, have a good night, hero."

I don't think Melifaro heard me. He had already curled up and was snoring peacefully. I covered him with a fluffy blanket, shook my head, and left the bedroom.

The Isamonians were still in the living room. They looked at me with alarm and insolence at the same time. I was going to continue my lecture on the subject of cleaning up but changed my mind. Melifaro wasn't a kid. He'll deal with them when he wakes up,

I thought. There were much more pleasant affairs waiting for me tonight.

❀

I was surprised at myself as I sped up in my amobiler. Holy cow! Did that unbelievable dark-eyed Tekki really exist? Her short silver hair—what an extraordinary color! Her sharp little beak-like nose and those helpless, tender lips—were they for real? Where had she picked up my favorite offhand manner of expression? I could have sworn I had made her up, that ideal woman of my idiosyncratic tastes. I had always been a guy with a wild and vivid imagination.

Life was getting curiouser and curiouser. Lady Melamori was swaying her hips in front of the white-haired result of a bunch of buriwoks practicing group mediation, and I was rushing off for a date with my own hallucination. We had all gone mad. Melifaro was the only sane person in the bunch: he fought, he yearned, he drank, and he slept like an ordinary guy.

But Tekki wasn't a hallucination. She was a very real woman, sitting over a tray with dinner from the *Fat Turkey*, fiddling with her pipe nervously, waiting for me.

Waiting.

For me.

Incredible.

❀

"Aren't you glad I'm back?" I said insolently.

"Of course I am. Someone has to eat all this. And I'm still not hungry. I can't eat when I'm nervous, and tonight was quite a night."

She spoke so nonchalantly, as if we'd known each other for at least a couple of hundred years. Her gaze was different, though: attentive, alert, and sad.

I really wanted to take her hand in mine, for starters. Instead, I stared at my plate. I'll be darned. Just when I thought I'd gotten rid of my timidity, life had to prove me wrong.

"Why did you come back?" said Tekki. "Do you really like it here?"

"You bet I do," I said. "There's no better place than this. Too bad the police took away the dead bodies: they really livened up the atmosphere. But even without them the place is really nice."

Tekki managed a crooked smile and touched her hair with a trembling hand. She hung her head. I was sure that she found my company very much to her liking, yet something was making her uneasy. I cast around desperately for a topic of conversation.

"Tell me about your family," I said. "You weren't joking when you said your brothers had all died and become ghosts, were you?"

"No, I wasn't joking. They did die. Or, rather, they perished. That's the word you're supposed to use when referring to violent deaths. They still exist, but their bodies are very different from those of the living. And their abilities, too. As I said, I still see my brothers sometimes. They live at—or, rather, they inhabit—our family castle. I'd love to move in there myself, but I find it impossible to be among them for too long. The living must live with their kind, don't you think? I like my brothers' current lives. They are as light and carefree as you and I could ever dream to be. They roam through different Worlds, stroll through the streets of Echo like you and me, and that's just a small part of what they do to entertain themselves. The other parts are still beyond my comprehension."

Tekki's description of life after death was so impassioned and riveting that I felt I wanted to become a ghost myself. It took quite a bit of effort on my part to nip that fantasy in the bud. Once, Sir Mackie Ainti, the old sheriff of Kettari and the most amazing of all the people I knew, told me that all of my wishes came true—sooner or later, somehow or other. I had had enough time to think about his words to conclude that my life was proof of his mind-boggling theory.

For starters, I reminded myself that I was quite capable of traveling between Worlds even while alive. Then I remembered that I wasn't especially fond of that ability. Not that I particularly disliked it—maybe I just hadn't gotten used to it yet.

While I was contemplating all this, Tekki stood up and went behind the bar. She returned with two glasses.

I didn't feel like drinking, but what I did feel like was seducing this amazing woman. At the very least, I was going to try. And it's not a good idea to begin by rejecting the drink she's just brought you.

"To you, Sir Max," she said, raising her glass.

"If you say so," I said, laughing. Then I added in the most gallant manner I could muster, "To you, Lady Tekki."

"But you must drink this all up," she said. "It tastes great, and it's not too strong, I promise."

I submitted and took a sip of the aromatic drink. It smelled of exotic blossoms and fragrant wild herbs. Tekki was right: the drink didn't taste strong, but it sent my pulse racing and took my breath away. No wonder, though—for the most beautiful woman in the Universe was sitting beside me, and I was foolish enough not to kneel before her.

I put the empty glass on the table. My head was going around in circles. Tekki's face seemed huge. It was obscuring the rest of the world. My heart stopped in my chest to savor the moment and suddenly exploded in pain.

Darkness surrounded me. I knew that this was death. The death I had always been afraid of. Except now I wasn't afraid of it—it just hurt like hell. The torture I was feeling was hard to describe. I felt as though I was being torn into millions of little pieces. My sinews were being shredded, my bones crushed with a stone crusher, and my heart ground up in a meat grinder.

At the very last moment I grew furious. I knew I didn't want to die. I was simply not going to give in to that ugly old man with his phony scythe! No way. I had great plans for tonight, and for tomorrow, and, to be completely honest, I had some darn good plans for the not-so-near future, as well.

I forced myself to speak. There was a part of me that realized Tekki was standing next to me—scared and bewildered. She's panicking, so she can't think what to do, and then it'll be too late, I thought.

"Call for Juffin," I said. "Call for Juffin Hully. Tell him I died. He'll . . ."

Darkness and pain enveloped me again, and I stopped resisting. To this day I can't remember what happened to me next. Maybe it's for the best.

※

Then I came to and almost lost consciousness again, this time from surprise. One doesn't die and come back to life every day, you know. And if, upon reviving, you find your body lying in bed with a woman . . .

"You're alive!" Tekki whispered, and burst out crying.

"Is that a bad thing?" I said. "What, you're not too keen on living men? I can die again, if you want me to, but please don't cry. Wait, when did I seduce you? I know I talk in my sleep sometimes, but I had no idea that even death couldn't make me shut up . . . I *was* dead, wasn't I?"

She laughed through her tears. "You bet you were. Sir Juffin went out to look for your second heart, because . . . Well, I guess it doesn't matter now."

It didn't matter, for sure, because Tekki put her wonderful face next to mine again.

❊

"I guess now you're not going to die anymore," she whispered a few minutes later.

Praise be the Magicians, she didn't leave. Instead, she curled up beside me and buried her nose in my shoulder.

Finally, I could look around. And I was completely horrified to see Juffin sitting in an armchair by the window. The orange light of the street lamps was falling on his calm face. It looked like the boss was looking at us very intently. I quickly pulled the blanket up to my chin. For a few moments I didn't know what to say, but soon I found all the words I needed, and then some.

"Look, we're good friends and all, and I don't keep any secrets from you, but this time you're going overboard. Why are you staring at us, can you tell me? Is what I'm doing so very amusing or funny?"

Juffin didn't say anything, nor did he move. I was completely beside myself.

"He's sleeping, Max," said Tekki. Tears were still falling from her eyes, but she was giggling. "He's sleeping with his eyes open. It happens. I told you he's out looking for your second heart."

"Right, the one I keep on the third shelf from the bottom in my bookcase," I said. "Well, well, I see everyone's having a great time around here."

Tekki's shoulders began to shake again, this time from laughter. I smiled. I had no strength to do anything else.

"But can you please tell me what happened?" I said. "Magicians only know when Juffin's going to wake up, and I still have no idea what's going on."

Tekki stopped laughing. Now she had to make considerable efforts to restrain herself from crying. "What happened? Oh boy, what a question! You turned all chalky white, told me to call for Sir Juffin, and died. But I didn't have time to send him a call, because he was already in the tavern. I have no idea how he got in. Then he grabbed you and me, and pulled us both up here to the bedroom. Max, I don't quite remember what happened exactly. I went crazy when I realized what was happening to you. And then your Juffin . . . I don't know how I was able to survive his stare." Tekki gave a sad sniff, and I stroked her hair.

"But you're all right now?"

"I guess," she said, and smiled again.

"Go on. What happened next?"

"Juffin said he was going to look for your Shadow so he could take its heart and give it to you, and he told me to finish what I'd started. He said there was a chance that might work, too, however small. And then he sat in that armchair and was completely still. I know that one can only find the Shadow in one's dreams, so I knew he was sleeping, and so—"

"Hold on a second," I said. "What did he mean, 'to finish what you'd started'? Started what, Tekki?"

"He'll explain it all to you," she said in a sad voice, and looked down.

I didn't like that one bit. "Look," I said, gently stroking her shoulder. "Let's get this clear: whatever you did, it doesn't matter. Because the grand finale was so wonderful that we're even, as it were. So spit it out, baby. And make it quick. Because I have a feeling I'm going to have to save you from Juffin's ire."

Tekki curled up and turned away. "I . . . I poisoned you," she said finally in a loud whisper.

"Poisoned me! But why? Am I that horrible? Or was it a vendetta? Did I kill one of your relatives? Are yōu, by any chance, the granddaughter of the late Hunchback Itullo?"

"Of course I'm not!" said Tekki, laughing her beautiful tinkling laughter. "You got it all wrong, Max. I didn't mean to poison you. I didn't know it would have this effect on you."

"'It'?" I was beginning to lose my patience. "Tell me what 'it' was or I'll die of curiosity, this time for good."

Tekki gave me a sullen look. "I slipped you a love potion," she said. "Goodness, I don't know what I was thinking!"

"You slipped me a love potion?" I laughed in relief. "But why? I was breaking my head all night trying to think of how to go to bed with you. Don't tell me you didn't notice. All my colleagues laugh at me, saying my feelings are always written in huge letters across my forehead."

"Really?" said Tekki. She seemed surprised. "Well, you did look like you were charmed, but I thought you were just being gallant. I had no idea you were flirting with me. I mean, I know I'm not much to look at, and all."

"Oh, but you are," I said. "I can't get my eyes full. You're just what my life has been missing. Do you understand?"

She nodded. Now she finally seemed to relax, and she reached over to take her skaba.

"Don't," I said. "Why?"

"What do you mean? Your boss is going to wake up sooner or later."

"Oh. I completely forgot about him." I laughed again, which was a mistake. I overestimated my capabilities. I was completely drained of strength. The orange twilight of the room started wheeling in front of my eyes.

"Are you all right?" said Tekki.

She had already stood up, and her worried eyes were following me from someplace far away. I wanted to say I was fine, but I couldn't utter a single sound. All I could do was smile because I felt so good. Darkness thickened around me, and I felt a pleasant, languorous warmth in my chest. I closed my eyes and let go, realizing it was useless and completely unnecessary to resist this persistent, tender force.

Then it was as if someone had flipped an invisible switch inside me. My strength returned to me abruptly. I opened my eyes, propped myself up on one elbow, and looked around. The world around me had changed, except that I had no idea what was different.

Tekki sat beside me, clutching my hand. It looked like she was preparing to mourn my sudden passing again. It was touching, but I hurried to reassure her: "Everything is fine now, dear. You can't imagine how fine I feel."

"I'll bet you do," said Juffin. "You just scared the bejesus out of a poor helpless woman and a half-witted old magician—and got a second heart at a significant discount. Sure, you're fine now."

"Juffin!" I said. "Will *you* tell me what happened to me?"

"Death happened to you. Other than that, nothing extraordinary."

"I figured that much. But why? And what's the story of that 'second heart' you took away from my Shadow? And how on earth can it get along without it, I should very much like to know?"

"Oh, don't worry about your Shadow. It can get along fine without much of anything," said Juffin. "As for the rest of the story, has the girl confessed already?"

"She has."

I smiled the widest smile possible and turned to Tekki. She was nervous again. Even Juffin's good-humored chatter seemed to throw her off balance. I squeezed her hand tenderly, hoping it would help.

"I see. So that's what this is all about," said Juffin. "You heartthrob lover boy, you. Well, long story short, the experiment has proven that our harmless love potion works as a lethal poison on you. It killed you almost instantly. I presume it wasn't pretty?"

"No, it was no walk in the park," I said. "I'm glad I've never been a chick magnet. I'll bet Melifaro gets a couple of glasses of that stuff in every tavern."

"It's not all that bad," said Juffin. "With your profession you won't be suffering from too much attention from women. Only the daughter of Loiso Pondoxo could have a crush on a guy wearing the Mantle of Death."

"The daughter of Loiso Pondoxo! The Grand Magician of the Order of the Watery Crow? The one you keep talking about all the time? Oh boy." I looked at Tekki in embarrassment. "I think today was one of the most exciting and interesting days in my life."

Then I got worried because I remembered something.

"Hold on," I said. "Aren't you guys some kind of mortal enemies or something? Juffin, didn't you bury her dad who-knows-where?"

"Whatever happened to my infamous dad, whom I only saw a couple of times in my life, doesn't matter," said Tekki. "By the way, during the Troubled Times, Sir Hully saved my life. He didn't come hunting for me when that overcautious old Nuflin declared open season on all the children of Loiso Pondoxo."

"I just didn't deem it prudent," said Juffin, "because it seemed that death only worked to the advantage of your family members. Plus, I had better things to do than hunt down innocent little girls. It wasn't my fault that nobody but me was up to the task. A dozen days later, His Majesty Gurig VII came to his senses and issued a decree granting personal immunity to all family members of those who had waged war on the Code. Nuflin was mad, naturally, but by that time he'd realized that it wasn't wise to run up against the king. So, I guess we have no grudges against each other, do we, Lady Shekk?"

Tekki shook her head no.

"Happy?" Juffin asked me. "Or do you want us to kiss and make up?"

"Don't even dream of it," I said. "Sinning Magicians, you two go back a long, long, dark way, huh?"

"Why, yes, we do," said Juffin. "Say, what are we going to do with the gal? Should we lock her up in Xolomi? On the one hand, she just murdered a government official of the highest rank. But, on the other hand, she put everything right. I didn't really have to bother with your Shadow. I could have just locked you two up in the bedroom and been done with it. She did a very good job and revived you without my help."

"How did she do it?"

"As if you don't know. I once heard that someone poisoned by a love potion must immediately seek the poisoner's embrace to survive. Granted, that pertained to the love potions of the olden days. Back then, they weren't as harmless as these modern-day concoctions. Still, I decided it wouldn't hurt to try even that, just in case. I didn't really expect it to work, but it did! By the time your heart was beating again, I already had your second heart in my hands. Since it's impossible to return to the Shadow what it has already parted with—unlike humans, the Shadow never changes its mind—I gave it to you."

"So I really have two hearts now?" I said.

Juffin nodded.

"Okay. The more the merrier, I guess. But what's the Shadow, and where did you find it?"

"Hmm, how shall I put it . . . I found it in my own dream, but that doesn't mean it's not real. Frankly speaking, no one truly knows what the Shadow is, but every person has one. The easiest way to find the Shadow is when you're asleep, and it doesn't matter whether it's your own Shadow or someone else's. Yours, by the way, is pretty good at playing hide-and-seek. It took me quite a while to track it down. The Shadow has everything its owner has, including a heart. Unlike us, thought, the Shadow can get along fine without all that junk. In fact, the Shadow is much better off without it—it feels lighter and freer. Do you follow me at all, Max, or is this an exercise in futility?"

"I don't follow you at all, but it's no exercise in futility," I said. "The sound of your voice is very soothing. So, how am I supposed to live with two hearts now?"

"The same way you did before, only better. You'll see. You're one lucky guy, if I do say so myself."

"I'm lucky, that's for sure," I said, winking at Tekki. "Unlike you."

"How come?" she said, startled.

"Because I swear in my sleep, spit venom left and right, work at night, and I'm a glutton. Oh, I almost forgot: on top of that, I'm the king of some tribe of nomads or other. Now do you see who you've gotten mixed up with?"

Tekki smiled. "Mother always told me I'd come to a bad end." Her smile vanished as quickly as it had appeared. "Wait a minute, Max. Why do you think I'd be interested in all that? Why are you so sure that I—"

"Who's asking you?" I said. "You poisoned me with your love potion. Now be so kind as to take full responsibility. I'll be needing a prolonged course of treatment. For the next six hundred years, at least, my life will still be in critical condition, so I'll be needing daily medical checkups. Then we'll see. Am I right, Sir Juffin?"

"If you say so," said Juffin, yawning. "Okay, now, put yourself back together. I'm expecting you back tomorrow at noon."

"At dusk," I said firmly. "Death is a valid reason for me to run a little late, don't you think?"

I tapped the tip of my nose twice with my right index finger, the favorite Kettarian gesture, meaning, "Two good people can always come to an understanding." Juffin melted right away. Then again, he wasn't particularly cold to begin with.

"You are a shirker, mister, but Magicians be with you. At dusk it is, then. Go ahead and live your life to the hilt. I'm going to get some sleep. By the way, I didn't even ask anybody's permission to leave work today."

"Ask mine," I said. "I'll let you go, I promise."

"Will you really?" said Juffin. Then he smiled at Tekki. "I hope to see you again under less dramatic circumstances, child. I'm sorry if I scared you, but when I realized just *what* had happened, I might have done something even worse."

"*He* scared me even more, to tell you the truth," said Tekki, nodding in my direction. "I don't remember much of the rest."

"All the better for you, then," said Juffin. "I suspect I didn't behave quite the way a good-mannered old gentleman should. Oh, and one more thing: if you are going to let this young man laze around in your bed all day, you're going to have to stock up on Elixir of Kaxar. He consumes that stuff by the crate."

"Oh, no," said Tekki. "Maybe he should buy it himself, then?"

"Him? No. He's also a cheapskate."

When we were alone, Tekki gave me a long, intense look.

"Are you sure you really want to stay here, Max?"

"Absolutely," I said.

"Strange," she said. "But why?"

"Because you are here," I said. "Isn't it obvious?"

"Is this a confession?"

"Don't be silly. It's much more than that."

"But do you even know who I am? All children of Loiso Pondoxo—"

"Did he have many children?" I said in an indifferent tone.

"I had sixteen brothers. We're all his illegitimate children, with different mothers, of course. But we get along very well, because we don't really have anyone but ourselves. Especially my brothers."

"And all of your brothers are ghosts now. That's great. I'm sure I'll get along with them, too, because I myself am Magicians-know-who from Magicians-know-where."

"I thought as much," said Tekki. "A man who changes the color of his eyes every minute . . ."

"Have you noticed already?"

"Have I? I've been staring at you all along."

"Why?"

I was quite openly fishing for compliments. Tekki noticed it and made a funny face.

"I had to be looking at something besides dead bodies."

"Speaking of dead bodies. I'm feeling hungry all of a sudden. Do you have anything I can peck?"

"You ate it all up, don't you remember?"

"O woe is me! I met the owner of the only tavern in this World that doesn't have any food on the menu."

"I can send over to the *Fat Turkey*."

"Forget about turkeys and Turks. Let's just say I'm on a postmortem diet."

"What are Turks?" she said.

But that would remain a mystery to her. I didn't have time to launch into geographical discussions, for I had just managed to reach her. To my delight, she had neither the strength nor the desire to resist.

❧

An hour before dusk I appeared at the House by the Bridge like a well-trained employee. I hadn't been able to follow Juffin's advice to get some sleep. Nor had I managed to get anything to eat. I was too busy.

"Oh, no," said Juffin. He immediately assessed the situation and showed me the door. "I hope you have enough strength left in you to carry yourself over to the *Glutton*. Go ahead and have a snack. I can't stand looking at you like this."

"He's not going to make it, for sure. But I can carry him over there."

That was the omnipresent Melifaro, chuckling behind my back. It looked like he wasn't suffering from a hangover.

"Just in time," I said. "You owe me one after yesterday."

"Uh-oh, did I make a mess?" said Melifaro.

"You bet you did. You broke all the dishes in that wonderful tavern and then fell asleep. They made me glue them all back together. I just finished."

"Oh, so that's what you've been up too all this time," said Juffin. "I never would have guessed. Look, boys, if you're going to stay here another minute, you won't have time to eat, so off you go."

"You're so strict today," I said, doing an about-face. The truth was that I did feel a little queasy.

"And take it easy, boy," said Juffin.

I felt his heavy stare fixed on my back as I turned to go.

"Hey! You look like a scruffy farm cat during mating season," Melifaro said as he sat down at our favorite table in the *Glutton Bunba*.

"Right you are, man."

I didn't want to argue. I was feeling too good for that. I wanted to send a call to Tekki and ask her how she was doing, but I withstood the urge bravely. I was afraid that if she heard my question, she'd be convinced she was dealing with a madman. It was crazy to ask how she was doing already, only thirty minutes after we had parted.

So I decided to attend to the matters at hand. I started devouring everything in sight. For the first several minutes I was incommunicado to the outside world. Then I gave a long and satisfied sigh, asked for a second helping, and fixed my gaze on Melifaro.

"Did you have fun this morning?"

Melifaro's face changed. "Why didn't you kill them, Max? It would've made me so happy."

"Well, I kind of hoped they'd follow my advice and clean up," I said. "And then I thought you'd be pleased to butcher them with your own hands."

"It was the worst morning in my life," said Melifaro. "I woke up with a headache and a heavy feeling in my chest. Besides, I had no clue how I'd gotten home and didn't remember how the evening ended. How did it end, by the way?"

"You broke a glass."

"Just one?" Melifaro was sad. "How unlike me. I'm ashamed."

"Don't fret," I said. "You can always make up for it. Better tell me what happened in the morning."

"Oh boy. So when I went down and saw those guys in their fur hats, I really did want to kill them. You know, if I had your talents—"

"Did they really stay until morning?"

"When I went down to the living room, they were right there, asleep in the armchairs. Guess what I did? The first thing I did was snatch off their hats and throw them out the window. But they didn't wake up. I went to wash up because I knew I had to calm down. By the time I came back, I almost found the situation amusing. I pushed and prodded those men in pink tights until they woke up, and I told them to get out. That got them talking, as you might imagine. Mostly about my brains, of course."

"Right. That's almost all they talk about. It's some kind of national obsession, I believe."

"Anyway, I tossed two of them out the same window as their hats. I hadn't expected it of myself. You should have seen them kicking and struggling. It was a hoot! Oh, and how they cursed . . . The third one left of his own volition."

"And what about Rulen Bagdasys?"

"Oh, he's another story," Melifaro drawled. "At first I wanted to kick him out with the others. After all, if someone's going to raise a ruckus in my house, it should be my own guests, not someone else's, right?

"Absolutely. You should invite me someday. I'll teach you how to raise the roof."

"Really?" said Melifaro. "And how, may I ask, are you going to do that? You drink almost nothing except for Elixir of Kaxar, which only makes you want to work like a horse."

"Only a sober man can get a good brawl off the ground," I said with authority. "No one can wreak more havoc and destruction than an absolutely sober man who wants to turn the world upside down."

"Hmm," said Melifaro. "Never thought of it that way. I'll have to try it sometime. Anyway, I decided I'd have to show this Isamonian the door. He could rent his own apartment and live as he saw fit. I was even prepared to give him some money just to get rid of him. But he started screaming something about my diminished mental capacities and other grievous shortcomings. Of course he didn't hear a word I was saying. Mr. Bagdasys suffers from a peculiar variety of deafness: he can hear himself, and the small pieces of information he's genuinely interested in. By the way, when I was explaining to him the rules of etiquette in the Quarter of Trysts, I was whispering yet he caught every single word.

"Anyway, about an hour into this, I was beginning to tire and then I . . . then I . . ." Melifaro started howling with laughter.

"Well, how did it end?"

I was expecting to hear him confess to committing involuntary manslaughter, and promised myself that I'd help my friend cover his tracks and get rid of any evidence. After all, I almost qualified as his accomplice: if I had taken Melifaro to my place on the Street of Yellow Stones, no one would have been hurt.

Melifaro, smiling from ear to ear, reached inside the pocket of his looxi.

"He's in here now."

He produced a signet ring with a large transparent stone. I stared at it, not quite comprehending what he was trying to say.

"Hold it up to the light," he said.

I did as he said, and . . . no way! A tiny Rulen Bagdasys was frozen inside the slightly greenish crystal like a fly in a piece of amber.

"My friend," I said, "I think it's time for you to pack up and move to Xolomi. I wonder how long your term's going to be for this."

"Dream on. It was just the seventh degree of Black Magic. Since cooks have been allowed to use up to the twentieth degree, such an insignificant breach of the Code can hardly qualify as a crime. Mere disorderly conduct, if anything. I'll be only too happy to pay the fine: it's worth every penny."

"He's alive, isn't he?" I asked.

"Of course he is. The trick is the same one you're so fond of, except that I hid him not in my palm but in the first thing that turned up. It was a little more difficult but much more efficient. I can let him out at any time, but I don't feel like it yet. Even without Rulen Bagdasys life is full of complications."

"You can say that again," I said. "Haven't you been tempted to flush him down the toilet?"

"I have to admit, that was the first thing I thought of. Then I calmed down and decided it wouldn't be wise to throw away a family heirloom. It's quite handsome, though, don't you think?"

"Sure. It's a nice little trinket. Give it to your brother—it will make him happy. Plus, it's going to make a great memento."

"No," said Melifaro. "I have someone else in mind as the recipient of this precious stone."

"Who?"

"All in due time, my friend. All in due time," said Melifaro mysteriously. "You'll see."

"I hope I'm not going to be the lucky one. I beg you, please don't let it be me," I said. "What I really want to know is what's going on in the search for 'filthy Mudlax.' I'm getting sick and tired of the whole thing."

"Oh, look who's talking," said Melifaro. "He's sick and tired, huh?

If anyone should be sick and tired, it's me. You barely make it to work these days. You're too busy polishing your crown, paying visits to your new friend Gurig, or spending time in pubs."

"Yes, with you, by the way."

"Okay, with me," said Melifaro. "Still."

"Look, quit grumbling and tell me what's going on with the Mudlax case."

"Yesterday, while we were out carousing, Sir Juffin had a quiet little conversation with the inimitable master of disguise, the dark legacy of the Epoch of Orders. Judging by the fact that Sir Varixa Ariama went home on his own and all in one piece, the boss was delighted with the results of the meeting. What we got out of the bargain was not just a detailed description of Mudlax's new face but also his home address. I already stopped in this morning—no dice, of course. He fled three days ago. It seems as though Mudlax disappeared the second the ship from Arvarox touched the Admiral's Pier. Was he able to smell his compatriots, or what? Anyway, I had fun interrogating his neighbors. They were very keen on describing what it was like to rub elbows with the fugitive king. Unfortunately, I had such a hangover that I couldn't enjoy their stories to the fullest.

"While I was collecting rumors, our buriwoks found eight more Arvaroxians on the streets of Echo. Sir Juffin had a heart-to-heart talk with every one of them. They didn't know much about Mudlax because they turned out to be his mortal enemies. Then again, they didn't exactly get along with the Conqueror of Arvarox, either. Also, they were about to kill each other. Such sweet, gentle people, these Arvaroxians. But where could that blasted Mudlax be? Do you have any idea?"

"If I were him, I'd try to commit some crime and get locked up in Xolomi," I said with a smirk. "The safest place for him, in my book."

"Brilliant!" said Melifaro. "Why didn't you say so before?"

"Say what before?"

"Your idea about Xolomi, of course!"

"Sinning Magicians," I said, rolling my eyes. "Relax. It was just a joke."

"Oh, it was just a joke, was it?" Melifaro was getting fidgety. "We should check your lead right away. Let's go over to Headquarters."

"You go," I said. "I still have a full plate."

"The third one," said Melifaro. "Fine. Keep stuffing your intestines, but I'm leaving."

"Can't you wait for, like, three minutes?"

"Three minutes I can wait. But I'm timing it."

Sir Juffin Hully was giving an audience to the "Sternlooking Master of two times fifty Sharptooths." I was beginning to view Aloxto Allirox as either our new employee or a distant relative from the provinces, one we all shared.

"Ah, it's great that you've come, boys," said Juffin. "Sir Allirox was just about to share his ideas on the whereabouts of Mudlax with us. Yes, of course, *filthy* Mudlax. Don't give me that look, Mr. Allirox. Please do go on, though."

"I told Thotta, my shaman, to ask the Dead God where the filthy Mudlax was. Thotta received the answer, but I did not understand it. I think this is because I don't know the city as well as the locals. Thus, I've decided to pass the words of the Dead God along to you. Thotta says that Mudlax is 'in the middle of Big Water, in a place that is easy to enter but impossible to leave.' Do you know of such a place?"

"Of course we do!" cried Melifaro. "Imagine, Sir Juffin, Max and I came to tell you the very same thing. The fellow is hiding in Xolomi. It's perfectly clear now."

"Did you ask a shaman, too?" said Juffin.

"Something like that," said Melifaro. "Max stuffed himself with food, entered into a state of trance, and performed some ventriloquism."

"Actually, it was just a bad joke," I said. "Or a good one."

"It's so nice of you to discuss work even when you're eating," said Juffin. "I'm touched." Then he gave Aloxto a compassionate look. "We're going to check this out. But if your shaman is right, you're going to face a long, long wait before the sweet hour of vengeance arrives. No one will let you or your Sharptooths into the Royal Prison. It's the law."

"I can wait," said Aloxto. "But first I need to find Mudlax—that's the most important task. Waiting is not the worst thing that can happen to a man."

"Really?" said Juffin. "Well, all the better, then. As soon as we find out something I'll send you a call. Oh, wait, how can I send you a call if you don't know Silent Speech?"

"I do now," said Aloxto proudly. "Lady Melamori has been teaching me. It is not very difficult."

"Talk about talent," I said with envy. "I still find it difficult."

"That's because you're not used to focusing on the task at hand, oblivious to everything else," said Juffin. "For the people of Arvarox it's the norm." He turned to Aloxto. "Even better, then. I'll send you a call once the situation becomes clear."

"Thank you," said Aloxto with a bow. "I should like to leave now, if you do not mind."

"Why should I mind?" Juffin was surprised. "As far as I know, only the Conqueror of Arvarox can appeal against your decision."

"It is true, but I was told that it is your custom to come to a mutual agreement on decisions with others. I believe you call this courtesy."

"We do," said Juffin. "That's exactly what we call it. That said, I really don't mind you leaving."

"Thank you. Good night, gentlemen." Aloxto bowed again and left.

"Our Melamori is demonstrating excellent pedagogical skills," said Juffin. "Who would have thought? What did Kamshi say, Sir Melifaro?"

It turned out that while we had been saying goodbye to Aloxto, Melifaro had sent a call to the new warden of Xolomi, Toiki Kamshi, former lieutenant of the City Police Department. He had already received an answer. The exchange, however, didn't seem to improve his mood.

"I'll tell you in a minute. Max, may I try your otherworldly smokes?" said Melifaro, sitting down on the window ledge. "I've found local tobacco revolting since I was a kid, and I desperately want to smoke."

"Here you go," I said, handing him a cigarette. "Hey, I'm expanding my clientele. First Boboota, now you. I should quit the Force and open up a tobacco shop. I won't have any competition, that's for sure. Except for Sir Maba Kalox, perhaps. But knowing him, he's going to get bored with it pretty fast."

"That he would," Juffin said, and turned to Melifaro. "Well?"

"Mmm, your smoking sticks are really good, Max," said Melifaro. "Right, Sir Juffin. Don't drill a hole in me with your stare. I digressed, I admit.

"Kamshi told me that they hadn't had any new prisoners lately, but just this morning they got a new one by the name of Bakka Saal. His description couldn't be further from that of Mudlax, but that's absolutely irrelevant, because you know why he was put in Xolomi? For the murder of Sir Varixa Ariama, the very same Varixa Ariama that—"

"I know very well who Varixa Ariama is," said Juffin impatiently.

"Oh, I'm sorry, sir," said Melifaro. "I got carried away."

"Who's on the case?" said Juffin. "Why didn't they report it to us?"

"They thought it was unnecessary. The murderer turned himself in to the Office of Expedited Reprisals. He just sent them a call and reported his own crime. The guys drove up to the scene of the crime, quickly filled out all the papers, and took him to Xolomi. Sir Baguda Maldaxan deems promptness to be the highest virtue among his subordinates, as you know. Now I think Mudlax—for it *must* be him—is facing about two hundred years in Xolomi. Our fair-haired friend had better move to Echo for good and keep his health in top shape. Otherwise, he's not going to live to see his moment of sweet, sweet revenge. There's no way Kamshi will let him—"

"Two hundred years, you say? Why so long?" Juffin interrupted him. "As far as I know the standard term for murder is five to six dozen years. Considering that he turned himself in, he can't get more than three dozen."

"Correct, but *also* considering that the murder was committed using White Magic of the hundred and seventieth degree, he's lucky that he didn't get put away for life," said Melifaro.

"Which degree?" Juffin was shouting. "The hundred and seventieth? Well, I'll be! Melifaro, take Kurush and rush over to Xolomi. We must be absolutely sure that the new prisoner is our 'filthy Mudlax.' Send me a call as soon as you find out anything. And remember: all we need from him now is his real name. Don't ask him any other questions. Magicians only know what he may do. What if he decides that it's 'easier to die'? It's best not to second-guess these Arvaroxians. Sir Max, get up. We're going out for a ride."

"Where to?"

"To the scene of the crime, of course. Better late than never. And I think we may need Melamori's help. We need to find the real murderer, the sooner the better."

"What do you mean 'the real murderer'?" I said. "Wasn't Mudlax—"

"Mudlax could easily kill his victim with his mighty 'flyswatter' or simply cut his throat," said Juffin. "Use your head, boy. Do you think a foreigner can handle Forbidden Magic, let alone the hundred and seventieth degree? I wouldn't be surprised to learn that he hadn't even gotten the hang of Permitted Magic. Only a very experienced Magician can handle the hundred and seventieth degree. I'm pretty sure the murderer was some wise guy from one of the old Orders. It's clear as—"

"You're right," I said. "But how come the guys from Expedited Reprisals didn't think of that?"

"They just didn't. It's not their job, by the way, to conduct interrogations. Usually, their clients go through us first, but this time it's going to be the other way around. How come you're still here and not in the amobiler?"

"Because I'm listening to you, and *you're* still here," I said, opening the door.

Juffin followed close behind me. "Finally, this Mudlax case is getting interesting," he said searching his pockets for his pipe. "It's high time it did."

There was no one in the house of the late Sir Varixa Ariama, the former Senior Magician of the Order of the Brass Needle.

"I'd like to know where his son's gone," I said.

"Good question, Max. A very good question," said Juffin. "I think we'll soon find out many things and get answers to many questions, including that one. But where's Lady Melamori? She should be here already."

"I am." Melamori was standing at the threshold. "For your information, I had to come here all the way from the New City. You should be proud of me."

"We are, we are," said Juffin in a placating voice. "Look around the house, my lady. Somewhere here there should be the trace of a very powerful Magician. Can you distinguish it from the rest?"

"Pfft. Easy peasy," said Melamori. "Max, don't just stand around loafing. As if you can't do it yourself—I know you can. And don't tell me I'm unique and irreplaceable because I'm not going to believe that."

"But you know how lazy I am," I said.

"Sir Max is loafing because as a Master of Pursuit he poses too great a danger for the suspects," said Juffin. "And I need our client alive and well. I prefer to get information from the original source. It would be sad if our monster's trail ended at the clean-picked skull of his poor victim. Besides, Max is too inexperienced to distinguish the trace we're looking for from others. So you *are* unique and irreplaceable, Melamori."

"Well, if you say so, I'll do it," said Melamori, flattered.

She took off her shoes and walked around the living room.

"Okay, this is the trace of the late Sir Varixa Ariama . . . This is Shurf's, and this is mine—I was here yesterday, too. Some other traces, nothing interesting. Maybe Baguda Maldaxan's boys. Oh, and here's where that 'filthy Mudlax' must have been hanging around. I told you that the trace of any Arvaroxian is different from the rest. Not significantly, but it is . . . Okay, here's someone else's trace, but he's not the one you're looking for. It seems he's very ill, but I may be wrong."

"Must be Ariama Junior's," I said.

"Possible," said Juffin. "We'll have to talk to him, too, but that can wait. I saw the young man. No Grand Magic about him, trust me."

"Sure," I said. "But I can't stop thinking about him. Maybe he's in trouble. I mean, since Melamori says he may be ill, who knows what could have happened to him?"

"Hmm," said Juffin. "Then it's best not to procrastinate. But who should we send on this case? You, Max, might accidentally kill the poor boy. Melamori's already busy. Should I try it myself? I used to be pretty good at it."

"Don't take the bread out of my mouth, Juffin," said Melamori. "By the way, I found the trace of another dead man. Pretty unusual, but the owner is dead for sure. Very strange, though. Are you sure there was only one dead body here?"

"We're not sure about anything," said Juffin. "But I have an idea. Do me a favor, Melamori, and step on Max's trace for a moment."

"Why?" said Melamori.

"Just do it for me, will you?" said Juffin.

"Okay."

She came to me from behind, shuffled her feet for a moment, and gasped. I turned around. I hadn't seen her that scared for a long time.

"This *is* your trace, Max," she said, her lips pale and barely moving. "When did you die?"

"Last night," said Juffin. "Don't fret, Melamori. He's more alive now that he ever was. You can take my word for it."

"I'm alive and kicking, Melamori, really," I said. "I'm not a corpse, I'm a good guy!"

"Phew! I don't like your jokes, gentlemen," said Melamori.

"Why do I have the trace of a dead man?" I asked Juffin in alarm. "I'm not a zombie, am I?"

"No, no. You're perfectly fine, Max," said Juffin. "But the trace is firmly attached to you body's memory of itself, and your body remembers its own death. Hence the confusion. But look at the bright side: it's an excellent disguise. You never know, it may come in handy."

"Who would I need to hide from?" I said. "I have no reason to hide from Melamori."

"No, not yet. But spend a few more years working for the Secret Investigative Force, and you're bound to end up with a few powerful nemeses. Just you wait," said Juffin. Then he turned to Melamori. "Don't be mad at me, my lady. I didn't want to upset you, but sometimes it pays for the Master of Pursuit to acquire new experience, don't you think? In any event, now you know that a dead man's trace can sometimes only *seem* like a dead man's trace."

"I'm not mad," Melamori said quietly. "But you really did scare me. Okay, I'm going to keep looking for the trace of that powerful Magician. But I don't think it's here. I've looked almost everywhere already."

"Are you sure?" said Juffin. "The body was found in the living room."

"It's not hard to move the body to another room," I said.

I had the age-old wisdom of myriad detective novels from my World on my side, so I didn't doubt for a second that I was right. To my surprise, though, Juffin didn't tap his forehead and exclaim, "Oh my, why didn't I think of that!"

Instead, he said, "That's a strange idea . . . Dragging a dead body around. Then again, people's heads are full of strange ideas. Let's give it a try. Where do you think we should begin?"

"How about the bedroom?" I said. "On second thought, scratch that. How about his workshop? He wouldn't be changing the appearance of his clients in the living room, I don't think."

"Indeed," said Juffin. "Melamori, step on the trace of that Arvaroxian. I just got word from Melifaro. He says that the new prisoner is, indeed, Mudlax, which I didn't doubt for a second. He also says that his new face looks nothing like the one Ariama described to me just yesterday. What is clear is that Mudlax came here to change his face again. And he got what he came for. His trace should lead us to that very 'workshop,' as Max has christened it. Where did you pick up this bureaucratic jargon, Max?"

"On the border of the County Vook and the Barren Lands, naturally. While I was sitting on my throne there, alone among the boundless steppes."

❧

Melamori shuffled her feet in the middle of the living room and then went downstairs.

"I wouldn't be surprised if Varixa Ariama's 'workshop' turned out to be the bathroom," said Juffin. "Very romantic."

We did have to cross a spacious room, in the center of which stood a toilet bowl. Melamori hesitated by the back wall and turned to us.

"There must be some secret passage here," she said. "His trace runs right into the wall."

"Interesting," said Juffin. "Well, a secret passage poses no problem."

He tapped the wall with his palm in a series of short chopping motions. A thin streak of pale light outlined the neat contour of a small door. The door opened with a mournful creak.

"It's not too happy about this," said Juffin. Then he made a gallant bow to Melamori. "After you, my lady."

Melamori had to stoop down to walk through the door and into a small, dark room. Juffin and I had to crawl on all fours to squeeze in.

"Ah, it's the same old story: the smaller the door, the easier it is to make it invisible," Juffin grumbled. "I'm only glad it's not a mouse-hole. Well, my girl, have you found anything interesting in here?"

"And how!" said Melamori. "An excellent trace. One of the best. I think Max is quite capable of standing on it. This person is unlikely to kick the bucket if he does. He's very, very strong."

"Oh, is he indeed?" said Juffin. "Well, if you're sure, then . . . Go on, Max. Try it."

"No problem," I said, making my way over to Melamori.

"Where's the trace? Ah, here we go, you don't have to tell me. Why did you say he was so powerful? I don't sense anything of the sort. Now, the sister of Sir Atva Kuraisa, on the other hand, she was one tough cookie. Remember her?"

"The problem is your oversized ego, boy," said Juffin laughing. "Like any professional Master of Pursuit, Melamori evaluates the strength of the trace's owner objectively. You, on the other hand, can only sense one thing: whether the owner is dangerous to you personally. Lady Tanna Kuraisa almost killed you, and you had a foreboding about it from the very beginning. That's why you avoided her trace. This guy, however powerful he may be, doesn't stand a chance against you, and that's why you consider his trace to be innocuous. Maybe your approach is more practical than the traditional one. After all, the only thing that matters is staying alive. How powerful the opponent is may be irrelevant. You don't have to be a Grand Magician to aim blindly from behind a corner and still manage to shoot your pursuer right between the eyes—just lucky. So I think you can safely go hunting. The sooner you track him down, the better. I know it's not completely up to you, but please try not to kill the guy, okay? I'm eager to talk to him. Melamori, what are you waiting for? Go back to the living room and step on the trace of Ariama Junior. You're on him now officially, since Max is having his premonitions."

❀

I felt I couldn't stay in one place. The sensation that I had begun to forget, pleasant and unbearable at the same time, made my feet move faster, and faster, and faster. I went back to the bathroom, then up the stairs. The trace, I soon realized, didn't lead upstairs. It swerved behind the stairs and broke off at the wall.

"Juffin," I called out, puzzled. "I think there's another secret door here. I could use your help."

Juffin examined the wall and shook his head.

"No door here. He left through the Dark Path. Not a problem for an experienced Master of Pursuit, really. If you can't figure it out, Melamori can follow him there."

"Right, but according to you, he poses no threat to me, and we don't know whether Melamori can handle him. So I'd better try it myself. Just tell me what to do."

"Hmm. You don't really need to do anything. Just stand here and wait for the trace to pull you. But you need to focus as hard as you can on your own feet. Imagine that you have nothing but your heels. Got it?"

"Of course not," I said. "But I'll try."

❀

Whoa! It was easier than I thought. The buzzing itch in my feet was so strong that I could think of nothing else. I seemed to have no choice.

A few minutes later I felt a cold wind blowing in my face. I opened my eyes and looked around.

I stood on the Bridge of Kuluga Menonchi. A stupendous view of Jafax, the main Residence of the Order of the Seven-Leaf Clover, opened up before me. The trace was pulling me farther ahead. To my astonishment it ran up against the Secret Door of Jafax. The problem was that only the members of the Order of the Seven-Leaf Clover could use that door. Okay, so this is what it comes down to, I thought. The murderer's in there, polishing the boots of Grand Magician Nuflin or attending to some matter of state, and then I show up, silly crime-snooper that I am. No, not a very clever idea. Not to mention that I can't even go through the Secret Door, sealed with a curse by Grand Magician Nuflin Moni Mak himself. Even Juffin couldn't squeeze through it. Although, come to think of it, Juffin probably could. I'd better call him for help. On second thought . . .

Then it dawned on me. Why bother Juffin when I had a good chance to get help from the holy of holies of the place I was trying to get into? Lady Sotofa Xanemer, the most powerful woman of the Seven-Leaf Clover, was Juffin's old girlfriend. And if I wasn't mistaken, she had a soft spot for me, too. In any case, I decided to grab the chance and send her a call.

Lady Sotofa, this is Max. I'm truly sorry, but I'm standing by your Secret Door now. Can you let me in?

Oh, what's happened, boy? Have you developed a passion for me and come to serenade me under the walls of Jafax? I strongly suspect you're tone-deaf, so let's leave well enough alone!

Well, you read my heart all right! I laughed. *But I have another piece of news. Bad news.*

"Just how bad is it?"

Suddenly the smiling, pleasantly plump old woman was standing right beside me. Magicians only knew how she'd gotten there. Lady Sotofa laughed and gave me a hug. As usual, I was surprised by the warmth and cordiality of this powerful lady.

She took my hand, told me to close my eyes, and walked on ahead of me. I stumbled behind. A few seconds later I felt the wet branches of a shott tree touching my face. I opened my eyes. We were standing in the beautiful garden of the Residence of the Order.

"Where have you been for a year and a half? Since you returned from Kettari you haven't shown as much as the tip of your nose in here."

"I haven't," I confessed. "I was too shy at first, and then—"

"And then you slept for a year. I know. Well, what's the bad news you were talking about?" said Lady Sotofa. "I doubt you were planning on kissing me by the light of the moon, which, by the way, just hid behind the clouds."

"I sure was!" I said. "But since there's no moon, we can just talk. Drat, though, I'm still standing on this trace! If only I could step off it for a moment, so I could explain all this to you."

"Let's do this: you keep following the trace—just don't rush. I'll walk right beside you, and you'll tell me everything you want me to know on the way. Speaking of which, why are you on the trace of our Order to begin with? Is this a new policy of His Majesty King Gurig? I find it hard to believe. Times have changed."

I quickly told Lady Sotofa about the events of the evening. She listened, and then became very serious.

"What a story! I'm glad you were smart enough to get in touch with me. I smell trouble with a capital *T*. You see, I'm absolutely sure that nobody here would soil his hands by killing that poor charlatan Ariama. Even if he did, why would a member of the Order of the Seven-Leaf Clover be covering his tracks? Our boys can get away with a lot more serious things."

"I'm sure they can!" I grinned. "Well, I hope we'll soon find out the truth. I'm getting the sense that we're almost there. You know how it is when a Master of Pursuit is closing in on the quarry."

"No, I haven't the faintest notion about that," said Lady Sotofa. "But I believe you."

※

"There," I whispered, pointing at a dense bush. "He's right there."

"Really?" said Lady Sotofa. "I'd like to know what a normal person would be doing, sitting in the bushes at night. There's no shortage of restrooms in here. Let's see . . . Oh, sinning Magicians! That's none other than Senior Magician Jorinmuk Vansifis, the new favorite of our Nuflin. Just a run-of-the-mill wheedler, in my book, but Magician Nuflin knows best, of course. Is he sleeping?"

"It's worse," I said gloomily. "Much worse, I'm afraid. Melamori overestimated his powers by a long shot. Or underestimated mine. I must have killed him. Juffin will bite off my head and spit it out in the Xuron. Mark my words."

"What if he does? Don't fret, boy. He's not dead; he fainted," Lady Sotofa assured me. She cautiously pinched the neck of the bald man, dressed in the blue-and-white looxi of the Order of the Seven-Leaf Clover, who was lying on the ground. Then she frowned suddenly. "Wait! This isn't Jorinmuk. He just looks a lot like him. I'd very much like to know what happened to the real Magician Jorinmuk. What a story!"

"You will know," I said, eager to demonstrate my gratitude. "I promise. As soon as we finish with this case, I'll send you a call and tell you everything."

"You don't have to. I prefer to think you'll come round again, whining plaintively by the Secret Door, and that we'll have a cup or two of kamra. Deal?"

"It's a deal. Thank you, Lady Sotofa!"

"Wonderful. Now retrieve your quarry and take him to Juffin. The old fox will eat him alive, I'm sure. It'll do him good, though. There must be some sunny days in the gloomy, monotonous life of the Venerable Head. Come on, I'll show you the way out."

The poor victim of my newfound talent found himself between my thumb and index finger. Lady Sotofa took me gently by the elbow and led me nimbly along the path, invisible in the darkness. When we reached the wall, she stopped and looked at me.

"How do you like your new heart, boy?"

"I haven't really felt the difference yet."

"No? That means the most interesting experience still lies ahead. You'll find it very handy, trust me. The daughter of Loiso Pondoxo did you quite a service. You like her?"

I nodded, embarrassed.

"Funny," said Lady Sotofa with a smile, revealing her charming dimples. "Who would have thought? Destiny is wiser than all of us, whatever people may think. But remember, boy, the children of Loiso Pondoxo are very different from ordinary people, even though you might not notice it immediately."

"I'm also very different from other people, don't you think?"

"You are," said Lady Sotofa, "but . . . Anyway, nothing's going to happen to you that you aren't equal to. Now, off you go to that old fox Juffin. And don't forget to visit me again sometime."

"I won't," I said. "And if I don't come for a long time, it means that I've grown shy again. That happens to me."

"Don't be silly," said Lady Sotofa, laughing. "Shy of me? Of all the nonsense! Don't you disappear again for a year and a half."

"I won't."

"Well, good night, then."

And she pushed me gently on the back. Just like that I found myself standing on the other side of the impenetrable wall surrounding Jafax. I sent a call to Juffin.

The mouse is in the trap, I said enigmatically. *Can you send an amobiler for me? I'm standing by the wall of Jafax.*

What on earth were you doing there?

I was flirting with Lady Sotofa but was rebuffed.

Were you? I'm surprised she still has some prudence left in her. Fine, I won't torture you with Silent Speech. We'll talk back at the office. The amobiler will pick you up in about fifteen minutes.

You should really let me give your drivers a master class. Fifteen minutes to drive here? I can walk faster!

Don't exaggerate. Walking will take at least half an hour.

❀

I made myself comfortable on the broad parapet of the Bridge of Kuluga Menonchi, lit up a cigarette, and began to wait. After a few moments of hesitation I sent a call to Tekki. I was worried she might be asleep already but hoped that a short conversation with me wouldn't be the worst thing that could happen to her.

Are you in bed already?

Not even close! I still have a ton of customers. Maybe they're waiting for you to appear, I don't know. They're looking at me like I'm a freshly resuscitated vampire. I can imagine the rumors making the rounds of Echo now.

How did the Echoers find out about it? Well, it's all for the best. Now I know nobody will be coming on to you, and that's cool.

Nobody has come on to me for the past hundred years. You were an exception. Granted, you only demanded food. The rest of it I had to do myself.

I'm working on that. I already have a long list of ways to come on to you. I'll read it to you next time I see you.

I'd like to believe it.

You know, it's not easy to deal with me. I may show up at the most inconvenient time. Tomorrow at dawn, for instance. Or earlier. Or later. Is that bad?

Very bad. But I'll manage.

That's what I wanted to hear. So kick out the remaining customers and go to sleep. Over and out.

What?

Over and out. It means goodbye. One of my bad habits. And it's infectious. You'll never be able to stop saying it now.

I see. Over and out, then.

❀

I saw the bluish headlights of an amobiler flashing at the far end of the bridge. Soon the amobiler drove up and stopped.

"Climb into the back seat, buddy," I said to the driver. "I'm going to give you the ride of your life."

He got into the back seat, and three minutes later I stopped the amobiler by the House by the Bridge.

On my way to Juffin's office, in the Hall of Common Labor, I saw Melamori. She was attending to a sad-looking young man with a bandage on his head, urging him to drink some reviving kamra.

"Ah, Sir Ariama Junior," I said. "How do you do?"

"Not so long ago he wasn't doing very well," said Melamori. "It's good that you insisted we look for him immediately, Max. When I found him he was on the verge of death. But Juffin is a true wonder-worker, so Sir Ariama is all right now. Aren't you, Sir Ariama?"

The young man nodded, and Melamori continued.

"That Arvaroxian hero—Mudlax, I mean—was waiting for him when he came home. He hit him over the head, then hid him in the bushes in the backyard. Either he got nervous, or just decided he didn't need any extra witnesses."

"In any case, you were very lucky, sir," I said. "That blow on the head saved you from running into some other clients of your father's who are much more dangerous. All's well that ends well, right?"

"Poor Father," said the young man. "I got along very well with him. Why did they kill him, I wonder?"

"His was a dangerous profession," I said. "I doubt people would want to change their faces just because the shape of their chin didn't match an ornament on their new looxi. Drink up your kamra and get well soon. Melamori, I'm off to see Juffin. I have some great news." I shook my left fist proudly in front of her little nose.

"Is he in there?" said Melamori, excited. "Great! Good night, Max. Juffin gave me permission to leave, so I'll be off soon. I'm taking Sir Ariama home, and then . . . Then I'm going to keep having fun."

"Good night," I said, nodding sympathetically. "Strange and wonderful things happen to people sometimes, don't you think?"

❀

There was a small, cordial gathering in Juffin's office. Sir Kofa Yox sat comfortably in my favorite chair, and Melifaro was sitting at the table, dangerously close to a tray with food from the *Glutton*. I think he was sleeping with his eyes open. I didn't remember ever seeing him so quiet before.

I poured myself some kamra and nestled on the window ledge.

"So what did you and Sotofa do at the Residence of the Seven-Leaf Clover?" said Juffin.

"Nothing that we'd be ashamed to tell the journalists," I said. Then I briefed my colleagues on the details of my hunt for the unknown villain.

"So, you're saying you found him in the bushes, without his turban and unconscious?" said Juffin. "That's just brilliant! Talk about luck. Okay, let's take a look at your trophy."

"Here you go."

The bald man appeared on the floor by Sir Kofa. He was still knocked out.

"The spitting image of Jorinmuk Vansifis! I don't even think the Great Nuflin would know the difference," said Juffin. "Kofa, would you be a good sport and let us take a peek at his real face? I'm curious."

"What a job," said Kofa. "To reverse the work of Varixa Ariama? A hole in the heavens above his grave—he was one of the best."

"And you *are* the best—don't be so modest. But cast some spell on him first, so he doesn't wake up. We don't want any trouble. We're sitting here in good company. I was just about to send for dinner."

"Perfect timing," I said.

"Okay," said Kofa. "Let me squeeze out the rest of my magic."

"'The rest of my magic,'" said Juffin. "You have enough magic for all of us here. You'll still be here when we've all retired."

"Maybe I will, maybe I won't," said Kofa. "Here goes nothing."

He bent over the bald gentleman. Melifaro blinked, gave me a blank look, and moved to the now vacant armchair. It did seem that he had just woken up.

"Where's Sir Shurf?" he said, bewildered.

"Where? He went home half an hour ago," said Juffin. "And so should you. You can't stay awake another minute."

"I'm awake now. I can't go anywhere now that you've sent for dinner."

"Suit yourself. The more people I torture with overwork, the more precious my memories when I get old."

§

"Look, a familiar face," said Kofa Yox standing up. "Juffin, you should be able to recognize this guy."

"Xekta Bonbon, the former Grand Magician of the Order of the Flat Mountain himself!" said Juffin. He looked almost tenderly at the sunken cheeks and furry eyebrows of the old man lying on the floor. "Well, I'll be! I thought he was digging in his garden somewhere in Uryuland and had long since forgotten about the Capital . . . I'm sorry, boys, but you must excuse Sir Bonbon and me. I guess I won't be staying for dinner. I can't wait to find out what on earth he was doing in Jafax."

"Are you going to tell me?" I asked hopefully.

"Of course I will. He's your catch, after all. Rather, yours and Sotofa's, which is even worse. The two of you can thrash the life out of me with all your questions.

"Right, gentlemen. Take care. Split my serving among yourselves. By the way, if I were you, I'd invite Lady Tuotli and Sir Blookey over. They've been working hard these days. Now they're probably dozing off at the Police Department, thinking life couldn't get any more boring than this. Don't you think it's a bit unfair?"

"I'll call them," said Melifaro. "Why didn't I think of that myself?"

I turned to him but only caught a glimpse of his orange looxi disappearing behind the door.

Juffin gently picked up Grand Magician Xekta Bonbon from the floor. Then, holding him like a drunk but dear relative, he dragged him over to the door.

"Are you going downstairs?" said Sir Kofa.

"Of course. You don't suppose Xekta will tell me his secrets in a friendly chat over a cup of kamra, do you? No, this interrogation calls for a great deal of magic."

I knew what he was talking about. In the basement of the House by the Bridge, among the numerous restrooms, there was a small and very uncomfortable room, isolated from the rest of the World by the joint spells of Sir Juffin Hully and the Grand Magician Nuflin Moni Mak. In that room one could exercise magic of any degree without fear of knocking the World off balance. I had been in that "lab" only once, on an excursion rather than on business: the highest degrees of Apparent Magic, for which the room was built, were way out of my league. As for more commonplace miracles, our office was as good as any other place.

Meanwhile, a sleepy courier had put numerous trays from the *Glutton Bunba* on the table. Melifaro returned in the company of Lieutenant Apurra Blookey.

"Where's Lady Tuotli?" I said.

"She gave us a concise lecture on the inappropriateness of parties during working hours, spiced up by a few expletives," said Melifaro. "Forget about her, that uncrowned Queen of the City Police."

"I don't understand what's gotten into her," said Apurra Blookey. "Kekki is a great girl. She should have thanked you guys for inviting her."

She's being shy again, I thought. I'll bet that's what it is.

I jumped down from the window ledge.

"I'm going to talk to her. Melifaro, friend, do me a favor. If I do come back, please aim your insults only at me, okay? I'm almost a goner, so you don't have to mollycoddle me. Lady Tuotli, on the other hand, has her whole life before her. Don't traumatize her."

"As if I'm some kind of baby eater!" said Melifaro, nonplussed. "I'm not that terrible."

"Ah, but you are. Trust me. And don't you dare go eating my food."

"I'll see to it that he doesn't, my boy," said Kofa. He was clearly on my side.

❀

I went to the half of the building occupied by the City Police. I tiptoed to the office that had once belonged to the late Captain Shixola and listened. Someone was sniffling inside. I decided not to go in but to send her a call first. No one wants to be seen crying.

Lady Kekki, I'm sorry to impose, but parties during work hours are the most interesting events, believe me. It's only for the sake of those parties that I'm still serving in this sinning outfit.

I sensed that my invisible interlocutor had smiled.

Your Silent Speech is so funny, Sir Max.

That's right, I'm a regular joker. As for the Silent Speech, I'm still not very good at it, so do you think I can come in?

For a long time there was no answer. Then the door opened. Lady Kekki stood in the doorway looking at me with her beautiful gray eyes, defiant and helpless at the same time.

"Has that madcap Melifaro been getting on your nerves?" I said. "He's a great guy, really. It's just that we're all—all the Secret Investigators, that is—a little crazy. His personal insanity can be a little wearying for some people, but you should try to ignore it."

"It has nothing to do with Sir Melifaro," said Kekki. "Granted, he's not the most courteous gentlemen on this side of the Xuron, but compared to General Boboota, he's not too bad."

With a great deal of pleasure I imagined Melifaro's reaction to Kekki's generous description of his character.

"Okay, but then why did you—"

"Sir Max, you are a very kind and good person," said Kekki. "You're quick on the uptake but . . . I'm afraid you can't help me. Please tell Sir Melifaro that I'm sorry for being rude, and tell Apurra not to be mad at me. But I think I'd better stay here in my office, okay?"

"Well, it's up to you," I said. "I, for one, don't think it's 'better,' but . . . Do as you please, Magicians be with you."

I turned around to leave. Then, all of a sudden, my new, second heart decided to show off its outstanding skills. It knocked ever so slightly on my chest, and I felt the hurricane of someone else's irrational emotions engulfing me. Another moment and I would have lost my head. I quickly remembered the breathing exercises promoted by Sir Lonli-Lokli. They did enhance my self-control, even though I hadn't been doing them regularly.

"I'm very sorry, Lady Kekki," I mumbled. "Honestly, I didn't do it on purpose. I'm not trying to meddle in your personal affairs, but why are you so afraid of Sir Kofa? He's an extremely nice man and—"

"Did you read my mind?" she said, shocked.

"No, no. I was simply engulfed by your emotions. Never mind, I didn't even have time to get to the bottom of them. Still, I shouldn't have let this happen. Forgive me, sometimes I just can't control my little quirks."

"It's all right," Kekki whispered. "My emotions—as though they're a big secret."

And she began crying like a child. I shuffled my feet in the doorway. I felt like an inept babysitter who'd just upset the child he was meant to be taking care of.

"Want me to cry along with you?" I said. "I'm pretty good at it, too."

"I think I can do it on my own, thank you very much," said Kekki, managing a weak smile. "It's nice of you to offer to keep me company. But you don't understand. I'm not afraid of Sir Kofa. I've been wanting to meet him since I was a child." She never stopped sniffling. "My parents had old newspapers, the very first issues of the *Royal Voice*. Among the latest news, it had a special column with old crime reports, a kind of chronicle from the Epoch of Orders. I couldn't stop reading the stories about Sir Kofa's exploits."

"I see," I said.

"No, you don't! I rejected a proposal to work at the Royal Court, fell out with all my relatives, and finally got this position at the City Police. All because Sir Kofa was once the general of the Right Bank Police—"

"And because our organizations share the same building," I said.

"That's right. But it didn't turn out exactly the way I thought it would. First, I'm terribly shy around him and always say silly things. Second, because of our boss, that idiot General Box, we're the laughing-stock of all the Secret Investigators. I can just imagine what Sir Kofa must think of me!"

"He's not thinking anything bad about you. If anything, it's the other way around. You should've seen him looking at you."

At that moment I was sure I was telling the truth. I'll go to any lengths to make a good person stop bawling.

"Are you serious?"

Her tears stopped for a split second and then began anew with twice the intensity. These, however, were tears of relief. I wanted to bite off my lying tongue. But didn't Sir Kofa brighten up when I mentioned the name of this stubborn girl? Or did he?

"So, what about the party, Kekki?" I said. "Will you change your mind? Everybody's waiting for you. We're good guys, you know. We all need to be friends."

"I . . . I guess I changed my mind," she said wiping off her tears. "Will you help me if I start saying silly things again?"

"Of course I will. I'll also start saying silly things, only louder," I said. "That's basically all I do, say silly things. In the breaks between brutal murders, that is."

Lady Kekki Tuotli smiled and passed her hands lightly over her face. It immediately changed, leaving no trace of tears.

"I can't change my face like Sir Kofa. Maybe I'll learn to do that someday. But what I can do is change it to look good without using any makeup," she said.

"Brilliant!" I said. "Will you teach me?"

"Are you joking?"

"Not at all. I really don't know how to put my appearance in order. With or without makeup."

❁

And we went back to the other half of the House by the Bridge. Lady Kekki was holding the fold of my looxi like a preschooler holding the sleeve of her older brother. It was too moving even for my unsophisticated tastes.

"There they are!" said Sir Kofa. "I was fighting for your servings like a hero of the ancient world, I swear."

"I don't doubt it for a second," I said, seating Lady Kekki in Juffin's armchair. Then I turned to Melifaro. "So they didn't give you the chance to play the villain?"

"No, but they gave me the chance to drink," said Melifaro. "If that ship from Arvarox doesn't sail back soon, I'll take to drink once and for all."

"It will sail back," said Kofa. "Are you that tired of them?"

"You bet! Now pour me another one. And don't look at me like a probation officer, Max."

"I'm only worried about my own leisure," I said. "Don't you think it'll be too much if I have to tuck you in tonight, too?"

Melifaro tried to sulk, but then he dropped the act and laughed. Sir Kofa and Lieutenant Apurra Blookey were smiling from ear to ear. Even Lady Kekki gave a shy giggle.

I didn't say anything funny, I thought. Is this just a normal reaction to the sound of my voice?

I took a bite off a still warm piece of pie and looked at Kekki. She didn't seem to have any appetite. Ah, *she's* the one who needs to have a few too many, I thought. Then she'll be fine.

"Sir Kofa, Lady Kekki and I need to have a drink," I said. "After the heated exchange we just had downstairs, we need to put things right. And I know of no better way of doing it."

"Were you fighting?" said Melifaro. "And who won?"

"It's a tie," I said. "We're going to take a short break and then give it another go. Right, Lady Kekki?"

"Well, if you think it's necessary, I don't mind," she said. Finally, I heard in her voice the hint of light playfulness that makes a person a fine interlocutor.

❀

I had told myself many times not to try to patch up other people's relationships. Too bad I'd always remained deaf to my own warnings. Sometimes a whole team of cartoon rescue rangers takes over inside me, and, led by Chip and Dale, they rush to save someone's ruined life. Back in the day, my charitable rescue operations had usually ended up a complete fiasco. Today, however, a glass of Jubatic Juice was all it took. The concoction had the most beneficial effect on Lady Kekki: she relaxed and finally began eating. I paused for a little while and sent a call to Sir Kofa.

You wouldn't believe it, but this exceptional lady here is crazy about you. Just stay calm, though. I don't want her to know I'm telling you this. She's been reading about your noble deeds since childhood, and it's been her dream to meet you. Now she's afraid of you, so have mercy on the poor girl.

Thank you for the good news, boy, replied Sir Kofa.

Then he said out loud, "Melifaro, my friend, what is it that you're looking at?"

"Look," said Melifaro, holding up his glass for everybody to view. A tiny green caterpillar was crawling across the outer surface. "Where did it come from?"

"Who knows?" I said. "Don't you think it just came to have a drink?"

"Well, sinning Magicians, nobody can accuse Melifaro of being greedy!"

He carefully took the caterpillar and put it inside his empty glass.

"There are a few drops left in there," he said. "Should be enough."

"Be careful, it's going to get drunk and come after you to beat you up."

"Me? Its benefactor? You're the ones it will go after!" He shook the caterpillar out of the glass onto the table, muttering, "That should just about do it." Lieutenant Apurra Blookey suggested that the caterpillar needed a chaser. This was all very amusing, but at that moment Juffin sent me a call.

Come down here, Max. I think you're going to find this interesting.

I slid off the edge of the table I had been occupying, retrieved the bottle of Elixir of Kaxar from Juffin's desk drawer, and took a substantial swallow. The drowsiness that the Jubatic Juice had brought on was gone in an instant. I nodded in approval, locked the drawer, and headed toward the door.

"Where are you going?" said Kofa.

"Juffin just sent me a call," I said. "And don't let the caterpillar get too drunk. It still has to become a butterfly."

"Do you think it will still be able to now?" asked Melifaro, genuinely alarmed.

"We'll just have to wait and see. Be good, my children. Listen to Sir Kofa and the mighty buriwok. I'm off to have some fun."

"And who's going to tuck me into bed? You said you'd take me home if I got drunk, which I did," said Melifaro.

I winked conspiratorially at the blushing Lady Kekki and left the office.

❧

Juffin was waiting for me downstairs by the small door to his "lab." He looked tired and preoccupied.

"It's best not to go in there," he said, pointing at the door. "It was such a nice room. What will I do without it now?"

"Put a spell on another one—you've got plenty of rooms here. What happened in there?"

"Oh, it was quite a show. After I did some magic, Sir Xekta Bonbon came to and answered all my questions. Then that noble gentleman realized he had nothing to lose and decided to challenge me to a duel. Very romantic on his part."

"And very imprudent," I said.

"Imprudent, yes. But he caught me off guard. I think he stood a chance of winning, but I'm lucky. I called you down here to show you what happens to a room where Apparent Magic of the two hundred and thirty-fourth degree has been performed."

"The maximum degree!" I said.

"I think so. There are grounds for believing that Sir Loiso Pondoxo used the two hundred and thirty-*fifth* degree once, but Loiso is such a legend you can never be sure whether what they say about him is true. Well, forget about your new relative for the time being, and look here."

Juffin pushed me toward the keyhole. I looked through it and was almost blinded by an unbearably bright emerald-green glare. There was nothing else to see there, only streams of light that looked alive, even angry.

"Yikes!" I said, turning back to Juffin. "Talk about pyrotechnics. Is it going to go on like this forever?"

"We'll see. Maybe not forever, but I'm afraid it's going to go on like that for a long, long time."

"What would happen if I tried to go inside?"

"Well, only the Dark Magicians know what would happen if *you* tried to go in, but I recommend that you not attempt that experiment. As for an ordinary person, he would simply vanish. Just like that mad Xekta did. He just vanished—or, rather, burned up. Blazed up from inside with that green fire and disappeared. To tell you the truth, Max, it was the first time in my life that I performed this trick."

"I'll be darned," I said. "I never thought there were things that *you* did for the first time in your life."

"I'm full of surprises," said Juffin. "Can I ask you to take me home? I'll tell you the details on our way, unless you've already figured them out."

"Not even close," I said. "Well, some of it is becoming clear. What's-his-name, Magician Xekta Bonbon—he decided to sneak into Jafax to settle an old score with Magician Nuflin. Am I right?"

"You are. Go on."

We were already upstairs and on our way out the door.

"Will Kimpa mind?" I said, getting behind the levers of the amobil-er. "After all, it's his privilege to drive you home."

"Kimpa is at his grandson's wedding in Landaland. He will be staying there for a long time. I spent almost an hour of my precious time persuading the old man that my one and only life will not go to the Dark Magicians in his absence, and I succeeded. But do go on, Max. I'm curious to see how closely your version corresponds to the actual events."

I started up the amobiler and went on: "Well, if I understand this right, Xekta disguised himself as a member of Nuflin's retinue. Which he did with the help of poor Sir Varixa Ariama. Then he finished off that hapless Sir Jorinmuk, whose face he stole. Right?"

"Right, except that he finished him off before, not after. Your logic fails you. Xekta couldn't know beforehand which member of Nuflin's retinue he'd be able to kill, and to do it so that no one noticed."

"Hey, that's right," I said. "So, he killed that unfortunate Sir Jorinmuk. What did he do with the body, by the way?"

"Just made it disappear. It's not a difficult trick, especially for someone like Xekta. He was a truly great magician, you can take my word for it."

"I'm sure he was," I said. "By the way, why did this Grand Magician Xekta Bonbon ask Sir Ariama to change his face to begin with? What with him being a great magician and all."

"Because the art of changing one's countenance requires not so much magic as it does years and years of practice. It's like embroidering with gossamer: you need more than just talent."

"I see. Then he killed Varixa Ariama to get rid of the only witness to his metamorphosis, right?"

"Right. Go ahead."

"No, now I'm going to ask you a few questions, whatever you might think of the limitless possibilities of my intelligence," I said. "Why couldn't Magician Xekta make his way into Jafax on his own? If I understand it correctly, he had a whole day. Another question: Lady Sotofa and I found him in the bushes in the garden of the Residence. What was he doing there all that time? Taking a leak?"

"Ha! There was only one way for him to get inside Jafax: through the Secret Door. Do you think it's easy to walk in and out of the Secret Door of Jafax? Unlike people, the Door really doesn't care much about what the person trying to go through looks like. What it craves is a good spell. After some time, Magician Xekta Bonbon did manage to walk through, but by that time you'd already stepped on his trace, so the poor old man was having trouble with his health. It's pure luck that Melamori was running late for her date and decided to give you her job. Any more questions?"

"Oh, I haven't even started! For example, I don't understand what that 'filthy Mudlax' has to do with all this. What's his angle? And how come he survived? How on earth did he get into Xolomi for someone else's crime? I know the arrest procedure. The magic wands of the guys from the Office of Expedited Reprisals work just as well as our magic gauges. If a person has never exercised a certain degree of Forbidden Magic, the wand will not light up when held over his head, and everyone will see that he's not guilty. Isn't that how it works?"

"It is," said Juffin. "You're absolutely right, Max. But unlike me, you've never had to deal with high-grade specialists like Xekta. A powerful magician is quite capable of projecting his guilt onto another person so that Baguda Maldaxan's subordinates never know the difference. Baguda himself could probably pick up on the hoax, but he hasn't come to the scenes of the crime for many years now. So it all worked like a charm.

"As for your other questions, you see, it was pure luck. Mudlax chose a very bad time to visit Ariama. I think he panicked when his subjects couldn't defeat Aloxto, so he decided to change his face again, just in case. When he came to Varixa Ariama, the Magician had just finished with Xekta. Xekta told him to work on his client and hid in the next room. He peeked and eavesdropped, though, and came to a few conclusions. Mudlax wasn't too specific, but Xekta figured out that he needed a good place to hide. He thought that he could use Mudlax's problem to his advantage. You see, leaving Sir Ariama alive wasn't a good option: he'd talk under pressure. Just killing him was dangerous— a Master of Pursuit would easily detect his trace. But this was his chance. Xekta waited for Ariama to finish with Mudlax's face and then emerged from hiding.

"You know, Max, it never ceases to amaze me what people can do in a desperate situation. You remember I had talked to Varixa Ariama the day before? And I could swear that his magic powers didn't extend much beyond his excellent skills in disguise. But according to Xekta, Ariama put up a fight worthy of the last hero of the Epoch of Orders. So the former Grand Magician had to sweat a great deal to defeat Ariama. I think he used Apparent Magic of no less than the hundred and seventieth degree.

"Then Xekta explained to Mudlax, who had been watching the battle of the titans, that Xolomi was the best hiding place. He offered him a choice: a horrible death or a perfect hideout for the next few hundred years. I think Mudlax figured that his death would give too much pleasure to the Conqueror of Arvarox. In any case, he accepted Xekta's offer with gratitude.

"Oh, look, here we are at my place already! Thanks, Max. I'm so wiped out, you can't imagine. Sorry for not inviting you to come in. I mean, you can come in if you wish, but I don't think I'll be up for a cup of kamra and a friendly talk."

"To be honest, I don't think I'm up to it either," I said, suppressing a yawn. "Then again, my shift only ends in the morning, right?"

"Well, you don't have to go back to work tonight," said Juffin, "but here's a piece of advice from me: go back to Headquarters. You'll definitely be able to catch some sleep there, and that's what you need now. You won't last much longer on Elixir of Kaxar alone."

"I can get some sleep at home, too," I said.

"Right, at home. Look, lover boy, do as I tell you, and everything is going to be all right. Good night, Sir Max."

"Wait," I said. "One last question. Why didn't Mudlax kill Ariama Junior?"

"That we'll have to ask Mudlax himself," said Juffin. "I think he just ran into a stranger in the doorway and thought it was an ambush. His reaction was almost instinctual. Then he either recognized Ariama Junior or saw some resemblance—I'm not sure if he'd seen the boy before or not—and decided to hide him so as not to raise the suspicions of the master of the house. Dragged him into the backyard and hid him in the bushes. I think that's plausible."

Juffin walked inside his house, and I went back to Headquarters.

Everyone had already left. The party had ended without me.

"All for the better," I said to the sleepy Kurush. "Did they give you a pastry?"

"Four pastries. But don't wake me up, okay?"

"I won't. I'm going to catch some sleep myself," I said. I sat in Juffin's armchair and put my legs on my own chair. It made a pretty comfortable makeshift bed.

"Why don't you do this at home?" Kofa's cheerful voice yanked me out of the realm of my sweetest dreams.

"Is it morning already?" I said.

"Almost. Boy, did we mess up the place last night. The junior employees will have one heck of a morning cleaning it up."

Sir Kofa put the jug with the remains of cold kamra on the burner.

"Tell me, Kofa, do you ever sleep?" I said, taking the bottle of Elixir of Kaxar from the top drawer. That was the only way I knew to revive myself quickly after just a few hours of sleep, which clearly hadn't been enough.

"I do, of course. But I got lucky with my body. Two or three hours of sleep are usually enough for me. Convenient, isn't it?"

"You bet," I said enviously. "I wish I only needed two hours of sleep every day."

"Be careful what you wish for. Both for you and for Juffin dreaming is an essential part of life. That's your strength and your weakness at the same time. In my life, on the other hand, I only focus on this wonderful World. Dreams mean nothing to me. So, it's unclear who's the luckiest of us here."

"I don't know, right now I'd like to change my body's habits, if only for a short time," I said. "It seems to need to sleep at least a dozen hours a day, and that's absolutely out of line with my plans."

"Go home and sleep some more."

"I'm going to. After a cup of kamra in your company."

"I've always liked good company," said Sir Kofa. "I owe you one, boy."

"In what sense?" I said, sipping the warm kamra.

"Thank you for telling me about Kekki. You know, I had no idea . . . Such a nice young lady, a hole in the heavens above her crazy head! But I'm old enough to be her grandfather."

"Grandfather, great-grandfather . . . what difference does it make?" I said with the tone of an experienced ladykiller. "By the way, if you were her age, she wouldn't have read about you in old newspapers. I think this is all very romantic."

"I think so too," said Kofa. "We'll see."

"The wisest words I've ever heard," I said. "Okay, since you don't mind, I'm going take my leave. If I can peel myself off the chair, that is."

"Go ahead. By the way, you and I haven't had dinner together for far too long. Don't you find it outrageous?"

"Utterly outrageous," I said. "As soon as that *Surf Thorn* 'foams the ocean' again, you and I will go celebrate that long-anticipated occasion."

"I know who's really going to be celebrating then: poor Melifaro. He's going to be living it up till the end of the year, I'm sure."

"Not such a bad idea—living it up for the rest of the year," I observed. "But, as Sir Anday Pu likes to say, 'It would kill me,' for sure.

Speaking of Anday, I haven't seen him in ages. Do you know what's happening to him?"

"The usual," said Kofa. "Throws around the money he gets from the *Royal Voice*, parties every night in expensive taverns, and complains about his miserable fate. Just what the doctor ordered."

"To think of how interesting other people's lives can be," I said, grinning. "I'm really going to be on my way now, though."

"You've been saying that for—"

"I'm gone!"

My head was spinning. Of course, I was going to see Tekki. Forget about sleeping.

When I walked outside it was still dark. I approached my new amobiler. Compared to the official amobiler clones of the Ministry, mine looked like a true monster. I had acquired it recently from an ingenious local craftsman. It cost me almost nothing: the guy was happy to get rid of it after failing to sell it for a dozen years. The locals were too conservative to handle such an unusual design, but I was happy. This "avant-garde" specimen very much resembled old automobiles from my World.

I stroked the green polished side of my beauty and took the driver's seat. I put my hand on the levers and felt something squeezing my throat. Everything went dark in front of my eyes, and I thought, That old buzzard Death is at it again. Why doesn't he go play with somebody else for a change?

I'm really getting sick of this, I thought. And then I stopped thinking. Fortunately, not forever.

I didn't die. I came to and found myself very much alive, if not kicking. Because kicking was a tad problematic. My hands and legs were tied. On top of that, I was wrapped up in something thick and heavy, which proved a hindrance to my plans for living life to the fullest. I think it was a thick carpet. Judging by the jolting and bumping, I was in a beat-up vehicle of some sort.

"What the heck is going on?" I said.

"Do not be angry with us, Fanghaxra, but you must return to your people."

Horrified, I recognized the voice of the gray-haired leader of my insane "fellow countrymen." First, I wanted to cry, but then I became enraged. Fortunately, I didn't do anything I would regret later. No Forbidden Magic of the umpteenth degree or whatever. I just cursed. And cursed. And cursed. I had no idea I knew so many swear words. Sir Juffin Hully, with his puny set of two thousand expletives, was a choirboy compared to me.

My subjects were deaf to my appeals, however, so I soon lost interest in my monologue and tried to come up with a better plan. Technically, my humble magical powers were more than enough to blow this caravan of Borderland dwellers to pieces, but to put my powers to any use I needed to free my hands. Without them I couldn't do more than spit venom. Unfortunately, the nomads had been farsighted enough to wrap me so tightly that it was extremely difficult for me to use any of my tricks.

I carefully moved the fingers of my left hand and tried to snap them. It worked. I was lucky that my kidnappers didn't have a complete file on me with the details of my "paranormal" abilities. If they had, they would have tied the ropes not only around my hands but also around all of my fingers.

I heaved a sigh of relief. Now I could act. The blasted carpet posed no obstacle to my Lethal Spheres, so . . .

But by that time, I had calmed down a great deal and didn't find the idea of massacring a group of peaceful nomads all that appealing. What I really wanted to do was to get rid of them and go back to the small cozy apartment above the *Armstrong & Ella*.

I decided to start with a little interview.

"Guys," I said in a stern voice, "what do you think you're doing? Let's imagine you took me home. Then what? Were you going to chain me to the throne? How was I supposed to reign, huh? With my hands and legs tied up? Because if you don't tie me up, I'm going to run back here on the first old nag I can find, I swear."

"Your feet must touch your homeland, Fanghaxra. Then your delusion will be gone," said the stubborn old man. "There are many cunning magicians among these Uguland barbarians. They put a spell on you. That's why you turned your back on your people. As soon as you step on your native soil, your heart will awaken."

The old man's voice lacked confidence, but I had no doubt he'd try to finish his bold experiment to remove the evil spell from me. No matter what the cost.

"If you don't untie me now, you're going to be very, *very* sorry," I said. "Do you want to try me?"

"Even you are not capable of breaking our snares," said the old man.

It sounded like he was trying to persuade himself rather than me.

"Well, that was a mistake," I said. "You've been warned."

❀

I tried to focus. I still didn't want to kill the earnest fellows. The nomads were few in number, proud, and rather sweet, and their stubborn attempts to make me their king were not so much annoying as they were flattering.

I tried my best to get rid of the rest of my anger and irritation. I knew already that Lethal Spheres followed my inmost secret desires, and that was great. All I had to do was tame my inmost secret desires, and all would be fine. I hoped that I had enough willpower to accomplish this feat. I just needed those stubborn dolts to do as I told them. And I wanted them to do it *now*, before they put their ridiculous crown on my poor head. A long voyage to the borders of the Unified Kingdom was not my idea of a good vacation.

A few moments later I decided it was time to act. I wiggled my numb left hand to let the blood flow and snapped my fingers a few times. Green fireballs passed through the thick pile of the carpet with a soft sucking sound. I could only hope that those dangerous clots of bright light were smart enough to find their targets without my help. Then again, sitting in that dark ravine, I hadn't exactly been aiming at the dead bandits from the Magaxon Forest, but still . . .

A soft ruckus outside signaled the successful beginning of my operation.

"I am with you, Master!"

The stubborn old man was probably the first victim of the attack. His voice was soon joined by a chorus of others.

"I am with you, Master! I am with you, Master!"

"Good," I said. "Now let me out of here."

The carpet was unwrapped and the nomads cut the thin but durable ropes that had made me look like a silkworm in a cocoon. Their hands were shaking. They looked at me amorously, their eyes staring at me from under their silly kerchiefs.

I rubbed my numb hands and looked around. The vehicle I had been kidnapped in was an old cart. It stood in the middle of a beautiful grove. Around it walked the nomads' moose, their antlers decorated with shiny thingamajigs.

Not without difficulty—my legs were still a bit numb—I got out of the cart and sat down on the ground. Then I gave my eccentric monarchists a long stern look.

"Never *ever* try to return me to my homeland. Especially in this manner." I looked at the old man. "How did you catch me, by the way? Come on, spill it out."

"With a lasso," said the old man. "We learned from people which of the strange magic carts belonged to you, and I hid myself under a seat. I'm very good with my lasso, Fanghaxra, so your life was never in any danger. I tightened it just enough for you to go to sleep."

"Really?" I said. "How convenient. Where were you when I was suffering from insomnia?"

"Forgive me, O Fanghaxra, that I was not with you during those days of hardship," said the old man, absolutely seriously.

I didn't know whether to laugh or cry.

"Fine. Go home, guys, will you? Some people are doing just great without kings, by the way, so it's not that big a deal."

"We cannot leave you, master!" said the nomads sadly.

"Oh, that's right. But it'll pass. One last order for the road, though. Well, not an order, really, just a piece of advice. Get rid of those darn headscarves. They look silly on you. Or at least tie them in a different manner. Let me show you."

The old man handed me his headscarf dutifully. I wanted to take off my turban but noticed I wasn't wearing it. It must have fallen off in the amobiler or wherever they had wrapped me in the carpet.

I took the scarf and quickly wrapped it around his head like a pirate's bandanna. Meeting Sir Anchifa Melifaro had apparently had a greater effect on me than I thought.

"Something like this. Got that?"

"We shall do as you say, Fanghaxra," said the old man.

And the dwellers of the Borderlands quickly began modifying their headgear. A few moments later I thought they looked pretty decent. They looked like a bunch of extras for a low-budget version of *Treasure Island*.

"Good, good," I said. "Now, listen to me very carefully. Get down on the ground, close your eyes, concentrate, and . . . You're free from my tyranny! Boom!"

A few moments later, the nomads stood up, scared and bewildered. Praise be the Magicians, though, they were now quite sane.

"What have you done to us, O Fanghaxra?" asked their gray-haired leader. "A man cannot do this to other men. Are you a god?"

"Oh boy. First a king, now a god," I said. "Forget it. I hereby adjourn this first and final meeting at my court. Goodbye, gentlemen, and have a safe journey home."

"Are you not coming with us?" the old man said sadly.

"Of course not. Did you ever think I would?"

"I had a hope."

"I told you that hope was a darn-fool feeling," I said. "Yet I have a hope, too. I hope you're going to do well, even without me. Go home, people. And I will, too."

I watched the caravan disappear in the distance as the thingamajigs on the antlers of their moose jingled and clanked, making a sad melody.

Then I shook my head a few times to clear it and sent a call to Juffin. The boss greeted me with a long monologue.

I'm glad you sent me a call, Max. I was just about to do the same and ask you politely whether you still remembered that you have a job. Your amobiler has been parked by Headquarters since morning, and you're nowhere to be found. How did you get home yesterday, I'd like to know? Did you fly? Actually, I'm willing to believe it.

You think I'm still in Echo?

Where else would you be?

Frankly, I have no idea, but this is definitely not Echo. Wait a minute, are you telling me you don't know? I was kidnapped.

Kidnapped! By whom?

My own subjects, if you'll pardon the expression. I thought everyone down at Headquarters was running amok in panic.

That's news to me! How come I didn't sense anything? When you overindulged in the love potion, I sensed it even before your body hit the floor.

Maybe you were sleeping like a log after your exercise with the two hundred and thirty-fourth degree of Magic yesterday. Besides, it wasn't a big deal. The guys didn't want to hurt me. I was unconscious and took a ride in some horrible cart. Other than that I'm fine.

Hold on a second. Run that past me one more time—are you still in captivity?

Are you joking? Do you think I can't handle a bunch of crazy nomads?

Okay, hero. I believe you want to get home now?

And how! Do you think you can send Melamori for me? Because I have no idea where I am. She can just stand on my trace and find me in no time. You know that it doesn't really affect me in any way. Plus, she now drives almost as fast as I do.

That's a very good idea. I think I can pull her away from her studies of the ancient cultures of Arvarox for a time. Okay, stay put and wait. I hope your loyal subjects didn't deposit you too far away. Send me a call if anything happens.

Like there's anything that can happen to me here.

Having finished with Juffin, I sent a call to Tekki. I should have been ashamed of myself: I had lied to her, threatening to return at dawn, and then disappeared for good. Not the best strategy for the beginning of a relationship. To my surprise, Tekki wasn't at all mad.

What swamp did the werewolves drag you off to, sweetheart?

I recapped a short version of the events for her.

I hope these things won't be happening to me every day, I said.

I'm not so sure. But never mind. It's fine by me.

Thirty minutes later I felt I might collapse in exhaustion. I could usually use Silent Speech for a few minutes without any problem, but then I began to tire. This was clearly too much for me, so I had to say goodbye.

I lay on my back and stared at the pale, almost milk-white sky. I felt completely happy—a state that was totally unusual for me. I fell asleep before I knew it.

I was woken up by the snorting approach of the amobiler. And just in time, because I had been dreaming that I was running away from a dozen grim-looking doctors with the faces of downright villains. They were going to stuff me with a bunch of pills that they said would help me get rid of my second heart. I, on the other hand, had other plans . . . A regular nightmare, in other words. I hadn't had nightmares in a long time, so I woke up in a cold sweat, happy that it had all been just a dream.

"What happened, Max?" said Melamori. She looked scared. "Were you in trouble? Why didn't you tell anyone?"

"No, no. I'm fine. Just a bad dream."

"That's not 'fine,' then," she said. "I decided to take your amobiler. I thought you'd be happy to come back home in it. Here's your turban, by the way. You should put it on—you're so disheveled. Was I quick?

Was I? Tell me. Was I quick? I got here before dark."

"You were," I said, looking at her pleased face. "You're getting better by the minute. You have every chance of winning our bet someday."

"Now I believe it, too," said Melamori. "Especially after this long, long drive. You know, the nomads managed to cover a great distance. I didn't expect to find you so far away from Echo."

"Then we'd better hurry back. Now it's my turn to drive."

It took me more than an hour to get back, even though I was breaking every imaginable speed limit. The nomads had, indeed, managed to take me pretty far. Apparently, their sad-looking moose were decent runners. On my way back, I entertained Melamori with a picturesque version of my kidnapping.

"So, what's your news?" I said.

"Oh, we've got a ton of it! They're keeping Mudlax in Xolomi. They only put him away for two years, though. For false evidence. Sir Juffin wanted to get his hands on Mudlax right away, but Kamshi was adamant. 'The law is the law,' you see."

"Yes, that's how Kamshi has always been. Only before he didn't have the clout to demonstrate his stubbornness to Sir Juffin Hully. Then again, stubbornness isn't such a bad quality for the warden of Xolomi."

"I'm not saying it's a bad quality. But do you know what's going on there right now? Aloxto is positioning his Sharptooths around the ferry crossing, because Kamshi wouldn't let them on the island itself. I'm sure they have orders to stare at the walls of Xolomi for two years and not even blink, making sure their 'filthy Mudlax' doesn't run away from them. Cute, isn't it?"

"It is," I said. "I should go have a look at that show sometime."

"You're going to love it," said Melamori, as if she were the artistic director.

Meanwhile, we passed the Gate of Kexervar the Conqueror. The amobiler glided swiftly through the dense gardens of the Left Bank.

"Wow!" said Melamori. "It took me much longer to drive there to pick you up. I'm never going to beat you."

"All in due time, my dear. All in due time. So, will those Arvaroxian beauties continue to entertain us for the next two years?"

"Well, yes and no. Fifty of the Sharptooths are staying to enjoy the view of the gloomy walls of Xolomi, and the others will return home, along with their 'sternlooking' chieftain. You see, Aloxto promised Toila Liomurik that he'd be back before the beginning of next year. He didn't know Mudlax would go to jail. The mighty Conqueror of Arvarox can't use Silent Speech, unfortunately, so there's no way of letting him know what has happened. In any case, the Arvaroxians are convinced that they must keep their promises. Aloxto is leaving in a few days and then coming back after two years to kill Mudlax with his own hands. Very romantic, don't you think?"

"I'll say." I looked at Melamori with sympathy. "Is that bad?"

"I don't know what to say," she said. "Maybe it's bad, maybe it's good. I don't want to think about it now. We'll see. Oh, are we back already?"

"What do you think?" I said proudly, as I stopped the amobiler by the entrance to the Ministry of Perfect Public Order.

"Good night, Max," said Melamori. "I don't think I need to go back to work today. Besides—"

"No need to justify yourself. This night is too beautiful to waste sweating away in Juffin's office. I'm going to skip work myself. I'm just going to show my tired face to the boss and make his heart weep with compassion."

"You're going to fail miserably," said Melifaro. "You look all right, Your Majesty."

She waved to me and disappeared around the corner. I watched her go and then went in to Headquarters.

"Nobody has ever stolen anything from me in my life," said Juffin with a smile. "Then some nomads up and steal my Nocturnal Representative. I hope you have avenged the soiled reputation of the Secret Investigative Force."

"You talk like a true Arvaroxian now, sir," I said, sitting down in my favorite armchair.

"I'm flattered, but I have much to learn from Sir Aloxto. Are you hungry? You look terrible."

"I can imagine. Melamori seemed to think things weren't all that bad, though."

"Melamori has always been a brave girl," said Juffin. "Especially lately. By the way, I had an almost two-hour-long discussion with Sir Korva Blimm. He thought I was stupid enough to interfere with the personal lives of my subordinates. I had to convince him otherwise. All in all, I can't say I spent my time any better than you did."

"I believe you," I said. "Parents can be unbearable sometimes. Are the Blimms really shocked about Melamori's affair with Aloxto?"

"What do you think?"

"I can relate," I said. Then I started laughing. "But you took care of it, right?"

"Sometimes I'm surprised at my own powers," said Juffin.

❦

After I told him in detail about my exotic little adventure and ate a huge piece of Madam Zizinda's special pie, Juffin decided that my weary, beat-up countenance wasn't something he wanted to look at right before bedtime.

"You should go get some rest, Max. It doesn't seem like we're going to have any work for a while, so you may be dismissed until the day after tomorrow. You deserve a rest after your 'coronation.'"

"You're not joking?"

"I am not joking. Unless something extraordinary happens, but I doubt it will. That's already behind us, I think."

"If anything happens, I'll be the first to know, because it'll be happening to me," I said, grinning. "I've been pretty unfortunate lately, don't you think?"

"You've been fortunate, too, if I understand correctly. But if I were you, I'd put getting my backside in trouble on the backside burner for the time being."

"I'm genuinely trying," I said. "Because if the trouble keeps piling up in that region, I'm not going outside anymore without my own personal bodyguards."

I was, of course, joking, but when I walked outside and went up to my amobiler I felt a little uneasy. Who knew what those nomads might do? What if they took it into their heads to return to Echo in the dead of night and start their antics all over again?

It looked like my premonitions hadn't deceived me. Squinting, I saw somebody's shadow in the back seat.

You're hallucinating, I thought, trying to reason with myself like a normal person. You're going to be seeing things like that for some time to come, so relax.

Autosuggestion didn't work: I was absolutely sure that someone was hiding in my amobiler. I took a bold step forward, preparing to spit or launch a Lethal Sphere—whichever came first.

"O mighty king of carts, grant me but a patch of your Land of Fertile Weeds!"

The dim orange light of the street lamps cast a pleasant shadow on Melifaro's happy face. I jumped back in surprise, put my hand over my two hearts, and laughed with relief.

"Man, you were playing with fire. I'm a bundle of nerves these days. I could have killed you!"

"Easier said than done," said Melifaro. "Want to buy me a cup of kamra?"

"You're in luck. I was just heading over to the *Armstrong & Ella*. Expanding the clientele of a beautiful lady is the foremost task of a noble knight."

"That's what I thought, Your Majesty," said Melifaro, and he bowed so low that he almost fell out of the amobiler.

I packed him back in and finally set out for where I had wanted to go for such a long time.

"I'm so happy you brought over your colleague, Max," said Tekki from behind the bar when she saw us. "I just happen to have a stack of old glasses I don't need anymore. Do you think you can break them for me, Sir Melifaro? You're so good at it."

"I'm not in the best form today, Lady Shekk, but since you're asking, I'll do my best, if His Majesty doesn't mind," said Melifaro. "You know, I'm afraid of making this tyrant angry. He could easily order his bare-bummed subjects to bury me in horse manure."

"Why bare-bummed?" I said. "They wear very cute shorts. I like them."

"Have some made for yourself, then," said Melifaro. "You will look irresistible in them. Better than that goggle-eyed Aloxto."

"I already look irresistible." I gave Tekki an apologetic look. "Now you know that you've fallen victim to a horrible fraud. We're not Secret Investigators. We're humble patients from the local Refuge for the Mad. They let us out from time to time if we behave ourselves."

"Really? Then you should behave yourself so they let you out more often," said Tekki, placing before us two cups of kamra, which really was the best kamra in the Unified Kingdom.

"I'll try," I said.

Melifaro listened to our exchange with great pleasure. "Finally, a place in town where I can have fun!" he said. "The future is looking bright."

The door creaked. Anday Pu was standing in the doorway.

"Max, a hole in the heavens above you! You don't catch a thing! Dinner is over once and for all," said the journalist. "Why did you refuse to become their king? They burn like comets out there where they come from! I could easily take care of your cats—it wouldn't kill me."

Melifaro was laughing so hard he almost fell off the high barstool.

"Is this guy also from your Refuge? Is his bunk bed next to yours, and did they also let him out for exemplary behavior?" said Tekki.

"You have such an astute mind, Tekki," I said.

❀

The next few days were the happiest days in my life. Even at work I didn't come out of the fog, thick as cotton candy, which turned the world around me into a blissful wonderland.

But one day, before an astonishingly beautiful summer sunset, I overheard a disturbing conversation.

"I must leave tomorrow." The whisper, coming from the Hall of Common Labor, belonged beyond any doubt to Aloxto Allirox because it was louder than a normal human shout. "But I do not want to leave. And yet—"

"And yet you must go, right?" I recognized Melamori's voice.

"Right."

"But you will come back. If only to kill Mudlax."

"*Filthy* Mudlax," said Aloxto.

"Of course. Two years is not that long, if you think about it."

"It's too long," said Aloxto. "Have you ever tried to count the days one must live to go though a year?"

"Believe it or not, I have."

"Yet you speak as though you have no notion of time. I do not want to leave, and I cannot stay. You do not want to come to Arvarox with me, or at least let me conquer another land for you, where you would like to live. I am completely lost, my lady. It's easier for me die, and I will. I swear by Toila Liomurik's armor!"

"Don't you dare give me any of that dying business," I muttered under my breath. I looked at Kurush. The wise bird was sleeping on the back of my chair. "Did you hear that?"

"No. What happened?" The buriwok opened one of its yellow eyes.

"That worshiper of the very tips of your feathers with a foghorn for a voice is going to shock Lady Melamori with the disgusting view of his dead body," I said. "I don't like it."

"That's his business," said Kurush.

"No, it's my business, too," I said. "First, I like him. Second, Lady Melamori likes him, which is even more important. Kurush, my friend, please do something. You're the only one he'll listen to."

"I'm going to fly away from you and settle in Arvarox," said Kurush. "No one will go waking me up there with their silly human demands."

"Do you think they bake good pastry there, too?" I said.

"That's the only reason I don't fulfill my threat. Fine, Max, if you really think I must."

"If only out of diplomatic considerations." I made a serious face. "Toila Liomurik the Conqueror of Arvarox will not be happy to learn that the beautiful Sir Aloxto Allirox—who slays the Kulyox Bird with just two glances and three compliments, if I remember correctly—kicked the bucket so close to the palace of His Majesty King Gurig. Who will bear the Third Chamber Pot to Toila Liomurik at the New Moon Feast right after his spouse and the Senior Cupbearer? Wait, what's this got to do with the cupbearer, I wonder?"

"You're completely mixed up, Max. No wonder, though. People always get mixed up," said Kurush.

He flew into the Hall of Common Labor through the half-open door. I climbed outside through the window that Sir Juffin Hully had charmed. I was the only one who could go through it unharmed. This time my exit went pretty smoothly, too. I didn't feel anything unearthly, but my heels were burning as if I had been running on hot coals. I examined them to make sure they were okay and then went for a little walk. Let them think that I hadn't even been at the House by the Bridge, I thought. In my book, if you want to do charity work, you'd better do it anonymously. Otherwise, it's not worth doing at all.

I returned a half hour later with a whole dozen pastries for Kurush—he deserved them. This time I used the door and walked through the Hall of Common Labor. Aloxto was still there. His expression was one of admiration and reverence—the consequences of talking to the buriwok, I assumed. The furry spider-like creature was purring gently on his shoulder.

"Where have you been, Max?" said Melamori.

"The only place I can be when someone asks me where I have been: somewhere where there's food. Spent an hour in the *Sated Skeleton*. Do you want to follow my example? It's a great place."

"Sounds good," said Melamori.

Aloxto Allirox looked at me with disbelief.

That's right, I thought. Those Arvaroxian heroes always sense when someone's telling an untruth. Now he's trying to figure out why I'm doing it.

Fortunately, Aloxto didn't deem it necessary to comment. I quickly bid the couple adieu and locked the door behind me. Kurush was already asleep on the back of my chair. I didn't want to risk waking him up again. The parcel with pastries from the *Glutton* could wait. The night was young.

§

The next day I had to go to work at noon. We were saying goodbye to Aloxto. *The Surf Thorn* was casting off before sunset, and the Bighearted Master of two times fifty Sharptooths demanded a grandiose parting ceremony.

Melifaro looked like the happiest person in the whole Unified Kingdom. He was sitting on the table swinging his legs, with a dreamy expression of delight.

"You look so much better now that Rulen Bagdasys is gone," I said. "Have you decided what to do with him yet?"

"Oh, *that* I decided a long time ago. But you no catch, Mr. Nightmare, as your rotund buddy has noted on many an occasion. Just wait, and you'll see it yourself."

"Okay," I said. I yawned and took the bottle of Elixir of Kaxar out of the drawer. I had gotten up quite some time ago. It was time to wake up completely.

Half an hour later everybody was assembled in the office. Melamori was the last one to arrive. On her shoulder sat Aloxto's spidery pet. It was visibly discombobulated by the change.

"That's some brooch you got there," said Melifaro. "A truly royal gift."

"This is not a brooch; it's a hoob. His name is Leleo. For your information, this animal is the keeper of souls of their entire clan. Did anyone ever give you a keeper of souls as a gift, Melifaro?"

"Magicians forbid, no!"

"Well, shush, then," said Melamori.

"Iron logic," said Sir Kofa. "Let me see your wonderful new pet, Melamori."

"I've read that these creatures can sing," said Lonli-Lokli. "Is this true?"

"Oh, they do. And how! But he doesn't always respond to my commands. He needs time to get used to me."

"A very human quality," said Juffin. "We all need time to get used to something new. Ah, here are our friends from Arvarox. Can you hear them? Oh, no, did Aloxto think they'd all fit into our reception room?"

The monotonous knocking of their inflexible capes could be heard coming from the street. I looked out the window and saw that Juffin was right. Aloxto had brought to the House by the Bridge all fifty Sharptooths who weren't keeping vigil by the walls of Xolomi.

"They are staying outside," said Melamori. "Aloxto brought them with him as . . . well, it's like dressing up for him. When a high-ranking Arvaroxian commander goes to a meeting that he considers an extraordinary event, he brings as many of his warriors as he can. Back home he would have come with 'five hundred times fifty' of them, in his words."

"Did he bring them along when he went out on dates with you, too?" said Melifaro.

"No, praise be the Magicians. You see, they don't consider a date to be such an extraordinary event."

Aloxto Allirox came in accompanied by only one of his warriors, a very young and very handsome man. He was about my height, which was already pretty tall. But next to his commander, he looked like a puny teenager.

"This is Thotta, my shaman," said Aloxto. I think he was a little nervous. "Thotta often speaks with the Dead God and almost always understands what the Dead God says. He will speak the words of the Dead God to you because my words will fail to thank you enough."

"I hope we will be able to appreciate the honor fully," said Juffin, surprised. His eyes were gleaming with curiosity.

"You will," said Aloxto.

You just don't know us well enough, I thought.

"The Dead God lets our commander give you his weapon as a gift," said the shaman. "You should know that the warriors of Arvarox never give their weapons to outlanders. It only happened once before, in the ancient times, when the Conqueror of Arvarox, Libori Fosafik the Invisible Head, gave his sword to your King Mynin. Our first gift is for you, sir."

Thotta gave Juffin a piercing look while Aloxto detached his "machete" from his belt.

"This sword is made from the fin of the biggest Ruxas fish that has ever been caught in the sea," Thotta continued. "The same sword was given to your King Mynin back in the day. I did not think I had the right to make such a gift to you, for only equals may exchange gifts. But the Dead God told me you would not be angry."

"Oh, not at all," said Juffin, accepting the "machete." He looked very flattered.

"The second gift is for the one who did not let the clan lose its commander." The shaman was now looking at Melifaro.

Aloxto handed him his lethal "flyswatter" and said, "You have seen this weapon in action. I made it myself from the tooth-ridden tongue of the Kydoo beast. This is truly a dangerous weapon."

"I have no reason to doubt it," said Melifaro, looking extremely pleased.

Then the shaman turned to Lonli-Lokli. "The Dead God favors you especially, sir. But he did not explain why."

"That's too bad," said Shurf very seriously. "I should very much like to know the reason for such goodwill."

"You do not need a weapon, for you yourself are the best weapon," said Aloxto. "But even you may need protection one day. I think my helmet is the sturdiest helmet under the sky. The six-thorn Uxunruk fish, from the head of which the helmet was made at my request, I caught myself."

"It is beautiful," said Lonli-Lokli, admiring the helmet. "A true work of art."

"Our next gift is for you, O master of many faces." The shaman gave a respectful bow to Sir Kofa.

Aloxto held out a sheathed object. "This is a death-bearing whip with two times fifty stings of the wild Zengo wasps," he said. "The stings are every bit as deadly now as they were when the Zengo wasps were still buzzing in their nests. But a wise man of your caliber will be able to handle them."

"I will try," said Kofa. "Whatever have I not handled in my life!"

"You, my lady, have already received the most precious gift," the shaman said to Melamori. "The Dead God said you would be able to keep the souls of our clan. He is pleased that our hoob will sing his songs for you."

"Will he really sing?" said Melamori. "So far, he's only been sulking and missing his owner."

"He will sing when I leave," said Aloxto. "The hoob does everything in its proper time."

"I know, you told me that. It's just that I think he wants to go back to you."

"The desires of only a few creatures under the sun who come into this World matter," said Aloxto. "And Leleo is not one of them. Neither am I."

The shaman now turned to Lookfi. I think there was even more respect in his voice now than when he spoke to Juffin. "You, who can speak with many buriwoks at the same time, will you agree to accept our gift?"

"Of course I will, gentlemen," said Lookfi with a shy smile on his face. "It is so very kind of you."

"When I set off on this journey, Toila Liomurik the Silver Bigwig, the Conqueror of Arvarox, took off his cape made from the thickest wool of the sheep from the King's Flock and gave it to me," said Aloxto. "He will be happy to know that his cape protects from the wind the one who protects the lives of more than two times fifty buriwoks. Please accept it, sir."

Then the shaman turned to me. "The Dead God knows you well, sir," he said. "He spoke to me at length about you, but I understood very little. The Dead God told me we have nothing that you could use. You have all you need. That is what the Dead God said."

"You sure know how to pick friends." Melifaro's voice broke the ringing silence. "That Dead God is bending over backwards to leave you with no gifts. What pettiness. Calls himself a god."

"It's all right," I said. "I'll deal with him personally next time I meet him." My colleagues smiled, but the two Arvaroxians looked at me with venerating horror.

"I truly wanted to leave some of my precious things with you, Sir Max," said Aloxto. "But it is beyond my powers to resist the will of the Dead God."

"You *have* left your most precious thing with me, Aloxto. I once had the pleasure of hearing one of your songs. It's safe to say that it's still ringing in my ears."

Poor Aloxto accepted my caustic compliment. "I am happy to know that you will remember me."

"You can rest assured that I will." This time I was being absolutely honest: things like that are hard to forget.

After Aloxto and I exchanged compliments, Melifaro turned to the shaman. "Do you think your Dead God would mind if I made a present to Aloxto? Or should I not even bother?"

"You may do as you wish. You saved the life of our commander and the honor of the clan. Any deed of yours will be considered a blessing."

"Great," said Melifaro.

From the pocket of his looxi he produced the precious signet ring with the tiny figure of Rulen Bagdasys frozen in the middle of the transparent stone. Then it dawned on me: that trickster Melifaro had decided to join together the two culprits of his short but deep depression and see what would happen.

Juffin noticed that I was putting up a heroic fight with laughter and sent me a call.

What's going on? Are you in on this?

Oh boy, let him tell you. This object poses no threat to Sir Aloxto's life, though, believe me.

I'd like to see anything that could possibly pose any threat to Sir Aloxto's life.

Juffin was tortured not by anxiety but by ordinary human curiosity.

There is something that can. A conflict between his wishes and necessity, for instance.

That's a good one. Okay, enjoy the show.

And enjoy the show I did. Melifaro was exercising his fine oratory skills.

"This is a magical object, Aloxto. You can wear it on your finger, or you can keep it in your pocket—it doesn't matter. But if one day you feel sad, throw this signet ring under your feet. The stone must hit the ground, the harder the better. You will see what happens then. I hope you will be greatly entertained."

Melifaro's tone was sad rather than mocking, although there was plenty of both emotions in his speech.

"Thank you. I think I will get to use your gift when the time comes."

Aloxto took the signet, admired the tiny Rulen Bagdasys frozen in the middle of the stone, and then put it on his pinkie. It was ridiculous to experiment with any other digit on his huge hand.

"This is a good thing, commander," said the shaman.

Juffin raised his eyebrows. He was sure that Melifaro would do something nasty to top it off.

"It is time, gentlemen," said Aloxto, nodding courteously. "I must hurry. The sooner I leave your city, the sooner I can return."

"I'll see you off," said Melamori.

"No. It is a bad sign if someone stays at the pier when the ship casts off."

"I'm not going to walk to the pier with you. Just to the Wall of Joxira Menka, the border of the New City."

"Thank you. It is very kind of you," said Aloxto.

I believe it never occurred to him that you could walk someone only halfway. If Aloxto were in charge of awarding the Nobel Prize, Melamori would have received it for her brilliant idea.

When they left I made a sour face.

"I didn't get a present," I pouted like a spoiled child. "I'm hurt, hurt, hurt!"

"Yes, but you got a compliment that I, for one, never got myself," said Juffin.

"What do you mean?"

"They said you have everything you need."

"And?"

"The ancient Sacred Book of Arvarox, all copies of which they burned about a thousand dozen years ago after they had memorized it, says that 'humans will remain humans as long they are lacking something,'" said Lonli-Lokli.

"In other words, they flippantly made you a god," said Juffin.

"And now their shaman will visit me every night, stand by my windows, and ask my opinion on the most important national issues?" I said. "Well, well. How were you able to read that burned book, Shurf? Are you that old?"

"No, but I have a decent library. I have a few rare editions, including one of the three remaining copies of the Sacred Book of Arvarox. There is some dark story connected with those three surviving copies. One of them was given to our King Mynin—"

"For educational purposes," said Melifaro.

"Something like that. Or some pirates stole them from Arvarox. In any case, there are only three copies remaining in the World, and I have one. A most interesting read."

"May I borrow it?" I said.

"You may, except that you never come to visit me."

"Oh, I will," I said. "We gods are busy folk, naturally, but I'm sure I can spare a few minutes for you."

Meanwhile, Melifaro was briefing Juffin on the unfortunate lot of Rulen Bagdasys.

"At first I was mad at both of them—the Isamonian and Aloxto. But then I accepted them, and even began to love them."

"Love them?" I said.

"Yes, imagine that. Granted, it was a strange kind of love, but still . . . I almost canceled the show altogether. Then I realized that Rulen

Bagdasys was quite capable of cheering up poor Aloxto. The warriors of Arvarox must appreciate rude jokes, and jokes don't get any ruder than those of Mr. Rulen Bagdasys."

Sir Juffin looked very happy. "Max," he said, "since you're a king and a god and all that, maybe you can let me have three days off work? Kimpa's gone. The house is empty and quiet. I want to get some sleep and maybe read a good book. I haven't had more than one day off in a row for more than three hundred years, I'll have you know. I'd like to try—maybe it's possible. I have no one else to ask for this."

"Permission granted. I'm not a tyrant, after all. But why didn't you ask the Arvaroxian shaman? He would have put in a good word for you with the Dead God himself. Who am I, after all?"

"That's quite all right," said Juffin. "You'll do just fine. Don't forget to pray to Sir Max every night, gentlemen. Order yourselves a good dinner at the *Glutton*. Do whatever you want, in other words. I'm going home. Boy, I wish you all had a blanket like mine!"

"Well, I'll be," said Sir Kofa, following Juffin with his eyes. "This Kettarian is going home to sleep before dusk *and* taking a few days off. I've known him much longer than you, lads, and I haven't seen him do anything like this before."

"In any case, Sir Juffin's words are an order," I said. "Say what you want, but a dinner from the *Glutton* will be on this table any minute now."

"Very good, son," said Kofa. "You must be a kind god. Would anyone mind if I called our colleagues from the City Police Department?"

"Along with Sir Boboota Box?" said Melifaro.

"Along with Lady Kekki Tuotli, my boy. And don't you dare smirk."

"Okay, I'll be serious and . . . what else does one do under the circumstances? Oh, yes, I'll be mournful," said Melifaro. He made the most dismal face his facial muscles could manage. Still, it didn't look very convincing.

The dinner was long, and we had a great deal of fun, except that Melamori never showed up. I realized that she wasn't up to having fun with us right then, and my heart went out to her. Or, rather, my two hearts—all I had at my disposal.

※

Melamori finally did show up, at around midnight, when I was alone in the House by the Bridge. I still had my night shift, after all.

She hesitated in the doorway of my office. My second heart immediately cringed from her pain and fluttered with a tenderness that wasn't mine, either. I tried my best to ignore the fits of my otherworldly love muscle.

"I think I did something stupid again, Max," said Melamori.

"People always do stupid things, as our mighty buriwok would put it if he weren't asleep," I said. "What *did* you do?"

"I got scared and didn't go to Arvarox with him, a hole in the heavens above it!"

"I would be scared, too," I lied, just in case.

"You? No, Max, you wouldn't be, I know it," she said. "Well, maybe you would be scared, but it wouldn't stop you."

"Maybe it wouldn't. But you'll still have a chance to put things right. There's nothing irreversible except death. Then again, even death can be considered just a minor glitch in the system. Take it from someone who's an expert in this matter. Come in, let's have a talk."

"That's why I came."

And we talked away until dawn. We talked about silly trifles and things that people rarely talk about—a little bit of everything. We were interrupted by the hoob, who had been asleep on Melamori's shoulder all night. He woke up and began to sing in a thin, sad voice.

"Look, he's singing," I said. "It's a good sign, right?"

"Of course," said Melamori. "Unlike Aloxto, I don't believe in bad omens, only in good signs. I think I'm going to go home now and sleep like a log. I never saw it coming really."

"It's been kind of obvious all along," I said. "I'm such a boring person that anyone would be falling asleep."

"Of course you are," said Melamori, laughing. "Have a good morning, Max."

"Have a good morning, Melamori."

I was incapable of making heads or tails of my own feelings, so I just put my feet on the table and lit a cigarette. Then again, were there any feelings to speak of?

Sir Kofa returned in the morning, looking pleased and mysterious, and let me go home. This time I was able to fulfill my old promise and show up at Tekki's at the worst possible time: an hour before dawn.

"Look, Max, you can go sleep at your place sometimes," she said in a sleepy voice as she opened the door. "Really, I won't mind. Don't you have a home?"

"I have two homes," I said. "The problem is that one of them doesn't have you in it. I checked."

❀

I finally managed to stay in bed as long as I wished—I woke up almost at dusk. I washed up and slowly went downstairs. I didn't have the nerve to tell Tekki that I liked to have my kamra in bed when I wake up. I thought that would be too much for her.

I walked into the tavern and froze in disbelief. Shurf Lonli-Lokli was sitting at the bar. Tekki was pouring kamra in his mug.

"You are a good sleeper, Max," he said.

It sounded as though he had been teaching me to sleep long hours and was now proud of the results of his mentoring.

"I'm trying my best," I said. "Have they already told you that this place has the best kamra in Echo?"

"No one told me anything, but I've just had the pleasure of confirming that claim in practice. I am here because I was looking for you. I wanted to send you a call, but I didn't want to wake you up. Then Melifaro told me that—"

"What happened to Melifaro? He gave you the correct address? It would have been just like him to send you to someplace like the *Grave of Kukonin*," I said.

"He tried to do something of the sort, but then Sir Kofa intervened. But I digress. I brought you the book you requested yesterday. It is best to give such things personally. It's a tradition."

"The Sacred Book of Arvarox?" I said. "Sinning Magicians, Shurf! I'd never part with such a rarity even for a minute."

"I wasn't going to give it you. I thought you'd pay me a visit and read it at my house, if you wanted to. But you see, last night I had a dream that the book asked me to give it to you," said Lonli-Lokli. "I thought I should respect its opinion. So, here you go."

He handed me a small, thick parcel.

I took it and started to unwrap it. I noticed that the ancient cover had clumps of fur sticking out here and there. Apparently, in its better days it was as furry as a kitten. I held the precious book in my hands. It felt too heavy and warm. No, it was hot! I barely had time to realize that my palms were burning like a bonfire before the book started trembling and vanished. *Poof!*—and it was gone. I looked at my hands in bewilderment. Fortunately, there were no signs of burns.

"D-did you see that, Shurf?" I said. "I swear I didn't do anything."

"Now I see why the book wanted to be in your hands," said Lonli-Lokli. He didn't look upset. On the contrary, he seemed glad. "Somehow, you relieved it of the need to remain in this World. Don't be surprised if the last two copies end up in your hands sooner or later."

"But . . . how? How did I do that?" I said. "And what do I have to do with this book, Shurf? Do you understand what's going on?"

"I understand some things, but not everything. I told you: you always get yourself into scrapes like this."

Lonli-Lokli looked at me with mild scorn. Or was it with sympathy? I still couldn't distinguish between the expressions on his usually imperturbable face.

"You're so bad at handling good things, Max," said Tekki, placing a mug of hot kamra in front of me.

THREE

THE VOLUNTEERS
OF ETERNITY

"YOU KNOW, PEOPLE DO CUT THEIR HAIR EVERY ONCE IN A while," said Juffin, as he came into our office. "Didn't you know that?"

Frankly speaking, I did know that, but I hadn't bothered to go to a barbershop. Instead, I had been tying my long, long hair into a ponytail and sticking it under the turban. The results were quite pleasing to the eye until I took the turban off. Which I had just done.

"Does the length of my hair really matter?" I said. "Take Sir Manga, for instance. He has a long braid, and I don't see anyone dragging him off to Xolomi for that."

"I just thought your lovely locks might be giving you some trouble," said Juffin. "It's up to you, of course. But enough about your hair. Tell me, have you read the papers?"

"I have," I said. "And I grieve. The crazy nomads who crowned me their king managed to defeat their enemies, who were wiser yet fewer in number. What are they up to now, I wonder? Is everything going to start all over again—they'll kidnap me, and I'll have to run away again, twice a year on a regular basis until I die?"

"The old Count Gachillo, Sovereign of the County Vook, sent a petition to His Majesty King Gurig the other day. Among other things, he said that an official delegation of your restless subjects has set off toward Echo. They intend to throw themselves down before our Gurig's feet and beg him to let you return to your homeland. In other words, if we want to call a spade a spade, they hope that His Majesty will command you to reign over them. The Dark Sack is thrilled. He thinks that now you're going to keep him company. He's too lazy to come to the Capital himself and finds it a bit too boring on his estate."

"Yikes," I said. "Say, will His Majesty really try to deport me? Deprive a fugitive fellow king of the right to serve at His Majesty's Royal Court?"

"Don't be silly, Max. No one's going to banish you from Echo, even if you wanted him to. But the king has another idea. One which, all things considered, may suit everybody."

"Oh, he does, does he?" I said. "What's the idea?"

"Imagine this: you agree to be king, put a crown on your disheveled head, and then appoint someone from that delegation to be vice king, prime minister, or vizier—whatever they want to call him. You, on the other hand, stay in Echo and continue to report for duty. Gurig will rent you some nice room, which will do for your palace. Your subjects will visit you a couple times a year for advice. That's it. Doesn't it sound great?"

"It sure does, but not to me. I'm sorry, Juffin, but I think I'm going to rain on your parade. I don't want to become a nomads' king. Uh-uh. No way. Period."

"Fine," said Juffin. "If you say no, then no it is. The show is canceled. It's too bad, though. It could have been a great thing. And Poor Gurig. He was so hoping you'd be good friends. He says it's his only chance to have such a companionable fellow king as a colleague. All the other modern monarchs are so bad tempered, and no one knows why."

"I know why. My temper would also turn sour if I became a king," I said. Then I asked Juffin again, just to be sure, "Juffin, you're not going to force me be a king, are you?"

"How can I force you do anything? You are a free man. If you don't want to be a king, you won't be a king. But if I were you, I'd give it a second thought. If could be a great opportunity, and one of the best jokes of your life, which is not too boring to begin with, I'll grant you that."

"But I've decided to quit joking and become as serious as Lonli-Lokli."

"Have you really? And what do you think your chances of success will be?"

"Not too great, I know, but I'll do my best. Anyway, I think I should have gone home a long time ago."

"I think so too. And why are you still here?"

"Because I'm talking to you, and you are here," I said. "On top of that, you're saying such unbelievable things that my head is spinning."

"Okay, I'll stop, then. But if you ever change your mind about the crown—"

"Never! Well, maybe if I really were a descendant of Fanghaxra's ancient rulers, I'd consider it. But look at me, I'm nothing but an impostor."

"But that's what's so great about the whole thing!" said Juffin. "It's too bad you don't understand global politics, the grand scheme of things."

"You're right, I don't," I said. "Anyway, I'm going home. I'm really sleepy."

"Sleepy, huh? Well, well, well. I'd like to see how you'll manage to get any sleep. I'd be willing to bet you're not even going home now."

"Wherever I'm going, I'm going to sleep there. I don't have the strength to do anything else. When I get up, I'm going to ask Tekki to cut my hair. You're right, it's beginning to look ridiculous."

"And you'll save on a trip to a barbershop," said Juffin. "Sometimes you can be very practical. All right, off you go, then, Your Majesty."

"Hey, quit that. I'm already dreading meeting Melifaro. I still don't have a snappy comeback."

"Don't bother," said Juffin. "You're at your best when you're speaking impromptu. Don't rely on canned jokes. You don't need them—take my word for it."

"I guess you're right," I said, and sprang down from the window ledge onto the mosaic sidewalk of the Street of Copper Pots. "I'll improvise, then. Good morning, Juffin."

"I'd rather you didn't jump in and out of this window," said Juffin. He looked out the window onto the street and shook his head, then looked back at me. "It's all very well for now, but you should have seen the kinds of spells and curses I applied to make this window absolutely impenetrable. It would be a shame if they did work one day. You know, just like that—out of the blue."

"Could that really happen?" I said, unnerved.

"Anything can happen. Next time don't be such a show-off unless it's absolutely necessary, okay?"

"Okay," I said, and hurried to my amobiler. I was wiped out.

Whatever was left of me managed to drive to Tekki's place, where I stretched my mouth in a pitiful parody of a gentle smile. Then I fell asleep right in the doorway of the bedroom. Poor Tekki rolled my useless body to the far corner of the bed and called it a day.

Alas, I didn't get enough sleep. Again.

"Wake up, Max!"

The voice sounded familiar. I was half asleep and couldn't figure out which one of my friends had turned into such an inhumane, relentless monster. I couldn't believe it.

"Aw, man," I groaned, trying to bury my head under the pillow. "I just closed my eyes."

"Don't exaggerate, Nightmare. I just came in, and your eyes had been good and closed for a long time."

I managed to open my eyes and stared at Melifaro, who was sitting cross-legged on my blanket, getting ready to shake me.

"For the love of Nuflin," I said. "Man, I hate you. What the heck are you doing here?"

"I live here," said Melifaro, making a face. "I had a heart-to-heart talk with Tekki and made her put on her glasses. She was finally able to see that I'm much handsomer than you. So, I'm moving in with her. This is my bed now. And you, mister, have to get up and rush over to Juffin's office."

I put my head between my hands, held it there a little while, and realized it wasn't helping. So I began giving orders.

"Great. Now, take my Elixir of Kaxar—it's on the window ledge. Yeah, that's it. Give it here. I want you to go down and tell Tekki that I'm going to expire if I don't get a mug of kamra. It's up to her whether she wants a dead government official of the highest rank in her bedroom or not. Tekki is a smart and prudent girl—I trust her judgment. Then I want you to bring the kamra to me, and wait while I drink it. And *then* I want you to tell me what you're doing here. Right now, I can't make heads or tails of anything."

I exhaled, took a big gulp of Elixir of Kaxar, and flopped back on the pillow.

Melifaro was completely floored by my insolence. He gasped like a fish out of water, looking for a stinging retort. Soon, however, he reconsidered and went back to fetch me my kamra. He probably realized that it was the only way to get me out of bed without resorting to weaponry and violence.

A few minutes later, Melifaro returned, bringing a tray with kamra. He still looked slightly bewildered.

"How come there's only one cup?" I said.

"You need two?" Melifaro said, surprised. "Wow, your royal 'we' seems to have kicked in."

"The second cup would be for you. For your information, I'm a hospitable person. You should have thought of that. Or are you the one who just woke up?"

"Here," said Tekki, bringing another tray into the bedroom. "Kamra for Sir Melifaro, and other mishmash for chewing and swallowing. He rushed back up before I could make all of this. He has separation anxiety and couldn't bear not being in your presence."

"Oh, I couldn't even dream of having breakfast in His Majesty's bedroom," said Melifaro with the tone of a court sycophant.

Tekki put the tray down on the blanket and frowned. "I always suspected that sooner or later Sir Max would turn my bedroom into a distant banquet room of the tavern. Looks like I was right. Now bread crumbs will be tickling me tenderly at night. Can't wait for the thrill. I guess that must be the domestic bliss that all young girls dream about."

"You were forewarned that I was a monster. Melifaro here warned you many times. He warns everybody. Day and night he runs around screaming, 'Help! We've got a Sir Max on our hands! A true monster!'"

Melifaro frowned, but Tekki listened to me with unconcealed delight. I knew I had to strike while the iron was hot. I mustered all my charm, assumed a repentant air, rolled my eyes back, and threw my palms heavenward in a martyr-like fashion. Tekki studied my face for a while, laughed, then waved and ran downstairs. And I realized I had finally woken up.

And that was good news.

❧

"Okay, what's going on?"

"Juffin's leaving," said Melifaro, his mouth full.

I went cold with apprehension. "What do you mean, leaving?"

Melifaro looked at my face, frozen in horror, and giggled with gloating delight. I concluded that nothing dire had happened and patiently waited for him to stop.

"Juffin and Shurf are leaving to grapple with the Spirit of Xolomi. For a dozen days or so," Melifaro said. "I have a feeling that in their absence you will have to take command of what's left of the Minor Secret Investigative Force. You can use this as an opportunity to test-drive your majestic plural, not to mention your regal responsibilities. That's going to be quite a show."

"Okay, now run that past me one more time," I said, "only this time, go slowly and start from the very beginning. What happened, what are the consequences, and what are we going to do about it?"

"Boy, are you a pain in the neck, Max. I don't know about Juffin, but you sure will do fine as Lonli-Lokli's replacement," Melifaro said. "Okay, Magicians be with you, let's take it from the top. A couple of hours ago, Kamshi, the warden of Xolomi and our longtime friend, sent Juffin a call. He said that the stones of Xolomi had begun to moan. That's a sure sign that the Spirit of Xolomi is going to be throwing a big party soon. Last time this happened was at the very beginning of the Code Epoch. It caused quite a panic back then. Nobody thought Juffin would manage to calm it down, but eventually he did. Look, Max, you'd better start getting dressed. Juffin asked you to come as soon as you could."

"When did he say that?"

"An hour and a half ago, at least."

"Are you saying that you were trying to wake me up all that time? I don't believe you."

"You should, though, because I was. More or less. First Juffin and I tried to send you a call, but you wouldn't wake up. It's the first time I've ever seen our Venerable Head break into a sweat. But to no avail. A half hour later, I realized it was an exercise in futility, so I sent a call to Tekki and asked her to wake you up. She said there was no way she was going to wake you up two hours after you'd gone to sleep, that it would be tantamount to suicide. She said if we were willing to risk our lives, we should go ahead and do it ourselves. Then I came over here. Meanwhile, Max, the time is ticking. So, please get ready."

I couldn't believe my eyes. Melifaro was so serious that I dressed in record time. I had never known myself to be so prompt.

"We can go now," I said.

"Praise be the Magicians," Melifaro said.

He gulped down the rest of his kamra and got up. I examined the bed—not a single crumb in sight. No "tender tickling" for Tekki tonight, I thought.

Tekki was sitting behind the bar, her head buried in the morning issue of the *Royal Voice*. The tavern was empty. Tekki still didn't have a cook, and there weren't too many customers who wanted to have a stiff drink on an empty stomach just before sundown in this part of town.

I waved goodbye to Tekki and left the establishment. Neither of us said a word out loud, since we preferred Silent Speech for our lyrical outpourings. And I didn't want to give Melifaro the pleasure of eaves-dropping on our billing and cooing.

※

"Here's the deal: I'm going to drive really fast, and in return you'll brief me on the Spirit of Xolomi and its R&R habits, m'kay?" I said.

"Do you mean to tell me you haven't heard of the Spirit of Xolomi?" Melifaro said, raising his eyebrows. "Some education you've got under your belt. Not up to the standards required in a royal family. But all right, start her up, and I'll tell you all about it since your ignorance casts a shadow on our ill-starred organization. Which has already been compromised to the limits.

"News flash number one: The Royal Prison of Xolomi is located on the exact spot that our scholars call the Heart of the World. I'll bet you didn't know that, either. Well, unlike you, the first king of the ancient dynasty, Xalla Maxun the Hairy, knew that very well. That's why he built his palace on Xolomi Island. It was clear from the beginning that the palace had a mind of its own. It was almost alive. It could tell friend from foe and didn't let outsiders inside. So Xalla Maxun and his descendants were well protected from disloyal magicians and other powerful rogues, who were a dime a dozen back in those days. The guys were all scrambling to plant their own backsides on the king's throne. You're the only one who's eager to reject a crown that you can get for free."

"Let's not digress," I said. "You said we didn't have much time, and I don't want to pester Juffin with questions. I don't think he's quite up to it now."

"You're right, he's not. Where was I? Oh, so for centuries everything was in top-notch shape, even better. And then our legendary King Mynin was born, and the palace rejected him for some reason. Long story short, right after Mynin's coronation, the palace became unlivable for the king. Mynin wasn't going to shed too many tears about it, so he built Rulx Castle, which you already know inside and out. Then he just up and moved there.

"During the reign of Mynin and the first Gurigs, what's now the prison was called the Xolomi Higher Institute and its graduates were powerful magicians. The idea was that they would serve the king and not the Orders. They say that back then, time itself flowed different within Xolomi's walls. The students would spend a whole century there, maturing, mastering the program of education, and then graduating, while only two years would pass in the World outside. But the king's efforts were in vain. In the beginning, the graduates of the Xolomi Higher Institute did exterminate a lot of the Ancient Orders, but almost immediately they founded Orders of their own, and the same old thing started all over again. By the way, your new in-law, Sir Loiso Pondoxo, was a student at the Institute. Which is, naturally, the best possible recommendation for it.

"Finally, one of the Gurigs—either the Fourth or the Fifth, I forget now—closed down the unruly Higher Institute. Then, some time later, our kings moved back to Xolomi. Everything went back to the way it had been during the time of Xalla the Hairy: nobody could enter Xolomi without the king's consent, and any form of magic was useless against the people inside its amazing walls. Which was pretty handy, given the times."

"How come they turned it into a prison?"

"Not too long before the Code Epoch, Xolomi Castle changed again. Now anyone can enter it, but nobody can leave without the warden's help. Not even Magician Nuflin himself, I believe. Not the best place to live, if you know what I mean. Well, of course you do, you spent a few days there yourself, remember?"

"That I'll never forget," I said, stopping the amobiler by the entrance to the Headquarters of the Ministry of Perfect Public Order. "But you never told me anything about the Spirit of Xolomi."

"Uh, you see, I don't quite understand it myself," Melifaro said. "I don't think anyone does for sure. You're already aware that Xolomi is not your run-of-the-mill fortress. It's more like a sentient being that is unlike anything we're used to thinking of as a living creature. It has a soul, or a Shadow, or whatever you want to call it. So, from time to time, it starts showing signs of life. And those signs of life are not something we're too happy about. We humans are such spoiled creatures, after all. We want a quiet life without surprises."

"Listen to Mr. Philosopher," said Juffin.

He had just come out to greet us, cheerful and glum at the same time. He surveyed me from head to toe. His stare was warm and heavy, so heavy that it even made me hunch my shoulders.

"This is how it works, Max. From time to time the Spirit of Xolomi wakes up and feels like dancing," said Juffin. "If its intensions ever come to pass, Xolomi will be razed to the ground, and I'm not sure anything else will be left standing, either. So we need to rein it in before it goes back to sleep, and that's just what Sir Shurf and I are going to do. We did this once before, about ninety years ago. It's not too difficult, but boy is it exhausting. Max, please pretend, at least, that you understand what I'm saying. I know you don't, but do it as a personal favor to me, all right? Now, I don't have much time, so let's talk about more important things."

"If you say so."

"Shurf and I will be gone a dozen days. Maybe a bit longer, I'm not sure. You won't be able to send us a call—our business with the Spirit of Xolomi requires extreme concentration. However, I'm absolutely confident that you will manage without us. Am I right?"

"We'll soon find out."

"Exactly. We'll soon find out. It won't require any special talents from you, but someone must make decisions from time to time. Whether the decisions are right or wrong doesn't matter so much, but someone has to be there to make them. I should be very much obliged to you if you took this responsibility upon yourself, Max."

"But why me? Why not Sir Kofa, for example?"

I wasn't showing off or bargaining. I honestly wanted to know why Juffin decided to make me deputy in his absence. I saw every other candidate as a much better alternative.

"Sir Kofa hates this kind of job. He had enough of it back when he was Police General of the Right Bank. And when I offered him a job in the Secret Investigative Force, he agreed on one condition: that he'd never be anyone's boss again. I gave him my word, and my word is the law.

"Okay," I said, still puzzled. "But mark my words, you might live to regret it."

"Might I?" said Juffin, chuckling. "All right, now take me to Xolomi please. I'm running late."

"You should have made me your personal driver from the beginning. It's one of the few things I'm really good at."

❧

"Don't worry, Max," said Juffin as he climbed into the back seat of the amobiler. "You're going to do just fine. If one of the guys needs a good wisewoman, send a call to Sotofa. She'll never let you down, you know that. If you need a consultation on some practical matters, ask Kofa. But what am I doing lecturing you? You'll figure it out, if need be. You've made your own decisions before without consulting me and I liked them. In fact, I like them more and more, but that's not really my point."

"What *is* your point, then?" I said. "Have you decided that I need some training before I ascend the throne?"

"Oh, will you please drop this throne business? Still, training, as you put it, is something that will do you good. May come in handy one day."

"Hmm. All right, then," I said as I stopped the amobiler by the ferry, which was about to cast off. "But you're going to have to deal with the consequences."

"It won't be the first time, will it? Oh, look, we're here already. I hope Sir Shurf's already in Kamshi's office. You don't have to walk me there, Max. The ferry won't go any faster even if you're on it."

"I don't *have* to walk you there, or you don't *want* me to walk you there?" I said in a voice that didn't sound like my own.

I had no idea what was happening to me. It suddenly seemed as if my personal universe was made of glass. And it was about to collapse and bury me under its crystalline shards. Something was missing in my picture of the World, the picture I had grown so used to. Something was missing—or something new had appeared. Something that shouldn't be there.

"What's going on, Max?" Juffin finally noticed that something wasn't quite right with me. "Of course you can walk me there, if you want to. Do you have more questions?"

I stepped on the ferry and shook my head. "No, I guess I don't. I'm just not feeling so great. And I won't even be able to send you a call. I'm feeling lonely and . . . scared. There, I've said it."

"Hey, look, Max! The ferry really is moving faster than usual. I guess I was wrong when I said your presence wouldn't make any difference," Juffin said.

"Are you joking?"

"No. Can't you see? This contraption is moving along like crazy. You know, Max, in my time I had it even worse. That was back when my tutor, Sheriff Mackie Ainti, told me that he was leaving Kettari forever. He said, 'Don't even think about sending me a call. Ain't gonna work. You'll only get a headache.' I thought that was the end of me. But, as you can see, it all worked out. As time went on, I became a pretty good sheriff of Kettari, and, between you and me, not the worst Magician in the Unified Kingdom."

"You're so modest," I said.

"It isn't modesty; it's undiluted pride. Don't hang your head, Max. You shouldn't complain. Just a dozen days—nothing to worry about. Oh, here we are now. Good day, Max. And try to get as much fun out of this as you can, okay?"

Without waiting for my answer, Juffin jumped off onto the pier and headed toward the gates of Xolomi Prison. Which, as it turned out, was a living creature. While I was watching him and trying to formulate an answer, the ferry pulled away from the bank of the Heart of the World.

"Okay," I said finally, watching Juffin's silver looxi disappear behind the gates of Xolomi. "It's a deal. I'll try to have fun."

Attaboy! Juffin's Silent Speech reached me so suddenly that I almost fell off into the water. *It's good to know that you're happy to do me at least one favor.*

When I returned to the House by the Bridge, I was a little more discombobulated than I could afford to be. I went into our office and sat in my chair, on the back of which Kurush was sleeping. I was planning to sit there feeling sad, but my chagrin was interrupted.

"O Sir Venerable Head! O mighty buriwok!" Melifaro's yellow looxi appeared before my eyes. "Command your loyal servant."

"I'm going to get mad and won't take you out for breakfast," I said.

"I already had breakfast."

"Then I won't take you out for lunch."

Melifaro said, "Oh, now *that* would be sad. Maybe you'll take pity on me after all?"

"Maybe," I said. "What other options do I have?"

"Will you take me out, too?"

Melamori was standing in the doorway.

"Okay, I'll take you out, too. On second thought, no. I'm going to send a call to the *Glutton*. Make them bring our lunch right here. I'm too lazy to go gallivanting about."

"I'm glad you're such a lazy bum," Melamori said. "Because Madam Zizinda is still a little scared of Leleo. I'd have to leave him at Headquarters, and he doesn't like that at all."

The furry spider-like creature perching on Melamori's shoulder was purring softly. The hoob had such a sweet voice that my heart stood still every time I heard it.

"I'm also scared of him," said Melifaro, hiding under the table. "So I'm going to have my lunch right here. Mark my words, miss, next time your beauty boy's going to bring you a nest of Arvaroxian wasps."

"And you're the ones who will be running for cover," Melamori said with a sting in her voice. Then she assumed the dreamy gaze of a girl imagining a romantic walk in the moonlight.

Melifaro got out from under his shelter, sat down in a chair, and put his feet up on the table. It was clearly my bad influence. The delivery boy from the *Glutton* knocked timidly on the door, came in, and began to clutter the table with trays of food. It's not such a bad start after all, I thought.

While we were eating, Melamori and Melifaro exchanged jibes. Melamori was on a roll. Toward the end, Melifaro was losing points, but he made a valiant attempt to save face.

"So, what's the plan for today?" he grumbled, as he was finishing off his dessert. "Command, Sir Nightmare. I humbly await your orders."

"Shush," I said. "I'm thinking."

"Really? Didn't you know you could do that."

"If you don't knock it off, I'll teach you how to do it, too," I said, and then turned to Melamori, who was giggling all the while. "Have you taken your hoob to the policemen's side of the building today?"

"No, not yet."

"That's too bad," I said. "It's been too quiet over there. General Booboota hasn't been shouting, and I haven't seen Captain Foofloss in a while. This won't do. The city policemen must be kept trembling in their boots. Off you go, then. I want to hear everyone screaming and shouting over there within five minutes. Got it?"

"Yes, Sir Max. They will be screaming and shouting shortly, sir."

"Good girl. And if Lady Kekki Tuotli faints, bring her back to her senses and invite her to your favorite café on the Victory of Gurig VII Square. Tell Booboota that I asked her to help us, or think up something yourself—I don't have to teach you. Sit there and have a chat. Beats loafing around Headquarters, anyway. You're friends with her, if I'm not mistaken?"

"You're not mistaken," said Melamori, smiling. "Max, I adore you. How about we dump that Juffin altogether? You're much better."

"You don't understand," I said. "If Juffin hadn't locked himself up in Xolomi, you and I could have gone to the ends of the earth together, if we wanted to. But now I'm too busy for that."

"Yeah, that's too bad," said Melamori. "But I still like your management style."

"That's obvious," said Melifaro with a trace of jealousy as she was leaving. Then he turned to me. "Okay, what pleasures do you have in store for me?"

"No pleasures for you. You, my friend, are destined to live a life of eternal sorrow. You're staying in the office. But try putting on an intelligent expression, okay? Send me a call if something happens."

"Where are you going?" Melifaro said.

"To Jafax."

"Are you kidding me?"

I made a face at Melifaro, and he snickered at me.

"I'm dead serious. Wait for me and try not to die of boredom."

"Deal," said Melifaro. "But in order to survive, I'll need a ton of kamra, and probably something stronger. I'll order a few stiff drinks in the *Glutton* and put it on your tab, okay?"

"If I were you, I would reconsider. You said yourself that your father was quite happy with the fact that he had three sons. I don't want to disappoint Sir Manga, but I may have to."

"Fine, I'll put it on Juffin's tab, then. You're here, and he's not," said Melifaro.

I shook a fist at him and left the office.

❧

I really did go to Jafax. I thought I'd use the opportunity to visit Lady Sotofa, since I'd promised her I would. Days were short, and there was no end of urgent matters to attend to, but I didn't want to look like a swine, throwing all thoughts of friendship to the winds.

A few minutes later I stood by the impregnable walls of the Residence of the Order of the Seven-Leaf Clover, just where, according to my vague recollection, there should have been one of the Secret Doors. I suppressed a sudden burst of shyness and sent a call to Lady Sotofa Xanemer.

Is that you, boy? she answered. *It hasn't been three hours since that old fox Juffin hid himself away in Xolomi and you're already in trouble? I don't believe it.*

I just wanted to take advantage of the situation to skip work and have a cup of kamra with you.

"And to learn a secret or two, while you're at it, eh?" said Lady Sotofa, who had suddenly appeared behind me.

"You read me like an open book," I said. "I never pass up the opportunity to learn something new at someone else's expense."

"Don't suck up to me, boy," said Lady Sotofa, laughing. "You don't have to because I love you anyway. Give me your hand, and I'll take you into the garden. You could have learned to open our Secret Doors already. It's not a difficult trick."

She took me by the hand and pulled me to the wall.

"Try not to close your eyes now. It's time you learned a few simple things."

For my obedience, I was rewarded with something extraordinary. I saw Lady Sotofa's blue-and-white looxi dissolve in the dark stones of the wall like sugar in a cup of coffee. Then the wall appeared so close to my face that I couldn't see anything. Or, rather, I saw too much: some barely noticeable scratches on the dark stones, small pieces of dust, and something else—tiny, nimble, alive, and, it seemed, even aggressive. The thought that this must be what germs looked like passed through my mind. Lady Sotofa laughed, a thin branch flicked me across the nose, and I realized that I was on the other side of the wall, in the Jafax garden.

"Oh, goodness me!" Lady Sotofa couldn't stop laughing. "'Germs'!" Dark Magicians only know how many novices I have taught to walk through the Secret Door, but I've never heard anything like this before."

I also laughed. Sure I had said (or thought) something incomparably stupid, but I was still pleased with myself. Sometimes we need to say silly things just to stimulate a warm and friendly atmosphere.

"Aren't you glad I came?" I said.

"And how!" said Lady Sotofa. She stopped laughing very abruptly and gave me a penetrating look. "You know, Max, your charm will be the end of you. Don't tease Eternity with your cute little smile. It'll backfire."

"I'm sorry?" I said, perplexed.

"Oh, never mind," she said, and smiled again. "I fancied I saw something. I'll tell you some other time."

"Some other time," I said, still bewildered. "I still don't understand."

"It's for the better. Come to my office and I'll treat you to some horrible kamra, brewed according to the recipe of the late great-grandmother of the current keeper of the *Country Home* tavern. You went there when you were in Kettari, right?"

"Oh yes, that was when Shurf left all our money in the back room. He just had to play some Krak, you see. But they had excellent kamra there. Don't slander your wonderful homeland."

"Oh my, you liked it?" said Lady Sotofa. "Then again, it's easier to love someone else's homeland than your own."

"That's true. My romance with my own homeland turned out to be a disaster."

"You're not the only one, so don't fret," said Lady Sotofa as she opened the door of a cute garden house for me. "Most people are born in places that are completely unlivable for them. Fate just loves to play pranks like that. Sit down, Max, and take a sip of this kamra. Praise be the Magicians, it's ready. When did I manage to brew it, I wonder?"

"Are you making miracles unbeknownst to yourself?" I said, tasting the thick, hot drink with pleasure. "I forget, Lady Sotofa, is it all right if I smoke here?"

"Only tobacco from another World," the wonderful old lady said sternly. "I find the smoke of our local tobacco completely unbearable."

"So do I," I said, producing a pack of cigarettes from the pocket of my Mantle of Death.

I was gradually running out of my Kettarian supplies, a generous gift from the old Sheriff Mackie Ainti, but this wasn't a big deal anymore. I had learned the lessons of Sir Maba Kalox very well, and could probably fetch a pack of cigarettes from the Chink between Worlds without too much sweat.

"So, what kinds of secrets did you want to learn from me?" Lady Sotofa said as she sat down across from me.

"Well," I said, "you're going to laugh at me."

"Oh, may that be the worst misfortune you suffer in your life."

"There are some things I still don't understand," I said. "First, what's the Spirit of Xolomi? Why does it feel like 'dancing,' and how are Juffin and Shurf going to rein it in?"

"They're just going to hold it by the head and the legs," Lady Sotofa said very seriously. "How else?"

"It has a head and legs?" I said.

"The Spirit of Xolomi has a head, legs, and other things that any respectable Spirit would have. As for your other questions, you know, Max, one can see the Spirit of Xolomi and observe its destructive power. One can even counteract the destructive power, which that sly old fox Juffin and his Mad Fishmonger have already done once before. I have no reason to doubt that they will be able to do it now. By the way, our ancient kings were able to tame the Spirit of Xolomi on their own, without any outside help. But this doesn't mean that a person is able to explain to you what the Spirit of Xolomi is, why it fancies throwing a party every so often, and why it would wish to leave its own abode in ruins, not to mention the entire City of Echo. Some things are simply beyond explanation. Are you disappointed?"

"But is it really that dangerous?" I said. "Are you absolutely sure that Juffin and Shurf can keep it at bay?"

"Of course they can. I wish I had your worries, boy," said Lady Sotofa, laughing. "You don't know Juffin very well yet. If he doubted his own abilities, he wouldn't even go there. He would have sneaked off to some other World and watched how it all ended from there."

"Really? He'd do that?"

"Yes, he would. And that shouldn't surprise you. Learn to see through people, boy. Someday you're going to need it. Now, what about question number two? Well, never mind. I know what you're going to ask. You want to know what you're supposed to do now since Juffin offloaded so much responsibility onto you, right?"

"Something like that, yes. But considering what you've just told me, it looks like it's not that relevant. You know, it never really occurred to me until now that anything could happen to this wonderful World, that it could end just like that, at the drop of a hat. Knowing that makes my problems at work seem—"

"Any World can end at any minute, and when it happens, it happens precisely in that manner—at the drop of a hat," said Lady Sotofa. "When you think about it, all other problems pale in comparison, don't you think?"

"I do," I said with a sigh. "You sure know how to cheer a person up, Lady Sotofa."

"Oh, my goodness, now this nice young man will suffer for the rest of the day," said Lady Sotofa, smiling. "Don't go borrowing trouble. Drink your kamra before it gets cold."

Three minutes later I got pretty tired of worrying about the fate of the World, and I laughed, to my own surprise.

"I think I know why Juffin made me his deputy. If the World could end any minute now, it doesn't really matter what kind of a mess I make in just twelve days."

"Quick learner, my boy!" said Lady Sotofa. "That's how I was going to answer your second question, if you had asked."

Soon, it was time to say goodbye to the wonderful Lady Sotofa. She walked me to the invisible Secret Door in the wall around Jafax.

"Don't bother yourself with the fate of the World," she said. "What you really need to do is to look after your shaggy, disheveled head. And remember, don't tease Eternity. It's already studying you with acute interest."

"Huh?" I shuddered. It was the second time this powerful witch with the manners of a loving grandmother had mentioned Eternity, which I was apparently "teasing."

"Never mind that," she said with a sigh, and suddenly gave me a quick hug, as if she were parting with a son going off to war. "Go take care of your silly duties, boy. And don't worry, you won't fail. Ever."

I went back to Headquarters feeling very confused. It was the first time that a conversation with Lady Sotofa had left a weight on my heart. But which heart? I wondered.

"Oh, here's our Venerable Head," said Melifaro, jumping down from my desk. He looked at me seriously, but his eyes were laughing. "Officer Melifaro reporting: nothing happened on my shift, sir! I mean, literally, nothing. Even the police are loafing. Kofa came by. He says that the citizens already know whose bottom is now occupying Sir Juffin Hully's chair. And they are almost sure that you kill people on the spot for the slightest misdemeanor. I guess Echo's criminals decided to take a break and wait for Juffin to return. They were used to him."

"Good, good," I said. "They should take their kids to the zoo, if there is one in Echo, which I doubt. They need a vacation like anyone else."

The accursed weight finally fell from my heart. I even thought I heard it hit the ground. The best remedy for metaphysical worries is two glances at Sir Melifaro before meals. And it's best to chase them down with something strong.

I said, "Has Kofa left already?"

"Of course. Our Master Eavesdropper-Gobbler is back at his post. He's probably munching away on delicacies in some tavern. I don't know what kinds of secrets he's uncovering, but I'm sure that when he moves his jaw, the walls start trembling."

"We should follow his example," I said, and beckoned to Melifaro with my index finger. "Let's go."

"Where?" Melifaro said, wrapping himself in his dreadful yellow looxi.

"To the *Juffin's Dozen*. I want to bring another client to that terrible Moxi. Maybe he won't smack me with his horrible ladle. What's more, I hope that surly man will give me a free drink since I'm going to do him a favor."

"Whoa, are these the new rules?" said Melifaro. "Did I hear you right? You're leaving your post during working hours, but you're not going to the *Glutton Bunba*? That's bold. Very bold."

"You heard right, mister. I'm the greatest hero of all times and places, didn't you know?"

This bravado was a sign that I was almost myself again—the flippant dimwit. Frankly, I was only too happy with that development. Given that the World could end any second now—ready or not, here I come.

※

I returned to the House by the Bridge about three hours later. I let Melifaro go "have some fun," as he put it.

Pondering the situation a bit, I realized that I was a lousy boss. My subordinates were loafing around Magicians knew where, and I was back in the office. Strictly speaking, it should have been the other way around.

"What's up, smarty?" I said to Kurush as I placed a parcel with pastries beside him. "Anything happen?"

"No," said the buriwok, digging his bill into a pastry.

Soon I was cursing myself for doing this, as I was trying to clean the sticky cream off his bill. An hour later, Kofa came in. He immediately grasped the situation and laughed a good-natured laugh.

"If you had your way, you would dismiss the entire City Police Department, too, and try to do their work singlehandedly. You're so humane it's almost disgusting."

"Is it really?"

"Oh, yes. Want a piece of advice? Order me to take your chair and go home. I'm sure Tekki's waiting for you."

"I'm sure she is," I said, and heaved a sigh. "Is my humanistic nature catching?"

"You might say that. I'll be honest with you, though: I'm going to keep Lady Kekki Tuotli company. Tonight is her shift, so you, Sir Venerable Head, are only going to get in my way."

"Well, well, well, I turned out to be a good matchmaker, huh?" I said enthusiastically.

"You are, indeed. Seriously, Max, you can go home with a clean conscience. Juffin, by the way, usually leaves work at around dusk."

"I guess you're right," I said.

I got up, smiled at Kofa, and opened the door. "Good night, Kofa."

※

The *Armstrong & Ella* was very crowded. It surprised me at first, but then I realized that I hadn't had the chance to stop in at dusk in a long while. Usually, I was just getting to work at this time of day.

On a barstool, dozing off, sat my friend Anday Pu. He had become a regular at this place recently. That in itself was surprising because Tekki served no food. Is he on a diet? I thought. Echo's star reporter was soused to the eyeballs.

"Am I dreaming?" said Tekki. "What a surprise!"

"You can say that again," I said, sitting on a stool next to Anday, who reeked of drink. "I thought I wouldn't make it back here for another dozen days or so, but the Heavens, assisted by Sir Kofa, had other plans for me. It's too bad this place is packed. To tell you the truth, I had some fantastic plans for tonight."

"They're leaving pretty soon," said Tekki. "I'm telling you, they come here every night with only one thing on their minds: to watch you flirt with me. Now their dreams have finally come true."

She was right. A half hour later the place was empty and Tekki and I were alone, serenaded by Anday's snoring.

"This guy can sleep all the way through until morning if you don't touch him," said Tekki, sighing. "No wonder, though, considering that he's been poisoning his body since noon today."

"What is his problem?" I said, shaking Anday by the shoulder. "What's wrong, you ancestor of Ukumbian pirates? Life is good—life in general, and yours in particular. Haven't you been burning like a comet for a little too long today, Blackbeard Junior?"

"You keep coming up with these otherworldly names for me," said Anday, still sleepy. "You still don't catch a thing."

"But I do," I said. "Depression again?"

"Max, would it kill you to buy me a ticket to Tasher?" said Anday. "I want to go south. It's warm, and—"

"And they appreciate poets there. I know, you told me. I'd love to think that they appreciate poets somewhere. How come you can't buy the ticket yourself? As far as I know, you get one heck of a paycheck from Sir Rogro. I'm afraid the newspaper will go bust just trying to keep up with your salary."

"It keeps disappearing. Somewhere. You know, those little round metal things. I just don't catch where," said Anday. "The dinner is totally over."

Tekki and I spent three hours and learned just two simple, indisputable truths: Mr. Anday Pu wanted to go south because it was warm there. And in Echo nobody can "catch" anything. The rest of the night, however, was ours and ours alone—something that I considered to be a rare and lucky event.

❀

A call from Sir Kofa Yox woke me up in the morning. I didn't get enough sleep again, but Kofa was very persistent.

I know it's unforgivable of me to call like this, but the sooner you come to the House by the Bridge the better.

Okay, if you say it's important, then I'm sure it is. Could you please order some kamra for me at the Glutton? *I won't be able to get any at home at this point.*

I already ordered it. Come on, Sir Max, show us your top speed.

"I will," I said out loud, addressing the bottle of Elixir of Kaxar would save my life once again. Back home in my World, where I had only black coffee at my disposal, I would have given up the ghost long before from chronic exhaustion, given my crazy schedule. Here, though, I was doing all right.

I dressed quickly and rushed downstairs. I got in my amobiler and took off at the speed of light. Then it dawned on me: something nasty had happened. Sir Kofa wouldn't have bothered me if it hadn't been something serious.

❀

"So, what is it?" I said as I stepped into the office.

Sir Kofa looked at me with genuine admiration.

"Only eight minutes! I timed you. You came all the way from the New City, right? I'm impressed, son."

"Mind you, it took me at least five minutes to come to my senses," I said, and poured myself some kamra. "But what happened?"

"The living dead have been spotted at the Green Petta Cemetery," Kofa said in an offhand tone. "The guard sent me a call. The poor guy was on the verge of fainting. He almost didn't get away. Nothing out of the ordinary, but we have to do something about the undead, and the sooner the better. We can't let that scum hang around the Left Bank."

"Are they hanging around already?"

"Not yet, but they're going to spread about soon, I believe."

"Are there a lot of them?"

"If there weren't a lot of them, I wouldn't have woken anyone up and would have dealt with them myself. The problem is that there are a few dozen of them already, and new ones keep popping up."

"Where are Melifaro and Melamori? Did you send them a call?"

"Of course I did. But unlike you, they move at regular human speed. They'll be here soon."

"If I get this right, we're going to go to the cemetery and tear them limb from limb," I said doubtfully.

Sir Kofa nodded yes. "That is precisely what we are going to do. Where are they coming from, I wonder?" he said.

"From the graves, naturally," I said.

"What's from the graves?" said Melamori, frightened. She entered the office briskly. Unlike me, she looked absolutely stunning. She had clearly had a good night's sleep.

"It's all very grave," I said mechanically.

A moment later, the silliness of the exchange dawned on us and we laughed.

"Is this a comedy club? It's bad taste to laugh like that so early in the morning," Melifaro said in a sleepy tone.

His bright-violet looxi was a perfect match for the dark rings under his eyes. He is definitely feeling worse than I am, I thought, not without pleasure.

Without saying anything, I handed him the bottle of Elixir of Kaxar. It wasn't an act of kindness on my part—I usually don't suffer from that. I did it in the interests of the case.

"Okay," I said, and gulped down the rest of my kamra. "Time to get down to work. Melamori, you're staying here and holding down the fort. We're going over to the Green Petta Cemetery, where we'll finish off those zombies. Then we'll come back here and have some breakfast together."

"Why am I staying here again?"

Sometimes Melamori can be a pain in the backside, to tell you the truth.

"Because I say so. And I am the law, according to the Borderland dwellers, an official delegation of which is approaching Echo as we speak." I winked at Melamori. "Think about it: we don't need to step on anyone's trace, praise be the Magicians. And making you fight those undead monsters is like hammering in nails with a microscope."

"What's a microscope?"

Melamori was no longer offended. Phew, it looked like I had managed to come up with a compliment that pleased her.

"It's a special contraption that you don't want to use for driving in nails," I said. "Sir Kofa, I'll feel so much better if you don't leave Melifaro and me to the mercy of fate. I have a peculiar fear of cemeteries, and I'll need you to hold my hand and calm me down."

"Of course I'm coming with you. I was planning on it. Why would you think otherwise?"

"Because you're still sitting in the chair, and I'm already on my way to the Left Bank, as it were."

"You're a quick lad," Kofa said, getting up reluctantly. "So much for my hoping to escape from Juffin the Quick and Nimble and all his candlesticks."

"He lent me some of them," I said.

"So very kind of him," said Melifaro. He was finally beginning to look like himself again.

§

I parked the amobiler at the cemetery gates and we got out.

"So, guys," I said hesitantly, "you can kill them, too, right?"

"Don't worry, boy," said Kofa. "We have a trick or two up our sleeves. You're not going to be doing this dirty business alone. Are you surprised?"

"No, not really, but I just wanted to make sure. Life's full of surprises, so I can't be sure of anything. Silly, huh?"

"No, not silly. Let's just say a little unexpected. You did guess, however, that of the three of us, Melamori was the only one who couldn't do it."

"Frankly, I just thought I needed to keep someone back at Headquarters. I'd leave Lookfi sitting in my chair, but as far as I know, he doesn't show up until after noon. The buriwoks have had a bad influence on him. It's too late to change the fellow now. And since we really didn't need a Master of Pursuit—"

"Admit it, you're as solicitous of our beautiful lady as her Uncle Kima," said Melifaro.

"What if I am?" I said. I looked around and stopped short. "Holy moly!"

Holy moly was right. The Green Petta Cemetery is one of the oldest in the city. It resembles a park far more than an actual graveyard. Against the background of this magnificent park, the crowd of naked, dirt-encrusted people looked particularly incongruous. Well, they didn't quite look like people, of course: people don't have such empty stares and unnaturally twisted joints, and their skin doesn't usually hang off of them in shreds like old newspapers.

The undead were sitting motionless on the crumbling gravestones.

They seemed not to notice us, though perhaps their dull eyes couldn't see anything, anyway.

"Not the most appetizing sight in the Universe," said Melifaro. "Max, just to let you know in advance, I'm getting smashed tonight after this spectacle."

"You can damage your body as much as you want, as long as it's not on my territory. Okay, guys, I don't know about you, but I'm going to start. The sooner we finish this the better."

I snapped the fingers of my left hand, and a bright-green Lethal Sphere took off from the tips of them. As soon as it touched the body of a living corpse, it exploded silently. The creature fell on the ground. Its sudden death surprised me. Until now my Lethal Spheres had been far less effective.

What surprised me even more was the indifference of the other living dead. They completely ignored everything that was going on. I felt a mixture of sick pity and disgust, something akin to what you feel when you kill a cockroach and its fragile chitinous shell bursts under your feet with a repugnant crackling sound.

Out of the corner of my eye I saw Melifaro stand on tiptoe, make a few pirouettes, crank up his arm, and throw several fireballs at the group of phlegmatic zombies. He looked like a bowler after a strike.

"Not too shabby, man," I said. I felt exhilarated and snapped my fingers again. This time my Lethal Sphere hit a flimsy creature with an earring made from an unfamiliar reddish metal.

"Say, have you tried one of these before, boys?" said Sir Kofa.

I looked around and saw Kofa clap his hands soundlessly several times. It looked like he was giving a rousing ovation to deaf performers.

"Don't look at me. It works remotely."

I looked at the group of undead. A few dark bodies stood up from the grass, swayed, and immediately collapsed to the ground.

"A strange trick," said Kofa. "No visual effects, but it kills anyone on the spot instantly. Well, almost anyone. It never worked on Juffin. He always managed to dodge it somehow. Praise be the Magicians that it was I who chased him and not the other way around."

"However many times I've heard the stories about you chasing him, I still can't believe it. You chasing Juffin, with the firm intention of killing him off? No, I just can't wrap my mind around it."

I shook my head and snapped my fingers a few more times. The ranks of the undead were getting thinner and thinner. They didn't try to run away or defend themselves. Frankly, it made me very uneasy.

"It's too bad they're not fighting back," I said, watching another one of Melifaro's dance moves. "I wonder why?"

"Right, the last thing we need is their heroic resistance," said Sir Kofa. "Not to mention that we're doing Lonli-Lokli's job. What, are you bored, lad?"

"I'm disgusted," I said. "If they were a little less torpid, I'd feel our actions were less inhumane."

"On the contrary, what we're doing is very humane," Kofa said. "You can't even imagine the degree of their suffering."

"I can, to a degree. Jiffa Savanxa told me a few things about them, and he was an expert on this, poor fellow."

I snapped my fingers again, never ceasing to wonder how effortless it was for me to produce something as incomprehensible as a Lethal Sphere. I didn't even need to focus: it just happened. It was easier than scratching my nose.

"I'm pooped. You can throw me in the dump. Better yet, take me home to bed," said Melifaro, sitting on the ground and wiping his forehead with the fold of his new looxi. "I've used up all my scanty resources for today."

"You could have stopped sooner," I said. "There are less than a dozen of them left. Kofa and I can take care of them."

"On the other hand, it's not that often that I get to murder so many people at once," said Melifaro. "You can be a villain day in and day out, but my life is monotonous, virtuous, and full of only kind deeds."

A few silent claps by Kofa marked the grand finale of our little excursion to the cemetery.

"Let's go, boys," he said with a yawn. "All's well that ends well. Now it's the mortician's job. I hope he'll manage without our help. Grave digging is not my line of work."

"Okay, then, you and I are going back to Headquarters, and Melifaro—"

"And I'm also going back to Headquarters."

"Oh, yeah? And I thought you were headed toward a dump or someone's bed—I forget in which order."

"I'll get there eventually, but first you're going to treat us all to breakfast. You promised."

"Well, since I promised, I will," I said. "Though it's easier to kill you than to feed you."

"Look who's talking," Melifaro said.

I could tell that the guy was really tired. Usually, his comebacks were snappier.

❀

"The Green Petta Cemetery is too ancient to be a quiet place," Kofa Yox said digging into his breakfast. "Now, the guard over at the Kunig Yusi Cemetery, on the other hand, can just sleep peacefully. Such things just would never happen on his turf."

"Is the Kunig Yusi Cemetery new?" I said.

"Very new. Newer than the New City. But those poor creatures we had to put to rest today had been lying in their graves for a few centuries. I wonder what ancient bastard needed them as actors in his sad show? The worst part is that we can hardly make him pay for it. Chances are he died of old age back in the days of King Mynin. I've never seen such ancient undead before in my life, Magicians' honor."

"Probably some Dark Magician from a dreary old legend put a spell on them, a hole in the heavens above his earnest head," mumbled Melifaro.

"You're in a strange mood," said Melamori. "I'm glad I stayed behind at Headquarters."

"Ah, but I think you'd have liked it, my lady," Melifaro said. "So many naked men in one place, and all of them so incomparably handsome. Our new tyrant deprived you of a great deal of pleasure."

"Oh, that is a shame, then," Melamori said. "But never mind, I'll make up for it. A naked man is not such a rare spectacle in this World. Besides, your beauty boys were dead, if I'm not mistaken. I'm quite old-fashioned in that respect. I prefer the living."

❀

Then everything started running like clockwork again.

Melifaro went home. He wasn't himself, though: launching so many Lethal Spheres so early in the morning had never been known to improve one's health. Melamori and I hung around doing nothing until evening and thoroughly enjoyed ourselves. Sir Kofa took a walk through town—just in case. Then he returned to Headquarters and almost resorted to force to make me go home. How sweet of him!

This time I was determined to get enough sleep, come hell or high water. I went to bed before midnight and woke up way past noon. What a privilege!

I was in the best of moods when I got to the House by the Bridge. Lookfi Pence was sitting in my office, looking quite puzzled.

"Oh, here you are, Max. It's unfortunate that Sir Kofa decided not to wait for you," he said with a shy smile. "He asked me to wait for you instead, and to tell you we're back to square one."

"Which one?"

I stared at Lookfi in distress for a few moments and then sent Kofa a call.

What's happening? Is it the undead again? Why didn't you send me a call?

There was no need to. Melifaro and I are managing just fine. These undead are the most docile creatures in the World. And you need to sleep occasionally.

Well, thank you, of course. But now I feel like a real dolt. Are you done, or still just beginning?

I'm almost done, only three more to go. Ah, now I'm done. Don't worry, boy. I took care of them myself today. Melifaro was standing by, just in case.

You're so very kind, Kofa. He really did go a little overboard yesterday. How about Melamori? Is she with you?

Yes, she is. She decided to take a look at the naked men. Melifaro's advertisement yesterday worked like a charm. Okay, Max. Set the table and get ready to welcome home the exhausted heroes. Over and out.

They returned in half an hour. Sir Kofa's face betrayed not a hint of exhaustion. Apparently, his murder methods didn't require much effort—that, or our Master Eavesdropper had an inexhaustible source of energy.

"Congratulations," said Melifaro. "Now you've become a real boss. We're doing all the work, while you sleep. That's the way to do it, your majesty."

"I can't say I didn't enjoy it," I said, and then gave Kofa a reproachful glance. "Still, you should have woken me up."

"I will next time," said Kofa. "I have a hunch that it will start all over again very soon. I can't say I like this whole affair, boys. It has a nasty odor to it, don't you think?"

"They sure do look nasty, I'll give you that," said Melamori.

She said it with such distaste that it seemed we were the ones who had brought those unsightly zombies into the light of day. It had been a team effort, no less, except that we had forgotten to consult her on the matter.

"Say, guys, were these the same undead from yesterday, or new ones?" I said.

"The same?" said Kofa, surprised. "Oh, I sure hope not. We did a darn good job dealing with the ones yesterday. It never occurred to me that today's undead might be ones we didn't kill all the way just a day ago. But you may be right. Anything can happen."

"In any event, this won't do," I said. "We need to quarantine that sinning cemetery somehow. Who knows, maybe our next batch of new friends will be friskier and will decide to go for a walk around Echo. Maybe we should send some policemen over there."

"Brilliant, Nightmare!" said Melifaro, laughing. "I can just picture the brave boys screaming and scattering if anything happened. Boy, you sure know how to arrange a program of light entertainment."

"If they're not scared of Boboota, I doubt they'll be scared of any other creature, living or undead. In any case, a few dozen scared policemen is better protection than one scared cemetery guard," I said. "So get on over to General Boboota's turf for reinforcements."

"Like he's going to give them to me."

"He will," I said. "Just tell him they're for me. Tell him I'm asking him very, very sweetly. Beg him if you have to. Come on, don't dawdle."

"Your word is my command, your wild borderland Majesty." Melifaro reluctantly got down from the table and bowed. "Do not be angry with me, O mighty ruler of bare-bummed eaters of horse dung. Gosh, you're such a big shot now."

"Break the policemen into three groups, depending on how many you manage to fetch. Tell them to take shifts, but I'd like to see as many people in uniform as possible hanging around the Green Petta Cemetery. Take them there and brief them about it—although there isn't much to brief them on. Anyway, think of something bombastic and earthshaking while you're strolling through the cemetery. Something that will make them feel responsible for the fate of the World."

"If you save the leftovers of your royal meal for me, I will soak the hem of your mantle with tears of gratitude, you monster."

And Melifaro rushed out of the office. I knew that bossing around a bunch of policemen would give him unique pleasure.

"Not bad, son," said Kofa. "I'm surprised I didn't think of it. Apparently, you can think straight and be good at it, sometimes."

"Yes, but only if I get enough sleep. It's not my fault that doesn't happen very often."

"What are we going to do about those disgusting creatures?"

Melamori said. It was clear she wasn't too fond of the "naked men."

"We're going to exterminate them," I said. "That's why I asked Melifaro to put guards there. At least we can be sure that they'll alert us right away, without any delays. It's too bad Shurf isn't here. His left hand is good at incinerating anything that gets in its way. Sir Kofa, do you, by any chance, turn things into ashes? It's much more sanitary that way, you know."

"Exterminate, yes. Turn into ashes, not my line of work, I'm afraid."

"Nor mine," I said.

"You seem to be discussing a very somber topic, gentlemen," said Lookfi suddenly. "Has someone died?"

Melamori and I laughed nervously, and Kofa shook his head.

"If only you were right, Lookfi," I said. "The truth is that the situation is much worse: somebody keeps returning from the dead."

"Oh, that really is bad," said Lookfi. "I know. I grew up in a cemetery. Nothing out of the ordinary happened during my time, praise be the Magicians, but I heard a great many stories about the undead."

"You grew up in a cemetery?" I asked, astonished.

"Well, I guess I didn't express it quite right," said Lookfi, "but I did spend much of my childhood in a cemetery. My uncle, Sir Lukari Bobon, wanted me to take over the family business. He was very disappointed when I enrolled in the Royal Higher Institute. So disappointed that he still refuses to talk to me. I cannot say that I lost an interesting interlocutor, though. He's always been somewhat lacking in erudition."

"Lookfi's uncle is an undertaker, and the most successful one in Echo, by the way," said Kofa. "You made the right choice, boy. It's much more entertaining to spend time with buriwoks than with the dead. Not to mention the undead."

"You are so very right, Sir Kofa. Oh, and thank you for reminding me. They've been waiting for me all day." Lookfi stood up, caught himself in the folds of his looxi, knocked over two cups, and finally bestowed his shining smile on us. "Thank you for the dinner, gentlemen."

And he left for the Main Archive.

"What did he mean, 'Thank you for the dinner'?" I said. "This is breakfast."

"As if you don't know Lookfi's habits," said Melamori, giggling. "But he wasn't too far off, if you think about it. People usually lunch at this hour."

✿

Melifaro returned an hour and a half later, glowing like a well-polished crown.

"It worked marvelously," he said. "The uniforms of the City Police look divine against the landscape of the cemetery. The spectacle is simultaneously didactic and majestic. If I were you, I'd go there right away."

"All in due time," I said. "I have a feeling we'll have plenty of time to get sick of it."

"Don't exaggerate, Max," said Kofa, looking out of the window pensively. "By the way, I don't think I can sit in for you tonight. Are you okay with that?"

"Of course, Kofa. I'll take the shift myself. I'll be the only keeper of the public order. After all, that was supposed to be my job from the beginning: to sit in Juffin's office at night doing nothing."

Sir Kofa went out for a walk in the city and even went overboard with joy. He caught a bearded pickpocket red-handed, even though hunting down such small fry was far beneath the dignity of the Secret Investigative Force. The pickpocket was fed to that ferocious animal General Boboota Box. It was his just deserts.

"I'll teach you how to clean pockets! Only instead of pockets you're going to be cleaning outhouses. And whatever you find there you're going to stick up your behind!"

I could hear Boboota's shouts even in my office, but I didn't mind. I began to miss them when it was quiet for too long.

"You look like a country hick who dreamed his whole life of seeing an Ekki Balbalao show, and whose dream finally came true," said Melifaro.

"I *am* a country hick. A simple, ignorant king from abroad—who, by the way, has no idea who Ekki Balbalao is."

"A hole in the heavens above you, pal! He's the best tenor in the Unified Kingdom," Melifaro said, shaking his head. "I'm not the most avid operagoer in Echo, but not knowing who Ekki Balbalao is too much, even for someone like you. What *do* you do in your spare time, monster?"

"Go out to taverns and chase women, frothing at the mouth," I said. Then I added, "Besides, I don't have any spare time because I spend my best years at work. Is he really that good?"

"He's okay," Melifaro said. "Actually, my leisure time is not that different from how you describe yours, except that I keep my mouth shut most of the time. And so should you. All in all, the strains of Balbalao's sweet voice don't reach my ears very often."

"We're so ignorant and uncivilized," I said. "No one would believe us if we told them."

"Sure they would," said Melifaro. "It's written across our foreheads."

Melifaro finished our discourse on the arts, saying that it was time for him to go. I stared at the sky, which was growing dark, and submitted to fate. The day had gone by amazingly fast, and I had a long, uneventful night of solitude ahead of me. Lookfi had left work at sunset, as usual, and Melamori had fled even sooner, Magicians knew where.

At around midnight, when I was beginning to doze off, Tekki's call reached me.

Max, it's awful! Just awful! That friend of yours, Mr. Pu, he's—

What, has he gotten drunk again and fallen asleep on his barstool?

I only wish. He is rather smashed, but he's wide awake. He wants to start something with me. He's all weepy, and he keeps trying to kiss my hand. It's pathetic. You know me, I could easily turn him into a pile of ashes without a second thought, but then they'd throw me in Xolomi. You would.

Don't be silly. I'd cover up for you and protect you, risking life and limb and my astronomical salary. Then again, it's not the best way to spend the rest of my life. Say, can you really turn him into ashes?

Sure. Why?

I wish I had your skills. You know, we just learned today that nobody but Lonli-Lokli can incinerate those sinning undead, but he and Juffin have left. Now we have to kill them and bury them, and then kill them and bury them all over again. I'm so tired of it.

Well, I don't think I can incinerate the undead. Those beasts are pretty tough. Even White Fire is useless against them.

White Fire? What's that?

It's the best and most reliable way of incinerating anyone. The one hundred and thirty-seventh degree of White Magic. One of the favorite tricks of my infamous daddy. Anyway, would you mind if I sent this tubby chatterbox to the House by the Bridge? You're probably bored out of your mind down there.

To be honest, I am pretty bored. All right, then. Send him over here.

You probably want to go to bed now anyway.

I do, especially since you might be showing up an hour before dawn.

Don't count on it tonight. But I agree, you have the right to live without Anday slobbering all over you. Fine, send Anday over here. Even pirates get the blues.

⚶

Less than thirty minutes later, a sleepy courier knocked on the door.

"A visitor for me? Small, tubby, pretty tipsy, and very sassy?" I said before the courier could open his mouth.

"You're exactly right, Sir Max," he said. After years of service in the House by the Bridge, he had lost his ability to be surprised. "Should I let him in, then?"

"I suppose, since he's already here. Go ahead and let him in."

"Max, I'm so very, very sad," said Anday, still in the doorway. "You sure don't catch what it's like to be very, very sad."

"Believe it or not, I do catch," I said. "I do that exercise at least a dozen times a day, trust me."

"What exercise?" Anday said, staring at me with his beautiful almond-shaped eyes. "What do you mean?"

"The exercise in sadness, of course." I poured him a cup of kamra. "Not exactly a drink you'd appreciate at this time of the day, but it'll do for a change."

"You can be sad, too?" Anday said.

He looked like an alchemist from the Middle Ages who had just been told there was no philosopher's stone. Anday hesitated, processing the information, and then corrected himself.

"So you do catch, Max! I'm sorry."

I didn't quite understand what he was sorry for but decided not to press it. The whole "catch" routine was beginning to get really old with me.

"Max, when you first met me I was hungry," said Anday, staring at his half-empty cup with disgust. "Today, I'm full. But this doesn't change anything: I must leave."

"For Tasher?"

"Tasher will do, I guess," Anday said. "It's really not too bad there. It's warm, fruit trees grow right in your backyard, and almost no one can read or write. That's why they catch how cool it is if you can. But I really need to go away. Doesn't really matter where, as long as it's away from here. Max, would it kill you to take a short walk with me? I'll show you a trick."

"A trick?" I said. "Can't you show it to me here?"

"No. I can only show it to you in the Quarter of Trysts."

"You know, I think it would be better if you just told me about it," I said. "I don't want to leave work for too long. It seems like tonight is going to—"

"I can't just tell you about it. You won't catch a thing then. You need to see it."

I pondered this for a moment and then agreed. I was curious: what kind of a trick could one show only in the Quarter of Trysts? Besides, morning was ages away.

"Fine, let's go. We can drive there—it'll just take minute. Will half an hour be enough for your trick, Captain Flint?"

"It'll be enough. You know, Max, when you call me these strange names, I don't catch anything. There's this joke—maybe you know it. A guy comes to a healer and says, 'Sir, I have lapses in my memory.' 'How long have you had them?' the healer says. And the guy says, 'How long have I had what?' Do you catch, Max? The dinner's over once and for all!"

I shook my head. I had heard the joke many, many years before. As with many other Echo jokes, this one repeated almost verbatim a joke from my homeland. Was Maba Kalox responsible for transplanting them from one World to another? It wouldn't surprise me in the least.

"Kurush, I'll be back in half an hour, and I'll bring you a pastry. Okay?"

"That means I should expect you back in an hour," said the buri-wok. "You're always late."

"But not today," I said. "I promise."

"It's not my concern," Kurush said sleepily. "It's *yours*. You people are full of contradictions."

"Right you are."

Arguing with Kurush was an exercise in futility. He was right. As always.

❦

I pulled over on the very edge of the Quarter of Trysts. Anday Pu jumped down on the mosaic sidewalk and pranced over toward the closest Trysting House, to the side reserved for Seekers.

"Hey!" I said. "Did you just want a free ride? You should have told me right away instead of scheming and luring me here with your talk of 'tricks.' I'm a busy man."

"Come with me, Max. My trick is right here. You'll catch everything."

Still burning with curiosity, I followed him.

Anday stopped on the threshold of the Trysting House, fumbled in his pockets, and turned to me, embarrassed.

"I'm sorry, Max. Could you lend me two crowns? I seem to have lost all of my shiny metal objects again."

"Sure," I said with a sigh, searching the pockets of my Mantle of Death. I always had some change in them. I knew whom I was dealing with.

"Will you pay for me, please? I'll pay you back tomorrow, or some other day."

He didn't sound like he was too sure that he would be able to.

Great, I thought. Last time it was that crazy Isamonian, now Anday Pu, totally smashed. When I go to the Quarter of Trysts I'm always in such dubious company.

"Here," I said, handing him two coins. "And listen. Next time you want to make me a couple of crowns lighter, you don't have to drag me all the way here."

"You no catch, Max!" Anday was almost crying. "Come with me, and you'll see."

"What do you need me for?" But I knew I'd go. Curiosity will be the end of me yet.

"Just stay here in the lobby," he said, opening the door to the Trysting House.

He handed the money to the proprietor and stuck his hand into a large vase of tokens that was standing on the floor. He pulled out a square ceramic token and showed it to me without looking at it.

"It's a blank, right?"

"Yes, it is," I said. "Hold on a second. Are you saying that you can guess the number? Or that you always pull a blank?"

"The latter. Now you get it. Good night, sir."

He gave an exaggeratedly polite nod to the proprietor, who had been staring at my Mantle of Death the whole time—I hadn't had time to change. I think the lady Waiters were very relieved to see me disappear into the darkness beyond the door.

"Would you mind spending another two crowns, Max?" said Anday. "I want you to be sure that I'm not pulling your leg."

"I do mind spending another two crowns, but just to be sure," I said, laughing, and produced the money from my pocket. "Some talent you've got, friend."

Anday didn't say anything. He took the money and shuffled along to the next Trysting House. The result was exactly the same, including the expression on the face of the proprietor when he saw the Mantle of Death.

"Okay, enough. I don't want to go broke," I said when we were back on the street. "I would have believed you if you'd just told me, though."

"You wouldn't have believed me, and I wanted you to catch," said Anday. "It's not the same."

"You're right, it's not," I said. "Hey, have you tried being the Waiter?"

"Many times. Same results. Forget about those Trysting Houses—it's not just that! I always pull blanks. It's the story of my life. You catch?"

"Let's go," I said. "Don't exaggerate, Captain Flint."

"You go, Max. I'm going to go to Chemparkaroke's. His Soup of Repose can calm down even me. About that ticket to Tasher, though. Would it kill you to buy me one? I'm asking because I know you're lucky. I'll bet you've never pulled a blank in your life."

"No, but I've pulled something much worse a few times, believe me. And why Tasher? Anyway, good night, Anday."

"And when the night ends, morning comes—the end of another workday." These words Anday Pu addressed not to me but to the lilac night sky over his head—a head stuffed with various sad and silly things.

❧

I drove back to Headquarters. I really wanted to get back on time at least once to make Kurush change his mind about me. My efforts were in vain, though. Kurush was sleeping peacefully on the back of the chair. I decided to follow suit. I settled down comfortably and fell asleep. I had a long dream about Blackbeard, who tried to convince me that Mr. Anday Pu was his relative.

Unlike Kurush, I wasn't a deep sleeper, so I woke up immediately when I heard the floorboards creak. A young boy in the uniform of the City Police was standing in the doorway.

"Sir Max," he said, startled. "They sent me for you. The cemetery—"

"Again?" I nipped a mournful groan in the bud—moaning and groaning could wait. I had more important business to take care of.

"Again," said the boy.

"Why did you come here?" I said. "You could have just sent me a call. Would have saved time."

"They told me to come," he said. "It wasn't my idea."

"Never mind." I took a gulp of Elixir of Kaxar, put on my Mantle of Death, and went down to the amobiler. On my way down, I sent a call to Sir Kofa. He answered immediately.

Again?

Again. I'm going to the cemetery. Come join me as soon as you can. I think we can leave Melifaro out of this today. These excursions take their toll on his health, and I'm counting on his standing in for me during the day.

I think I'd better call him. He can just stand there and watch. Just in case.

Up to you. See you.

I got into the amobiler and grabbed the lever. The young policeman stood nearby, shuffling his feet.

"Hop in, I'll give you a lift," I said. "Don't be afraid, I don't bite."

The boy got in the back seat and we took off.

"So, why did they send you to me?" I said, without much interest.

"Lieutenant Chekta Jax said that sending you a call would be a breach of duty," the policeman whispered. "A subordinate must not interrupt the train of thought of his superior with Silent Speech."

"The train of thought, you say?" I said. "Well, well."

The boy would make a good Captain Foofloss, I thought. He won't make another General Boboota, though. He's not absurd enough.

I looked at the kid and said, "Listen to me very carefully, and pass this on to your colleagues, sir. If it's about work, you can send me a call at any time of day or night. And never mind subordination, even at the risk of being demoted to janitor— Oh, come on. No one's going to demote you. It was a joke. I always make bad jokes in the morning."

"I'll remember that," said the policeman, shocked, not by what he feared was my premonition but because I had called him "sir."

"Better tell me what's going on there," I said, looking at the sky, which was getting lighter by the minute. "It's too early for action today."

"There's a horrible new creature there now. I don't know what it's called. Lieutenant Chekta Jax told me to go get you immediately, so I didn't have time to take a good look at it."

"All right," I said, suppressing a yawn. "Let's have a look at it."

I pulled over by the gate of the Green Petta Cemetery and dashed to the scene of the crime.

"Sir Max, there they are! I ordered the boys to open fire with the Babooms, but they're useless against them."

I had never seen Lieutenant Chekta Jax so bewildered. He pointed at the crowd of undead with a trembling finger. Their disheveled appearance not only disgusted me, it bored me to death. Everything looked exactly the same as it had two days ago.

"Of course the Babooms are useless against them," I said, yawning. "And, by the way, next time just send me a call. No need to stand on courtesy, Chekta. What if they'd started to scatter?"

"They . . ." Chekta trailed off.

"They what? Are they scattering already?"

"Well, no, but sometimes they get up and start ambling around among their graves."

Chekta sounded very uncertain, but I was too busy to pay attention to such minor details.

"Right. Now, tell everyone to get out of the way," I said. "The quicker the better."

Praise be the Magicians, I didn't have to say it twice. A moment later two dozen policemen were already in retreat, shuffling their feet some distance behind me. If anything, they were too quick. Then again, if I were them, I'd also want to be a safe distance from the battlefield. When some Max the Terrible is about to exterminate a bunch of no-less-terrible creatures, a prudent man hides in the cellar.

❀

My Lethal Spheres didn't let me down. The zombies fell on the ancient gravestones left and right. Out of the corner of my eye I caught a glimpse of red metal glinting in the rays of the rising sun. I turned my head in that direction and recognized—no, not the creature itself, for I couldn't tell one from another. I recognized the large earring that one of them wore.

The same ones, I said to myself. I knew it. It's been the same ones all along.

❀

"I'm so sorry, lad. I'm running late today," Sir Kofa Yox said behind me. "Sinning Magicians! You're almost done. How did you manage?"

"Not sure," I said in a raspy voice, and slumped down on the grass. It was too much for me. Sir Shurf Lonli-Lokli had once told me that firing three dozen Lethal Spheres at one go was just about the limit of human capability. I had just fired at least four dozen.

"What was the hurry?" said Kofa.

He clapped his hands a few times quietly, took a stroll to the pile of immobile bodies, and returned, happy with what he had seen.

"Was that all?" I said.

"Yes. When is all of this going to end, is what I'd like to know."

"It may never end," I said. "Today I realized for certain that these are the same guys as the first time. And probably the same as yesterday."

"That's news! What makes you so sure? Do you remember them that well?"

"I remembered one of them from the first time. He was here today, too."

I realized that I didn't want to sit on the wet grass any longer. It would be much better to lie down on it. And if I could close my eyes, too . . .

"Uh-oh, I see you're completely wiped out, son," said Kofa. "Ah, here's Sir Melifaro. Just in time."

"It took me just half an hour," said Melifaro. His voice seemed to be coming from somewhere far away. "I don't exactly live in the neighborhood. Max, do you like sleeping outside? Is this a custom in the Barren Lands? Do you lie down on the ground, cover yourself with a young concubine, and put an old nag under your head instead of a pillow?"

"Not funny," said Kofa. "You should take him home. I'm sure his bed is a lot drier than the grass."

"Hold on, guys." I made a colossal attempt to stand up. The attempt failed, but at least I was able to support myself on one elbow. "We've got to do something about the bodies," I said. "Burn them, maybe."

"I think I know what you mean, boy," said Kofa. "I don't think that . . . On the other hand, it won't hurt it if we try. Leave it to me, though. I have so many assistants here." He waved his hand in the direction of the policemen.

"That's great. Then do whatever you want with me. Sinning Magicians, it was so stupid of me not to take along the Elixir of Kaxar. I knew where I was going and why."

"May I humbly touch thy royal body?" said Melifaro. "I would never allow myself such liberties, but you are lying on the dirty, unwashed grass like a sack of your beloved royal horse dung."

"I think the grass has been washed," I said. "Why else would it be wet?"

Finally, I settled myself on the back seat of the amobiler, and Melifaro grabbed the levers.

"Take me to my place on the Street of Yellow Stones," I said. "Tekki's already seen me dead once—I think that's enough. She'll think that this is my usual state."

"Fine, if you say so. But you look very much alive to me," Melifaro said.

"Not for long," I said, and it was lights out for me.

I simply fell asleep. I slept soundly, the way only a very drunk man can sleep. Praise be the Magicians, Melifaro was kind enough to haul my body all the way up to the second floor, and not drop it in the hallway.

※

I woke up a bit past noon. I even had the strength to get up and take a bath. I didn't feel sick, just nauseatingly weak, like you feel sometimes during a bad cold. The weakness was gone after just one gulp of Elixir of Kaxar, and I was back in business.

On the table in the living room sat a jug of kamra. The delicious smell let me know that Tekki had made it and brought it over to me. Only she had such spices in her kitchen. All I had to do was to warm up this godsend of a drink. I took a sip of it and immediately sent Tekki a call to express my gratitude.

I didn't expect you to get up so soon, she answered. *Sir Melifaro said your entire Royal Harem was visiting you and that I shouldn't disturb you before evening. By the way, you can tell him that I bought his joke. You'll be delighted to see his reaction.*

I have a better idea. I'll tell him that my entire Royal Harem did visit me right after he left. He'll be green with envy.

Yeah, that's a good one, too. Will you be able to crawl to my place today?

If Sir Kofa and my harem let me, I'll definitely come. But later. Right now I'm not sure which World I'm in.

Ah, that's something no one knows for sure.

※

I got dressed and went to the House by the Bridge.

"Another dead man is alive!" Melifaro said, hiding from me behind the chair. "This will never end!"

"What's worse is that one living man is going be dead soon," I said. "What's with that story about my harem, man? What if my girlfriend didn't have a sense of humor?"

"Oh, come on," said Melifaro. "Your girlfriend not have a sense of humor? Impossible."

"It's happened to me before. More than once, mind you."

"Stop scaring me. I've heard enough scary stories already," Melifaro said.

"Is Kofa here?" I said.

"Why would he be here? He's been gone since morning. Probably gobbling down Xator Turkey in some *Rowdy Skeleton* or other. He said he'd be back, though. You can send him a call."

"Not now. I just wanted to know about the cremation yesterday."

"It went okay, as far as I know. They poured the red Yokki tar on the bodies, burned them like firewood, and buried the ashes. They say it stank like all get-out. Chekta's nose is permanently shriveled from the smell."

"I'll bet it was something to behold."

"It sure was."

"Where's Melamori?"

"Believe it or not, she's working. Someone bought an ancient figurine at the Murky Market and it disappeared a half hour later. Melamori set out in the company of three tough policemen to trail the guy who sold it. Not the worst entertainment in the world. Relax, she's all right. I just talked to her. She'll be back soon."

"Max," said Kofa, who had just walked into the office. "If I were you, I'd go home to rest right away. Nothing is happening at the moment, and it would be a shame if you weren't in tip-top shape tomorrow."

"Do you think tomorrow it will start all over again? Even after you burned them?"

"If the one who turned those poor creatures into what we had to burn was any good at it, cremation isn't going to stop them," said Kofa. "And I have reason to believe that whoever accomplished it was a true master."

"Great. What are we going to do then?" I said, almost beside myself.

"I told the policemen to stay there and keep watch," said Kofa. "If the undead should want to party once more, we'll have to return and kill them again. And again. And again, until Juffin gets back. I'm sure he can put them to rest once and for all."

"How about the Main Archive?" I said. "Has anyone tried looking in the Main Archive? Maybe the buriwoks know some way to—"

"What do you take us for?" said Melifaro. "Lookfi and I began digging for information yesterday. We spent all morning there, too. Nothing. Nada. Nothing even remotely similar has ever happened in this city before."

"Okay, then, we'll just have to wait for Shurf and Juffin." I was beginning to come to terms with the fact that the disgusting extermination of zombies would become a daily routine, like morning exercise.

"Then I'd better go get cleaned up," I said. "A sack of horse dung can't be a deputy of the Venerable Head of the Minor Secret Investigative Force, as far as I know."

"I am absolutely free tonight, so I can sleep in your chair," said Kofa. "I'd be happy to hold down the fort."

"Okay, but please send me a call if something happens," I said. "My sense of responsibility requires me to take part in every collective sacrifice."

"I will," said Kofa.

۞

The living dead, huh? I said to myself. The feeblest plot of the worst B movie. Why the heck should I be dealing with this plot every day when I had grown sick and tired of it long ago from TV?

This monologue cheered me up. Besides, I was visited by a vague, crazy thought, which hadn't quite taken the form of an idea . . . Even a weed needs time to grow roots and become strong. A few days, though. No more.

The rest of the day I spent spiffing myself up and pulling myself together, and I took my time with it. There's nothing more satisfying than playing the exhausted hero. If I had my way, I would do it day in and day out. But this time the play ended before midnight, when Kofa sent me a call.

Guess what, Max.

Okay, I'm on my way. It's getting worse, don't you think? It's happening more and more often now.

You can say that again.

۞

This time, Kofa and I arrived at the Green Petta Cemetery at the same time. The policemen seemed much more frightened than they had been the day before, probably because it was happening at night. By the dim light of a sliver of moon, the group of naked creatures looked much spookier. Even I shuddered at the sight.

"You take it easy today, Max," Kofa said. "You overexerted yourself yesterday. I can do it alone very easily."

"I don't doubt it for a second. Your method is much more efficient. You should teach me someday."

"All in due time," Kofa said. "You see, Magic that doesn't drain your energy takes a long time to master."

"I'm a quick learner," I said.

"Are you, indeed? You have so many virtues, lad. Who would have thought? But today I'm going to go for something different. I think you're going to like this trick even more. I daresay you haven't seen anything quite like it before."

From the pocket of his looxi Sir Kofa Yox produced a small pipe, examined it very carefully, and lit it up.

For a few minutes he just stood there smoking. I could only admire his deliberate puffing. Then I realized that all this time Kofa had only been inhaling. He hadn't exhaled the smoke a single time.

Then Kofa walked toward the group of undead, who were shuffling around aimlessly. He stopped a few feet away from them and exhaled a cloud of thick reddish smoke. There was so much of it that it was as if a whole peat quarry were on fire inside Kofa's chest. I closed my eyes instinctively, then opened them and saw the undead fall to the ground. In a matter of minutes, Kofa's magic smoke had killed almost all of them.

"There's that one with the earring again," I said, spotting the reddish glow of metal. "You were right, Kofa. Burning them was absolutely pointless."

"The worst part is that they're coming more and more often now, as you may have noticed," said Kofa. He wiped his forehead. "I shouldn't have tried showing off. That trick with the smoke takes a lot of energy. And all that just to find out a few hours later that the trick was in vain. We need to think of something else. Pretty soon we'll just have to move here permanently. Unfortunately, our almighty colleagues aren't going to be back for a long time."

"Maybe I can ask Lady Sotofa Xanemer to help us," I said hesitantly.

"I'm afraid that she won't be much help here. The Order of the Seven-Leaf Clover doesn't like dealing with death and the dead. It's not so much that that they loathe it as that they don't know *how* to deal with it. It seems to be their only weakness."

"Well, we're out of luck, then. There is Sir Maba, of course."

"Maba Kalox?" Kofa said. "He's not too keen on helping Juffin out, even though they seem to be friends. But go ahead, try him."

I sent a call to Maba Kalox.

Don't fret, Max. Your problem is not a problem at all. In a few days' time you'll see for yourself.

If I don't fret, Echo will be crowded with undead very soon. The Echoers will be thrilled, I'm sure.

You talk just like Juffin. Neither of you can stand Echoers, but the very thought of something threatening their dormant lives keeps you from sleeping at night. It's up to you, though. If you fancy this storm in a teacup, who am I to stop you from making your own mistakes?

After that Maba Kalox fell silent. That was his way. Any further attempts to establish communication with him were fruitless and ended with me breaking out in a sweat.

"Kofa, you're clairvoyant," I said sighing bitterly. "Our magnificent Sir Maba Kalox said we shouldn't fret because, you see, our problem is 'not a problem at all.' And that was that."

"Maba Kalox never speaks idly," Kofa said. "He's very enigmatic and sneaky—and this time he's being extremely sneaky. I wish I knew what he meant by that."

"Maybe he meant to say we shouldn't kill them anymore?" I said. "Maybe we should let them roam the streets and wait for something extraordinary to happen."

"I'm afraid this is not the kind of experiment we can afford to make," Kofa said. "But 'don't fret' sounds very appealing to me."

❦

We went back to the House by the Bridge, waited for Melamori to arrive, planted her in Juffin's chair, loaded the responsibility for everything in the world on her fragile shoulders, and went home. It was clear that we needed to use every opportunity we could to relax and get some rest.

Another call came at sunset. This time Kofa and I took Melifaro with us. The undead had begun to seem like annoying old acquaintances. The daily battle in the cemetery was a dull routine, and my feelings about it lacked so much as a hint of metaphysical trepidation.

"Wait a minute, guys," I said. I thought I had found the solution to the problem. "What if we tried talking to them? How come we didn't try it right away?"

Melifaro grinned, and Kofa shrugged.

"Because . . . Go ahead and try it."

I approached a group of the undead. I looked for the one with the red earring. I almost thought of him as an old classmate.

"What's the deal, guys?" I said. "Why do you keep rising from the dead? Maybe we can help you?"

My "classmate" with the earring stared into the distance, as if he didn't even notice me. His buddies also ignored my interrogation.

"Well, say something already, darn you!" I said.

One of the undead shuddered, turned to me, and opened his toothless mouth. "U-u-u-u-u-uh," said the creature very seriously.

"Thank you very much," I said. "That was extremely informative."

"I think the first round of diplomatic negotiations is over," said Melifaro. "Now, let's get down to business."

And that's just what we did. Several moments later it was finished. Or was it?

It's like I'm being forced to act in the worst possible soap opera, I thought, as I drove my coworkers to the Right Bank, away from the Green Petta Cemetery that we had all grown to hate. How many times do we have to kill these repellent living dead? Where are my silver bullets? Wait, silver bullets only work against werewolves and vampires. How do you kill the undead? Sprinkle them with holy water?

That last idea seemed so good to me that I almost crashed into a large Vaxari tree that grew near the House by the Bridge. The daft idea vanished from my crazy head for the time being.

"Go get some rest, guys," I said. "I'm on duty tonight. I have to be useful every now and then."

"I don't need any rest," said Melifaro. "And I'm not in the mood for it."

"Okay, you can stay, then. We'll order a nice dinner, munch away the hours, and feel sad," I said. "Kofa, do you want to join us?"

"No, thank you. I'm going to visit a few taverns and listen to what people are saying. Undead or not, life goes on. Who knows what may be happening in Echo?"

He passed his hands over his face. His new countenance remained immobile for a moment. Then his thick red eyebrow shot up in a sly arch.

"Bon appétit, boys. Have fun."

"Fun is all we need now," said Melifaro.

And then it dawned on me. Just like that, all of a sudden. The way it usually happens. "Sculptures . . . What are sculptures made of in Echo?"

"All kinds of materials," said Kofa. "I've never been too keen on applied arts, however."

"You're probably thinking of erecting a monument to yourself," said Melifaro. "It's high time you did."

"All right," I said. "Kofa, your tavern-hopping will have to wait, I'm afraid. Step into my office. There's something I want to discuss with you."

❀

"Here's what I think," I said. "As I see it, we don't need to destroy our visitors from the next world. What we don't want is that those nimble fellows start roaming the streets, right?"

"Right," said Kofa. "I thought that was obvious."

"I know, I know," I said. "That was just a prelude. Now, listen to me very carefully. I think we can turn our pesky friends into statues. Pour molten metal or something like that over them. Some craftsman will know what would work best. Then we can leave them alone until Shurf can incinerate them for good."

"Brilliant!" said Melifaro, laughing. "But why incinerate them? It's conceptual art! The sculptures will be an excellent embellishment on the Left Bank. Better yet, let's auction them off."

"Wait, stop laughing for a second, Ninth Volume," I said. "Let me talk to a reasonable person. Kofa, what do you think? Can this be done?"

"We should try it, at any rate. It's a wild idea, but—a hole in the heavens above you, Max—why not give it a shot? We'll be needing professional advice, though."

❀

For the next several hours I felt like a true boss. My subordinates ran around Echo's shops and studios recruiting volunteers. They even got Sir Lookfi, whose responsibilities normally fell within the vaults of the Main Archive, on board. I was loafing around in the office. Sir Kofa thought that my Mantle of Death would not necessarily further mutual understanding between the sculptors and us.

There was, however, one task I could manage. Melamori left the hoob with me. His appearance could also throw off our volunteer helpers. For the first two hours Leleo missed Melamori and wouldn't eat the crumbs that I offered him. Then hunger got the better of him. He gobbled down his treat and purred softly. This small achievement made me very happy.

I listened to his sweet purr, thinking of our upcoming deliverance. Yet thoughts about holy water were still wandering through my poor, crazy head. The problem was that there was no way to get hold of holy water in the Unified Kingdom: there were no churches, no priests, no religious superstitions.

If my plan with sculptures doesn't work, I'm going to have to fumble around in the Chink between Worlds, I thought. Who knows, maybe I'd be able to fetch a crucifix or something like that. Or should I run home real quick? There is a lot of that paraphernalia there. After all, I didn't learn to travel between Worlds for nothing. I wasted a whole year on that trip. There must be some good that I can do for society with all my training in True Magic, after all.

These thoughts seemed like innocent fantasies, inconsequential plans that would never materialize. But I derived a great deal of pleasure from such musings.

"Max, I'm back." Melamori was standing in the doorway. "How's my Leleo doing? Has he missed me?"

"No, he hasn't. He's been with me. I fed him, too."

"Aw, you traitor, you," said Melamori, laughing. "I thought he only took food from my hands."

"He also thought so at first. But then he realized that hoobs can be wrong. Well, did you manage to recruit anybody?"

"Of course I did. I brought you all the apprentices of Mr. Yuxra Yukkori. Yuxra said he'd come, too, when he finishes some work he's doing. But trust me, this is not going to happen for another dozen years. Mr. Yuxra Yukkori is the most leisurely person in the Universe. Once he did some work for my father. For six months he kept telling Korva that it wasn't going to work—that's Yuxra's favorite way of getting started on a job. Then he worked for two years and fashioned something that was all wrong. But Father liked it so much he agreed to take the piece anyway. Then Mr. Yuxra Yukkori said that he was so proud of his work that he didn't want to sell it. Long story short, my father paid three times the amount they had originally agreed on, and became the happy owner of a sculpture that didn't fit inside the house. Yuxra Yukkori hadn't bothered to stick to the original dimensions, either."

"A true artist," I said. "That's the way to go, I say. You know, Melamori, perhaps it's for the best that Mr. Yuxra Yukkori is busy. We have a lot of problems already. I hope his apprentices are more sane."

"You bet they are. He's really cruel with them. You know, I think geniuses make the biggest tyrants."

"You're right about that," I said. "Okay, you can take your hoob and go home. I'm sure you're about to collapse."

"Well, not quite. But I'd be happy to go home and lie down, read a book, and eat ice cream. But if you go back to that cemetery again, who's going to stay in the House by the Bridge? Kurush?"

"I haven't decided yet. Either Kurush or Melifaro. I'll see about that."

"I'm so glad I don't have to drag myself to the cemetery," Melamori said. "I hate dead bodies. The ones from the Magaxon Forrest at least bore some resemblance to people."

"They did," I said. "I think your hatred toward the dead is hereditary. Kofa told me that the dead are particularly loathsome to your relatives in the Seven-Leaf Clover."

"That's true."

Melamori sat Leleo gently on her shoulder and left. I felt like a kind uncle.

❀

Half an hour later, Sir Kofa and Melifaro returned in the company of a team of Echo's finest sculptors. Lookfi Pence sent me a call, boasting proudly that he had managed to send a few "true masters" to the House by the Bridge. You might have thought I was going to order them to cast my own bust in bronze. After his report, Lookfi asked me if he could go home. Of course I let him go. He had already worked overtime, which, according to Sir Kofa, hadn't happened in more than seventy years. We had enough people already: the sculptors were crowding the reception room.

"I think I should treat them to dinner at the Ministry's expense," I said. "What will Sir Dondi Melixis say? I'm emptying the Treasury much more rapidly than Juffin does. The sculptors' fees alone are going to be astronomical."

"He will say, 'Thank you very much, Sir Max,'" said Kofa. "And you know why? Because he lives on the Left Bank, just a few minutes' walk from the Green Petta Cemetery. In a sense, we are guarding our Dondi's well-being."

❀

Sadly, our volunteers didn't have time to dine at our expense. Lieutenant Apurra Blookey sent me a call: it was happening again.

"The Treasury has been saved, huh?" said Melifaro.

"Yes," I said. "Which was to be expected, at the rate these guys are regenerating."

Again we went to the Green Petta Cemetery. Boy, was I sick of that route. A cavalcade of official amobilers of the Ministry of Perfect Public Order followed us. We had just enough vehicles to fit in all the sculptors, along with the materials and tools of their trade.

"Stay with them," I said to Melifaro. "What a way to pass the time—hanging out behind the cemetery gate while we're dealing with the undead. I'll call you when Kofa and I have finished. Cheer them up while you're waiting. You're good at that."

"I *used* to be good at it," said Melifaro with a sigh. "I haven't been myself lately."

※

Kofa and I got down to work. A few minutes later it was finished, and I sent a call to Melifaro. He came with the group of sculptors. To my delight, they looked curious rather than scared.

"It seems we *have* been reduced to driving in nails with a microscope after all," I said. "Never saw it coming. All right, gentlemen, it's show-time. May the Dark Magicians be with you."

"We can't manage here without them, that's for certain," said Kofa, sitting down on a gravestone beside me.

"What's with those microscopes, Nightmare?" said Melifaro. "You've been going on about them for quite some time. What do they look like?"

"Oh, it's a well-guarded secret," I said. "What I'd like to know is, would Madam Zizinda agree to send our dinner down here to the cemetery if we asked her nicely?"

"You're full of brilliant ideas today," said Kofa. "Let's find out."

Madam Zizinda turned out to be a fearless woman who valued a steady income above all else. Twenty minutes later we were all munching away. It was the strangest picnic in my life. The three of us sat comfortably on gravestones, and moments later we were joined by Lieutenant Apurra Blookey and the other policemen. Our heroic sculptors left their work from time to time, came up to us, and grabbed a piece of Chakatta Pie or a glass of Jubatic Juice. Not only did they feel comfortable, they had also cheered up considerably.

"Look, this one is a true beauty!" Occasionally, one of them showed us his creation proudly. The sculptors poured liquid stone on the zombies, which quickly hardened in the open air. The results could easily have served as the top draw at some infernal art biennial.

"Is that liquid stone hard enough?" I said to one of the sculptors.

"Harder than the natural stone," he said. "You won't regret it."

But I felt uneasier by the minute.

"You don't like your own idea anymore?" said Kofa compassionately. "It happens. Don't be sad. I'm almost sure this is going to solve our problem."

"That's the thing—almost. Anyway, we'll see about that."

۞

By the morning, our helpers were finished, and they went home.

"Shall we go?" said Melifaro, jittery with impatience. "All's well that ends well. I think we've made a great gift to our beloved city, gentlemen. This will make one heck of a tourist attraction. They look like souvenirs from the Epoch of Orders. They don't make them like that anymore."

It really was a scene to behold. The stone-clad bodies of our restless undead comprised a phantasmagorical sculpture group. But I found it very unsettling. It was too realistic. I expected the lifelike stonework to start moving again at any second.

"You go ahead, fellows. I'm just going to sit here a bit longer," I said. "I have this strange feeling in my heart . . . my two hearts, that is. After all, it was my crazy idea, so I need to deal with the consequences."

"What are you talking about, Max? What consequences?" Kofa said. "It was an excellent idea. By the way, according to my estimations they should have started coming alive again already, but . . ."

He approached the figures lying on the ground and looked at them long and hard. Some minutes later, he turned to me and said, "Sinning Magicians, Max! You were right!"

"Are they moving?" I said, horrified.

"It's starting again? Well, a hole in the heavens above this blasted World! The predictability is killing me," said Melifaro with unexpected vehemence. Where had his benevolent spirits gone? I wondered.

"Either I'm hallucinating, or . . . Yes, they are definitely moving. No need to stare at them—the movement is almost impossible to discern with the naked eye. This liquid stone isn't bad. Not bad at all," said Kofa.

"You don't seem to be too worried about it," I said.

"Why should I be? Of course they've revived again, but they're hardly able to stir at all, and that's wonderful."

"I guess you're right," I said. "Let them twitch all they want. At least they won't run off now, which was what we wanted to prevent, I suppose."

"That's the spirit," said Kofa.

Melifaro was smiling again. His bad moods were the most volatile substance in the world, praise be the Magicians.

I pondered the situation and said, "Still, I think I'm going to stay here. It would be rude to leave our innocent policemen alone with these newfangled sculptures. Who knows what's going to happen? You've earned the right to get some rest. Melamori will be staying at Headquarters, and you can join her when you feel up to it."

"As you know, I just need a couple of hours of sleep," said Kofa. "Then I'll help her."

"And I, as you know, need much more than just two hours," said Melifaro. "I'm taking a vacation. I've had it up to here."

"Deal," I said. "You're on vacation, then. But only until noon."

"You are a tyrant—nay, a despot," Melifaro said. "I don't envy your subjects."

"Sure. When the delegation of nomads arrives in Echo, will you be a good sport and lecture them on my autocratic atrocities? Maybe they'll change their minds about me. Good morning to you, guys."

They left and I stayed, half asleep on a gravestone. A new shift of policemen had just arrived, headed by Lieutenant Chekta Jax. They were staring in horror at the sculptural group, the authorship of which I attributed to myself deep down in my two hearts.

I decided to play it safe.

"Chekta," I said. "Send one of your boys to the city. We need a rope or a thin metal wire. At least two hundred yards. The more the better. I'll explain what to do with it when I wake up.

I stretched out on the lush cemetery grass and fell asleep. I dreamed I was going back to the World where I had been born. I think I was on the same streetcar that had once taken me to Echo. This time, though, I had to pay the fare, and for the life of me I couldn't remember where those "little round metal objects," as Anday Pu put it, had gone. The ticket taker was leaning over me, threatening to throw me out if I didn't pay—out where, as far as I knew, there was nothing but complete and utter emptiness. I heard a menacing cough from the driver's cabin. In the dream, my situation was getting worse by the minute. If I hadn't been lucky enough to wake up, I would have been a goner for sure.

I awoke to a clamor of loud chattering. The policemen had brought the rope and wire. It took me a while to remember why I'd asked them to fetch it. When I woke up I was absolutely certain there was only one thing that could put the undead out of their misery forever: holy water. Magicians only knew which particular low-budget horror film I had gotten this idea from, but my idée fixe seemed to augur a bout of upcoming madness.

This time, however, I managed to drive my obsession away and even remembered what I was going to do with the ropes.

"I want you to do some work for me, boys," I said. "I want you to tie up those sculptures. Tie their legs and arms. Tie them tightly, like you'd tie a real criminal. Mind you, I'm not going to help you, so you're going to be on your own. It's in your best interests to do your job as well as you can."

The policemen got down to work. Lieutenant Chekta Jax walked around them looking dissatisfied, and barked out unnecessary orders. I wanted to intervene, but then I thought, what business did I have poking my nose into the way he treats his subordinates? He wasn't going to change. It was a sober and reasonable thought, but it was too unlike the regular thoughts of the Max I liked to be. I was about to start brooding about the matter, but then I dropped it altogether. It was clear that I was just tired. Too tired for that kind of self-scrutiny.

"It moved!" I heard some young policeman scream. "This statue, it—"

"Shut up!" said Chekta. "Keep doing what you were doing and stop talking nonsense."

"It's not nonsense," I said quietly. "They are moving. That's why you are tying them up, not because it gives me some kind of perverse pleasure."

And I lay down on the grass again. Lieutenant Chekta Jax looked at me in disbelief but didn't say anything.

An hour later, the policemen had finished the job. The stone-clad bodies of the undead lay on the ground, their legs and hands bound. I was free to go home, which I did very happily.

❀

On my way, I mustered my remaining strength to stop by the House by the Bridge. To my delight, Sir Kofa Yox was already there.

"I told the policemen to tie them up," I said. "Now they can twitch and jitter all they want. Juffin's going to be back in a week, and everything will be fine then."

"A week? What's a week?" said Kofa.

"Just seven days," I said. "There's a strange place where people have devised this peculiar way of counting days."

"Just don't tell me that's the way they do it in the Barren Lands," said Kofa, smiling. "I don't like prying into other people's secrets, but I'm tired of pretending to be an idiot."

"Fine, then I won't bother telling you that that's the way they do it in the Barren Lands," I said.

"Good. Go get some sleep, Max. You look exhausted. I think you can relax now that you've told the policemen to tie up our fidgety friends."

"But if anything happens—"

"If anything happens, I'll send you a call. I promise. Now, scram, and go dive under your blanket."

❀

I went home to the Street of Yellow Stones. It wasn't Tekki's fault that the undead kept coming back to life, so it wouldn't be fair to make her suffer having to contemplate my gloomy face—which definitely wasn't all that attractive at the moment.

Even though I was wiped out, I couldn't sleep. I tossed and turned and thought about my little bedroom on the Street of Old Coins. I would surely have fallen asleep there in no time. All I'd have to do was close my eyes, and the Door between Worlds would open . . . A feverish fog appeared before my eyes, purging the rest of my thoughts. I was burning up. That's not good, I thought.

I thrashed around under the covers for about three hours. Then I went down and took a bath, and drank a whole glass of Elixir of Kaxar. It was an overdose, but I was feeling wretched. I had begun to forget that you could feel like this, and that you had to struggle against it.

After I downed the Elixir, the good spirits that I hadn't even dared hope would return came back in almost no time. I lit up a cigarette and sent a call to Sir Kofa.

I can't sleep. Very unlike me. What's up in the cemetery?

I guess you might say it's fine. Our petrified friends try to budge from time to time, but to no avail. So you should try going back to sleep.

344 / **MAX FREI**

I wish I could. I think I'm going to go back to the House by the Bridge. Beats staying at home.

And I began to dress.

꽃

Everything was quiet at work. Melifaro was sitting on top of Juffin's desk swinging his legs. Even that idyllic sight couldn't put me at ease. I was on pins and needles.

"Remove the stick from your backside and let it air," Melifaro taunted.

"Right, right," I said absentmindedly. "I'm going to the cemetery to see how things are going over there."

I didn't even hear Melifaro's answer. What had gotten into me? All my thoughts had evaporated except for a single idea that went around and around in my empty head. This was the idea of the holy water, which I could only obtain in my homeland, "the land of my ancestors." Why am I suddenly so preoccupied with my homeland? I wondered. I usually can't even stand thinking about it. But look at me now!

The Green Petta Cemetery was very quiet. The stone statues, their arms and legs bound, lay exactly where we had left them. Horrified, I wondered how those poor creatures must feel. Blessed are the poor in imagination! Now I simply *had* to conduct the experiment with the holy water, the sooner the better—if only to put them out of their misery. Slowly but surely, I was becoming obsessed.

꽃

I left the cemetery determined to go back home to my half-forgotten and none-too-cozy World. I could get a few gallons of holy water in the nearest church—that wouldn't be a problem. Clichéd plots should develop according their own strict laws, I thought. And I am the only person in the Unified Kingdom who knows these laws inside and out. That's why I have to be the one to draw this protracted horror story to a close. While I'm at it, I'll give the guys a treat. I've been meaning to show them a few good movies. The only thing that this otherwise perfect World is missing is great movies.

This time I was operating completely on autopilot. I didn't send a call to the wise Lady Sotofa or to Maba Kalox. I don't even think I would have asked Juffin's advice if he had been around. I didn't need advice. I was afraid someone would try to talk me out of this insane trip. Back then I was sure that the idea of this short visit home was all my own. It never occurred to me that this might not be the case.

❧

"What's wrong, Nightmare? Are things that bad at the cemetery?" Melifaro said in a worried tone.

I looked around and realized that I had somehow managed to return to the House by the Bridge without noticing it.

"Uh, no. No worse than they were in the morning," I said. "But while I was there I had another idea. I think I know how to get rid of those poor dead fellows once and for all."

"Sweet," said Melifaro. "How?"

"It's not too difficult, but we'll need a special magic potion that you can't buy in your average magic potion store. So I'm going to go get it. The sooner I leave the better."

"And how far do you have to go to get it, may I ask?" Melifaro was getting suspicious.

"Pretty far. But I'll be back soon. I should be back by morning. Maybe even sooner, though you never know beforehand with these things."

"Are you sure it's absolutely necessary? It's not the end of the world, you know."

"It is," I said stubbornly. "We just got used to it, but in fact it is the end of the world. So, good day to you, pal."

"Max, are you really coming back soon?" Melifaro was visibly worried.

"Come on, do you think you can get rid of me that easily? Dream on. You won't even begin to miss me."

And I hurried out of the Ministry of Perfect Public Order. I left my amobiler parked at the entrance. My little house on the Street of Old Coins was a stone's throw away—no more than ten minutes, if you walked fast. And today I was rushing like a bunch of Mutinous Magicians was hot on my heels.

❧

My first apartment didn't look like it had been abandoned, even though I had only been there once, and only for half an hour, in the past year and a half. No stale air, no oppressive atmosphere, not even a layer of dust. That was a miracle in itself.

I ran upstairs to the small bedroom. If I had understood Juffin's laconic explanation correctly, this bedroom was my personal entrance to that unfathomable place the boss referred to as the Corridor between Worlds. Through the Corridor I could get to any place I wished. For example, I could get to the World I had happened to be born in, the World from which I had fled not so very long ago, obediently following Juffin's instructions. Back then, though, I had used a regular streetcar.

I had reason to hope that a year of wandering through the labyrinth of unknown Worlds, of which I could hardly remember anything, had not been in vain. I was certain I'd be able to find my way home—and, even more important, my way back to Echo again. That was why I walked into the trap voluntarily. I lay down in bed, closed my eyes, and finally relaxed. Sinning Magicians, what was I thinking?

And then, what happened, happened. I yawned and fell asleep, certain I was going to dream of the mysterious Corridor between Worlds, the place where there was nothing, not even me—although I would have to be there, of course, for where else could I be? And among the infinite Doors to endless Worlds, I thought I would find the Door to the World I was looking for, and then open it, and . . .

I woke up on my couch under a thin checkered blanket. I was cold, because it was the end of fall, and the heating wasn't working. I pulled the blanket up over my head to keep warm and tried to remember my dream. I had been dreaming about something wonderful, something completely improbable and mind-boggling, something . . . I couldn't quite remember what.

Now, looking back, I realize that my sudden awakening under my old checkered blanket might have been a worthy finale to my suicidal plan. Somehow I managed to forget absolutely everything that had happened to me. I thought I had just fallen asleep on that couch a few hours before, in the morning, as usual, and so hadn't gotten enough sleep. My dream, though, had been extraordinary, absolutely incomparable.

Fortunately, I never allow myself to forget my dreams. That part of my life has always been more important to me than the waking part. Since childhood I've had a clever method of retrieving my dreams before they slip away. I relax all the muscles in my body, close my eyes, and allow myself to doze off—not to fall completely asleep but just to doze off so that I find myself on the fragile, intangible threshold between dreaming and waking. A tried-and-true method.

It worked like a charm. Boy, did it work! All the memories of my life in Echo poured down on me. All of them at once. It was like swimming in a waterfall: it wasn't a question of whether you'd get wet but of making sure you didn't drown. There were too many details for my feeble mind to cope with, and the details were so real, so sweet . . .

Being the nitwit that I am, when I remembered the details of my life in Echo I thought it was just a dream. A long, fantastic dream that had, nevertheless, ended. I had never walked the mosaic sidewalks of Echo, never sat in the *Glutton Bunba* with Juffin Hully. Because Juffin Hully didn't exist. The others had never existed, either. All that existed was my endless loneliness and the boundless tenderness I felt toward my made-up characters. That's right, *characters*. That's why Sir Shurf Lonli-Lokli, the Master Who Snuffs Out Unnecessary Lives, the Mad Fishmonger, my imperturbable comrade in the most incredible and dangerous adventures, so resembled the famous Charlie Watts. And that's why Sir Kofa Yox looked like Commissioner Maigret. In what old Hollywood movie about a boxer had I seen Melifaro's handsome face? Even Lady Melamori—my unfulfilled, breathless romance—looked a little like a young Diana Rigg. It all made sense now. I had no idea I was such a cinephile. And Tekki . . . Well, if you think about it, she resembled me. I don't know from what associative cellar I had salvaged her black eyes and silver curls, but her manner of speaking was exactly like my own. There were no two ways about it. And the others? Where the hell did they come from? Who cares? The imagination of a delirious mind works in mysterious ways. However crazy our dreams may be, we wake up sooner or later.

Sooner.

Or later.

We. Wake. Up.

My right hand grasped the hard upholstery of the couch. I broke a few fingernails, but it seemed to me that the pain was coming not from my fingers but from the leather upholstery. I writhed like a dying animal, but a totally different kind of pain was tearing me apart. What does a man feel when his Universe is collapsing? Or, worse, what does a demiurge feel when the Four Horsemen of the Apocalypse ride roughshod over his new-made World? The time had arrived for me to find out.

I still don't know how I managed to withstand the horrible gnawing pain in my chest, to drive away the hordes of predatory rats that were eating my poor heart alive. I beat my head on the wooden armrest, hammered my ribs with my fists, bit my lips until they bled, and howled quietly, shuddering at the savage sound of my own voice. The whole nine yards.

※

Then I calmed down. Without waiting for the signal from the brain that had gone awry, my body began doing the famous breathing exercises of Lonli-Lokli. Magicians only knew how many jokes I had made about them in the past.

Let's make a deal, I told myself. You're going to get up and wash. Then you're going to make some coffee, drink a cup or two, smoke a cigarette, and put your thoughts together. Then, if you still feel like howling, you can do it till the cows come home. All right?

I tried to get up. My legs felt like they were made out of cotton, and I swayed back and forth. It was better than agony but worse than a bad hangover. I stayed upright, though, made it to the bathroom, and got into the shower. For a few seconds I stood under the stiff stream without realizing I had turned on the cold water. I howled and turned the hot water tap. All the better, I thought. I would never have agreed to subject myself to such extremes of my own volition.

After the torture of the alternating cold and hot water, I wrapped myself in the same checkered blanket (I had never had a bathrobe) and went to the kitchen to carry out the rest of my survival program. I stared blankly at the electric coffee maker, trying to figure out what it was. Then I remembered, and even recalled how to use it. The peaceful bubbling noise of the machine sent a jolt through my mind, and it spat out another piece of useful information: people brush their teeth in the morning. I saluted my mind, did an about-face, and returned to the bathroom.

While I was brushing my teeth, I examined my face in the mirror. Something was wrong, although I couldn't quite put my finger on it. I put the toothbrush back on the shelf and looked with disgust at the unshaven chin of my reflection. What I saw was pathetic: week-old stubble and long, tangled hair reaching almost to my shoulders. The only thing missing was a mammoth's bone between my teeth.

Then it struck me. I knew what was wrong with my reflection—it was the hair. It couldn't have grown that long, because just a week ago I had gone to Victor's to get a haircut. He had just gotten an electric hair-cutting gadget. I should be sporting a neat, short haircut, I thought, and there's no way my hair could have grown that long in a week. People cut their hair once in a while—wasn't that what Sir Juffin said at the very beginning of my wonderful long dream? And then I remembered some charming old lady, the powerful witch Lady Sotofa Xanemer, who told me to look after my shaggy, disheveled head. My *shaggy* head. I was onto something. All I needed was to figure out why my hair looked as unattractive as—

Off you go to the kitchen, I told myself. We had a deal, remember? First you drink your coffee, then you go insane, if that's what you really want to do.

So off to the kitchen I went.

On the way it occurred to me that I might have gone to Victor's not a week but a whole year ago. Maybe I had amnesia? That possibility was comforting. Compared to everything else that was happening to me, it sounded sane and made a lot of sense.

I took the *TV Guide* from the table. No, the date seemed right. It was November. You can't confuse the dreariness of that month with anything else. The year was the same year it was yesterday. Also, according to the guide, yesterday they aired the last episode of *Twin Peaks*. That's correct, my dear Watson. After the TV show I was going to go for a walk on Green Street, because Sir Juffin Hully from my dreams said that—

I broke into a cold sweat and sank down on the stool in the kitchen. But of course, last night I went to Green Street, and then there was that mysterious streetcar 432. Holy cow! And the streetcar took me to another World, where, as it turned out, I felt right at home. It wasn't just that I felt good there. It was *right*! It was *the way it should be*! I was in my element there. I was indispensable there. God almighty! If I told this to anyone here, they would just laugh. Me, indispensable? Getting along without me is the easiest thing in the world. That's what they do from morning till night, day in and day out. And they do it very well, let me tell you.

Drink your coffee, I said to myself. Who else do you think I made it for?

I stood up, grabbed a cup, poured some coffee, took a sip, and almost spat it out. Looks like I'm losing it, I thought. I forgot that I usually take sugar in my coffee.

I found the sugar bowl and put a few funny-looking white cubes in my cup. Now the coffee tasted heavenly. My head started spinning at the long-forgotten smell. I lit up and stared at my reflection in the dim screen of an old TV set. My reflection gave me a vague sense of hope. "Hope is a darn-fool feeling," someone had once told me. That someone was Sir Mackie Ainti, the old sheriff of Kettari, another imaginary town where I had once spent some marvelous moments.

I finished my coffee, poured myself another cup, and decided it was time to begin an investigation. If I was going to think anyway, I might as well start thinking logically. I could deal with my unruly locks right now. The phone was just an arm's length away. Granted, in this apartment everything was an arm's length away, no matter what corner you retreated to. I wavered a bit before making the call, then brushed my doubts aside. Victor was also an oddball, and he had long ago gotten used to my eccentricities.

Thank goodness Vic was home. He picked up almost immediately, as though he had been waiting all day for my call.

"Hi, who is this?" he said after my incoherent variations on the theme of good morning.

"It's Max."

"Jesus, man! I didn't recognize you. What happened to your voice?"

"I don't know. I picked up some wicked germ," I said. "I wanted to ask you something."

"You wanted to? You don't want to anymore?"

I couldn't contain a smile, even though I didn't feel like smiling.

"Vic, did you give me a haircut with your miniature lawnmower about a week ago?"

"Bad conscience, huh? Have you finally decided to pay me for my job? What's my fee?"

"The standard lawnmowing fee, naturally. But you're not going to get rich, considering the minuscule area of my head," I said. "So, did you or did you not give me a haircut?"

"I did. But I disagree with the proposed fee. You see . . ."

I exhaled and mopped my forehead. Vic was saying something on the other end of the wire, but I couldn't focus. I already knew what I wanted to know. Now I had to figure out what to do with this new information.

"Max, is everything all right?" said Vic. "I'm talking and you're totally silent. It's usually the other way around. That 'wicked germ' of yours, is it serious?"

"No, I don't think it is," I said, surprised at the mixture of happiness and hysteria in my voice. "Thanks, Vic. I'll call you back later, okay?"

"Okay," he said. "Call me any time you want. I can't deprive you of that pleasure."

I hung up. One of the flimsy postulates of my not-yet-formed theorem had just been proven. My wonderful dream began to sound more and more like reality, although I still couldn't wrap my mind around it. And who could?

"Quit whining, mister," I said to my scruffy reflection. "There's something else besides your haircut. How many hearts were pounding in your chest when you were dialing Vic's number? One or two? Huh? I say two."

I finished my cold coffee and stared at the linoleum floor, darkened with age. Then I conducted an experiment. I spat on the floor and looked at the results: an ugly black hole on a smooth gray surface. My infamous venom, which required that I wear the Mantle of Death, was still with me. Very interesting.

I should go out and test it on somebody, I thought with a nervous laugh. If he dies right away, than it was all true. If he just punches me in the face, then . . . Oh, well, since I don't have a potential victim, I'll just use the floor.

Another small black burn appeared on the floor next to the first one. Then I snapped the fingers of my left hand. How were my Lethal Spheres doing? The Lethal Spheres were doing great. A tiny blob of blinding green light rolled through the kitchen and burst when it hit the wall. That's right, there's nobody to kill here, I thought. Except for the cockroaches, but they had prudently scurried away.

So all of my dangerous talents were still with me. I could relax and forget about any further experiments. Regular people don't juggle little fireballs in their kitchens and burn linoleum with their spittle. And then I realized, with relief and horror at the same time, that there was no *me*, and hadn't been for quite some time. Sitting in my kitchen was Sir Max from Echo. Ladies and gentlemen, meet the very real Max the Terrible. He had left his Mantle of Death on the floor of the bedroom on the Street of Old Coins. And he was in trouble.

But unlike my good old friend Max, who had had a haircut just a week ago at his friend Victor's, *Sir* Max from the Minor Secret Investigative Force of the City of Echo was capable of handling any metaphysical problem, big or small. In any case, that's what I was hoping.

The revelation was so powerful that I tried to ignore it. That was the only way to save whatever was left of my sanity. I took the bag with coffee from the shelf again, poured fresh water in the coffee maker, and turned on the TV. If there was anything I had learned from spending years at the epicenter of magic, it was the art of remaining aloof.

Interesting things were happening on the TV screen. Airplanes were taking off, fat men in suits were shuffling around, loud sounds resembling human speech came from the speakers. Then a homely middle-aged man with an intelligent expression told me that the president of the United States had flown to Japan for some reason.

"That's very wise of him," I said, lighting up another cigarette. "To Japan, you say? Well, well. It's high time he did."

The anchorman responded by trying hard to unsettle me. He very warmly broached the subject of the lowering of the exchange rate of the dollar against the Japanese yen.

"Oh, really?" I said. "Well, what about the exchange rate of Kumonian doubloons, huh? See, since morning I've been feeling uneasy in both of my hearts about the state of the Kumonian currency."

While I was bickering with the TV, my mind tried desperately to reach some balance. It failed, but it was better than not trying at all. By the time a lively lady in a blue sweater started blaring out some phantasmagorical sports news at me, I had realized two things. First, I had almost certainly lived in Echo for some time. My hair, venomous spit, and other charming attributes clearly testified to that, whatever the stubborn and prudent half of my personality might think about it. Second, I desperately wanted to go back. It wasn't just a matter of wanting to. Going back was the only solution to this unbearable situation. It was my only chance of survival.

I put down the empty cup on the table and went to get dressed. I needed to take a walk and collect my thoughts, which I can't really do when I'm sitting still. I'm much better at it when I'm on the move.

When I went into the hallway I realized I didn't have any warm shoes. Of course, I had been wearing my one and only pair of boots when I boarded the streetcar that had taken me to the wonderful Capital of the Unified Kingdom. Now they were lying there in one of my numerous closets—a souvenir of sorts from the homeland. I had no choice but to put on a pair of canvas sneakers—not exactly the footwear one would choose for walking in a cold November drizzle. I was lucky I hadn't taken my coat with me, as well.

After thinking about it, I decided to buy new shoes. I wasn't what you would call wealthy in this World, far from it, but at least I didn't have to economize, praise be the Magicians. I still had no idea how I was going to get out of here, but one thing I knew for certain: I wasn't going to stay here for long. No way. Besides, I was worried that my honestly earned talents might pave the way for a brilliant career in crime. One Lethal Sphere, and any bank teller would be willing to throw millions at my feet. Sure beats robbing 7-Elevens with women's tights pulled over your head.

By the time I got to the shoe store, my feet had turned into thick, barely usable frozen clumps. This informed my choice of new shoes. I had two basic considerations in mind. Number one, they must be warm. Number two, they must be very warm. And in addition to that, they had to be warm and waterproof. I didn't even give a thought to the price. I shelled out almost half of my savings for the new shoes. I threw my old sneakers away in a garbage can and grinned. If there was anything I'd never be able to get used to again, it was poverty.

I tried to estimate how much I was being paid in Echo for the services I rendered to His Majesty King Gurig VIII. I got mixed up for a few moments, numbers dancing around in my head, while I tried to figure out what the purchasing power of one Unified Kingdom Crown was. Finally, I arrived at some astronomical number: my salary was about a million US dollars or more a year.

Well, that's the most persuasive reason for returning as soon as possible, I thought, going back out into the unpleasant drizzle. Where else can you get paid that much to do your favorite work?

I wandered around aimlessly. The city where I had lived for several years now seemed a very strange place. High-rises, asphalt sidewalks, the roar of the engines of public buses—it all looked surreal. Most peculiar of all (and, frankly, very annoying) were the faces of the passersby. I had already gotten used to the faces of the inhabitants of another World. Compared to them, the faces of my compatriots looked quite unattractive, although I couldn't put my finger on what exactly was different about them.

Walking outside hadn't calmed me down. On the contrary, at some point I felt even worse. I had just gone down into an underpass. When I stepped on the dirty concrete floor of that dreadful catacomb, I understood the full horror of my situation. It was clear to me that I had no idea how I was going to return to Echo. It looked like I had only had a one-way ticket. Goodbye, my hopes. Fare ye well, and please tell Sir

Juffin Hully that he got mixed up with a total moron. Now, could you please try not to make too much noise driving nails in my brand-new coffin? Thank you.

The pain in my chest returned and brought me to my senses. Both of my hearts went crazy and attacked each other like fighting roosters. I think I must have been crying. In any case, some unidentified wet substance was making its way down my cheek. A fat woman in a red coat looked at me like I was mad, and gave me a wide berth. I *was* mad. Completely insane. Insane in the membrane.

It took me only a few seconds to hit rock bottom in the final circle of my very own hell. But when I did, my spirits soared. I remembered that I had my personal Door between Worlds in this city: the wonderful, handy little streetcar that was probably still running down Green Street. If I remembered correctly, Sir Maba Kalox had said that the Door was still open. Of course, a maniac murderer had once used it, and Juffin and I hunted for him high and low throughout Echo. But if he could use it, there was all the more reason I could, too. After all, the Door had been created for *me*. It shouldn't be a problem for me to use it again.

I laughed with relief. It looked very much like a fit of hysterics. Passersby, I'm sure, were amused, but I ignored their mistrustful looks. Someone's magnanimous hand was wiping off the writing above the Gates of Hell, the writing that read "Abandon All Hope, Ye Who Enter Here." It turned out that the dire warning had been written in plain chalk, not in letters of fire. My future again glowed with the bright lights of a fair. Hopes that had almost gone were now returning like swallows to their nests in spring. My head was spinning, this time because I was happy. I had to crouch down on my haunches—this sudden change of spirits had drained me of strength.

"Are you all right, young man?" A pleasant middle-aged woman was nudging me. "Are you all right?" she said.

"Don't pay any attention to me," I said. "I've simply gone mad. It happens sometimes." And I laughed again.

"I've never seen anyone so happy about such a turn of events. Well, I guess you're going to be fine, since you haven't lost your optimism," she said.

Her voice sounded familiar. No, not her voice but the intonations. Did I speak like that sometimes?

I raised my head to look at her, but she had already gone. Dozens of people were walking past me, and a dog was barking somewhere nearby. A moment later I realized the dog was barking at me. An angry man in a sweatsuit was trying to restrain a huge German shepherd on a leash. The hairs on the dog's back were standing on end. I shuddered, got to my feet, and went up into the street.

The rain had almost stopped. I walked slowly down the street slowly toward my house. I felt calm and light. I knew what I had to do, and I was not going to waste another minute. This walk did me a great deal of good, I thought, and now it's time to go back. After all, I had promised Melifaro that he wouldn't even begin to miss me. I had to keep my word.

I was very hungry and bought a hotdog. There was too much fat in the hotdog, and the bun was tasteless. I ate about half of it and threw the rest on the sidewalk. The bun attracted the attention of several sparrows, and a large bold crow hopped over to it. It was sure the hotdog belonged to it alone, and was now pondering how to bring this idea home to the sparrows. I smiled and walked away. Inside me, everything was peaceful and quiet. This mood was not really in keeping with the circumstances of my official visit to my homeland, but I deserved a break.

❦

I returned home and opened my small, shabby refrigerator. The failed culinary experiment with the hotdog on the street had only stimulated my appetite. Fortunately, I found cheese and some vegetable in the fridge. Nothing too exciting, but it was better than the disgusting hotdog.

After my little snack, I turned on the coffee maker again. While the alchemy of turning bitter and inedible seeds into a heavenly drink was taking place in the corner of the kitchen, I decided to experiment with Silent Speech. After my trip to Kettari with Lonli-Lokli, I knew that sending a call to someone in another World was virtually impossible. *Virtually*, however, did not mean *absolutely*. The question was: Whom should I start with?

Most of all I wanted to talk to Juffin, but that was clearly outside the realm of possibility. If time in the Unified Kingdom flowed at the same pace as it did here, Juffin was still trying to appease the mysterious Spirit of Xolomi. On the other hand, if time in each World had a mind of its own . . . Should I try it? I thought. But my second heart, the origins of which were still a mystery to me, had already contracted, suggesting that my attempt would fail. I could relax: that wise muscle was a very good adviser.

Then I remembered Sir Maba Kalox. The powerful, retired Grand Magician was an experienced traveler between Worlds. Maybe he'd want to chat with me as a fellow voyager? We could discuss a few common professional issues. I listened to the radar of my heart, but this time it was puzzled and silent. Perhaps it had no idea how the experiment would end.

I wasted almost half an hour trying to reach Sir Maba. This resulted in little more than a great quantity of perspiration spread evenly across the surface of my body.

I gave up with loud sigh of desperation and poured myself some coffee. What a marvelous concoction it was! It was the only thing I truly missed in the Unified Kingdom—although, come to think of it, there had been a brief but memorable time when I had had excellent coffee almost every day, thanks to Mackie Ainti, the old sheriff of Kettari. I remember him calling my favorite beverage "liquid tar," and asking me if I'd get sick from drinking it. Still, he was kind enough not to deny me a second helping. Hold on a minute . . . But of course! Mackie Ainti. Why didn't I think of him before? Mackie was the only person whose help I knew I could rely on in any World.

Mackie was . . . Frankly, I didn't really know who he was, that man with the red mustache and a face that was already a little blurry in my memory. I didn't doubt for a second that it would be easy for him to chat with me no matter where I was. The only thing that mattered was his mood, which worked in mysterious ways.

I put the cup aside and took a careful look at my reflection in the dim TV screen. The eyes of my distorted reflection shone with a cold light that frightened me. That was probably a good thing, I thought. A man with a pair of ordinary, dull eyes would hardly be capable of discussing the technical details of a magical journey from one World to another with an inhabitant of that other World.

I sent a call to Sir Mackie Ainti. Almost immediately I felt crushed by an immense weight, as though I had temporarily switched places with the muscle-bound Atlas said to support the heavens. But I was happy: the sensation was almost identical to what I had experienced when I communicated with Mackie on my return trip from Kettari to Echo. One doesn't forget such things easily.

Tough, huh? Mackie's Silent Speech betrayed a hint of compassion. *My apologies, Max, but I can be a pretty overwhelming interlocutor. Then again, everybody's got his faults. You're in trouble, I reckon?*

I suppose I don't have to tell you much. You probably know it all already.

More or less. Your World took you back. It happens.

Well, it didn't exactly take me back. I was all my fault. I—

Hold it right there. The last thing I want is to listen to your crazy theories. And it's for your own good. The only thing you should keep in mind is this: your World took you back, no matter what you think about it. It ain't that simple. It breaks down like this. There's a few hundred people in your World who know that you're living among them. I can't say they're really concerned about you, but you are a part of their lives. They're sure you're going to show up at work tonight. If you don't, they'll call you at home and you'll pick up the phone. If not tonight, then maybe tomorrow, or in a couple of years. Sooner or later you'll resurface, and for your acquaintances this is as obvious as the sky above. They don't even think about it. They know it. It ain't easy to just up and disappear. Their memories of you are what bind you to their reality, the World you were born in—the place you're supposed to be living until the day you die. That's how your mighty compatriots think about it, without even realizing their own mightiness. Too bad we can't put their powers to good use. But I digress. Get a load of this, Max. It ain't that difficult for you to return. You'll manage. You'll figure it out. Your kind always does. But remember, someday your World will take you back again. And again, and again. Until you're able to convince it that you don't exist anymore. Got it?

No, not really. Mackie, it's really hard for me to talk to you. Well, you know that already. Maybe you could just tell me what to do?

I just did. You need to convince your World that you don't exist. Convince everyone concerned, and do it in dead earnest. Your idea about the streetcar is a mighty good one. Keep working on it. But be prepared for a surprise. I reckon you forgot about the coachman. Whatever you call him. Is there a special word for what he does?

It's okay, I understand what you mean. He's called a driver. Sir Maba Kalox called him a Tipfinger. He told me something about him, but I didn't understand.

I can just imagine Maba's "explanations." Of course you didn't understand a lick of what he said. But that don't matter. Just remember that you shouldn't be afraid of him. Beating him is as easy as Chakatta Pie. Especially for you. But don't kill him—ask him a few questions first. He's your chance, Max. Be careful with him, though. The Tipfinger is the most cunning creature in the Universe. Or one of 'em . . .

His words were beginning to trail away. The weight was becoming unbearable. It was a miracle that I had managed to sustain the conversation for so long. Silent Speech had never been my strongest point.

Thanks, Mackie. These were the last words I could squeeze out. I decided not to postpone the words of gratitude for another time since I wasn't even sure that "other time" would ever come.

Happy to oblige. Don't fret. You'll pull it off. Just remember—

What I was supposed to remember would remain unknown because the invisible steamroller had smashed me against the kitchen wall. For some time I didn't exist in any World at all, but then I came to. My clothes were soaked with perspiration. I knew, however, that I had gotten off easy.

※

I went to the bathroom, took a shower, and put my wet clothes in the trash. I didn't think I'd be needing them anymore. No matter how hard it was to talk to the old sheriff of Kettari, talking with him had removed a huge weight from my shoulders.

Mackie doesn't speak idly, I thought. If he says I'll be all right, then I'll be all right. He approves of my idea to take the streetcar back to Echo, so that's great. If he says it will be easy for me to beat that creature in the driver's cabin, then it will be. He even says it will help me somehow. Perfect. If Mackie says so.

Now I felt like someone who had just bought a plane ticket or won the trip of a lifetime. I was counting the hours before my plane would take off, and I thought I should probably start packing.

Well, that was, of course, a metaphor. I didn't really have to pack anything to take back to Echo. I was taking no souvenirs. I doubted I'd want to keep a memento of this trip home and look at it during long winter nights. If anything, it would become a recurring theme of my future nightmares. But never mind, I'll get over it somehow, I thought. I didn't even want to take a packet of coffee with me. To the Magicians with it, I thought. Next time I go to Kettari to thank Sir Mackie Ainti, I'll get some at his expense. After all, I'm already used to kamra. It's a great thing, so I think I'll stick to it.

There was, however, one thing that I wanted to take back to Echo with me—not so much for myself as for Juffin and my other colleagues. I had been wanting to show them a good movie. I had been dying to see the expression of otherworldly curiosity on Sir Juffin Hully's face when the "Columbia Pictures Presents" credits appear on the TV screen.

Thank goodness there were VCRs, TVs, and cute, fat videotapes in my homeland. And thank goodness I had learned a nice, useful trick: I could easily take with me just about anything I wanted. Even the Statue of Liberty. All I needed to do was to shrink it down to almost nothing and place it between my left thumb and index finger. That was a piece of cake for me. Then again, what would I do with that Mother of All Exiles when I was back in Echo?

I was looking forward to exercising the tricks of my trade. I imagined with relish how I would carry off the entire stock of a video store in my mystical fist. Then it occurred to me that there was no need to rob a store. There was a video collection in this city that, until recently, I had considered mine. And what a fabulous collection it was, in spite of my humble income. One day, about a year before my departure to Echo, I had lost the entire collection along with my girlfriend. My former girlfriend, that is.

I poured the rest of the coffee into my cup, lit up, and pondered the breakup. It was a fairly nasty story. Nothing that stretched the limits of the imagination—just a regular nasty thing that regularly happened to regular people. The present-day me couldn't care less about that stupid page in the history of poor Max. I'd seen worse things happen to him. But the possibility of restoring justice intrigued me. That was my favorite pastime. If I could have my way, I'd be restoring justice every hour on the hour.

I looked at the clock, then at the calendar. Saturday, six p.m. Perfect. Just what I needed. At this hour Julia was usually home studying French. She would definitely run off somewhere later, but not before eight. Praise be the Magicians, her habits were absolutely invariable. It was habits like hers that kept the world going. I had had the opportunity to study her habits well for about two years. Two very good years. It's too bad the finale turned out so ugly. It fell far short of what would make a good soap opera.

When we first started seeing each other, I couldn't believe my eyes: could there still be such wonderful girls roaming the surface of this planet? She got almost all of my jokes, even those that were more risqué. Frankly, the risqué jokes were the ones she got best. Back then we laughed like crazy every day. She was always overjoyed to see me, and didn't get too upset when I disappeared for several days. That—combined with a clever face, beautiful eyes, and an independent spirit—was worth a great deal to me.

Everything was great. Life seemed not just tolerable but wonderful. I warmed up, relaxed, was tame enough to be hand-fed, and even purred occasionally. Would the two of us be able to turn human existence into a wondrous event? I wondered. If the relationship had lasted any longer, I probably would have learned to answer that question with a short and unequivocal "yes" rather than indecisive mumbling.

Then one day, my girlfriend told me that, sure, we were having a great time together, but . . . That ellipsis, as it turned out, meant that I had to learn a great deal about human nature, and I had to learn it the hard way. I learned that my beloved would soon be sharing her life with a so-called real husband. Free love, mind you, was all well and good, but a woman's got to think about a family and children. My constant presence hindered the realization of her matrimonial plans. So, I was told, we could keep seeing each other, but not as often. My one true love needed time to prepare for her happily-ever-after.

I'm afraid my reaction to the news was like that of an extraterrestrial. You might have thought I had never heard anything like it before. I felt I had been betrayed. The woman I trusted more that I trusted myself had swapped me for some abstract family happiness and the "maternal instinct." That's what I told her. Not the nicest thing to say, I realized, but all the other things that were on my mind then were even worse, and I never knew how to keep my mouth shut. In hindsight, now I know that it wasn't the worst breakup in my life. I've had worse. Much worse. But back then it all looked very different to me.

Long story short, I left and slammed the door. I disconnected the phone and tried to get myself back in shape for a couple of months. All of my love affairs had ended in a similar fashion. I should have gotten used to it by then. Everything has its price, and if you resolutely refuse to accept certain fundamental principles of human existence, don't be surprised when, sooner or later, people stop accepting you. They will extricate you gently from their lives, like a healthy organism rejects a foreign body, in the interests of survival.

But Julia was more than just another cute girl in a long line of short love affairs. I thought she was my good friend, and a wonderful exception to all possible and impossible rules. To hear from her the exact words I had heard from the others was a hit below the belt. And what a hit it was. I had always been an incorrigible idealist. It was even surprising that I could forgive representatives of the human race their daily trips to the bathroom.

For two months I was in a homemade hell, replete with crushed plans and childish resentments. Then I slowly began to pull out of it. Usually, I rehabilitate much faster. As Sir Mackie Ainti said, I am a survivor. Two months of high-quality agony was my absolute record. My affair with Julia had been worth it. At least I thought it was.

When I returned to life, I began missing my movie collection.

I should say that before I met Julia I hadn't had any movie collection to speak of because I had never had any decent equipment to watch movies on. I had never made much money and was a poor saver. In this regard, I had to agree wholeheartedly with Sir Anday Pu, that descendant of Ukumbian pirates, who often complained that "those little round metal objects" kept disappearing.

Julia had a top-of-the-line VCR and just a few lousy videos: her mom's favorite soap operas, a few action flicks, and her French lessons. She studied the damn language constantly, with all kinds of multimedia aids. I had never heard her put her knowledge to any use, though.

In a sense, Julia and I had achieved a kind of harmony: every time I went over to her place I bought a new movie. Over time, she even had to buy a special storage rack for them because the tapes tended to crawl around the house like cockroaches. I was absolutely sure that I was buying the movies for myself. One day, I thought, I'd buy my own VCR, but for the time being, I can relax and watch my favorite movies at my girlfriend's. What could be better?

Two months of deep depression greatly reduced my daily needs and expenses, so I managed to save a fair amount of money. Some of it I planned to spend on a VCR so I could watch the movies in my collection again. Not out of the corner of my eye, in bits and pieces, like before, but very attentively. Every movie from beginning to end. I had to kill time somehow.

The collection was in a nearly inaccessible place, however, and I had to address that issue. One day I managed to bring myself to call Julia. I said I was going to come over to get my tapes. "Okay," she said. I mustered my will, clenched my teeth, and went over to her place.

She greeted me in the doorway, saying firmly that it wasn't very nice of me to take the presents back. I could hear her mother clearing her throat significantly from the living room. Julia must have invited her for moral support.

"What do you mean 'presents'?" I said. "I bought the movies to watch with you, and—"

Her reply made it obvious that she was not going to give up the disputed property. "It's only fair," she said. "After all, you came over almost every day and ate my food. And food costs money. Probably even more than the tapes. Plus, I don't understand why you need them. You don't even have a VCR, and you're never going to get one. You're too frivolous. Granted, it's not so bad. In fact, Max, it's your best quality."

So we thrashed it out.

It was ridiculous and unfair to call me a sponger. I had never come over to see her empty-handed. I always brought her something: aromatic teas in small paper bags, tiny cookies that melted in your mouth, fruit, or sugarcoated flowers. I loved giving her presents, and I couldn't afford anything more extravagant than those little things.

Maybe she was right when she said I was living in a dream and had lost touch with reality. It had definitely never occurred to me that when I got up to make a sandwich in the middle of the night, a calculator began whirring inside the head of the woman I loved. That blow was the hardest. It was the ultimate and irreversible crash of my illusions. Who cared about a movie collection? I turned around and began walking downstairs, not bothering to wait for the elevator.

The last thing I heard was Julia's almost inaudible sigh of relief. But of course. She'd managed to keep the property that she'd grown accustomed to considering her own. And as far as she was concerned, I could go to the nearest junkyard, where I belonged.

An invisible and impenetrable barrier grew up between me and the rest of the world. Reality bore no connection to me anymore. It remained somewhere far, far away. And it wasn't really so bad. In any case, I finally stopped feeling bad. Or sad. Or anything at all.

Julia called a week later. She told me not to be angry and asked me if I wanted to see her. I said no. Then she called a few more times, saying she was sad that I hadn't been coming over to see her. I said I was too busy, but maybe next week, or in a month . . . Her voice didn't inspire any emotion in me anymore. I didn't understand what this strange woman wanted from me. Why the hell was she calling?

I never got around to buying a VCR. Even thinking about it made me sick. Half a year later, on a cloudy November day, I saw Sir Juffin Hully in my dream. That was when my life here ended once and for all.

✸

I finished my coffee in a single gulp and went to the bathroom to shave. I decided to drop in on Julia unexpectedly, like premature death, without bothering to call her first. Who knew what kinds of excuses she'd come up with? I just needed to get into her living room for a few minutes, and then . . . Surprise, surprise.

I must say I wasn't feeling anything even remotely resembling vengeance. I was possessed by a cold curiosity and an uncontrollable, merciless happiness that scared even me a little bit. I was going to have fun, and my mysterious second heart was telling me I was doing the right thing. Go ahead and do it, it told me. I didn't know what kinds of principles governed that cryptic muscle, but it sure didn't have an ax to grind with Julia. When my affair with Julia was at its lowest point, I still made do with just one heart, like everybody else.

I dressed very carefully, eliminated the remains of the stubble on my chin, and gathered my hair into an elegant ponytail. Boy, did I look suave! All the eighth-grade girls would swoon.

Having finished admiring myself in the mirror I went outside. I wasn't planning to return home again. I didn't dare think that my search for the streetcar on Green Street might not pan out. Granted, I had grounds for optimism: if Mackie said I was going to be all right, there were no two ways about it.

I walked up the stairs to the sixth floor. I couldn't trust elevators anymore. It was pretty odd, but I had already learned to respect my own oddities and premonitions. They didn't just come out of the blue.

When I caught my breath again I rang the doorbell. I felt like laughing. It was too funny. Then again, I've always tended to go a little overboard with everything.

The door opened. Julia stood in the doorway fiddling with the collar of her checkered blouse, as if she couldn't decide whether to button it up to be out of harm's way or leave it as it was. She chose the latter. Attagirl.

I smiled a warm smile. It turned out I was darn happy to see her. The bad memories didn't matter anymore. But I wasn't going to change my mind. My whole collection—my favorite movies, which I had carefully selected; the junk that I had bought on a whim; and the movies I hadn't gotten around to watching—all of them were going with me to Echo. That was the only thing that mattered to me now, and I knew it was *right*. That vague notion popped up in the midst of my uncertainty more and more often. A new soloist had emerged in the choir of voices that had been mumbling incoherently in the dark corners of my mind. Unlike the other voices, this one was strong and confident.

"You look different," Julia said finally.

She seemed glad to see me, too, but something was stopping her from displaying it openly. But of course, it was Sir Max from Echo visiting her today, and Julia hadn't had the pleasure of meeting him yet.

"Must be my hair," I said. "Can I come in? I won't be long. Really."

"Yes, of course."

She stepped aside, allowing me to pass. I produced a small parcel from the pocket of my coat.

"Got some tea for you. I don't think we've had this kind before."

"Right," she said, fiddling absently with the parcel. "Let's go to the kitchen and I'll make it. You're not mad at me anymore?"

"I dropped the whole getting-mad business long ago," I said. And it was true. "To tell you the truth, I don't even remember why I was supposed to be mad at you. So it's all right."

Julia went out to the kitchen, and I hesitated in the living room by a new rack with a TV, VCR, and a great number of videotapes. Not long before I had been expelled from this heaven, there had been more than a hundred. Now there must have been even more, but not by many. Julia wasn't a spendthrift—she wouldn't waste money on silly things.

I carefully pulled the power cord from the outlet and unplugged the other cables. Now the rack was ready to be placed between my left thumb and index finger. This could wait, though. First I was going to have a cup of tea in the company of a nice girl. Now Julia awoke in me a feeling of—no, not of passion but of genuine sympathy. As for the calculator in her head, well, what did I care about the problems of the inhabitants of this World, which had long ago become strange to me? It's no bed of roses here, as I had come to understand. Tough for them, but life goes on.

"Come in here, Max. It's cozier," Julia said from the kitchen.

I obeyed. She had already put the kettle on and was busy opening the parcel with tea. A small white rat was sitting on the kitchen table.

"A new friend, huh?" I said.

Julia quickly grabbed the rodent and put it in the breast pocket of her checkered blouse, as though I were in the habit of snacking on little rats.

"This little girl is afraid of strangers," Julia said.

"That's very smart of her," I said. "We strangers are a peculiar bunch. So, what's new?"

Julia talked and I listened to her with half an ear. She seemed to be doing fine, although my lengthy absence hadn't seemed to facilitate the creation of another family unit. Why had she wanted to break up with me, then? I thought.

The tea wasn't very good, though maybe I had just forgotten the taste of hot tea. After I finished one cup, I realized that I had had enough. I was beginning to get bored. Also, I couldn't believe that what was happening was real. We resembled characters from, say, episode one hundred eighty of some soap opera. And Julia was giving me strange looks. No wonder, though. She had known the Max I used to be very well. Of course she was a little suspicious of this new one.

"Well, I'd better be going, then," I said.

"Sure."

She frowned, and then said cautiously, "Why did you decide to drop by?"

"I don't know," I lied. Then I decided to say something that was a little closer to the truth. "I guess I just came to say goodbye."

"Are you going out of town?"

"Something like that," I said. "Yeah, I guess I'll be going out of town."

"Okay, then. Good luck. Thanks for dropping by."

The tone of her voice implied that I was the one who had left her. And, scoundrel that I was, I had also pinched the silver spoons from the chest. It was amusing.

She got up and went through the living room. I followed behind. When I was walking past the rack with the TV I executed my best trick. One very subtle motion of my left hand, and the entire thing disappeared into my fist. The heist was so quick and soundless that Julia didn't even turn around.

"Well, so long, honey," I said, and walked out of the apartment.

The expression on my face must have been ominous because Julia looked away, scared, and took a step backward when she was letting me out. I did manage to turn around and give her a tender kiss on the nose, though. I had been dying to know what Mr. Judas Iscariot felt at the moment of his historic kiss. If he was anything like me, he enjoyed it immensely.

I walked down all the stairs again. Deep down in my heart I was hoping that Julia would dash out onto the landing to inform the world about her loss. Moreover, I was really counting on it. I anticipated a flood of accusations and imagined, not without pleasure, how I'd offer to turn my pockets inside out—maybe there would be a TV in one of them. Let's see, where did I put it?

But nothing like that happened. Poor thing must have fainted dead away. Or maybe she was calling the police. Then again, maybe she decided that all was vanity and vexation of the spirit, after which she sat down in the lotus position and started mumbling some mantra suited to the occasion. You never know what a person will do when she encounters the uncanny and inexplicable.

There was a small commotion on the landing of the fourth floor—some repairmen and a few curious preschoolers. Well, what do you know? The darn elevator was stuck between floors. I was doing quite well if could foresee such a small mishap.

Then I took a long walk through the city. I got a bit wet, and very cold, but that didn't take away from the pleasure of the walk. In the night, the city looked alien and, because of that, very beautiful. Much to my surprise, I realized that I could fall in love with it, given enough time. Maybe it was because night transformed the cityscape, and maybe it was because I finally felt I was a complete stranger on these broad streets. It is easy to love strange places: we take them for what they are and demand nothing but new experiences from them.

To warm myself up, I had some coffee with cognac in a cozy little bar, the name of which I don't remember. I started to thaw out, and even felt like having some dinner. This was beginning to resemble the life I had gotten used to in Echo: a nice long dinner in a cozy tavern before I set out looking for my next adventure. Today, I was going on another dangerous trip: catching the streetcar that traveled down Green Street, following an unmarked route. I really hoped that this story would have a happy ending, just like the others before it.

I looked at my watch. Soon it would be midnight. Time to stop stuffing my belly and get out of here. I asked for the check, paid, and walked out. Time almost stopped dead in its tracks. It seemed as though none of my movements would ever be completed. The foot in my new shoe moved so slowly toward the ground that it felt like the asphalt was a mirage, a metaphysical carrot receding endlessly before a lazy donkey.

Yet I managed to walk, step after step. I moved forward feeling the cold tickling of Eternity on the back of my head. The very same Eternity that I wasn't supposed to be teasing. Darn it, I thought. Lady Sotofa could have put it a little more clearly. If she'd just told me, "Don't even think about going back to your World, Max," I would have listened to her. At the very least, I would have tried. The most absurd thing was that the whole time I had never once thought about the holy water that was supposed to be the reason for this crazy trip.

When I got to Green Street, the electronic clock on top of the telephone company glowed 11:11. I remembered that I had always considered such symmetry to be a good sign, and turned away quickly so as not to see how the symmetry would shatter when the last digit turned to two. That, according to the same superstition, would have canceled out the good luck.

A moment later I heard the streetcar bell. The streetcar rumbled just like it had the first time, almost two years ago. On the other hand, though, it had just happened yesterday. Anyway, the last thing I wanted to do now was to try to comprehend the flow of time. I prefer not to have any particular opinion about such complex matters.

My head started to spin, but I managed to suppress the nausea fairly quickly. I inhaled and exhaled a few times, as Shurf Lonli-Lokli had taught me to do. Darn it, I thought. When I'm back in Echo, I simply must treat him to a good dinner. I owe him a big one. His breathing exercises have saved my life and sanity many times today already.

The moon looked out from behind the ragged edge of a cloud for a split second, and I could make out a familiar sign informing me that I was standing at the stop of the streetcar following route number 432. The number was the same. Praise be the Magicians, my Door between Worlds seemed to favor predictability over surprise.

The streetcar appeared from behind the corner and slowed down as it approached the stop. Everything was going according to plan. Better than I had dared hope. This mysterious express streetcar that followed the most improbable route between Worlds was at my service.

This time, however, I was going to have to negotiate with the driver. Sir Maba Kalox called him a Tipfinger. If I remembered correctly, he had said that a Tipfinger comes out of nowhere and feeds on our fears, anxieties, and premonitions. Sometimes a Tipfinger takes the form of a person and wanders around visiting his friends, scaring them by throwing fits, or just looking at them askance. Also, Maba told me that I had created the Tipfinger in my streetcar myself. Why on earth would I have done something like that? And how did I manage it? To tell the truth, I have done a lot of stupid things in my life. Some were even worse.

Okay, I thought. A Tipfinger it is, then. Whatever. I smiled wickedly and stared at the driver's cabin. There he was, the Tipfinger, with his broad face and thin mustache. I couldn't believe that two years back this ridiculous creature had scared the bejesus out of me. It was my luck that he had disappeared almost immediately, and I had mustered up courage to get into the streetcar. Looking back now, I realize it was the only right thing to do.

The streetcar stopped. The door at the front of the streetcar opened silently, and I dashed inside. This time the creature didn't disappear. The streetcar wasn't moving and the ugly mustached creature looked at me with bored indifference.

"Just the man I was looking for," I said. "I'm going to teach you a lesson, pal. I'll teach you how to scare novice travelers between Worlds. It's bad manners to scare newbies, didn't you know that?"

The driver didn't say anything, but his face was undergoing a transformation. The mustached face slowly disappeared into a misty blur, and a few moments later it took the shape of another face. Grand Magician Maxlilgl Annox, the short-nosed apparition from Xolomi, was staring out at me. Then his face faded away, too, and now the piercing blue eyes of the late Magician Kiba Attsax were fixed on me.

I immediately realized what was going on.

"What? Are you trying to remember who it was that scared me not so long ago? Not going to work, pal. Just this morning I lost myself, but then I managed to find me again. I don't think anything or anyone can scare me now. I'm in a very good mood tonight."

I raised my left hand. Sure, it had a long way to go to match the death-dealing hand of Shurf Lonli-Lokli, but I always made do with what little I had.

"Do not waste your Lethal Sphere on me," the creature said quietly.

Now his face didn't look like anyone or anything, although an infinite number of vaguely familiar faces appeared through the shimmering mist that surrounded the Tipfinger's head.

"Don't waste it on you, you say?" I said, laughing, reveling in my own powers. "I'm a miser all right, but I can stand the loss of one for your sake."

"It is your choice—you gave me my life, you can take it back—but whoever takes away the life of a Tipfinger must replace him. This is the law."

The creature's tone was listless and indifferent. It seemed that he didn't care much about his fate. One of my hearts knew somehow that the Tipfinger wasn't lying. The other heart was silent. It probably knew that no one was asking its opinion.

"Fine. We'll do without Lethal Spheres. I'm not bloodthirsty. Step out for a second. Let's have a talk."

I was completely calm now. I didn't feel like laughing, smiling, or even smirking. I was very tired and could think about only one thing: how great it would be to curl up on the rigid seat, close my eyes, and not open them until this wonderful vehicle delivered me back home to Echo. As for the Tipfinger, Mackie had told me that he could help me convince the World I was born in that I didn't exist anymore. And I was beginning to guess what Mackie had meant by that.

%

The creature came out of the driver's cabin and sat down on the front seat. I noticed that his body, too, had no definite shape. The Tipfinger was neither thin nor fat. Or, rather, he was thin and fat at the same time. The outlines of his body, which was quite anthropomorphic, trembled and faded away.

The doors of the streetcar closed and it finally began moving.

"Is this streetcar going to Echo?" I said.

"It will go where you want it to go," said the creature.

"Okay. That's not too bad."

I gave a sigh of relief. God knows why, but I was still burdened by doubts, which I tried to ignore. I was so tired of uncertainties. I was generally tired.

"If I understand correctly, you can take any shape?" I said.

"Yes. I can look like whatever people around me want me to look like."

"More like what they *don't* want you to look like," I said. "You feed on our fears, don't you? That's what I've been told, anyway."

"This is also true."

"Well, it's your business," I said. "But I didn't make the Universe, unfortunately. If I had my way, everything would have been much simpler and much more pleasant. Now, tell me something. If I've got this right, you can't decide what you will look like. Our inner fears dictate the shape you take, whether you want it or not, right?"

"Right," the creature said.

"And if I tell you to take *my* shape?" I asked. "I don't mean to say that I'm scared of my own face. I'm simply asking whether you can become my double. Can you do this?"

"I can," the Tipfinger said.

His tone was as listless as before, but now there was a glint of excitement in his eyes.

"Excellent. Then I want you to take my form and go to some place with a lot of people. Downtown somewhere. But what's important is that you become a *dead* Max, and the sooner you do it the better. Is this possible?"

"It is."

"Great. Oh, hold on a second. I think poor Max has to die right on the job. There are a lot of people at the editorial office now. And there won't be any problem identifying me. Gosh, I can just imagine what a ruckus there's going to be there." I couldn't restrain a malicious smile. "That's it, then. After they bury me—you, that is—you're free to do whatever you want to forevermore. Got it?"

"You are setting me free forevermore?" said the Tipfinger.

Ah, where was his melancholy now! He stared at me with eyes that were already starting to resemble my own and laughed.

"Thank you. I could not have counted on such generosity. I will do as you say. You can trust my word. You can trust any words uttered between Worlds. Did you know that?"

Gee, I said to myself. What's with the elevated spirits?

The creature's indeterminate face had turned into my own. I smiled—I was a pretty handsome guy after all. Too bad this new Max was going to die almost immediately. Maybe I should have asked the Tipfinger to live out my boring life here and grow old? No, that would have been too much to ask. I didn't want to entrust the remains of my reputation to this strange creature. Besides, there is something romantic in any sudden death. And I've always been such a show-off.

My doppelgänger looked at me with unconcealed compassion.

"You are very unlucky," he said. "You didn't know of the true power of words uttered between Worlds, and you gave me freedom by mistake. You also did not know that he who frees a Tipfinger must take his place. To kill me or to set me free—in fact it is one and the same. I do think you are going to like it, though. On the paths a Tipfinger roams you will find the most frivolous kind of power. Deep inside you have dreamed about this all your life, and now it will come to pass. Goodbye, Sir Max, and thank you."

. Now both of my hearts were knocking against my rib cage. They knew I was in deep trouble. I had fallen into the most ridiculous trap, from which, it seemed, there was no way out. Damn it, I thought. I knew my chatterbox of a mouth would be the end of me.

And then I was alone, and I felt that it didn't matter. I was no longer Sir Max from Echo. I didn't know who I was, and frankly, I no longer cared.

"Time to go for a walk," I said out loud, taking the driver's seat.

My streetcar moved along into the unknown. My passion for high-speed driving was still with me. The air, knocked flat onto the tracks, screamed as if in pain. Thick clots of darkness crawled onto the windshield, and I kept muttering *faster, faster,* not knowing what I was running from.

At daybreak, I found myself standing outside in the middle of a street. It was a broad central street in a German town. I knew it was a German town from the signs on the stores. The tracks ended here. They just stopped as if they had been cut off.

I stood on the smooth asphalt and watched indifferently as the magic streetcar disappeared, like an old ghost for which there was no need anymore. I felt no regrets about it. Something in me knew that now I could get to any destination I wished without boarding any dubious vehicles. These creatures, one of which I had just become, could open Doors between Worlds as easily as I had once opened the secret door to the Ministry of Perfect Public Order. I could go to Echo right this minute, but I didn't want to go back there. I did remember that wonderful city, to which I felt connected both through my destiny and through necessity. Even the tender feelings I felt toward the people I had left behind were still with me. I missed them, but my feelings did not matter anymore. That morning I knew beyond the shadow of a doubt that creatures like me were destined to be lonely, and I did not mind. It was the way it was.

I was overwhelmed with my power, but I had no particular desires. There was only someone else's vague but insistent thought that it was "time to go for a little spin," and an irresistible urge to keep moving. I didn't have the faintest idea of the rules of the game I had been sucked into, so I had to learn them fast, and learn them the hard way.

I went for a walk. I no longer belonged to the World I was born in, but it seemed that this World belonged to me. The round cobblestones of the street that my new shoes were treading whispered their history to me. I have to admit that it was too boring to listen to very carefully.

I walked into a cozy pub. It was called *Nuremberg* or *The Nuremberger* —something like that. The old waitress looked at me with horror, and also with vague hope. I wish I knew whose face it was that smiled at her and ordered a cup of coffee.

I finished my coffee and walked out into one of the narrow streets of old Nuremberg. A cold wind blew from the river. It resembled the minty wind of Kettari, the way the shadow resembles the object that casts it. But that mysterious resemblance left me cold. I didn't care about the poor old Max who had fallen in love with the bridges of Kettari. Now I was much more interested in my recent discovery. Interesting, I thought. So that's how it works. I'd better remember it.

That morning I had discovered one of many fantastic new ways of traveling. It turned out that all I had to do was enter the first bar, restaurant, or even bakery I came across that had some geographical location for a namesake. I had to stay there for a while with my back turned to the window. That was important. Then, when I walked out, I would find myself standing under a different sky, on a sidewalk or street in the place the eatery had been named after. I was completely enchanted by this.

If I wanted to, though, I could always take a train, a plane, or a car. My pockets were always full of everything I needed: money, ID, tickets, and other papers. These fraudulent documents proving that I belonged to the world of people appeared in my pockets just as I needed them, so I could fool anyone.

It wasn't so bad. No, not bad at all. In fact, what had happened to me exceeded my wildest notions of the miraculous. I envied myself.

I could go to a cheap Mexican diner on the outskirts of Berlin, then walk outside into the sweltering heat and melting sidewalks of Mexico City. I could walk through the heat of that city and follow my feet to the cool *New Yorker* bar. The mustached bartender would shudder when he looked at me. I wasn't surprised—everyone did that if I didn't turn my face away in time. Where was my famous charm now?

To hell with charm, though. I could have a cold beer in the *New Yorker* (remembering to sit with my back turned to the window), then push open the thick glass door and walk out onto the streets of the real New York, in the very heart of Greenwich Village. I would stop there and visit a neat little place called *Club 88*, not because I wanted to throw myself into a distant adventure but just for my own personal enjoyment. It's not just by chance that the number in the name of the place is the number of keys on a piano. In the evening, a virtuoso pianist taps on the keys. Behind the bar, a black woman dressed in men's clothing hums the blues in an oddly familiar raspy voice while she mixes cocktails and dumps out the cigarette butts from identical white ashtrays. The *Club 88* regulars are not what you'd call yuppies. They smoke like chimneys, giving the lie to another Great American Dream. Naturally I sympathize with them. I only regret that my ever-changing face, obedient to their fears, scares these merry "outcasts." The barstools next to mine are always empty.

From New York, praise be the Magicians, I could go anywhere: every possible geographical location has been immortalized on the innumerable signs of New York cafés, bars, diners, and other eateries. Flattered, the international community pays New York back in kind. Almost anywhere in the world, you can find a bar or restaurant that bears the name of that new Babylon. And so New York became a transportation hub for me. I visited it more often than any other place. I rarely lingered a long time, however. Too many geopolitical temptations.

In those days, I finally came to appreciate the World I had been born in, and which I had been none too fond of. I realized it was a magnificent place. The smell of lime trees in bloom on the outskirts of Moscow was to die for. Then there were the hot winds of Arizona, the bracing moist air of London at night, and the resinous breeze of the Baltic Sea coast, whose white sands were covered in thin, dry pine needles. Not to mention a bike ride through the empty Amsterdam streets on a Sunday morning, a merry flute player on the Charles Bridge, the rounded tops of the Carpathian Mountains, the aroma of Parisian coffee houses, the discontented chattering of an agitated squirrel, the round black eye of a swan about to tear off a piece of bread from the hand of a leisurely nature lover . . . I doubt I'll ever sit down to make a complete inventory of all the wonders of the World. And who was the idiot who decided there were only seven?

I had to admit that the World I was born in was all right. There was nothing wrong with it. There had been something wrong with *me* while I belonged to it. It really made no difference where I was. It just didn't matter.

If there is anything that matters, it is the creature out of whose heart you look at the world around you. I had the chance, a unique chance, to look at my former homeland with the eyes of a very peculiar and strange creature.

There was, however, one false note in this wonderful symphony of my new existence. At times, that note sounded quite harsh.

While I was enjoying the new possibilities and playing this exciting game, something deep inside me knew that Sir Juffin Hully wouldn't have agreed to join me on my trip if I had invited him. I knew it even during the days when I accepted my strange destiny and was almost happy with it. I would probably have become completely happy, if the creature I had become had been capable of happiness.

Back in those days, I would have forgotten my own name if it hadn't seen it everywhere I went, on seemingly every sign, billboard, or notice. All those Maxes, Maxims, and Maximilians followed me day in and day out, as though there were no other names left in the world. Their ubiquity prevented me from forgetting myself completely.

Once, on the menu of some diner in Germany, I saw something called Strammer Max in Mirrors. Curious, I ordered it. The mirrors turned out to be a cold fried egg on a piece of rye bread. In addition, there was a thick slice of finely cut ham on the plate. It wasn't particularly tasty, but it had a positive effect on me. Sir Max from Echo woke up somewhere in the depths of my soul for a few minutes, and said in a very persistent tone that he wanted to go home. Soon, I said, brushing him off like a nagging child. Sir Max retreated into the darkness, but from then on, his formerly sound sleep of a baby became the light, anxious sleep of an old man.

It was in that diner that I decided to commit to paper everything that had happened to me as Sir Max from Echo. I covered several napkins with my writing and liked what I had written. I somehow felt that as soon as I finished writing, the wonders and mysteries would let me go back to the same place that that guy, who had become almost unfamiliar to me, wanted to return to. And then he would be happy, and I . . . I would be free forever and ever.

❀

I'm still not sure what I did while traveling throughout the planet. My memory still can't cope with the chaos of things that happened to me during my wanderings. It is unable to sequence the episodes and put the elements of the mosaic into a single, coherent picture that it can store away. What is clear is that it is much easier for me to recollect the events that happened after I had the Strammer Max and began to take notes.

That day I built the first flimsy rope bridge that connected me to my past. The mosaic pavements of Echo slowly began to take shape as objective reality, however unreachable. I no longer needed to dash away from a TV screen showing another installment of *Mad Max*. I no longer needed to stare at the neon sign of the Max Men's Clothes department to remember that it had once been my name. Now I didn't forget for a second who I had once been. And that was a lot.

More and more often now I paid attention to the obvious fear in the eyes of my random interlocutors. What's more, I derived less and less pleasure from it. I felt weary of my strange obligations. But for the time being I wasn't able to retire. Once you take the place of a Tipfinger you've set free by mistake, you are obliged to travel the world with a whole pack of intimidating personas. And quit whining—this isn't the worst thing that can happen. Some only get to wander around the dank basements of some ancient castle as ghosts. Would you rather do that?

I learned a great deal about human fears. The most ridiculous and ludicrous of my discoveries was connected with bicyclists. My own bitter experience proved that most bicyclists are afraid of hitting pedestrians. They rarely realize the true depths of their fear, but feeding fuel to their panic was part of my job. Once I was outside, some bicyclist always hit me. I don't think that anyone or anything could really hurt me in those days, but the regular collisions with bicyclists were extremely annoying. Thank goodness automobile drivers didn't have such fears. Well, they did, but far less frequently. I was run over by a car only four or five times, not more.

Sometimes I got into bigger trouble. I will never forget one tall, blond girl from the *Red Elephant* restaurant in the center of Erfurt, Germany. A force, which it was best not to antagonize, enticed me to follow the young woman into a dark alley. The alley was so narrow that two people couldn't walk through it if they were holding hands. They could only walk single file. I had to kill the blond girl because for the entire evening she had been possessed by the thought that the man she was staring at through the thin walls of her glass would follow her into the alley and kill her there. Blood, she thought, would clash with her light-green jumper.

Sometimes, though, I think that I remained seated on the barstool on the second floor of the *Red Elephant*, and that she just dreamed the assault. I don't know how I managed to crawl into her nightmare, but it seemed quite plausible. At least I like to think it was.

Nevertheless, that bloody sacrifice—real or imaginary—did me a great deal of good. It was that night, when I was having a dinner on the second floor of the *Red Elephant*, that I first sensed that my incredible but meaningless new life was coming to an end. I had almost finished my notes. I reread them, and recalled Echo and the people who were waiting for me there with piercing clarity. There was no doubt that good old Sir Max had woken up and was now groping around, bewildered, in the farthest reaches of my inner being. He still needed time to shake off the sweet and perilous stupor, and time was something we both had. We could frivolously squander this precious treasure, the way he—no, the way *I*—had squandered the crowns I had earned at the service of His Majesty King Gurig VIII, wandering in and out of the antique shops of the Right Bank. I was even more heedless about time than I was about money, for you always feel it's easier to spend something that doesn't belong to you.

One day I was in New York again. I took a short walk around the evening streets of SoHo and stared at the illuminated windows of picture galleries. I felt like having a cappuccino and went to the nearest Italian restaurant. That night everything was a little different. Something had changed in my life, and I liked the change. At least the black-eyed bartender looked at me with an indifferent smile. My face didn't touch any strings deep in his soul.

What are you doing here? I thought. How much longer do you think you're going to be here? Until Mommy calls you back home because the dinner's ready?

I laughed with relief. My internal monologue sounded a lot like Sir Max's confused thoughts. Were we together again?

Suddenly someone bumped into me, and my barstool started teetering. I couldn't keep my balance and tumbled off it into the embrace of a nice elderly gentleman. The gentleman wore an elegant gray hat, which was strangely in keeping with his foppish, dark-brown leather jacket.

"I beg your pardon," he said. "I was staring at my reflection in the mirror. I can't decide whether I look like a World War II pilot or not. More likely I just look like a lunatic."

I smiled. God only knew what was going on in the head of this eccentric stranger. Nice guy, I thought. I really like him.

"You knocked me down like a true flying ace, that's for sure. You can paint another cross on your plane. But you should exchange the hat for a headpiece with goggles."

"You're absolutely right. We pilots don't wear hats like this. Here, you take it. It'll go well with your coat," he said. He took off his hat and placed it on top of my disheveled head.

I blinked, slightly taken aback. Gosh, I'd forgotten what it was like to be taken aback. It was a strange but, quite frankly, pleasant feeling.

"Gee" was all I could say.

The stranger nodded and took a few steps back to enjoy the view.

"I like it," he said. "Keep it, young man. This hat suits you. When I left home this morning, my wife told me, 'Ron, I'm sure you're going to lose something today, and my premonitions have never failed me. You know that. So go ahead and lose something, but for crying out loud, lose something that's not worth much.' Now she'll be happy because I have fulfilled her wish. Have a nice day, young man. Drink your horrible black drink with cream. I can imagine how much caffeine there is in it."

I watched him as he was leaving, and then sat back down on the tall barstool to drink my coffee. The young bartender smiled at me.

"Ron is an eccentric, like most artists. But he's a good man," said the bartender in a conspiratorial tone. "He's a regular here."

"That's good, because you've got great coffee," I said.

"Oh, no. He never drinks coffee. Only a little bit of a good wine."

"Well, there's no caffeine in wine, that's for sure."

I paid for my coffee and slid down off the stool. I walked out and found myself in Rome just before dawn. I had come here a few times, to the great joy of the local pigeons, which I fed almost everything that happened to be in my pockets. Did the name of that restaurant have the word *Rome* in it? I thought. And then I thought that it would be great to get some rest. For the first time during my wanderings I felt tired and sleepy. I sat down on a bench by a fountain and lit up a cigarette. Then, it seems, I dozed off.

§

I woke up because I was cold. I looked around and saw that I wasn't sitting on the bench but standing on a large stone bridge. The cold wind from the river chilled me to my bones. Drat, just a moment ago I was hot, I thought. My coat was way too heavy for taking walks through Rome. Even in the winter it was too warm for the Eternal City.

Clearly, I wasn't in Rome. But where was I? The town felt vaguely familiar, especially the cold wind that so resembled the minty wind of Kettari. What if . . . ? I thought.

But of course I wasn't in Kettari. I was in Nuremberg. I had been there once, right at the start of my crazy odyssey.

"I really have to go home now," I said to a seagull flying past me.

The bird shouted something back in a harsh, raspy voice. It looked like it was agreeing with me and was saying, "Fine. Scram, then."

I unstuck myself from the stone railing and walked slowly across the bridge toward the sad-looking figures, green with age, of beasts guarding the plaque with the name of the bridge. I looked at the plaque and laughed. It turned out I had just been standing on the Max Bridge, or the Bridge of Max, translated literally.

"It sure is nice to be so popular," I said to a solemn-looking bronze Chimera. "What don't they name after me these days!"

Someone laughed a tinkling laugh behind me. I turned around and froze. There stood Tekki. She looked much older than I remembered her, but I didn't notice it right away.

A hurricane of thoughts rushed through my head. Of course, Tekki was the daughter of Loiso Pondoxo himself. She could easily pull a trick like this. But why did she look so old? Had I been away from Echo for *that* long? How long? I wondered. Two, three hundred years? A thousand?

I froze in horror. Could it be that the lives of people who at one time couldn't do without me *did* somehow go on without me? While I was wasting precious time hanging out in stupid cafés and restaurants, drinking gallons of coffee and absorbing other people's fears, the people who needed me were living, feeling sad and happy, and *dying*, without ever having seen me again. Time had played a dirty trick on me. It had carried off all my colleagues, and now everything was over for me, because . . . Because it was not they who couldn't live without me, but *I* who couldn't live without them!

This was so shocking that it actually did me good. It was like a bracing cold shower for my burning head. The chilly wind from the river dispersed the last remains of the creature that I had, for some reason, been for so long.

Now I was the Max I had been before. Only the old Max could have sat down on the sidewalk to stare at a beautiful stranger and go all to pieces because he had taken her for a beautiful girl from another World.

"What are you doing here, Tekki?" I said in a hoarse voice. "And what happened to you?"

"I'm Theia," the woman said. "And nothing happened to me. Did you think I was someone else?"

I was flooded with relief. Of course it wasn't Tekki. Just a sweet lady, around fifty, who looked a lot like Tekki but was far from being a replica of my beloved.

"I did think you were someone else," I said. I wasn't croaking like a dying goblin anymore. I was squeaking like a buoyant teenager.

But it *was* my voice—no two ways about it. And what was even more important, these were *my* confused feelings. Eternity was no longer holding me hostage. I desperately needed a mirror to make sure that my face was the face of the good old Max. But did it really even matter?

"I'm sorry, would you happen to have a mirror?"

I was smiling ear to ear. It was the stupidest smile I could muster—I had tried as hard as I could.

"I would," she said.

"May I have it for a second?"

The woman rummaged around in her purse for a long time and then handed me a small, chipped pocket mirror. I grabbed it and peered into it. From underneath the brim of the hat given to me by Ron, that funny New York artist, a guy who looked a heck of a lot like Sir Max from Echo was staring back at me. The only thing missing was his turban.

"Guess what?" I said. "You just saved my life. May I buy you a coffee?"

Instead of calling the police or trying to run away from a strange, possibly crazy man, this nice woman nodded, shaking her short, curly hair. Her hair was silver, just like Tekki's, but for another reason. It had been silvered by age.

"You know," she said, "I think life costs somewhat more than just a cup of coffee. I insist on a glass of good wine." She looked at her watch and frowned. "I am running a bit late. But all right, if I'm going to be late, I should be at least thirty minutes late. There's something small-minded about running just five minutes late, don't you think?"

"I do," I said.

Quite frankly, right now I couldn't help agreeing with everything.

"There's a nice place nearby. Very American. No bouquets with blue-and-white Bavarian ribbons or any of that nonsense."

"Sounds great. I'm sorry, what is your name, again?"

"Theia," she said, shaking her head. "All right, let's go before I change my mind. I may be making a big mistake. I still need to visit my friends and say hello to them. I don't think I'll have time for more if I want to catch my train to Munich. Isn't this terrible?"

"It sure is."

My recent agitation was so draining that I had almost lost the ability to speak. I could only meekly agree with whatever she said.

"This way," said Theia, turning from the embankment onto a small street with only a few buildings. "We're here."

The place was "very American." Perhaps too American for my

tastes. The design was pure, sterile white. Nothing to feast your eyes on.

"It's hard to believe, but they have very good French wine here. The only thing that can tempt me," said Theia.

"Great," I said.

My head was spinning, and I wasn't feeling too great overall. I still couldn't collect my thoughts, even though it was high time I started thinking about how I was going to get back to Echo. I still had no idea.

"Get yourself some strong coffee," said Theia. "How long have you been up? Your life, which you say I saved, still seems to be hanging by a thread."

"Well, it's not so bad," I said. "You're right, though, I've been up for too long. But I'm going to make up for it. I just need to get back home. As soon as I can."

"Home?" said Theia. "That's a very good idea. They're waiting for you there." She smelled the wine in her glass.

I shuddered. She spoke as if Sir Juffin Hully himself had told her in detail just last night about how everyone was waiting for me. No, it couldn't be.

The waiter brought me my coffee. Theia finished her wine, lit a cigarette, and looked out the window, lost in thought. Her silence was comfortable and didn't make me feel at all awkward. Then she looked at her watch again.

"Now I really must go. Soon I won't even have to bother going back to the station. My train leaves in less than three hours. Thank you for the wine. It was the most unexpected invitation in my life."

"Mine, too," I said. "But I'm not as crazy as I look."

"Who knows?" said Theia, laughing a wonderful laugh. "When I saw you on the bridge you were talking to a stone lion."

She waved, walked out, and strode quickly toward the river. I followed her with my eyes. My savior was slightly pigeon-toed, but it suited her. A woman with such beautiful legs could afford to walk however she liked.

❀

I ordered another coffee and a bottle of mineral water. I wanted to organize my haphazard notes, my report to myself about my life in the Capital of the Unified Kingdom. I felt like kissing every page. These memoirs had kept me from disappearing forever—the notes; and the funny "pilot" Ron, the original owner of the gray hat; and that wonderful Theia, who looked so much like Tekki.

When I finished sorting out my notes I noticed it had become dark outside. I sighed, ordered more coffee, lit up, and forced myself to think about the most crucial thing at that moment: How was I supposed to get back to Echo?

Now I felt that this trip was going to be smooth and easy as never before. But what was I to do to find the right door? The door that would lead me to the Corridor between Worlds, to the threshold of my favorite bedroom on the Street of Old Coins? I was exhausted from my wanderings. I wanted to find the right answer on the first try, and I didn't even know where to start. I wished someone would give me a clue!

I almost fell off the chair, crushed by a tremendous weight, like a huge, invisible steamroller. I heard the voice of Sir Mackie Ainti in my head.

Any door opened in darkness will lead you where you want to go. It must be very dark so the visible World doesn't interfere with the invisible. That's all. You would have figured it out sooner or later, but I couldn't bear looking at you sweating over it, partner.

Mackie! I'm so glad you found me! Don't disappear now. Please. I'll endure the strain of talking to you as long as you wish.

That's what you think. You're not in the best shape, partner. So you'd better go home. That's enough miracles for you.

I could almost see the smile of compassion hidden behind his thick red mustache.

The heavy weight gave way to weightlessness. I was sad. Mackie had cut it way too short this time. I never asked him how many years I had been wandering around, and I still desperately needed to know that. But he had told me the most important thing. The only right answer that I would have spent an eternity trying to find.

All I needed was a door and complete darkness. That was it. It would be easy. I would simply rent a room in a hotel, pull down the curtains, turn off the lights, and all the darkness of the night would be at my service.

❈

I walked out into the street. My feet took me back to the river. Then I turned right, crossed a narrow lane, stopped by the Old Town Hotel, and rang the doorbell.

They had a room for me. The contents of my pockets were still in perfect harmony with my needs, so a few moments later I walked up to the third floor and turned the key in the lock. A few dim lights were on in the hallway, so instead of the Corridor between Worlds, I walked into a small square hotel room with a window that took up half the wall. Without turning on the lights, I flopped down in an armchair, closed my eyes, and took a breath.

I was a few steps away from Echo. I just had to take these last few steps, and tonight I'd be showing Sir Juffin Hully some *Tom and Jerry* cartoons—the best way to apologize for my sudden disappearance.

In bewilderment, I looked at my palm, where the storage rack with video equipment and my movie collection was still safely secreted away. How in the World was I supposed to show cartoons to my boss when there were no electrical outlets in Echo? Echo had no electricity! Major bummer.

I felt like crying from disappointment. My magical gift that I had been carrying around the world was completely useless.

Then it dawned on me. Ah, my head was still worth something after all. I turned on the lights and looked around. I found two outlets, right by the door. That's exactly what I need, I thought.

I shook my left hand and the bulky storage rack landed gently on the floor. I plugged the TV and the VCR into the electrical outlets, pulled down the curtains, returned to the door, and once again hid the storage rack between my thumb and index finger. To my surprise, the trick worked like a charm. It was a little strange to see two black power cords extending from my fist to the municipal power grid. I wonder what it will look like after I leave? I thought. The innocent room cleaners will probably faint when they see two wires disappearing into nowhere. Then again, as Lady Sotofa Xanemer would put it, I wish I had their problems.

I turned off the lights and pushed open the door to the hallway. The door opened not into the hallway of the hotel but into the Corridor between Worlds. At least that was what Sir Juffin Hully called this strange place that held absolute emptiness in thrall. It was surprisingly easy for me to find the Door into my bedroom on the Street of Old Coins.

❦

I opened my eyes and looked around. I was lying on the soft, fluffy flooring that served as my bed in my old house on the Street of Old Coins. It was dark, but I could see in the dark no worse than the natives of Uguland.

Two short black cords were still coming out of my left fist. They vanished into nothingness, but they didn't look like they had been cut off. They faded away and turned into black misty blurs. The cables restricted my freedom a great deal, so I hurried to shake my hand. The storage rack landed right on my blanket. Well, it looked like there wouldn't be much room left in the bed. No big deal, considering that I wasn't planning on ever using it for sleeping. There were plenty of places in Echo where I could spend the night, and it would be quite some time before I'd want to travel between Worlds again. At least that was what I thought back then.

"What's that you brought with you?" said Juffin.

I had no idea whether he had just appeared out of nowhere or walked through the door.

"Juffin! Gosh, am I glad to see you!"

I was so happy. Then I remembered my recent scare about the caprices of time and decided I had to deal with it once and for all. I had to have the answer immediately.

"How long have I been away?" My two hearts were beating like crazy.

"About four dozen days," said Juffin. "Forty-nine, to be exact. Goodness, Max! I knew that once I turned away for just a moment, you'd go on vacation. That's so like you. Where were you, if you even know yourself?"

"Only forty-nine days?" I laughed with relief. "Sinning Magicians! Just forty-nine."

"Were you scared?" said Juffin.

"You bet."

My laughter could easily have turned into a sob, so I shut up and did a few breathing exercises courtesy of Sir Lonli-Lokli. I took a few deep breaths and calmed down. I knew I wasn't going to cry. Not now, anyway.

"I'll tell you the whole story, but let's go somewhere else," I said. "I'm a little scared to stay in this darn room. What if it decides to take me away again? I desperately need to walk on the multicolored stones of our sidewalks and pavements. And I've almost forgotten the taste of kamra. Then we'll come back here and I'll show you something you've never seen before in your life. You're going to like it, I promise. But first I need to get outside."

"Well," said Juffin, "if you say so. I think I already know where you're headed to refresh your memory of the forgotten taste of kamra."

"To the *Armstrong & Ella*, of course," I said, putting on my black-

and-gold looxi and the Mantle of Death, which I had been missing as much as everything else. "But you must go there with me. The only way I can apologize to Tekki for being away for so long is to bring along a good customer."

"As for Lady Shekk, she was the only person who didn't panic about it," said Juffin. "To tell you the truth, when Maba told me you were nowhere to be found—not in any of the Worlds at all—I felt the ground sinking underneath my feet. That hadn't happened to me in a long, long time. But your girlfriend kept smiling mysteriously and saying you were going to be all right."

"She did?" I said. "Who would have thought? According to the genre of tragic romance she should have fallen down unconscious and then come to, only to die of happiness in my arms. It's great that Tekki doesn't go in for melodrama."

"Are you sure you want to walk?" said Juffin, opening the door for me. "It's a long way to the Street of Forgotten Dreams."

"I know, but I'd still rather go on foot," I said. I carefully put my foot on the mosaic sidewalk. What if it disappeared? But no, the motley colored pebbles were very real.

While I was away, wandering Magicians know where, fall had come to Echo, and it was beautiful—better than all other seasons, which are also magnificent. A gust of wind from the river almost tore the turban off my head. I laughed.

"That's right. A strong, cold wind from the Xuron is exactly what I need right now. Maybe then I'll finally realize that I really see you, and I'm not dreaming."

"Does it really matter whether you're dreaming or not? What's important is that you do see me," said Juffin. "All right, then. If you want to go on foot, we'll walk. Today is your day. You can be as spoiled as you wish. You know, you look different. Older, maybe?"

"Maybe," I said with a sigh. "Magicians only know how much time I spent there. And I promised Melifaro that he wouldn't even begin to miss me."

"Yes, that was an example of poor judgment on your part. He did miss you. But you know Melifaro. He's a whirlwind. He's always ahead of himself."

"You're so right, Juffin," I said, surprised at the mixture of tenderness and causticity in his voice.

Then I remembered something and gave Juffin a puzzled look.

"Whatever happened to the undead? I never got around to bringing any holy water. I completely forgot. Gosh, that's so typical of me. That was the reason I went on the blasted trip in the first place."

"Well, let's just say that that dubious potion was just a pretext, but you probably knew that already. There are many ways of going insane when two Worlds begin to claim their rights to you. Anyway, that was the worst idea you could have come up with, Max. Your so-called holy water can't hurt any evil spirits in your World, much less ours."

"Are there evil spirits in my World, too?"

Then I remembered whom I had turned into when I was there and blushed.

"I'm sorry, I said something stupid again. I guess evil exists everywhere and takes many forms."

"Is this the opinion of an expert?" said Juffin with a wink. "I should very much like to know what you were doing there all this time. And why couldn't Maba find you? Usually, if he does something, he does it well, and thoroughly. What was happening to you there, do you remember?"

"You know, I'm afraid I really didn't exist and really was nowhere to be found. You see, I was a Tipfinger," I said. "By mistake, my chatterbox of a mouth set free the creature that had been driving my streetcar. Remember Sir Maba telling us about him, and telling me that sooner or later I'd have to deal with him?"

"You bet I do," said Juffin, shaking his head. "Some news, huh? All right, no need to explain anything. I don't think your incoherent story is capable of satisfying my curiosity. Praise be the Magicians, I have quite a few methods of learning about all the details myself. That's why you're spending the night at my place tonight. Chuff will be thrilled, as you might expect."

"That would be great, but what about Tekki? Don't you think she'll object?"

"Maybe she will, a little," said Juffin. "I love it when people object and stand up to me. It makes life so much more interesting."

"You've always been a tyrant and a despot," I said, smiling. "But seriously, what happened to the undead? I really want to know because, boy, did they wear me out!"

"I can imagine. Bad timing, huh? But you were great. Kofa still can't calm down after what you did. I think he wouldn't mind if you stayed in my chair forever. Your working methods rattled him to the core. Especially all those breakfasts, lunches, and dinners."

"Are you making fun of me?" I said.

"A little. As for the undead, they're quite all right. I'll introduce you to them tomorrow."

"To the corpses?"

I was so surprised that I didn't notice the thick trunk of a Vaxari tree. I bumped my head on it and moaned.

"They are not corpses. I guess I was wrong—you haven't changed at all," said Juffin, laughing. "That's the good old Max I know so well. Anyway, Sir Nanka Yok, Grand Magician of the Order of the Long Path, desperately wants to meet you. He's very eager to meet the man who almost ruined his plans, and then made things right again."

"Plans? What plans?" I said. "He's a bit confused, your Nanka Yok. I can guarantee you that while you were away, I wasn't fighting any Magicians, grand or not so grand."

"You still don't get it, Max. Whatever happened to your quick wit?" Juffin shook his head in disapproval. "There were no corpses. What you saw at the Green Petta Cemetery were the members of the Order of the Long Path. A few dozen millennia ago, almost as far back as the time of Xalla Maxun the Hairy, they voluntarily descended underground to become immortal. Don't ask me to explain how they did it. I'll let Nanka himself tell you about it. He's quite fond of confabulating on this subject."

"Fond of *confabulating*?" I said. "When I tried to communicate with him, all he said was 'U-u-u-u-u-uh.' That was the end of our fruitful confabulation, if I remember correctly."

"But of course," said Juffin. "They needed to stay on the surface a few days to become human. Instead, you kept killing them: you burned them, you buried them, you did Magicians-know-what with them. So they had to start all over again, every time. But your idea about the statues was only to their advantage. They simply stayed in their stone clothing a few days and finally became human. Nanka himself, however, had already visited Kofa at the House by the Bridge and explained to him what was going on."

"But how?" I said. "Did he walk around Echo clad in liquid stone? I'm sure it was quite a spectacle. Too bad I missed it."

"Oh, no," said Juffin. "Nanka had escaped from you earlier—not from you but, rather, from the police. Lieutenant Chekta Jax lost him, but was afraid to tell you."

"I'm going to kill him," I said.

"Easy does it, boy," said Juffin. "I've already discussed the matter with him, so your little vendetta can wait. He's already been put through the mill. By the way, you should have caught a glimpse of a guilty secret in the depths of his eyes. You'll learn in due time, I suppose. Sir Nanka Yok is indeed a powerful creature. A true Grand Magician, one of the Ancients. Even in the twilight state he was in, he managed to escape the terrified policemen and crawl off to a safe distance beyond your firing range. Then he lay in the bushes for about six days. When he had finally become human, he went straight to the House by the Bridge."

"But how did he know about the House by the Bridge? As far as I know, it didn't exist back when he was alive."

"A hole in the heavens above your scruffy head, Max! As you might have guessed, a creature as powerful as Magician Nanka Yok was easily able to read the minds of the policemen who were hanging around."

"Of course. I guess I'm not in the best shape right now. Mackie was right."

"You saw Mackie?" Juffin's eyebrows shot upward and almost disappeared underneath his turban.

"No, I didn't see him, but I talked to him. Twice. Once at the very beginning of my foolish undertaking, and then again recently, right at the end. The second time, Mackie sent me a call himself and told me how to get out. Maybe I could have figured it out myself, maybe not. I don't know. But I think I'm forever in his debt."

"Well, I'll be," said Juffin. "That sly old Mackie Ainti never helps anyone. Congratulations, Max. His affection for you knows no bounds. The fundamental philosophy of my dear mentor has always been to leave people to their own devices and watch what happens."

"I'm just lucky," I said. Then I added, "You know, Juffin, I was in such a scrape that I think even Mackie got curious."

"You can bet he did. I am burning with curiosity myself. I can't wait for you to start dozing off so I can learn all the details of your fact-finding expedition."

"I'm sure I'll be dozing off sooner than you think," I said, yawning. "I just need to say hello to Tekki and then hit the sack. I feel like I haven't slept for years. Maybe you'll be able to find out about that, too."

"About what? About how long your were awake?"

"About how many years I spent there," I said. "I feel I've been away for a very, very long time. Much longer than forty-nine days."

"I'm sure I'll be able to find that out," said Juffin. "We're here, Max. Don't you recognize the place?"

"Of course I do," I said. I smiled and rushed through the slightly open door of the *Armstrong & Ella*. How could I not have recognized it!

"What swamp did the werewolves drag you off to this time, sweetheart?" said Tekki, smiling at me from behind the bar. "Sinning Magicians, you're under convoy! Sir Juffin, are you taking him to Xolomi? How sweet of you."

"Don't get your hopes up," said Juffin. "I'm not going to let him loaf around in Xolomi. He's had enough loafing for years to come. But don't get too excited, girl. Even if this connoisseur of long walks has managed to drag his feet to your tavern, he's not likely to be in the kind of physical condition you're counting on."

"I see you've become good friends," I said, giving Tekki a hug.

"Oh, goodness! You reek of other Worlds. I could smell it a mile away. Still, better that than somebody else's perfume," she said, burying her face in my shoulder. "Of course we've become friends. I needed someone's shoulder to cry on, and Sir Juffin's looxi was just the thing to dry my tears."

"Right," said Juffin, settling down on a barstool. "If anyone, it was I who cried on her shoulder and dried my tears with the fold of her skaba. And wise Lady Shekk stroked my hair and told me you were going to be all right."

"And I was right, as you can plainly see," said Tekki, bending over a small burner. "I know why you're here, sweetheart. And it's not for hugs and kisses. You're dying to have a mug of my kamra."

"I am literally dying to have it," I said, sitting down next to Juffin. "But you're wrong about hugs and kisses. They go very well with your kamra."

"I so want to believe that," said Tekki with a smile, and she raised her eyes to look at me.

Her eyes were so sad that I couldn't feel the floor under my feet, no matter how much she smiled. For a split second, her face seemed much older to me. It looked so much like the face of the kind lady from Nuremberg that I almost fell off the stool.

"So it was you, Tekki?" I said, quietly. "You caught me chatting with the stone lion on the bridge and then gave me your pocket mirror. Or did I just imagine it?"

Tekki didn't say anything. She put a jug of kamra before us and turned away. She went to great lengths to show me that she had no idea what I was talking about.

"I knew you'd be bold enough to send your Shadow after him, girl," said Juffin. "I was almost sure of it."

"My Shadow?" said Tekki. "What are you talking about? I have no idea what you mean. You must be mixing me up with my infamous daddy again, sir."

Her black eyes looked at us warily and even flashed a bit with anger.

"Okay, you can keep your secrets," I said. "I just wanted to thank you . . . or your Shadow."

"I don't have any secrets, I'm telling you." She was smiling again, and her eyes were no longer wary or sad. "How do you think I could have pulled that off, Max?" she said. "I'm not too keen on running after men myself, and to send my Shadow chasing after them—that would be simply ridiculous."

"Not after 'them,' just me," I protested.

"Well, it might chase after you," said Tekki, quite unexpectedly. "But my Shadow would never be so frivolous as to drink wine in the company of a stranger. Even one as cute as you. It must have been someone else's Shadow."

"A cute one, huh?" I said.

My hearts were beating like crazy. So she knew that I had treated Theia to a glass of wine. Not tea or coffee or beer, but wine. She can say all she wants about just guessing, and I'll pretend that I believe in coincidences, I thought.

I took a small sip of kamra from my mug and smiled. Forget coffee. Nothing could be better than Tekki's kamra.

Half an hour later, I couldn't keep my head up or my eyes open. I could hardly move my tongue in my mouth.

"I wish you knew how much I love you guys," I mumbled, falling asleep.

I could have come up with something less banal, but as I already mentioned, I wasn't in the best shape and couldn't manage anything but the truth.

"Right, now you only have to marry us both," said Juffin, and he laughed so loudly that the panes in the windows trembled. But even that didn't wake me up.

In my sleep I heard Juffin talking to Tekki. He said something about taking me with him solely because it was absolutely necessary.

"Solely because he is absolutely insidious," I mumbled to their utter delight. Then I fell asleep for good. I slept so soundly that poor Juffin, I'm sure, had to drag me to the amobiler by the scruff of the neck. Then again, he could have dragged me by the feet. I wouldn't put it past him.

I woke up because someone was licking my nose. I couldn't remember Tekki ever doing that to me before. Where have I ended up this time? I thought, opening my eyes.

Chuff, Juffin's fluffy canine with the endearing face of a bulldog, was sitting on my chest. I laughed and kissed him on his small, moist nose.

"Well, I'll be. Not only did you occupy my bed, you also stole the heart of my trusty old dog."

Sir Juffin stood in the doorway shaking his head.

"Sinning Magicians," he said. "I was obviously better off without you. What's true is true."

"Let this be a lesson for you. Next time you'll think twice before taking me away from my beloved, especially after a long separation."

"I'll keep that in mind," said Juffin. "Then I'll write a book. A popular guide to handling Sir Max. It'll be a big hit among university professors and petty criminals."

"So, what do you think about my adventure? Did you get to the bottom of it?" I said, trying to remain serious. I didn't succeed. I still couldn't believe that what was happening was real. It was simply too good to be true.

"Quite an adventure it was, let me tell you," said Juffin. "In all honesty, you should quit the Minor Secret Investigative Force and found your own Order. It's too bad the Epoch of Orders has been laid to rest once and for all."

"So, we'll just leave everything the way it is, then?" I said. "Do I have thirty minutes to wash up and get ready?"

"Ten minutes," said Juffin. "It's almost noon, and I'm still babysitting you. Knowing you, you won't leave the house without a mug of kamra, so I don't know when we're going to get to Headquarters. And everybody's waiting for you there. Sir Melifaro is itching to give you a shiner, I'm sure. Your disappearance shook him to the core. He was gloomy and sad for almost a dozen days. It pained me to look at him. I'm willing to bet that you're going to have to pay dearly for it now."

"I guess I am. I'm going to have to hide behind the back of Sir Lonli-Lokli. I once saved Shurf's life, so it's time for him to return the favor."

I set a meaningless personal record and managed to dip myself into all eleven pools in Juffin's house in just under ten minutes. I put on a black skaba while my body was still wet and took a close look at my reflection in the mirror.

I didn't see anything extraordinary there. I did, however, look somewhat older. I could make out a few shallow but visible wrinkles at the corners of my mouth, and there was another much deeper vertical crease between my eyebrows. But it was still my face. Well, almost. I looked closer. Yes, there was something indeterminate, something unfinished in my face now. Something that didn't quite let me focus.

"Do you like what you see, handsome?" Juffin asked from behind my back.

I looked around, embarrassed. "It's not bad. But don't you think there's something wrong with it?"

"Let's eat breakfast," said Juffin. "Do you remember what your friend Mackie looks like?"

"As if it's possible for anyone to remember his face. You know that yourself," I said, heading upstairs into the dining room. "Wait, are you saying that it's the same with my face now?"

"That is exactly what I'm saying. I can only assume that when he was young and foolish, Mackie got himself into similar trouble. Funny."

"You're flattering me."

"Me? Whatever gave you that idea? Teasing you, perhaps. But let's get on with the matter at hand, shall we?"

"With great pleasure," I said. I took a few big gulps of kamra and shoved a pastry into my mouth. "So, how long was I there, Juffin? I'm very curious."

"You always have a very keen interest in things that don't matter," Juffin said. "You were knocking about in that World for almost nine years. But I don't think time made a mark on you. Take your hair, for example. It didn't grow much longer, and I'm willing to bet you never made it to a barber. Am I right?"

"I don't think I ever passed a barbershop the whole time I was there. But gosh, nine years!" I shook my head. "My inner clock swears it was no more than a year."

"Then you've got a lousy inner clock, my boy," said Juffin. "Well, everyone has his faults. I sure am glad that time flows at different paces in different Worlds. Nine years would have been a little too much."

"I guess you're right," I said. "But at some point I got pretty scared when I thought a few hundred years had passed since I'd left Echo. I almost went crazy with grief. What else did you find out about me?"

"Everything. Including something you'd forgotten yourself. If you don't mind, I'll reveal this for you in small portions, and I won't start today. What you really need to do now is try not to think about all of this. There are plenty of interesting and exciting things in the World, and you'll need a great deal of time to reconcile yourself to your own might."

"My *might*?" I said.

"That's right. I think I know what you are capable of now, but you don't have to know it just yet. No need to rush. Unless you're planning to found a new Order, of course."

"I'm not," I said. "I don't have time for that. Plus, you know that I'm not an ambitious guy."

"That I do know. And I hope you're going to stay that way."

"Juffin," I said plaintively, "just tell me that I'm all right, and I'll stop bothering you. I won't ask you any more questions."

"You are all right, indeed, Max. More than all right. In any event, the World you were born in will never try to reclaim you again. So it's unlikely that you're going to go through something like that adventure any time soon. Maybe another adventure—but no man can ever know anything beforehand, and you and I are still people, Max. Now, try to busy that disheveled head of yours with other kinds of problems."

"As you say," I said. Then I remembered about my surprise for Juffin and almost yelped from excitement and anticipation.

"What's with this cunning glint in your eyes?" Juffin said. "Oh, yes. You said something about miracles and wonders yesterday. They have something to do with that ugly stick of furniture that you brought with you from your homeland, right?"

"Exactly," I said, smiling dreamily. "I think I'm going to torture you until tonight, though. This will be my little revenge. You have your secrets, and I have mine."

"I think you're going to give up first," Juffin said. "I can hold mine in, but I'll bet your secret will defy you before sunset."

"Maybe it will, maybe it won't," I said.

"Time will tell. In any case, I don't think I'll have a minute to spare before sunset. While I was busy rummaging through your precious brain, I lost a great deal of time. Let's go, Max. Today, I'll let you drive my amobiler. I've already warned Kimpa."

"I can't believe it. The old man agreed to entrust me with the cargo of your precious self?"

"Quite right. I told him this would be in the interests of the Unified Kingdom, and Kimpa, as it turns out, has a keen sense of civic duty."

Once I was behind the levers of the amobiler, all metaphysical problems vanished from my poor head. I was enjoying life—and fast driving—to the fullest. Juffin was happy too, I think. The sharp outlines of his face gave way to a peaceful smile every now and then.

"I think Echo is the most beautiful city in all the Worlds," I said as I stopped the amobiler by the Ministry of Perfect Public Order. "Even that place I created near Kettari is not quite on par with it."

"Don't speak too soon, Max," Juffin said. "You haven't seen Cherxavla yet."

"What's that?"

"A charmed city on the Uanduk continent, in the heart of the great Red Xmiro Desert. I think you'd like it. Anyway, let's go in. Are you ready for a long, painful death from suffocation?"

"Depends on whose arms I'm going to die in. If it's in Lady Melamori's arms, I'd be only too happy. Shurf's or Kofa's will also do. If it happens to be in the arms of General Boboota, I'd hate it. He's not my type, to say the least. But I'm sure he missed me, too."

We walked through the cool, empty hallways of the Ministry. I enjoyed breathing in the mild, familiar, but very distinctive smell of the walls of the House by the Bridge.

This idyll was interrupted in the rudest possible manner when something heavy launched into me from behind and gripped me in a headlock. I plummeted to the floor and cried out from the shooting pain in my knee. Out of the corner of my ear I heard Juffin's laughter, which suggested that it was a well-rehearsed accident.

"Now you're my trophy. I'm going to take you home and hang you on the wall, along with the other spoils." Melifaro was sitting on my chest with the happy air of a victor. "Did I scare you?"

"What do you think?" I said, smiling from ear to ear. "You also hurt me."

"It's all right. I hurt myself, too." Melifaro laughed. "A true hero such as yourself could have stayed on his feet."

"I could have. But if I had, you wouldn't have fallen and hurt yourself, which wouldn't have been half as funny. It's all right now, though.

You know, I expected a bear hug from you, but boy, you totally overdid it."

"That was my sweet revenge," Melifaro said, helping me up. "I wanted you to feel exactly what I felt when I was standing in the doorway to your bedroom. Soon after you left, I remembered the crazy look in your eyes and began to worry. Then Melamori and I decided to take a walk down your trace and make sure you were all right. We followed the trace to your former apartment on the Street of Old Coins, only to see you vanish from under your blanket right before our very eyes. Can you imagine what we felt?"

"Good golly," I said. "But I wasn't exactly sunbathing at the beach all that time, either. Trust me."

"Really? Well, that's a relief. Makes me feel so much better," Melifaro said.

"Gentlemen, we have much more comfortable rooms at our disposal here in this building," said Juffin. "Or do you prefer to stay in the hallway?"

And we moved to our side of the Ministry.

"It was very wise of you to decide to return," said Shurf Lonli-Lokli, getting up from behind the desk in the Hall of Common Labor. "There was something inappropriate in your absence."

"Sinning Magicians, Shurf! I couldn't put it better than that myself. 'Inappropriate' is just the word. You are a master of eloquence."

"It is the result of subjecting the thought processes to many years of self-discipline. You will get the hang of it in another ninety years or so, I'm sure," said Lonli-Lokli. Then he smiled and winked at me.

"Good golly, Shurf! What's this I hear, irony? Do my ears deceive me?" I said. "Gosh, it's so great to see you all."

"It's great to see you, too, Max," said Melamori.

"No, my dear Melamori. It's not just 'great' to see me. It's wonderful."

"I have to say that we were a little bored here without you," said Juffin. "But let me tell you something, lad. You're going to have to treat us all to a good lunch at your own expense. I can't let you put dents in the Treasury anymore. After we paid the sculptors you hired, Sir Dondi Melixis kept giving me meaningful looks for at least a dozen days. Maybe after lunch we'll be magnanimous enough to forgive you the irreparable blow to our nervous systems."

"I've always known that I'd never be a rich man," I said. "And now I have to stuff your bottomless bellies, in addition to my own. Speaking of bottomless bellies, where's Sir Kofa?"

"Our Master Eavesdropper-Gobbler has already reserved a table for us at the *Glutton* and has been waiting there since yesterday evening," Melifaro said with a laugh.

"Then let's go," I said. "Who am I to make Sir Kofa Yox wait?"

When we were leaving we ran into Lookfi.

"Sir Max, what a surprise!" he said. "I haven't seen you in a few days. Have you been sick with a bad cold or something?"

"Or something," I said, bewildered. Sometimes all the wonders of the Universe paled in comparison with Sir Lookfi Pence's absentmindedness.

Then I felt I had entered the sweetest dream of a hopelessly lonely wishful thinker. Even better. The taste of Madam Zizinda's half-forgotten house specials, combined with the faces and voices of people I had almost lost, and then found again . . . I felt I was dreaming, but that it was a good dream. And that the dream was *right*. It had nothing in common with the dangerous dream I had had for nine years—or forty-nine days, depending on who was counting.

We returned to the House by the Bridge and Sir Juffin Hully dragged me to the reception desk, where a blue-eyed young man in a rich, dark-green looxi was sitting. The stranger studied me carefully, his blue eyes shining from underneath his black turban. His stare felt even heavier than that of Sir Juffin himself.

"Max, I'd like you to meet Sir Nanka Yok, Grand Magician of the Order of the Long Path," said Juffin. "I told you about him yesterday."

"Do I look a little too young?" the stranger said with a smile, contemplating my bedazzled face. "I already see the downsides of my new countenance. No one wants to take me seriously."

"In my book, that's more an advantage than a downside," I said. "It's even better when nobody takes you seriously. No one gets in your way."

"Perhaps you're right," the Grand Magician said. "Yet it is difficult for me to get used to my new circumstances. In my former life, before I took my people to look for power along the paths of the dead, everyone took me seriously. Very seriously, indeed."

"Well," I said, "ever since it was mandatory for me to wear the Mantle of Death, everybody's been taking me seriously, too. But it doesn't offer any comfort or facilitate inner peace. If anything, it's the other way around."

"Ah, a true conflict of Epochs," said Juffin. "So quaint. I'm afraid I'll have to disappoint you, however, Sir Nanka. Nuflin Moni Mak, Grand Magician of the Order of the Seven-Leaf Clover, takes you very seriously, and it may come with a few provisos. Yesterday morning I talked to him about you. Nuflin is prepared to offer you and your people all you need to lead a comfortable existence, even more than that. But under one condition: you must stay away from Uguland."

"We weren't going to stay here, anyway," said Magician Nanka with a cold smile. "We don't need the powers of the Heart of the World, Sir Hully, as I have already told you. Furthermore, we have a vested interest in maintaining the balance of the World. We like to be alive, and we are going to stay that way for a long time. We really don't have a preference in terms of our habitat."

"The Order of the Seven-Leaf Clover is prepared to offer you some of its lands in Gugland," Juffin said.

"On the *other* side of the bay, naturally. Well, I guess we'll have to make do with the lousy Irrashi kamra, then. That's all right, though. I've been in worse situations. Your Grand Magician Nuflin is truly a master of precaution. It's amusing to see how much this World has changed."

"It has changed, indeed," Juffin said. "But you said it didn't matter to you where you lived, if I understood you correctly. Sir Max, you're in charge of this matter now. Magician Nanka's people may stay in Echo for another dozen days. If, however, they don't leave the Capital after this period—"

"We intend to leave tomorrow," Nanka Yok said. "Don't try to scare me, Sir Hully. That is completely unnecessary. We are not planning to wage war with anyone. We are going our own way."

"I wasn't trying to scare you. I'm simply offloading some of my responsibilities onto Sir Max. I apologize that I'm doing this in your presence."

"No need to pretend," said Nanka, smiling at both of us with a radiant, friendly smile. "Your logic is very transparent. You want me to know that the man my people consider the most dangerous person in the city is going to oversee our departure from Echo. I would have done the same, if I were you. But I assure you, there is no need to worry about us. Do you think one can return from a trip like ours and still be interested in such petty things as nominal power?"

"One never knows," said Juffin. "My job is to warn you."

"Your job, you say? I know what your job is," said Nanka Yok, narrowing his eyes slyly. "Your organization resembles some sinister Order much more than it does the police, or even the Secret Police."

"We're not sinister," I said. "We're very harmless folks."

"Harmless you say, Sir Max?" said Nanka Yok. "By the way, I must thank you for not leveling your full power against us. I must confess there was a moment when I thought the immortality we had acquired along the paths of the dead would be torn away from our weak hands. Your Lethal Spheres—I've never seen anything like them before. If you had truly wanted to get rid of us forever, you could have done so. We are lucky that you are not really fond of killing. Every time you experienced a momentary doubt, it left us a slim chance."

"Silly me," I said. "I went on a trip for holy water, even though I was a hair's breadth away from defeating you. But I'm glad that you're all right now."

"Your idea of turning us into sculptures was simply marvelous," Nanka Yok said. "It saved the lives of my people. But if we *had* been the undead, we really wouldn't have been able to hurt the citizens of Echo. I must say, I was worried that my people were going to wear their stone clothes forever. That strange new formula turned out to be very strong. I thought they might have to stay like that until Sir Hully returned. That would have been extremely dire. Even thought we are immortal, we can still suffocate."

"Jiminy!" I was horrified. "How did you manage to get out?"

"With the help of one kind man. What was his name again, Sir Hully?"

"It was no other than Sir Lukari Bobon, our Lookfi's uncle," said Juffin.

"The cemetery guard?" I said.

"Not the guard. He's an undertaker. Thank goodness he can't hear you, or you would have gained a mortal enemy. Anyway, he happened to possess a very useful secret: a formula that destroys liquid stone. It comes in handy in his line of work."

"So he and Lookfi finally made up?" I said.

"Yes. Their reconciliation lasted for two days, and then they had another fight over something. I believe it was over the family property."

"I can't imagine Sir Lookfi Pence fighting with someone."

"Anyone would fight with Sir Lukari Bobon," Juffin said. "He's a very hotheaded gentlemen."

Grand Magician Nanka Yok must have been a little bored with our conversation. In any case, I wasn't surprised when he got up to say goodbye.

"We're leaving tomorrow," he said. "Gugland sounds as good as any other place. It really doesn't matter. I believe we'll meet again someday. Secret paths never cross just once."

"I hope that it won't be the worst event in our lives," said Juffin.

"Goodbye, Sir Nanka," I said. "I'm glad that I didn't do my job very well."

When Grand Magician Nanka Yok left the reception room, Sir Juffin Hully said to me, "I would still like you to keep an eye on them. Make sure they leave tomorrow. I don't think they're going to make any trouble—they have more important things to worry about now—but you never know with Grand Magicians."

"Especially the ancient immortal ones," I said.

The rest of the day, Sir Juffin Hully was on pins and needles. I had been ready to crack and divulge the secret of the "ugly stick of furniture" long before dusk. But the boss kept getting sidetracked by all kinds of problems. I spent the day wandering aimlessly around the Ministry, going from room to room with an expression of happy torpor on my face, as though I were just visiting.

Finally, Juffin dashed out of his office. On his way out, he explained something about "pressing matters" to a gentleman whose looxi signified that he belonged to the Royal Court.

"Let's go, Max," he said, yanking the fold of my Mantle of Death so hard that I had to run after him if I wanted to keep my clothes on.

"What happened?" I said when we were outside.

"What happened? We're going over to your place to investigate your new 'miracle.' The sun set a long time ago, by the way."

"Oh, I see," I said. "And I thought you had some 'pressing matters' to attend to."

"This *is* my pressing matter. Don't worry, boy. I had to get rid of that bureaucrat somehow. Come on, let's go."

I didn't fret a single bit when we were going up to my bedroom on the Street of Old Coins. My trust in Sir Juffin's power was limitless. Frankly, some of the other people I had become acquainted with—Sir Maba Kalox, or Sir Mackie Ainti, the old sheriff of Kettari—were probably much older, more experienced, and more powerful than my boss. But Juffin—the man who had had the crazy notion to transport me from one World to another, and who had thrown me mercilessly into a bog of wonders—had forever become the mean average between the Almighty and a kind uncle. In his company, I was prepared to go anywhere in this World or the next.

❀

"What's this, Max? Where did you get the hat of King Mynin?" said Juffin, surprised.

He was holding the gray hat of Ron, the New York "pilot." I laughed so hard that I had to sit down on the part of the floor that passed as my bed.

"Juffin, what are you talking about! This is just a regular hat. Granted, it's from another World, but that's all the more reason that it can't belong to your legendary king."

"King Mynin's hat looks exactly like this one," Juffin said stubbornly. "Considering that it once disappeared along with Mynin himself, this may very well be it, Max. I wouldn't be so sure, if I were you."

"You can have it," I said. "I think its former owner, whoever he might be, would be glad to know it belonged to you now."

"Thank you," Juffin said. "You see, I have seen this hat in my dreams for many years. Who would have thought that you would be the one to give it to me as a gift?"

He took off his turban, put on the hat, and paused for a moment, listening to his feelings. The hat suited him. Then Juffin smirked mysteriously, took the hat off, and laid it carefully on the shelf.

"Well?" I said.

"You'll understand when you grow up," said Juffin, acting like the "big kid" on the block. "Well, come on. Show me your 'miracle'. I can't wait to see it."

I walked to the storage rack and flipped the switch. I held my breath. A little green light indicated that the first power line between Worlds was in full working order. Only then did I realize the degree of madness of my experiment, and finally allowed myself to be surprised. Then I grabbed the first videotape I could reach from the shelf and carefully inserted it in the slot. It was swallowed into the mysterious darkness of the machine.

"Come on, baby," I said. "Don't let me down."

It didn't. A few seconds later, the screen turned red, and then the good friend of my younger days, the African lion that had sold its feline soul to Metro-Goldwyn-Mayer Inc., roared its velvety roar. When I saw the credits, I had to laugh. Juffin and I were about to watch the *Tom and Jerry* cartoons.

Then I turned around to look at my boss. There was no doubt about it: this was my moment of glory. I never thought I'd live to see the day when Sir Juffin Hully's jaw dropped in astonishment.

"Motion pictures, Juffin. The movies," I said. "I told you about them once, remember? When the maniac from my World was running amok in Echo, I told you that I'd seen such things in movies many times. But this is even better, in a sense. These are cartoons."

"I thought as much," Juffin said with a nod, sitting down on my blanket. "Max, step aside, please. I can't see anything."

I sat down next to him and stared at the screen. Watching *Tom and Jerry* cartoons with Sir Juffin Hully—there was something surreal about it.

"I think we should call Sir Kofa," Juffin said a half hour later. "We can't keep this all to ourselves. Moreover, the exploits of these animals remind me of the good old days when he was chasing me. Goodness me! I think I'm getting sentimental."

"Go ahead. But if I were you, I'd make the employees of the Minor Secret Investigative Force take a vow of silence, and call them all over here. It's a sin to deprive them of this pleasure."

"It *is* a sin, you're right," Juffin said. "Do you have more of these . . . movies?"

"I have plenty. You know what? How about I just teach you how to use this thing? I'll show you where the other cartoons are, and then I'll leave. Because it's really unfair. Tekki's waiting for me, and I'm sitting here with you watching cartoons."

"'Cartoons,'" Juffin said in a dreamy voice. "You're right. You show me how to use this thing, then scram."

"Sweet. Now I get to teach *you* some miracles," I said.

"Quit showing off and get down to it," Juffin said.

It only took me about ten minutes. I had a very talented boss. I have to admit, back in the day it had taken me at least half an hour to get the hang of the VCR.

❀

Then I left Juffin watching cartoons and drove over to the New City, to the Street of Forgotten Dreams. I wanted to get to the *Armstrong & Ella* as soon as I could.

I thought that Tekki would be alone in the tavern—well, not counting the cats, of course. But the place was much more crowded than that. Sitting on a barstool was Sir Shurf Lonli-Lokli himself. His snow-white looxi was flapping in the draft like a sail. Next to him sat Melamori. She looked like an innocent schoolgirl, but the lively hoob was crawling up and down the bar. Tekki gave Melamori's pet mistrustful looks, but she had already fed it some breadcrumbs.

"You know, Nightmare, we really enjoy carousing at your expense," said Melifaro. He had already mounted himself on top of the bar, and was sitting there dangling his feet. "And since we were sure that you'd show up sooner or later—"

"Your colleagues have already spent half a dozen crowns," said Tekki. "So pay up."

"Put it on my tab. I promise I'll shake down Sir Dondi Melixis for ten Royal Crowns. I'll tell him we called an emergency night meeting. And he'd better believe it."

"A hole in the heavens above you, Max," said Melifaro. "I'm going to cry."

"I'd like to see that. But I don't believe in miracles," I said. "Not that kind, at least."

"Why not, sweetheart?" said Tekki. "I can bring him an onion."

Melamori looked at Tekki and they both giggled.

Every cloud has a silver lining, I thought. My absence seemed to have made them good friends. Who would have thought? Even without getting too deep into our complicated love affairs, it should be noted that Lady Melamori Blimm belonged to the clan that had been connected with the Order of the Seven-Leaf Clover since time immemorial. Tekki was the daughter of the late Loiso Pondoxo, Grand Magician of the Order of the Watery Crow, their mortal enemy. Sure beats the story of the Montagues and the Capulets.

Either Melamori had decided to join the Reading Max's Mind Club, or she just noticed the expression on my face. She shook her head.

"We became friends long before that, Max," she said. "Where do you think I used to go after work at dusk, when you stayed on in Headquarters?"

"I don't know. Did you come here? Why didn't I notice anything?"

"That's what we wanted to know, too," said Tekki. "We were so curious that we even decided to see how long you could go without noticing what was happening right under your nose."

"It could have gone on forever," I said. "I live like I'm in a waking dream. What's more, I manage to forget my dreams from time to time."

"I never thought you realized your weaknesses so clearly. This is worth many words of praise," said Lonli-Lokli pompously.

Melifaro laughed so hard that he fell off the bar. Perhaps, he might have managed to keep his balance if I hadn't tugged his leg. I listened to an avalanche of the foulest curses coming from his mouth, nodded in approval, and sat down next to Sir Shurf.

"Thank you, friend. You are the only person who praises me, however seldom."

"And I serve you kamra, which is also worth something," said Tekki, putting a steaming mug before me.

"Guys," I said, looking at this jolly crowd. "If I could die for you, I'd choose not to. Why? Because I wouldn't meet you in the next World. I know for sure you wouldn't be there. I've checked."

✿

I didn't get to sleep until morning, and that in itself was a miracle. I think I fell into a dead faint that just faded into something resembling sleep. At noon, I was woken up by Sir Juffin Hully's call. Talk about déjà vu.

Get up, wash up, and come here right away. But don't bother looking for me at the Ministry.

Why do you think I would look for you there? You're on the Street of Old Coins, of course.

How insightful. What's with the attitude? Did you not get enough sleep again?

Can I ever get enough sleep with you guys around? I suppressed a yawn and stretched my arm out to grab the bottle of Elixir of Kaxar. *Okay. I'll be there in an hour.*

Half an hour. I know how fast you can drive if you want to.

"Sinning Magicians," I said out loud, crawling out of bed. "Now that's what I call tyranny in its most vile form. Roman emperors couldn't even dream of this. Speaking of Roman emperors, it may very well be that Juffin has already watched *Caligula*. Now he'll have a whole new repertoire of ways to torment his subordinates. I hope I'll just be executed, quickly and painlessly, as an act of mercy to an old friend."

"Who are you talking to, Max?" said Tekki.

She brought a jug of kamra and my clothes to the bedroom. She had never spoiled me like that before.

"What have I done to deserve this?" I said.

"I have a few customers downstairs, and I don't want you to scare them all off. Sir Juffin just sent me a call and warned me that something terrible was about to happen because he'd just woken you up."

"So, he's been concocting a terrible conspiracy behind my back," I said. "You know what? Close down your place and come with me."

"What about the customers?"

"Customers, schmustomers. Decent people don't go to places like yours this early in the morning," I said. "Come on. You're going to love it."

She didn't object. Now *that* was a miracle.

"Have you vowed never to let her out of your sight again? Did you put a spell on the poor girl, you monster?" said Juffin.

It seemed he hadn't gotten any sleep, but he looked quite alert. Sir Kofa Yox was dozing next to him. On the TV screen I saw the face of Special Agent Dale Cooper, the character who had once "seen me off" on my trip to Green Street. Juffin had entered the *Twin Peaks* phase. I knew that he was going to spend a long, long time in my bedroom.

"I'm afraid that now Tekki will want to stay here, too," I said. "Here's a fellow victim for you."

"What is this, Max?" said Tekki, squeezing my elbow.

"This is the biggest miracle I can conjure. And no Forbidden Magic, mind you," I said.

"You don't say," said Juffin. "The indicator goes well beyond ten. It's okay, though. It's not going to destroy the World. Max, I called you to say that—"

"Let me guess," I said. "You remembered that you hadn't taken a vacation in a long while, right?"

"Very insightful. Yes, I think I deserve a little vacation," Juffin said. "All the more so because last time you made a pretty good deputy."

"Don't suck up to me," I said. "I knew this would happen. I'm willing to bet that I'm going to be giving orders to my reflection in the mirror because the entire Minor Secret Investigative Force will end up in this bedroom sooner or later. Fine, it's a deal. But my girlfriend gets to sit in the front row. I'm off to plant my backside in your armchair."

"Excellent," said Juffin. "Oh, don't forget to go down and admire the spectacle of the vestiges of the ancient Order of the Long Path saying goodbye to the streets and squares of Echo. If they refuse to leave, deal with them like the fat lady usually deals with the poor cat Tom at the end of every episode."

"Can do," I said, turning around to leave.

"Hold on, Max. Look what we can do now."

Juffin produced a huge cartoonish hammer out of thin air and immediately smashed it against Kofa's head. Kofa, who had been snoozing, woke up. His head vanished completely in between his shoulders, and his headless body began to hop around the room. Tekki squeezed my elbow even harder. I didn't blame her. I felt like squeezing somebody's elbow myself, for moral support.

Juffin was laughing so hard that some of the tapes fell off the shelves.

"And that's just the beginning," he said. "You can't imagine how much practical wisdom I have gained from watching those didactic animal stories."

"Max, I'm staying," said Tekki. "I simply must know what has driven these respectable gentlemen to the brink of insanity."

"I hope you'll manage to stay sane yourself until evening," I said. "Speaking of the evening, Kofa, could you find it in your merciful heart to sit in for me tonight? Just a couple of hours, maybe?"

"But you can just sleep in the armchair, son," Kofa said, surprised. "It's much more convenient. Just think, why would you want to go back and forth between the Old City and the New?"

The next dozen days passed almost exactly as I had expected. Sir Juffin Hully never showed up at the House by the Bridge. My other coworkers spent most of their time on the Street of Old Coins. The unbending Lonli-Lokli and I pulled our own and everyone else's weight. Lonli-Lokli's sense of duty outweighed his curiosity. Besides, Shurf realized that the wondrous spectacle was not going to disappear, and measured doses are a tried-and-true way of extending pleasure. The other members of the "Order of the Silver Screen" exercised no self-control whatsoever. Even Tekki at some point decided to ask one of her neighbors to work in the tavern. As though she wasn't the one who had come up with a dozen excuses when I suggested that she hire an apprentice so that her business wouldn't interfere with our regular nightly walks. And it hadn't been all that long ago.

Finally, life got back on track. At any given time you could still see one or another of the Secret Investigators in my old bedroom on the Street of Old Coins, staring at the TV screen. Lonli-Lokli was the only one who had devised a schedule for himself and followed it rigorously.

He watched one movie, picked at random, every three days. No more, no less. The others admired the steely self-restraint of our professional killer, held him up as an example, but secretly felt sorry for him.

Nevertheless, the days of understaffing eventually passed, and Sir Juffin Hully granted me not one but three Days of Freedom from Care. I spent them in the most wonderful way possible: I went over to Tekki's place and finally got as much sleep as I wanted. It wasn't difficult to do because the lady of my heart still spent her evenings on the Street of Old Coins, watching rapturously as the ghostly events unfolded in the depths of the screen.

❦

On the evening of the third day, I woke up right after sunset and went down to scare the customers of the *Armstrong & Ella* with my grumpy face. I had no other plans for the night.

A surprise was waiting for me downstairs. Even two surprises. Surprise number one was Tekki, who was standing behind the bar. She was here and not "at the movies," where I had planned to pick her up (bodily, if necessary) and take her out to breathe some fresh autumn air. Surprise number two was Sir Juffin Hully himself, sitting on the barstool. There were no other customers in the tavern—not too many Echoers were eager to spend an evening in the company of Sir Venerable Head.

"Don't tell me you missed me," I said. "Something happened, right?"

"Nothing to write home about," said Juffin.

Tekki threw me a conspiratorial glance and set several little glasses with drinks and a large empty mug in front of Juffin. He nodded and carefully poured the contents of the glasses into the mug. Then he snapped his fingers a few times above the mix. A red flame flared up above the liquid. Juffin swallowed the flame with unconcealed delight. Two streaks of steam came out of his ears, and his turban began jumping up and down on his head like the lid on a kettle of boiling water.

"Impressive, isn't it?" he said.

"I see," I said. "You've gone gaga over cartoons."

"In my opinion, they are much more realistic than the movies, which depict so-called real people. In any case, I seem to keep picking out movies with the silliest, most improbable stories. Maybe I'm just unlucky. There are these strange fellows who try to travel to other planets in huge, bulky contraptions—what do they call them?"

"Spaceships?" I said, chuckling.

"That's right. Any child would know it's much easier to use the Corridor between Worlds for that, if they're really so eager to leave their planet. Then yesterday I watched a tragic love story about a nice but emotionally disturbed man, also named Max, by the way. First he was either a policeman or a prisoner possessing some secret power—I didn't quite catch that. Then he found himself an easy night job. I still don't understand why he and his lady kept trying to scratch themselves with sharp objects. Although they both looked quite happy. To tell you the truth, I don't find it strange in the least that they were shot in the end. The circumstances of their lives reeked of some botched Forbidden Magic."

Listening to Juffin's synopsis of *The Night Porter*, I was on the verge of fainting. Tekki had to give me a glass of cold water, and I swear I wasn't pretending. Well, almost.

"Juffin," I said when I was able to control my tongue again, "you'd make the best movie critic of all times. If you're interested, I can organize the publication of your reviews in some popular magazine. You'll become a cult figure back in my homeland. Still, what happened, and why are you here?"

"As I said, nothing to write home about. His Majesty wants to meet you tomorrow afternoon. He still intends to coax you."

"Coax me?" I said. "Coax me into what?"

"Oh, you must have forgotten already. The old story with your 'subjects.' They did arrive in Echo and have been occupying the Palace Garden of Gurig for at least a dozen days, waiting for the opportunity to kiss your lower appendages. His Majesty, however, is drooling over the thought of enlisting your help in annexing the Barren Lands to the Unified Kingdom. He has a clever plan, according to which you would have to reign for just a couple of years without even leaving Echo. But you're against playing such games in principle, as far as I know. Don't worry, Max. The king won't try to coerce you. But you must go a talk to him at least once, simply out of courtesy. What are you laughing at?"

I was laughing because I remembered how horrified I had been the last time the subject was raised. What I had worried about most was that my orderly and predictable life would have to undergo change. I'd wanted to leave it all as it was, not touch it, not even dust anything off. Yet my life still crumbled, very unexpectedly, and I was the one who caused it.

"I was just thinking about what a fool I was," I said when I had laughed myself out. "I got scared at your suggestion that I play an unfamiliar game with rules I didn't know, and then I ended up playing a dozen unfamiliar games with almost no rules whatsoever."

"Are you saying that you may change your mind?" said Juffin, raising his eyebrows. "That's news to me! Are you getting wiser?"

"I'm not sure," I said. "Maybe I'll change my mind, maybe I won't. It all depends on what I think of His Majesty's 'clever plan.' Anyway, I used to be against any games of this sort, but now . . . In short, I'd like to familiarize myself with the rules of the game before making a decision."

"Goodness me, Max!" said Juffin. "You've grown up fast. Excellent. Meet me at the Ministry tomorrow morning, then."

"At the Ministry?" I said. "Are you sure you don't mean to say the Street of Old Coins?"

"I say what I mean. In the morning, I won't have much time for anything. Kofa brought me a whole bunch of counterfeiters. Black Magic of the seventy-second degree—only to get hold of a couple of bags of crowns. Can you believe it? I have to have a heart-to-heart talk with them. As for the Street of Old Coins, I'm on my way there now. I'm going to watch more cartoons. Maybe I'll learn a couple of new tricks."

"You're going to need them," I said. "The counterfeiters will be ecstatic when you start smashing their heads with your hammer."

"I left the hammer way behind. Another excellent thing has captured my fancy now. I believe it's called dynamite. Unfortunately, that trick is way too destructive. I've been thinking about a way of eliminating the dangerous aspects while retaining the special effects. Good night, guys."

Juffin jumped down from the barstool, looked around to make sure that we were alone in the tavern, and turned himself into a striped ball that bounced all the way to the ceiling, then disappeared.

"Looks like I got a bit carried away choosing the videos," I said to Tekki. "I should have foreseen what *Tom and Jerry* would lead to."

"You're right," she said. "But I like him that way."

"I do, too. Let's go for a walk and have breakfast while we're at it. No need to stay here since Juffin has scared off the rest of clientele that I wanted to scare off myself."

"At sunset, normal people usually have dinner," said Tekki, laughing.

The next day, Juffin and I went to visit His Majesty King Gurig VIII in Rulx Castle, where he had retreated at the first gust of chilly autumn wind. The Winter Palace had its own rules. In particular, when we went in we had to put on loose capes made from thin metal mesh.

"This is supposed to symbolize being captured," said Juffin. "Before the Code Epoch, however, these meshes were far from symbolic. Granted, Rulx Castle had a great number of other traps, as well. The times demanded it."

"You know," I said, shuddering, "I have a feeling that those traps still exist. Maybe they're just asleep and dreaming, but it's only for now. I'm almost certain they're sniffing the air and checking me out."

Juffin nodded. It wasn't clear whether he was agreeing with me or just surprised at my fancy.

We climbed onto the palanquins, and the bearers took us to the Royal Reception Hall.

His Majesty King Gurig VIII came out to greet us only a few seconds later. After the ceremonial exchange about the weather (which we all found quite agreeable), the king pointed at a small table crammed full of jugs and some dishes. He looked very proud.

"Not too long ago, gentlemen, I won a resounding victory over my Master of Ceremonies. The old man retired. The new Master of Ceremonies, praise be the Magicians, is not so stubborn as to deny his king the right to serve food to his guests wherever he wishes, be it the Reception Hall or the bathroom. I am very happy. The Dining Hall is not the coziest room in the castle. I personally cannot bring myself to partake of food there."

"Never a truer word spoken, Your Majesty," Juffin said with the tone of an expert. "Every time I'm in there I feel I'm about to drink a cup of someone's blood."

"Yes, the blood of some rebellious but appetizing vassal," said the king. "I suspect that it was quite customary among my illustrious ancestors."

Gurig VIII finally looked at me and winked slyly.

"Well, Sir Max, are you ready to become my colleague? Juffin warned me that you would put up resistance."

"To the last drop of my blood," I said, laughing. "Tell me what you have in mind. Sir Juffin told me you had some clever plan."

"A plan is a plan," said the king. "We will tell those nice people that you agree to become their king, but matters of the utmost importance do not allow you to leave Echo. Thus, you are to reign over them in absentia, as it were, while remaining in the Capital of the Unified Kingdom. Your goodhearted but ignorant compatriots will put a crown on your head and go back home completely happy. Naturally, you will have to have a castle of some kind where you will receive their representatives, but that will be my concern. I thought that if you should agree, my Furry House would be at your disposal."

"The former library of the Royal University?" Juffin said. "It's a good place, Max. You're going to like it."

"This is all hunky-dory, but how am I supposed to rule them?" I said. "Over the course of my life I have mastered a few professions, but being king is not one of them."

"Oh, do not be concerned, Sir Max. You will not have to fill your head with such trifles. Your subjects will be far away from you, along with their problems. As I understand it, they will be sending their messengers to you, as none of them has mastered Silent Speech. My employees will write your 'Royal Decrees' for you—after all, it's their job. That is all. Well, perhaps you'll need to survive a few exhausting receptions. They don't happen very often, however. Otherwise I would have followed my poor father and met the Dark Magicians already. Last but not least, this game should be over very soon. I hope it will not bore you. I expect it to end in about two years' time."

"How exactly will it end?" I said.

"It's quite simple. You will announce that you have become weary of your royal duties and will transfer your lands to my care. Thus, the Barren Lands, that thorn in my side, will become another province of the Unified Kingdom. This is far more humane than allowing County Vook to wage war against those poor souls. The old Dark Sack would wreak such havoc over there that the Barren Lands would, indeed, become barren. With your help, however, this operation can be a completely painless one. I assure you that it will benefit your countrymen."

"I have no doubt that what is good for me will be good for them," I said. "And I am fully satisfied with being a subject of the Unified Kingdom."

"I am happy to hear that someone is fully satisfied with it," said the king, laughing "Certain people love to indulge in jeremiads."

"Well, I'm just a simple and naïve barbarian from the Borderlands," I said. "I don't even know what *jer-e-mi-ads* are. Must be some Capital City trick."

❦

When I left the Royal Reception Hall I was almost a king.

"I can just imagine what Melifaro will do when he finds out," I said to Juffin. "He'll just explode with mirth."

"You should be happy if he explodes. Otherwise, you'll have to have a lot of patience."

"True that. Listen, Juffin, what does His Majesty want with those Barren Lands? There's hardly anything there but my subjects' yurts and their famous horse dung. Or am I completely clueless about imperial politics?"

"You are," said Juffin. "Okay, here's Political Geography 101 for beginning monarchs. Have a look at this."

He produced a small World map, embroidered on a piece of leather, from the pocket of his looxi.

"The Barren Lands separate the Unified Kingdom from the friendly County Xotta. Its rulers are dying to become loyal vassals of His Majesty King Gurig VIII. I think they're simply tired of wars with Kebla Principality—they've been fighting for about eight hundred years now, and it doesn't look like they're going to stop any time soon. A province like County Xotta would be a desirable jewel in the crown of any empire. His Majesty, if he had his way, would love to reign over the entire continent, and then some. Just to outdo his late father."

"That's right. I read once that the offspring of celebrities always have complexes like that. I hope His Majesty doesn't begin to enjoy this too much. I'll have to hop from one throne to the next for the rest of my life, or until there are just three of us left: His Majesty King Gurig, myself, and the Conqueror of Arvarox. And I don't think I'll be sitting on his throne anytime soon."

"You never know, maybe you will. Do you want to look at your would-be castle?" Juffin said when I was behind the levers of the amobiler.

"The Furry House? Sure. By the way, why is it called that?"

"Because it is a furry house. You'll see."

The former library of the Royal University was located in the Old City right between the University building and the editorial offices of the *Royal Voice*.

"Great, now Sir Rogro and I will be neighbors," I said.

When I saw the tall building I smiled: it was covered from top to bottom with a coniferous vine. This must be Echo ivy! Only the windows and the very top of the pointy roof could be seen under the thick layer of furry growth.

"This ivy will look great in combination with the stubble on your chin," said Juffin. "You were made for each other. Well, how do you like it?"

"I like it very much. It looks much cozier than Rulx Castle."

"Of course it does. For centuries, this building was occupied by very nice students along with their very nice tutors, and dozens of generations of royal ancestors, which you never had to begin with."

"Magicians forbid! What's in this building now?"

"This was once a library, but it was closed long ago. So there's really nothing in it now."

"And the books, what happened to them?"

"Well, maybe there are a few of them left. Some decrepit ancient folios and other old junk."

"Remind me to ask that they not be taken away. I've always wanted to have my own collection of rare antique books."

"And now you have them," said Juffin. "Okay, you can make yourself comfortable here if you wish. I have to go back to the Ministry. Does Your Majesty remember that he must be at work tonight?"

"His Majesty does remember this unfortunate fact," I said. "When I'm king, I'm going to send you my ministers and have them work for the good and prosperity of the Unified Kingdom. Oh, and tell Melifaro to take it easy, or I'll forbid him to watch cartoons until the end of the year."

"I think his personal favorites are your silly movies about policemen," said Juffin. "He tries to guess how they will end. The sooner he can guess, the happier he seems to be. I think his latest record was a minute and a half after the movie began."

"Well, I'll be!" I said. "Looks like the boy is not a lost cause after all."

Juffin was gone and I was left standing on the threshold of my future royal residence. Praise be the Magicians, this political intrigue now seemed silly and ridiculous to me. Which it was.

I really liked the Furry House. In time, I thought, I can turn it into a very nice, if capacious, abode.

I roamed the empty rooms of the former library, walked up to the third floor, and then entered a small watchtower. It smelled of dampness and dust, so I flung open the window. The fresh wind from the Xuron will only do a place like this good, I thought.

I looked out the window and shook my head in astonishment. It overlooked Echo, and the view was simply dazzling. The Furry House was one of the tallest buildings in the city.

I sat on the window ledge and looked down on the mosaic pavements of Echo and the silver ribbon of the cold Xuron. The beautiful magic city from my childhood dreams was real, and had become the geographical center of my new life. I had once lost it, and then found it again, only to realize for a second time how incredibly lucky I was. I felt I owed a debt of gratitude to the unfathomable powers that ruled over my destiny.

I decided that I should thank them. Right that very moment. It's best not to postpone such things. I leaned out the window as far as I could without falling and screamed "Thank you" at the top of my lungs, addressing it to the heavens, where, according to popular belief, those hypothetical "forces" reside. Having shouted to my heart's content, I sneezed a loud sneeze and then, relieved, laughed at this unexpected finale.

"That's right, buddy," I said to myself out loud. "Keep the pathos down."